DARK HEART

SILVIA AVALLONE

TRANSLATED BY LUCY RAND

Silvia Avallone was born in Biella in 1984 and lives in Bologna. She has published the international bestseller Acciaio (2010), which was a Premio Strega finalist and adapted into a film, *Marina bellezza* (2013), *Da dove la vita è perfetta* (2017) and *Un'amicizia* (2020). Her novels have been translated in over thirty countries worldwide.

Lucy Rand was shortlisted for the TA First Translation Prize for *The Phone Box at the Edge of the World* which she translated while living in Japan. She has also translated novels by Italian authors Paolo Milone, Irene Graziosi and Emanuela Anechoum. She now lives in Norwich.

DARK HEART

SILVIA AVALLONE

TRANSLATED BY LUCY RAND

MANILLA PRESS

First published in Italian as CUORE NERO in 2024 by Rizzoli
Published in agreement with MalaTesta Lit. Ag., Milano
First published in the UK in 2026 by
MANILLA PRESS
An imprint of Bonnier Books UK
5th Floor, HYLO, 105 Bunhill Row,
London, EC1Y 8LZ

A CIP catalogue record for this book is
available from the British Library.

Hardback ISBN: 978-1-78658-470-0
Trade paperback ISBN: 978-1-78658-471-7

This book has been translated thanks to a translation grant awarded by the
Italian Ministry of Foreign Affairs and International Cooperation.
Questo libro è stato tradotto grazie a un contributo alla traduzione assegnato dal
Ministero degli Affari Esteri e della Cooperazione Internazionale italiano.

Also available as an ebook and an audiobook

1 3 5 7 9 10 8 6 4 2

Typeset by IDSUK (Data Connection) Ltd
Printed and bound in Great Britain by CPI (UK) Ltd, Croydon CR0 4YY

The authorised representative in the EEA is Bonnier Books UK (Ireland) Limited.
Registered office address: Block B, The Crescent Building
Northwood, Santry, Dublin 9, D09 C6X8, Ireland
compliance@bonnierbooks.ie
www.bonnierbooks.co.uk

For my husband Gio

And silence everywhere; only in gusts
From distant gardens where the leaves are shed
You hear the fragile falling. Time of ghosts,
Cold summer of the dead.
Giovanni Pascoli, *November*, translated by E.J. Scovell

Reality demands that we also mention this: Life goes on.
Wisława Szymborska, *Reality Demands*, translated by
Stanislaw Baranczak and Clare Cavanagh

PART ONE

Two Solitudes

1

THE NOVEMBER MONDAY WHEN Emilia and her father started on the track called Stra' dal Forche, climbing up through the chestnut forest that separates Sassaia from the rest of the world, was the Day of the Dead.

Riccardo thought that somewhere like this, a tiny, isolated hamlet, wasn't the right place to start a new life – not for his daughter, not after what had happened, and not alone. But Emilia, convinced, strode on.

The sky was a dazzling blue that morning. The air had been cleansed by the rain of the night before, drawing attention to distant details. A particular light fell on things: it felt as if nobody could ever die and no story ever end on this flawless ridge of earth.

In reality, though, it had all come to an end some time before. The cowsheds were dilapidated and the Black Madonna in the roadside shrine had been disfigured by bad weather. Father and daughter pretended not to notice the signs of decay along the way as they sweated, not saying a word. They had waited so many years for this moment that now they were afraid speaking out loud would somehow break it. The mule track was covered in a thick blanket of wet leaves that silenced their footsteps.

Their own heartbeats were the only thing they could hear, booming from effort, emotion and fear, amplified by the silence that crouched all around them, alive, among the roots and the branches.

Every so often, they put their suitcases down to catch their breath. Their lungs were not used to the mountains: they were lowland people who had only ever gone there on holiday, and that was a long time ago. They had cramp in their legs and backs but there was no other way to get to Sassaia: no tarmac or dirt road, nothing anywhere close to driveable. They had had to leave the car in Alma, the last outpost of civilisation, and continue on foot as if it was the 1950s. And since seventy years on from then nobody (bar a few rare exceptions) would settle for having to walk through an entire forest to pick up some milk or a packet of cigarettes, they passed only a couple of magpies and a squirrel, with no trace of a human.

Their worries for now were focused on the house and the state they would find it in. Riccardo had sent a distant relative, a discreet man, to check it over a few weeks earlier and he'd found the predictable problems. The boiler was old, as were the pipes, and he wasn't confident they would make it through the winter. Some of the shutters were in bad shape and the draught would threaten the heat from the stove. The electric wiring had been compromised in places by mice.

Emilia, understandably, hadn't wanted to postpone the move. She had reiterated that she'd get by, she'd sort it out herself. Aldo, the relative, had done all he could to prepare for their arrival. He'd given the place a clean, replaced a few cables, covered over some cracks. But he had made it clear that the majority of the work would require an electrician – a good one – who was willing to venture all the way up there. Right now, the prospect of lighting candles in the pitch black of the evening, the darkness typical of a village with no streetlamps, was making them both feel a bit uneasy.

Halfway up the road they sat down on large rocks that seemed to have been put there especially for people to rest on. The midday sunlight pierced through even the trees' lowest branches, illuminating the last leaves still attached and hitting the fallen chestnuts, polished like pearls.

'If you hurry and collect a dozen kilos or so,' her father said pointing at them, 'you could survive for weeks.' Then he added, ironically, 'You'd be fine even if you get snowed in this winter, which is quite probable.'

Emilia stretched out a leg and prodded a spiky, damp-soaked husk with the toe of her boot, not responding to the provocation.

'It was always impossible to convince Aunt Iole that bread was better than chestnuts,' Riccardo continued, shaking his head. 'A true valëtta. Do you remember?'

Yes, but she didn't want to. Emilia's weak point, and this is important, was dead people. And it so happened that Aunt Iole was dead. She had died a few months after 'the event'. Of sorrow, they said.

She wondered how she'd be able to live day in, day out in a house that belonged to a person she didn't want to think about, a house filled with her furniture, her table-cloths, her ornaments. And how, twice a day, she would walk this mule track that was once a cheery path she skipped up and down as a girl, but had since become a hill steep enough to make her lungs explode. Up and down, summer and winter. To do the shopping, to look for a job and, assuming she found one, to go to it. She realised that in making your dreams come true, you betray them too.

'You'll get used to it,' her father reassured her, reading her mind. 'Your calves will be this big.' He laughed. 'And if you decide it was a crazy idea, like we've all told you, I'll come and get you. Even if it's tomorrow.'

'There won't be any need.'

'Changing your mind isn't the same thing as weakness.'

'So you say,' Emilia replied curtly. 'Anyway I know how to unblock a pipe, I can paint. I even did all right in woodwork. I can make myself a sled for winter.'

She flashed her trademark smirk, the one she'd picked up in the same place she'd learned to file, to saw, to tell a textbook lie, and to draw the perfect outline of a land-scape with a single brushstroke.

'Seriously,' Riccardo went on, getting irritated now. 'The snow worries me. What about when you get snowed in, with a phone that doesn't always have signal? Aldo says there is some signal, in a specific spot in the kitchen, but I want to check . . . What will you do, if it doesn't have signal? Light a beacon for the forestry service helicopter?'

'Papa,' Emilia sighed, 'I lived without a phone until two days ago.'

The chestnut trees were full of nuts that nobody would collect. There were woods as far as the eye could see and bare rock protruded up beyond the trees. Strewn in the middle, either wrapped in dark shadow or struck by cold light, were nine or ten clumps of houses, of which the smallest was Sassaia.

Father and daughter looked at them in silence. Then Riccardo turned to Emilia with an intensity that might have been hope. And on his sorrow-marked but handsome face, still young at fifty-nine, she found a forgotten memory: the trust she'd glimpsed on her first day of school, when he'd held her hand as they walked up to the gate of Collodi Primary. There were no other children with their dads, and for her too it was completely new, because Papa was always working, travelling, even at the weekends. Yet – she understood later – he had always been there.

Whatever happens, Emi. Whatever happens . . . you are and you will always be my daughter.

'OK,' Riccardo resolved, dabbing his eyes, 'let's try and get to this shack before nightfall.'

He picked up the cases, leaving the lightest shopping bags for her, and led the way along the inhospitable Stra' dal Forche, which was becoming hard to make out.

They hadn't set foot up there for almost two decades.

On their arrival down in Alma, their Ravenna-plated Volvo was immediately noted. They hadn't even finished parking at the entrance to the village when Emilia caught a subtle stirring out of the corner of her eye. Some windows were suddenly bolted, others opened a crack. It might have just been paranoia, as her father insisted. But when they got out of the car, a stout woman with an apron tied around her waist came out of the grocery shop to observe them. And she didn't say hello.

Then, when they asked the only other two people they came across for directions to Sassaia – the path wasn't on any signs or maps, and they could no longer remember where it began – they were regarded with such suspicion that Emilia immediately began to regret it. One man kept walking, without responding, staring at them as if he recognised them. The other enunciated three stiff words with such hard consonants and closed vowels that they effectively communicated just one thing: outsiders were not welcome here.

I wonder what they were expecting: there has never been tourism in Valle. Being there means either that you have proven blood ties, or that you're an intruder, a meddler, and therefore not welcome. Their suitcases and their full-to-bursting shopping bags announced that they were here to stay. But their family connection to this place had faded, and it was better not to dredge it up again in case someone began to piece things together, to remember, to spread the word – to vilify, like humans always did at any opportunity.

Their clothing didn't help. Emilia, though she no longer was one, was dressed like a teenager in ripped jeans, purple Dr. Martens and a fluorescent green ski jacket. Her father looked like something out of a Simenon detective novel in his elegant grey coat, starched trousers and cashmere gilet. Neither one of them bore any resemblance to the gloomy old men from around here with their indignant dialect, scruffy beards and felt hats that fell over their eyes.

As Emilia glanced around the village square, it slowly began to come back to her. She had come here in the summers of her childhood to run errands with her aunt and for certain religious holidays, she now remembered, which they spent in the restaurant over there, Le Betulle, of which only the sign remained. The grocery shop, however, was still in business and still sold everything from bread and cleaning products to farming tools. Bar Samurai was also hanging on, acting as both a newsagent and a tobacco shop. Further down, there was the post office which – according to the sign stuck to the door – opened on Mondays, Wednesdays and Fridays from 8 until 12. The church, the town hall and the school made the final components of the square.

That was everything.

What the hell am I doing here? Emilia wondered now, confronted with the reality.

She didn't need God, or to go back to school, nor did she need newspapers. She only needed cigarettes. She took one out of the packet in her pocket and lit it. She took a long, deep drag because she was starting to feel scared. There was one iron rule in her life: you did not go back on your word. Because if you did, you were a rat. Her father didn't know that: he hadn't moved in such brutal circles. But she had learned it down to her very bones.

While Riccardo persistently sought directions, she wandered over to the fogged-up windows of the Samurai to get a look inside. The clientele, absorbed in playing cards, all looked to be between sixty-five and ninety years old. Marta's voice came into her head:

Think of the men, Emily. So many men!
We'll snap them all up, never get married.
We'll fuck, just fuck, one after the other!

A smile slipped onto her lips: if only you could see the men, Marta.

Eventually a shepherd passed by – Rivetti I think – with a flock of sheep and a couple of dogs. It was he who pointed Riccardo in the direction of the stone steps carved out of the earth right between the bar and the shop, so well hidden by the withered brambles and hydrangeas that you'd never find them if you didn't know they were there.

The nettles that pushed through between one step and the next were thriving in a way Emilia had never seen before. They seemed to want to bar the passage of fools like her who thought they could move to a place like this. A place as rejected as this. A place that didn't admit anyone who was young and alive. A place where the houses were eighty per cent uninhabited, forgotten, empty. But that was exactly her reason, wasn't it?

On the final stretch of the climb, Emilia decided not to trust in what she had seen down in Alma, or in the fatigue of her legs, but in her instinct. Which was, admittedly, pretty out of shape. But there was one thing Venturi had told her that was right: 'We do not have power over our desires, we must only find the courage to listen to them.' And she had listened to them, session after session, sedative after sedative. The will to move to Sassaia had remained steadfast even when Venturi went back to being mean: 'When a person has your history, Emilia, she chooses a big city, a metropolis where she can get lost among the crowd. Not a tiny village where she'll be immediately pinned down.'

'Nobody remembers,' Emilia had replied. 'They're all dead.'

'Exactly. You want to live with the dead? Because if that's the case, it's very significant.'

Fuck you, she had thought in response. She had got up and left. Because that was a really mean question and, to quote Marta, Venturi was 'a frigid bitch with a stick up her arse'. So why was she still thinking about it?

She was breathless now. Her father also couldn't keep up the pace. It felt like the mule path would go on forever, like there would be no houses at the end, like nobody could possibly live there in a century like this one. But all of a sudden, in the middle of the forest, there appeared a white sign with black letters that read:

SASSAIA, Fraz. di ALMA

And the ramshackle houses of her recurring dream suddenly materialised. Stone constructions with slate roofs, remaining upright only by clinging on to one another. They were inflamed by the sun. It shone with such intensity that it felt like June, not November. In that light, even the mountains looked new. Maybe even she could become new here. And Venturi would be only a memory, in the past like everything else.

Here, finally, was *the after*.

2

THE RESIDENTS OF SASSAIA that year amounted to two.

One, Basilio Raimondi, was sixty-four but seemed infinitely older. He had never been married or engaged, had always lived alone up here, becoming a man of so few words he could easily pass as deaf and mute. In Valle people called him *il* Basilio, *the* Basilio – names are always preceded by the definite article in these parts – and though he was greeted with friendly familiarity, most people were privately convinced that he wasn't normal.

The other inhabitant, not dissimilar to Basilio, was me.

Neither of us was aware that a third person was about to intrude on our silence. A young woman with red hair and freckles. If we had known, I'm not sure what we would have done to defend ourselves. Perhaps nothing, perhaps we would have just been more prepared and the surprise would have been less traumatic. It probably goes without saying, but if a person decides to live in an abandoned village, it's because they want to leave behind the season of their life in which things happened. In which events crushed them, dislodged them, changed them. If we'd known about Emilia's arrival, we wouldn't have slept that night. In fact, from that day on, like people say happens with the arrival of a child, I stopped sleeping.

I had been at the cemetery that morning. I'd gone down to Alma at seven to avoid meeting anyone as I wiped a chamois over the oval photographs and changed the dusty old plastic flowers for fresh chrysanthemums.

My sister didn't come. Another year that she hadn't even bothered to come up with a feeble excuse in her short message, and I wasn't surprised. I didn't even know where she lived anymore. How long had it been since she stopped coming back? Stopped sharing the responsibility of the dead, the stacked burial niches, the stepladder, the candles? Stopped calling?

It was normal for her to keep her distance now.

I headed back around half past eight – I remember every detail from that day – and ate a beaten egg yolk, raw, with sugar for breakfast. I should have had a shower and trimmed my beard, which was now down to my collarbone, but I didn't want to. They all called me 'the Bear', but they knew I was harmless.

One time, Ofelia raised her hand in class and asked, in front of everyone, 'But sir, how old are you?'

On that occasion the beard served to conceal my smile.

'Because Michele says you're thirty, but Marco says you're fifty.'

The others hissed from behind their desks, 'Ssh, stupid!'

I laughed inwardly and responded, 'I'm eighty.'

Since November 2nd was a holiday, I made the most of it and repotted the cyclamens and read late into the morning. Only after noon did I decide to correct the children's homework, which was an essay entitled 'My Best Friend'. I went up to my study on the first floor and sat down at my desk where the lined pages were waiting, diligently stacked one on top of the other. The first was Martino Fiume's, and I automatically raised my eyes to the sky.

Twelve years old, repeating year five of primary school for the second time. The first line was promising: 'My best friend is Misty, my dog.' But the second didn't live up to the first: 'I found him in a hole and he was little, abandoned, baking like mad.' I sighed, took the blue pen I used for serious mistakes from my pouch and circled *baking*.

'Wrong spelling, Martino,' I said out loud. Living alone, this is one of my methods for making the silence more bearable. 'I know you won't need to be able to spell out on the mountain pastures, but you have to learn it for me anyway.'

I wrote the forms of the verb *to bark* in the margin with the correct spelling. *Write out fifty times*. I had just lifted the tip of my pencil off the paper when I heard two voices that weren't mine or Basilio's.

I spun round towards the window.

It was a man and a woman and they were chatting and laughing. Their footsteps were moving in my direction, then stopped right below my window. The sound of keys, a door opening. I became aware of my heart, an organ I rarely considered, beating loudly in my chest – as if I'd been caught in a bear trap.

We never heard voices in Sassaia.

Apart from the period between the beginning of July and Ferragosto in mid-August, when the relatives who had inherited houses and not managed to sell them came to get some fresh mountain air, the silence was absolute. Other than partridges, eagle-owls, wild boars, roe deer and red deer, nobody ever ventured up here. Not even the priest came anymore, nor the binman or postman. You had to go and collect your correspondence from the post office in Alma, and as for rubbish, you tried to accumulate as little as you could and carry it down once a week. There was someone who came to check the houses hadn't collapsed after heavy rains, but he came alone – he didn't speak, he didn't laugh.

I got up from the desk, moved over to the window and peeked out through a gap in the curtains.

I couldn't see anyone. I was either disappointed or relieved, I couldn't decide which. Standing there, stock-still, my ear tensed for potential other sounds, I imagined how I looked from the outside: a misfit, a misanthrope. Vulnerable enough under my stained clothes, bristly beard and musky smell to feel threatened by the mere presence of two strangers.

I felt ashamed to be spying in that way. Yet I pulled the curtain aside and stuck my head out of the window into the alley. I noticed that the door of the house opposite was wide open and there were two big suitcases on the doorstep.

Then, I don't know why, I suddenly recalled that I hadn't only assigned an essay with the title 'My Best

Friend' to my pupils, but had also been assigned it myself by Miss Irene when I was in year four. I had written, verbatim, 'My best friend is my sister. She runs faster than the boys and she climbs trees quicker than the squir-rels. Her legs are muscly and covered in bruises, but if she gets a cut she doesn't cry, because she is a rock and is always the bravest.'

I got a 9. I always got a 9. At that time everyone was convinced I had the brain of a genius and an extraordinary future ahead of me. A bit like how they said Basilio, as a boy, would become a great artist, and he ended up painting houses.

I put the essay and my sister back in my memory cellar, where it was cold and dark, where they needed to stay. I pulled myself away from the window and returned to the desk, made myself correct the errors, and let spelling and syntax triumph over my turmoil. But the fact that heart and memory rebelled against my rules was a clear sign of the turn things were about to take with the arrival of Emilia.

They threw open the shutters of the French doors on the first floor and pushed a mattress onto the balcony to air.

I'm using the plural but it was actually only him moving the mattress, the covers, the cushions, and beating them right in front of me. She wisely remained hidden inside for all the remaining hours of daylight.

I forced myself to concentrate on Martino Fiume's dog and infantile handwriting, but through the curtains I kept catching glimpses of the outline of the middle-aged man, decidedly overdressed, who was plumping, shaking out, and vexedly shouting about the mites that the stuffing was certainly infested with.

I wondered what that mattress could mean. A couple of nights, a week? An inspection way ahead of the summer season, or had they decided to sell Iole's house? I was certain of only one thing: nobody would be moving to Sassaia. Especially not a city dweller like him, with his white shirt and the cufflinks glinting on his wrists. Who, in this day and age, could possibly live without satellite TV?

And that was indeed the first obstacle: television.

For however much Emilia raged and despaired as she turned over every room, there wasn't one, and there never could be.

At this point, I'll let myself get on with marking homework while we slip quietly into the house across the alley to reconstruct events as I would later hear of them.

Emilia was convinced she remembered Aunt Iole spending hours in front of the TV in the evenings. She could even recall that her favourite programme was *Inspector Derrick.*

'You're mixing her up with your aunt in Ravenna . . .' her father responded.

'Literally everywhere has a TV!'

'If that's your reasoning, literally everywhere has tarmac roads!'

Emilia dropped onto the bottom step of the winding staircase, prey to a discomfort she hadn't seen coming.

She didn't care about the condition of the minuscule bathroom out the back which was practically an icehouse, or the bedroom with no electricity. She was used to spartan living conditions and had never complained. Picky was the worst thing you could be in certain environments. She had never begged for any luxuries but television wasn't a luxury, it was salvation: the lifeboat that kept you afloat when tensions rose, and voices, then hands; when depression ravaged and dragged you down, down, down.

'It's hardly a tragedy.' Riccardo appeared at the bottom of the stairs with a downplaying smile. 'It just means you'll read more!'

Emilia curled her lip in disgust. She thought of the time she'd been convinced to participate in a reading and writing workshop – for the brownie points she'd get from it, nothing else. The teacher was a middle-aged writer who used big, fancy words and spoke of good feelings and rosy prospects. In the middle of the second session, Emilia had experienced such irritation – it was epidermal, like a prickling all over her body – that she put up her hand. She rarely revealed her thoughts but in this situation she felt such an urgent need to interrupt the woman's flow of bullshit that she exclaimed, 'Are you telling us that words will cure us? That reading a book can redeem us? Do you think we're morons? Get out of your life and come here and live ours.'

Marta had been proud of her. She whistled magnificently with two fingers in her mouth. Everyone else whooped and clapped. The writer went bright red. Then Emilia stood up, victorious and indignant, and left the class. Later on, Marta put an arm around her shoulders and gave her a kiss behind the ear that was worth a thousand times more than the brownie points.

'Pa, we have to buy a TV. Now.'

'Do you know how long it will take to go down to the city and back? And then we'll have to find an electrician – there's no aerial here.'

'But I can't sleep without a TV. It's impossible.'

Her father shook his head: 'I told you this was a silly idea. The psychologist said it, the social worker said it . . . Let's go home.'

'What the hell are you on about?' Emilia shouted.

Her face was flushed, eyes open wide. Life was a fragile drama, suspended over an abyss, and she was forever at risk of slipping into it. 'What fucking home are you talking about?'

Riccardo stayed calm and tried to reassure her. 'Just for a couple of nights, nothing's going to happen.'

'I will never, *ever*, go back to Ravenna!'

'Well then let's find a hotel halfway and re-evaluate things from there.'

'I want to stay here.' Emilia was on the verge of tears. 'Why can't you get that into your head?'

Riccardo looked at her severely. 'So show me you're an adult, forget about your *Big Brother* and your *Celebrity Survivor* and all the other rubbish you watch. Instead of complaining about what you haven't got,' he passed her a bleach spray, 'get on with cleaning the bathroom.'

They both set to cleaning in silent anger, so as not to think, I believe. He checked that there really was a spot in the kitchen where you could get phone signal, and that the stove, the boiler and the fridge all worked. She ruined her lilac nails scrubbing the bathroom tiles, scratching away the black from all the grout lines. Aldo must have had a very relaxed idea of 'clean'.

After the bathroom she went into the room that would be her bedroom. She took in the flowery wallpaper stained with damp, a gypsum doll with perplexed glass eyes sitting on an upholstered chair, and a dark inlaid wooden bed that looked like it belonged in a Catholic school, or perhaps to some solemn couple practising chastity.

I will never be able to sleep here, thought Emilia. She lifted up the brass candleholder from the bedside table, the candles and the matches that Aldo – who would never have talked to people about her situation – had left there to conquer the night. Emilia studied them for a while and realised this was going to be a serious challenge.

Then Riccardo joined her, bringing the old hemp bedsheets back inside, the thick wool cover that weighed a ton, the pillows and the mattress, and together they made up the bed and swept the squeaky floorboards, preferring to anchor themselves in objects rather than arguing again. They would tackle the jungle of a garden at the back later, and the attic which was one big cobweb. For now they tried to enjoy the chestnut-scented air, warm and falsely springlike, that entered through every window along with my gaze.

They stopped when the sun started to hide behind Monte Cresto. 'Let's have a sandwich,' her father said, 'and then I'll be off.'

Emilia felt the earth disappear beneath her feet at the words 'and then I'll be off'. She reluctantly followed him down the narrow staircase into the ground floor kitchen that, like all the kitchens in Sassaia, was dark and damp and more like a tavern than a kitchen.

She helped her father slice the bread and peel the slices of prosciutto from their wrapper, biting her tongue to stop herself from saying 'stay'. They sat down with their sandwiches on the sofa, the same one on which Aunt Iole had spent hours, days, years, without ever watching television. Was it possible? In the rectangle of light that streamed in through the window they listened to themselves chew and swallow, incapable of talking.

Maybe, she thought, he too was reliving 'the trauma of separation'. One of Venturi's favourite phrases. God knows how all those professionals – successful women, righteous career women – had a diagnosis for every problem. Emilia had wanted to go back to the writing course to raise her hand again and say: 'Miss "Reading Heals", listen to these four words – "the trauma of separation". Can you explain to me what the fuck they mean? Really, *in the real world*?' Every time she heard someone say them, they sounded cold, useless. She was there, and she was bad. And badness is red hot. It burns you at the root, annihilates you.

They each left half of their sandwich because they weren't hungry. They drank two glasses of ice-cold water.

Her father forced himself to make a joke: 'The first decent reason to move to Sassaia,' he said, nodding at the glass. 'I'm going to try and make us a coffee with this water – I wonder if it'll boil.'

It was such a natural thing that a daughter of her age would go and live alone, in a place that she had chosen for herself, about which she had been stubborn to the point of exhaustion. But the fact of the matter was this: there was nothing at all natural about their story.

'This moka pot can't have been used for fifteen years.'

That was it, that was the problem: fifteen years. Or rather, fourteen years, four months and nine days.

They waited for the coffee to bubble up. It was undrinkable, even after they added two heaped teaspoons of sugar. Her father placed the two porcelain cups in the washing-up bowl then looked around in search of one last tea towel to dry up. Then, with a sad smile, he surrendered.

'Well, I'll be off then,' he repeated. 'Four hundred kilometres is some way. If I get stuck in traffic I might not get back in time for the dinner I was telling you about.'

'You don't have to excuse yourself.'

They were used to not living together, and now it was no longer because they didn't have a choice: they had chosen not to. Emilia felt a new anxiety rising under her sternum. A feeling like a little death, but that also contained – and this was new – a shiver of adrenaline.

Riccardo gathered up the wallet, watch and keys to the Volvo that he'd left on the sideboard. 'Listen,' he said, 'don't waste time, find things to do: start straight away, tomorrow morning, handing out your CV down in town. And make good use of those two bars of signal. Call me if there's anything at all you need. Don't be proud, don't dig your heels in. I can be here in four hours.'

'I'll be fine,' Emilia repeated. She stood next to the table, leaning on it with one hand because her legs were shaking.

'I know. I just don't want anything to happen to you.'

Emilia frowned. Just a moment ago she was crumbling and now she suddenly burst out laughing. 'Pa, are you serious? What do you think is gonna happen to me *here*? What *more* can possibly happen to me?'

Everything had already happened.

Riccardo didn't laugh; he stretched out his arms. She let herself collapse into them. They held each other tight and both closed their eyes and breathed heavily. Then her father, his cheek wet with tears, said: 'Emi, we've done it.'

They let go of one another. He put his coat on, turned around and left without saying goodbye, because there was no way to say it. And when he left with a torch in his hand, because the sky was already darkening, when the sound of his footsteps on the cobblestones of Sassaia were swallowed by the forest, Emilia found herself in Aunt Iole's old kitchen, under a cone of electric light from the single bulb, alone.

She immediately looked at the door.

The bolt, the lock.

She could open it and leave whenever she wanted. At any moment, any time of day or night. Without asking permission. Without having to earn it. She could just get up and leave.

The thought chilled her.

It set her alight.

It sent a faint shiver of excitement down her spine.

She tiptoed towards the door like a thief, her heart beating fast like it did after an orgasm.

She pressed her fingers to the handle and made to push it down.

Not yet, she told herself.

She leaped up the stairs like a little girl. She put candles into the brass holder and lit them all. She opened up her case and pulled out her little portable stereo with the CD player that was among the objects that were dearest to her in the world. She took it into the bathroom where there was electricity and put the plug into the socket. She felt the music flow through her body.

No new life was possible and she knew it: the future ended years ago. But this CD was her favourite.

She pressed play and turned the volume up as high as it would go, and then went back into the bedroom and started to dance, swinging her hips, hair down, as she sprayed Vetril on the glass of the French doors and the mirror that sat on the chest of drawers. For the first time in the history of Sassaia, disco music spilled out through the deserted alleyways, between the abandoned houses, frightening the animals, raising Basilio's head – and mine, which had done nothing all day but eavesdrop and spy.

Finally I saw her.

It was a scene so moving it broke my heart.
A girl.
Dancing.
By the light of a candle.
With a bottle of detergent in her hand.
In the house across the way.
Lost, together with me, in the mountains.

3

Can you believe I haven't gone outside yet?

The same happened to me on day 1, don't worry. I watched the door for like 10 hours, then burst out of it at 1a.m., ran into the first pub I saw and pulled a 21-year-old!

There are no pubs here, just rocks . . .

Emilia, standing, stretched her body towards the almost three bars of signal as she exchanged messages with Marta, compulsively, like a child entranced by a new toy.

I'm scared it'll be like that time in Piazza San Francesco, do you remember? I nearly fainted.

Yeah, you fainted and I had already found the ganja.

Emilia laughed out loud. First leave permit, first joint! God how I'd love to be you.

Every single night when I get home and roll myself a joint, I think about it and smile. You are you. You're magical, Emi.

What you up to?

Before even reading all of Marta's words, Emilia was typing back. She couldn't slow her thumbs down. She still couldn't believe she could send messages one after the other without her credit running out. Her life had paused with SMS, and now she had the Internet on her phone.

What do you think I'm up to? I'm going to work.

Shit, I need to start looking for a job . . .

I'm expecting great things of you, you know. More than just finding yourself a cute lumberjack.

Seriously, how can I make myself go out?

Just think about when you couldn't.

Marta was three years older than her, but she belonged to the category of creatures who have been so beaten by life, and who have so resisted the beatings, that they become ageless. 'When she speaks, silence', the newbies were warned on their first day. Unlike the psychologists, writers and various other privileged people whose unsurprising degrees were framed and hung on the walls of the office just for show, no one would ever have guessed that Marta would go to university and finish it. She was the first in the history of that place. She was pure substance. More than that – she was the example.

When they came to tell her that her mother had died, she sat on the edge of the bed for a day and a night, not eating, not drinking, not shedding a tear, serene as a Buddhist monk. She stared at the ceiling the whole time, unreachable by anyone's words. Then she took her little box out of a hole in the mattress, found what she needed, and made a deep incision across her belly button. Then, her T-shirt covered in blood, she opened her chemistry book.

Just think about when you couldn't, Emilia reread.

Do you ever think about it? she asked.

All the time, Marta wrote. *I think about Giada, about Yasmina, about Afifa, about Myriam.*

Each name was a little stab of tenderness.

I friended Afifa and Myriam on Facebook and we write often. Giada is a skipper on a boat just off Elba. Yasmina has had a son. You should look them up too, now that you can.

It was nine in the morning. Glorious sunshine drenched the island of rocks that Emilia had washed up on. The sky was a blank sheet of blue, without a smudge of a cloud. It hurt her eyes to look at it. She hadn't closed them all night.

She was wedged between a cement-hard mattress and a similarly heavy cover, and wrapped in sandpaper sheets that stank from the decades spent in a closed wardrobe, face to face with the abyss.

Emilia had forgotten the hell of the absence of sound. Or worse, the absence of all sound except her heart.

In the life she had come from, the television chattered tirelessly until 11:30 p.m. and then began the secrets, the noises of bodies, the flushes of toilets, the heavy breath of Marta, of Myriam, of Afifa.

There was another lifeline in that past: the glow of the streetlight that shone into the room until the sun rose. Even in the middle of the night, she could open her eyes and find the other girls' photos stuck to the walls, her watercolours, their communal posters of Luke Perry and Brad Pitt – both wearing nothing but tight jeans that stretched snugly over their bulges – and the blanket-covered silhouettes of her fellow wayfarers who, like her, either weren't sleeping or else woke up continuously throughout the night. She could cling on to them and feel safe. But here, it was just black and silent, like the inside of a coffin.

I don't have a TV, Marta. Last night was hell.

Nights will always be hell for us, little Emily. Get some pills. Or a man who knows how to fuck.

Emilia smiled. I'll go into town and see what I can find.

She waited in vain for another message from Marta, squeezing the phone between her hands as if she could juice another couple of words from it, but they didn't come. She noticed that the word 'online' had disappeared from under Marta's name and chic photo: her sitting in a fancy bar with a cocktail in hand, all smile and miniskirt. Who would've thought, twelve, thirteen years ago, that Marta would metamorphose into this beautiful, normal woman?

Emilia understood that her friend, the only one she had decided to keep in the *after*, had gone into the lab and would remain out of her reach for the next seven or eight hours.

She plonked herself onto the sofa.

Now what? she wondered.

Now you go out, for fuck's sake.

'Draw me a heart.'

One morning many years before, in the little room behind the infirmary with a window that looked out onto a plane tree, a bald man with round glasses who was generally considered to be a luminary had pushed a white sheet of paper and pencil across the desk. Emilia smirked arrogantly and said: 'I am not doing that.'

'Draw me your heart.' He raised his bet with a sly smile.

Emilia continued to put up resistance because that was her universal approach to the world of adults. After half an hour of irritating silence, she grabbed the pencil and started scratching at the white page with hurried lines, some heavy, some light, as she saw in her mind's eye the bed on the fifth floor of the hospital, second room on the left, that had been glued in vivid detail to her retinas on that last day of 1997.

Her heart must have turned gangrenous once and for all in that silent room, suspended like a celestial body over a city fervent with New Year's preparations. It must have stopped between the lifeless green walls, with the long morphine drip, the smell a person releases when they unravel from the inside, turn yellow, rot, and eventually go cold; together with the novel she had been given a few weeks before that lay on the bedside table, with a bookmark inserted in it which would forever remain halfway through; the pair of black-framed glasses folded next to it, the glass of water, the tortoiseshell hair clip.

Emilia's heart had stopped and then restarted, but only in appearance, as if to deceive everyone. In reality it had turned blue and purple, bruised, the colour of eye bags.

And another thing that had stopped were her dreams. On that day, Emilia had completely stopped dreaming, whether she was asleep or awake, which for a girl of thirteen might be the worst thing that can happen. Black nights. Black days, hollow like a dead tree trunk. Time that became empty, punctuated by sedatives and antidepressants. Until, all of a sudden, two decades later, without warning or reason, they started up again.

One single dream: recurring, monothematic, full of serenity and light, of creeping vines and wide-open shutters, rivulets of water, chestnut trees, flickering stars in the dense petroleum of her life.

But what I really want to write here is that during the meeting with the luminary, in one of the sessions intended to establish her psychiatric profile, Emilia had pushed back across the desk the exact outline of the organ as you see it in anatomy books, with the right and left ventricle, the arteries that pump and the muscular tissue that contracts, and, right in the middle, a big hole, blackened so hard with the pencil that the paper had torn.

The professor picked up his glasses and nodded with satisfaction. 'Has anyone ever told you that you are very good at drawing?'

Emilia pulled on her boots and jacket and stood at the door.

She waited.

She felt one version of herself splitting her sides laughing and another almost peeing her pants. She turned the key: click. Just a click, faint and lovely like the tweeting of a bird. She caressed the handle while biting her lower lip until it bled. Then she took a deep breath and pushed down hard. The door opened wide and . . . Boom!

The world.

There, at arm's reach, all of it.

'Holy shit.'

She crossed the threshold. She bathed in the light and the air that tingled on her skin. She took a step, then another and another. She began to run through the thirty or so uninhabited houses of Sassaia like an oversized, graceless little girl, over the cobbles inlaid with moss, down the deserted alleyways, leaving the door open wide behind her since nobody could steal anything, tell her to be quiet, reprimand or punish her. There was wind. There were thousands of chestnut trees flaunting their dry leaves that were about to fall. A bell tower stood tall and solitary. The mountains ate the sky. She was just about to start crying, her lungs and eyes exploding, when two phrases boomed around her mind:

You have to forgive yourself for being alive, Emilia.

No, there is nothing more I can do to deserve it.

Emilia recomposed herself. In three minutes, she had already run around half the village. She recognised the stone washhouse from her dream, the one where Aunt Iole spent her Saturdays soaping and rinsing the sheets, chatting with friends in a dialect that was as inaccessible as a tangle of brambles.

There were no longer any women sitting on the benches or bent over scrubbing. There were no longer children playing hide-and-seek or tag around them. The silence, however, wasn't empty. In fact it teemed with the calls of birds; lizards among the shrubs; a robin in the distance.

Emilia turned back, walking slowly. She passed her door and closed it. She noticed that the house opposite had some beautiful white and fuchsia cyclamens on the windowsills and nice curtains that fell over the open windows, and concluded she must have a centenarian for a neighbour. She intended to postpone meeting anyone for as long as possible. She would omit her surname or, if forced, provide a false one. No, no . . . definitely not a relative of Iole Innocenti!

She completed her tour of the other half of the village and ended up in the church piazza. 'Piazza' is a grand word; it was more like a small courtyard. The door of the church was bolted with two crossed planks, and the bell tower didn't have a clock – or a bell, for that matter. Emilia carefully observed every detail and was astounded by how clearly she remembered it all, down to the water fountain with ivy climbing up one side; it was as if the summers of her childhood had never ended. As if, here, the *before* was still intact.

She continued, passing in front of Basilio's lawn, seeing his geese and chickens. Again, she shooed from her mind the nuisance of another resident she'd have to meet, to whom she'd have to justify herself: 'Good afternoon, my name is Emilia . . .' She thought of the possible lies: 'I'm here to do some research, a doctoral thesis on depopulation . . . I shan't bother you. No boys, no drugs, I guarantee!' At the same time, it occurred to her that in a place like this, light years away from the law, she could grow a whole greenhouse of marijuana. And she knew people who could sell it: she could contact Afifa on this Facebook everyone kept talking about.

Sassaia was so coiled up in itself that it made her feel safe, as if she was in an amniotic sac. The streets were as narrow as carpet runners, the houses clung tightly on to one another, their stone sides like arms. But when she got to the edge of the village, where the path to Piaro begins, she emerged unexpectedly onto a panoramic viewpoint.

A natural terrace, looking out over the valley. It seized Emilia and exposed her suddenly to the vastness of the mountains, the autumn, all that endless sky above her head. She felt herself spinning; she felt like a minuscule piece of debris lost in infinite space. She lost her breath, and the earth beneath her feet, and fainted.

I was on my way home from school. It was a Tuesday, which meant I only had to teach the first two lessons. At breaktime I said goodbye to the thirteen pupils in the only primary school class in Alma, leaving them to run around in the playground with my colleague Patrizia, and headed up into the woods. Usually, if I didn't stop to gather chestnuts or mushrooms, I was home by eleven. I was tempted that morning, but I didn't; I wanted to stop in at Basilio's to buy some eggs instead. That was the only reason I cut through via the viewpoint and found her.

I didn't recognise her from the night before. She looked so defenceless, curled around herself, that it was hard to tell her gender, her age. She looked like a discarded bundle of rags.

I remained at a distance and heard myself shout: 'Hey! Is everything OK?'

She twitched. Then squinted and staggered to her feet. Her outline was twisted and clumps of sweat-soaked hair stuck to her forehead. She brushed the earth off her jeans, slapping her thighs and buttocks. It must have been about twenty degrees where we were, in full sunlight, but she was wearing a fluorescent green ski jacket. I was in shirtsleeves. I must admit I thought she was a patient escaped from the facility that had recently been opened in the next town down from Alma.

Then she looked up and saw me.

She was like a rabbit in the headlights.

I saw her whole face properly then, and began to put the pieces together: the sinuous silhouette of the night before, swaying, painfully seductive in the soft light of the window opposite, now became this wild girl, dishevelled and, in all sincerity, less beautiful than I had imagined.

Not that I was looking for anything. Keeping myself at a distance from certain matters was an ironclad rule I had set myself. They were merely muddled fantasies to help myself sleep more sweetly.

Only now there were no curtains. No glass, no windows between us. I couldn't help wondering whether I smelled of the forest, whether she could smell it. I experienced a stabbing discomfort. She did too, it seemed, because she hot-footed it away.

She turned her back to me and ran, like my pupils at the sound of the bell. As if she had seen a monster.

I stood stock-still for who knows how long. I was disappointed, in her and myself. Why did I avoid certain situations? So I wouldn't have to feel like this? Misunderstood. A moron. A guy who people at high school said would go to some prestigious European university, and instead still lives where he was born. Who was the only one to come back.

What had this woman come to Sassaia for? I hoped she would leave, that she would pack her bags immediately. I felt rage. So much rage that I forgot all about the eggs, about Basilio. I got home and slammed the door.

Then I submerged my head and my beard under the scalding jet of the shower. I rubbed the soapy sponge into every corner of my body. Despite everything, I was alive.

4

THREE DAYS AFTER OUR first meeting – if you can call it that – Iole's kitchen was stagnating in a cold, still silence. The air was already tainted with cigarette smoke and solitude. Lying on the sofa, having had a lunch of Coca-Cola and crisps, Emilia phoned her father and before he'd even managed to say hello, snapped: 'Wasn't that bastard Aldo meant to come this morning with the electrician?'

'Good morning, Emilia, how are you? I'm well, thank you. For the record, you don't decide you want something, click your fingers, and it's done. It doesn't work like that, especially not up there. You can listen to the radio while you wait.'

'There is no radio, I've checked.'

'I gave you a book.'

'Are you taking the piss?'

'Calm down.'

'No I will not calm down!' Emilia exploded. 'I haven't slept for four nights, I'm going crazy!'

She was having a tantrum – what a luxury. She would never have dreamed of doing that in the other place. Not her, nor the other girls. If you felt a bout of anger or frustration rising up and you couldn't contain it, you cut your arms with the blade you kept under your mattress.

Or banged your head against the wall until you felt a stream of blood trickling down over your nose. Until someone came who you could beg for a dose of Rivotril.

'I'll post you the prescription from the doctor and you can go to the pharmacy and get some sleeping pills,' her father replied.

'I'm not taking pills anymore. I made a vow.'

'Christ!' Riccardo lost his patience. 'Then I don't know what else to say to you! We're repeating the arguments we had when you were a teenager.'

When exactly was I a teenager? Emilia thought.

'I just want a TV. It isn't hard.'

'Have you been down to the city?'

'Yes.'

'Don't lie to me.'

From the moment her father's footsteps disappeared at the edge of Sassaia on the evening of the Day of the Dead, she had produced nothing but dirty clothes, a sink full of coffee-encrusted cups, empty crisp packets, and cigarette butts strewn everywhere. She hadn't even tried to live. She realised this against the soundscape at the other end of the phone: empty, the sounds of traffic in the city where she was born, rhythms punctuated by the timetables of offices, factories, schools, the ordered time of others. Of everyone but her.

'I told you I went.'

'That wasn't our agreement, Emilia. We agreed you would start making up for lost time immediately. You can't be up there doing nothing all day.'

Her father was on loudspeaker while driving. Emilia could hear that he had put the indicators on and was slowing down. She imagined that he was so saddened and irritated that he had looked for a place to pull over and curse in peace. The thing she hated most about herself was how easily she disappointed him.

'Don't tell me what to do. I will no longer put up with people giving me orders.'

'If you want to be left in peace to manage your life, you have to demonstrate that you're capable. Find a job, be independent. You promised me you would go down to the city on Tuesday. Today is Friday and we are still talking about the television.'

'OK!' Emilia yelled. 'I'll go to the job centre and sell them my soul!'

She hung up and switched off her phone.

She immediately regretted everything she had said and not done, but making mistakes was how she operated. She flipped the cushions on the sofa in a desperate search for her torch and keys. After that first expedition around Sassaia, she had barricaded herself in the house with the curtains shut so she wouldn't be seen by or have to interact with the other inhabitants of the village, especially the bearded man who had caught her out already.

She had spent hours on the phone to Marta, exchanging messages and little faces: *Do you remember all the times I slapped you when you didn't want to study?* her friend threatened her. *I'm not afraid to come there and do it again.* And scant minutes on the phone to her father, lying excellently. And that was everyone, because there were no other numbers in her contacts.

She had listened to dance music while lying on the sofa imagining she was someone else, standing on a podium in a nightclub, young and sexy, smoking, soaking the filters with saliva – *'You don't smoke, magical Emi, you give blow jobs to cigarettes'*. She had played the CD from the beginning to do aerobics, abdominals, thighs and glutes, like old times. She had moped about, masturbated, talked to the darkness: 'Go die, arsehole.'

That's enough now, Emilia told herself. She found her torch and keys, which had ended up in the crack of the sofa in a burrow of dust and crumbs. She put them in her bag. She checked she had her wallet. Then she went to the bathroom and looked at her face in the mirror.

She had bags under her eyes, which were lifeless like the eyes of the fish in ice boxes lining the jetty in Marina, and her skin was so pale her freckles stood out like lentils in milk.

She thought of Rita and their last meeting. The way she had pulled Emilia to her bosom like a mother to say goodbye. 'Call me, that day,' Rita had said. 'Do you promise? Because I guarantee you that day will come, and you'll be ready. You will live where you want to live, you'll start again. Call me, please.'

Emilia brushed her wild frizzy hair violently. She splashed handfuls of water on her cheeks, pinched them to give them a bit of colour and tried to mask herself with cherry-red lipstick and abundant mascara.

She said to the mirror: 'Freedom is hell, Rita. And I am not a person who keeps promises.'

She pulled a top on over her ripped jeans, tied a studded leather jacket around her waist, picked up her bag, armed herself with all the determination she had in her body, and headed towards the Stra' del Forche.

The idea of bumping into those people who looked her up and down and detected her rottenness almost made her turn around, lock herself in the bathroom with a razor blade and lapse into old habits, but she had decided to act. She owed it to her father.

The intertwined branches of the chestnut trees formed a frescoed ceiling above her head: a swaying mobile of brown, orange and yellow leaves and sudden glimmers of light. It reminded her of the sky in the mechanical nativity scene she loved as a little girl, with its papier-mâché sun and stars and comet. When she marvelled at that scene, crafted by the local residents' association, and felt the hands of her parents on her shoulders, their love, she felt she could trust herself and the world.

She stopped treading carefully and launched into a sprint down the mule path, spreading her arms wide. She risked tripping at every bend but she didn't care. The speed was exhilarating, liberating. *Marta*, she wondered, *how can I be more like you? Why didn't I follow you to Milan? Why didn't we live in the same flat? Sleep in the same bed?*

Because here we're all in the same boat, but each of us has our own black hole that we have to bear.

Emilia emerged from between the nettles, dishevelled with her tote bag and big boots, and peeked through the gap between the bar full of old men and Rosa's grocery shop. The descent had taken her less than fifteen minutes.

And now she was here.

She crossed the piazza and headed straight for the bus shelter. *What day is it today? Friday.* She ran her finger down the timetable. *What time is it? 2:45, good.* She checked the timetable again. Not good. She had missed it. By ten shitty minutes. And the next one, the last one, was at 6 p.m. Too late to get to the city, do what she had to do, and be home by a decent time. She lit a cigarette and turned on her phone.

She wrote to her father: I'm sorry.

The piazza was deserted. A car drove through every so often. Emilia watched them roll by, mostly three-wheeler Piaggio vans or rusty pick-ups, full of tools for the fields or cattle. She put her cigarette out on the back of her hand and lit another one. Then her father replied: *No, I'm sorry, I shouldn't have put pressure on you. You'll get there.*

She loved him. And the love hurt.

Because the world was full of model daughters who had disgusting dads: who beat them, or touched them, or some who even fucked them – she had met dozens of daughters like that, not least Marta. And Emilia, who was the worst of them, had somehow won the 'perfect dad' lottery.

She took a photo on her phone of the timetable for the only bus that crossed Valle: four trips on weekdays, two on weekends and national holidays. She promised herself she would catch it on Monday morning at six. She promised herself she would be highly productive next week. That she would clean toilets, shovel manure, serve pizza – anything she could to bring a wage home, to spend as soon as possible on a train ticket to Milan, to Marta. First, though, she had to solve the sleep problem.

Pointless looking for a herbalist to buy some valerian, let alone an electronics shop. But she was in Alma now, and didn't want it to be a wasted trip. She looked around. Of course there was absolutely nothing. Then her gaze paused on the sign of Bar Samurai with its scuzzy windows.

She smiled. *Why didn't I think of that earlier?*

Perhaps because it had been such a forbidden thing, alcohol – even at Christmas, New Year's, or Ferragosto – that the possibility of it had been pulled out at the root. They had managed to procure the odd joint on the rare occasions they were allowed out – just two quick tokes before stuffing their mouths with minty chewing gum – but a bottle of vodka would've been impossible. Even a shot was unthinkable.

The last time Emilia got drunk was at the end of her first year of high school: a kid's party at a pizzeria on the beach, with a midnight curfew. The party started badly – no one wanted to sit next to her for the pizza – and ended badly, on the slippery deckchairs between the collapsed umbrellas where everyone had retreated to except for her and one other person, of whom she couldn't remember a single detail.

She just remembered they had gone off to one side and drunk, drunk, drunk, and an old lifeguard had tried it on with them. She spent all the money her dad had given her on mojitos and, in the end, when she got home, he had held back her hair so it didn't end up in the bottom of the toilet along with her soul.

Sixteen years later, the opportunity had materialised again and the coast was clear, free of a sign saying 'extremely *verboten*'. She just had to walk about ten steps – and Emilia walked them with glee. The range of possibility had, for a decade, sat between zero and zero point one. And now, all of a sudden, it had rocketed up to a hundred thousand.

When she got to the front door she waited for someone to open it. Then she told herself she was being an idiot and walked in.

Cherry-red lipstick. Jeans you could see her legs through. The mischief and hunger of a person who, since that party in high school, had drunk only Coca-Cola, Fanta and water while her peers continued to get buzzed on the beach, lose their inhibitions, sing with guitars around bonfires, couple up, fuck each other.

She burst into Bar Samurai resolved to claw back a meagre sliver of that lost time, without delay and without looking anyone in the eye. At this momentous entrance, the most introverted, timid and savage old men of Valle raised their heads from their card games to look at her, *the foreigner.*

Emilia sat down at the bar and ordered one amaro, thank you.

Nobody made any effort to hide the fact they were staring at her. Nobody said ciao, hello, good afternoon. Piero, who was drying glasses, sized her up with a slow, investigatory look. Then, without making a sound, generously filled a glass and put it down in front of her.

Everybody returned to their games of poker, *scala quaranta* and *scopone* as if nothing had happened. But in fact, *everything* had happened. A woman. Drinking at three in the afternoon. Alone. And nobody knew who she was! And she had that lipstick on! It was such an exceptional event that not in a single kitchen, bedroom or cowshed would anybody speak of anything else for weeks.

The intruder, whose age, residence and genealogy everyone was secretly guessing, took small sips, absorbed, her legs crossed. She savoured the goodness of the alcohol as it burned her oesophagus, tickled her stomach, relaxed her nerves one by one, clouded her mind. And it was such a relief to release her grip on herself, the memory of being her, the weight of being her, that as soon as she had finished her first glass, she ordered a second.

Unfortunately, just as Emilia's head was spinning so much that she couldn't stand up, Patrizia and her friends walked in. Immediately noting the sensational novelty, Patrizia almost died from the thrill. So much so that she phoned me later on to tell me all about it.

She'd used the opportunity to return to her favourite topic: 'We should go out for dinner one of these evenings.' To talk about our lesson plans, 'nothing more than that', and to discuss Martino Fiume: 'How many times is it OK to make a pupil retake?' I skated around it and made my hundredth excuse, which she refused to accept like all the others. It didn't work. The following Monday at school, while I watched the children in the playground and heard nothing, all she did was talk talk talk about that strange woman who had struggled to pull a banknote from her purse and couldn't pick up her change, who had stumbled from the barstool to the door and then tripped down the first step. Who was obviously an alcoholic. Who was almost certainly a prostitute, or one of the headcases escaped from Villa Sorriso. A criminal. A witch. Because I did know, didn't I, that women with red hair were witches?

I found the woman bent over vomiting near the old washhouse.

The mountains had turned dark. The peaks of Cresto, Mucrone and Barone had hidden the sun that was thinning in the west, but the last light still filtered through, imbued with pink. The birds had retreated to their branches. The air had turned cold. Gusts of damp blew in from the woods, and leaves lay pulped on the floor. I stopped in my tracks.

I had been on the phone to Patrizia, so I knew. I admit that I went out that evening not so much for my usual walk as out of a concern that at that point I wouldn't have been able to name: the fear that this stranger, coming back up Stra' dal Forche in a sorry condition, might get hurt.

I observed her body as it convulsed. Without the shell of her ski jacket, her body was pale and thin. She couldn't have weighed more than forty-five kilos; her bones jutted out through her clothes. I was astonished she had made it all the way up to Sassaia this drunk.

I waited while she stood up straight, plunged her head into the freezing water of the wash trough and reopened her eyes.

'Better?'

She focused in on me, not frightened this time. She ran her hand across her forehead and nodded before collapsing heavily onto the bench.

The water gurgled, Basilio's geese honked in the distance. Her lipstick was smudged.

'I went on a bit of a binge.'

'I think the whole of Valle might know about it by now.'

She smiled and shook her head. 'I'm a mess.'

With her eyes closed again, locks of wet hair dripping over her shoulders and the childlike smattering of freckles on her nose and cheeks, she looked like a weary Pippi Longstocking.

'You're safe here,' I said.

'That's why I came.'

She opened her eyes. They were forest green, apple green, bud green; specked with yellow; beautiful. But absolutely devoid of light, like two dead stars. They unsettled me. And when I realised that we were actually looking at each other, even talking, I felt suddenly embarrassed, like in those dreams where you find yourself naked in the middle of a crowded square.

I gave her a cursory jut of my chin and dragged myself clumsily in a random direction – not that there were many to choose from. I wanted to disappear into the trees.

'Wait,' I heard her call.

She walked towards me with small steps, keeping a distance between us for which I was grateful.

'You live here, right?'

I nodded.

She squeezed her bag strap between her hands and looked like she was struggling. 'I know what I'm about to say is going to sound very strange. And that I might look very strange to you, as well as drunk. But I assure you I am lucid, I swear . . . it's just that I can't sleep.' She dropped her bag to the ground and began to move her hands in the air. 'I'm not used to this silence, it's boring holes in my ears. There's no TV, no radio, no nothing, and I need to hear voices, people speaking. Because I've always had that, I've never slept alone.'

I thought she was being very dramatic.

'There's a man who's gonna bring me a TV soon and it'll all be better. But in the meantime . . .'

I didn't dare tell her that no house in Sassaia had a TV, nor would any house ever be able to use one.

'. . . but in the meantime, I'm asking you for a favour. And I beg you not to think badly of me. Would you come to my house this evening and talk until I fall asleep?'

I remained frozen, holding my breath as she piled unlikely sentence on top of unlikely sentence. I was suddenly startled. 'We don't even know each other!'

'I know, I know!' She seemed like she was acting, but was desperately sincere at the same time. 'I promise you I'm not crazy, I'm just exhausted. I can pay you for your time, or do you a favour in return. I won't need you for long. I get into bed, you talk to me. About goats, about astrology, whatever you want. Then, as soon as you see that I'm asleep, and I think I'm gonna go quickly tonight, you can leave.'

I couldn't believe it. She was asking me to go to her house after dinner, into her bedroom. I didn't even know her name, nor she mine. I could have been a pervert, someone with bad intentions, someone who rapes women instead of someone who used to pay Gisella once a month at Le Piane Hotel in the middle of the paddy fields.

'I'm sorry, ignore me.' She waved a hand in the air, wiping away the question she had so laboriously constructed. 'Forget it.' She picked her bag up off the floor, red in the face.

She was so disappointed and embarrassed, a sensation I knew all too well, and I did something I hadn't done with anyone for a very long time: I felt her pain.

'OK,' I responded, against my better judgement. 'I'll come over later, after dinner.'

5

ONE DAY NEAR THE end of September in 2001, Rita had said: 'Let's find the good and start from there.'

'If I've ended up here, evidently there's never been any good,' Emilia had replied, entrenched behind her usual wall of boredom.

'Nobody is all bad. Even the people the papers call monsters – paedophiles, terrorists, mothers who murder their children – have a shred of humanity somewhere.'

'Yeah, sure.' Emilia laughed, fiddling with her packet of Winston Blues.

'Go ahead and smoke. But it's not like you have many options: you've got to start somewhere.'

Emilia reached out across the desk, grabbed her social worker's lighter which was covered in stickers of cats, lit a cigarette and sank back into the chair.

'I've already signed up for school; what more do you want?'

'The life we're talking about is yours. You're not doing me any favours by studying. I already have a job, a degree, a house: I know who I am. It's you who has to make some decisions and find something to do.'

'You're talking as if I have a future.'

'I'd like you to give it a chance – you're only seventeen!'

Emilia leapt up from her seat. 'Don't take the piss, Rita. Who the hell's gonna hire me after this? Who will rent me a house? Who will want to be my friend, my boyfriend? Who will ever forget?'

'Oh, how you run!' Rita started laughing. 'Slow down, one step at a time. Let's think about this school year for now, OK?'

How, Emilia thought, *can there be a remedy for the irremediable?*

'Can I tell you something?' Rita stared at her calmly, her elbows resting on the desk and her hands together as if in prayer. 'It feels impossible to you now. But I promise you everything passes. And, if it can't pass, it changes.'

Of the dense crowd of people the state had laid out before Emilia to try and salvage something from the wreckage – professionals who certainly didn't aspire to any grand redemption, but would've been happy with minimal but real change – Rita was the only one who immediately broke through her sealed emotions, which were at that time considerably dulled by psychiatric medication.

People said social workers tore children away from families, that they were evil, scowling, sadistic witches. But Rita just seemed like a sincere and pragmatic woman.

The first time they met in her office on the ground floor with a view of the sports field, it was the middle of summer, forty degrees, and Rita, energetically fanning herself, put her cards on the table with very little preamble. 'You don't need to use formal language with me, but I'm not your friend. We are here to face what happened, and I won't ask you to do anything until you feel ready. No Jung, no Freud. My goal is to extract a concrete project from your current difficulties, and keep it simple. Oh, and in my office, you are allowed to smoke.'

Emilia liked her immediately. For the permission to smoke and the promise to keep it simple; because when you find yourself in the middle of an enormous shitshow, before diving into the remote depths of your subconscious, you need a floor to stand on – and, yes, a Winston. She also liked Rita for her backcombed hair, which was platinum blonde like Pamela Anderson's, and her voluptuous bosom, also worthy of an American TV actress, framed by a generous neckline. For the off-trend fuchsia-pink lipstick that melted in the humidity, and her dramatic stilettos. Finally, for her Bologna accent, which Emilia adored.

From that day on they met twice a week, and Rita never turned up in anything less than a flowery silk dress or a canary-yellow, powder-pink or emerald-green pantsuit. She always looked dressed to meet the Queen of England, not a wretch like Emilia.

This was the only meeting in which they had ever bickered. Emilia was still in a profoundly dark phase. She didn't even open her mouth with Ms Venturi. It was the period in which she sat alone at a table in the canteen and watched the others eat, without speaking, without even touching the bread. She had started, timidly, to talk to Marta, in their room in the evenings: the odd sarcastic comment on a TV programme or on their surroundings. But her mind was still absorbed by a single preoccupation: finding a battery, a blade of any length or a shoelace long enough to hang herself from the tap in the shower. The words 'future', 'good' and 'after' were enough to drive her mad.

Then Rita caught her off-guard: 'OK, don't tell me what's good in you. Tell me what you like.'

'What I like?' Emilia failed to hide her surprise. 'Uh . . .' She shrugged her shoulders.

'There must be something . . .'

She smiled with all the arrogance she could muster. 'Life!'

'Umm . . .' Rita stayed composed. For a moment her ultra made-up face crumpled into condescension and a holy patience that said: *You think you're original? You all say the same – 'life' – and lo and behold, you've all thrown it down the drain. I'm sure you're one of the best but do you know how many wretched girls like you I've seen come through here?*

'And if we wanted to try for a ballpark . . .' She coughed. 'A school subject, a sport?'

'I hate sports and I hate studying.'

'So why did you enrol in high school?'

'Because if I didn't it would've broken my dad's heart. Even more, I mean.'

'And if you had to do something for yourself? Because you wanted it?'

The 'you' hit her straight in the face. *Who the hell are you, Emilia? Are you still in there?*

And that verb, *want*, pierced her in the only demilitarised zone of her soul that remained.

She squashed her cigarette in the ashtray and decided to take the question seriously. The fact was that there was nothing simple about 'likes' and 'wants'. Because on one hand she didn't deserve to breathe, let alone have fun or enjoy something. But on the other, she was being forced to live, to occupy herself with something more edifying than the cuts on her arms and legs. It was a contradiction in terms: of society, but also of herself. Because she was dead inside, but she was still alive.

She looked out at the city, its towers and bells, beyond the sports field, the netting, the walls. That city had been her promised land since she was a little girl. Going up on the local train at the weekends had always been a source of unbridled joy for her, to visit a museum, attend a concert or Liberation Day celebrations: they were days when she would wake up at five to pack her rucksack by herself and lay the table for her parents' breakfast.

She never could have imagined that one day she would live there for real, not as a university student as she had dreamed, but as a wreck of a human who was already rotten at seventeen, greasy hair tied with a saggy elastic, pimples, and nails chewed down to the quick.

'I like sitting by the window and drawing the rooftops of Bologna,' Emilia admitted. 'Villa Aldini and San Luca and the hills that blur towards Modena. Either in pencil or with watercolours.'

Rita's face brightened. 'And will you bring them with you next time, these drawings?'

'Meh, if you really want to see them . . .'

'What else do you draw?'

'Whatever I can see from the window: a bit of church with a hill behind, the balcony of the building opposite. Once, when they brought us oil paints and canvases . . .' her defences had inadvertently come down, 'there's a place in the mountains in Piedmont where I used to go for summer holidays when I was little, and on the canvas I painted one of those mountains and hung it over my bed.'

'Really, you, the seaside girl?' Rita innocently let slip.

Emilia stood up. Her dark, sad, dead eyes were suddenly hard like rocks, injected with a black light. She pointed at Rita. 'I hate the sea,' she snarled. 'I'll be happy if I never see it again.'

'Why?' Rita wasn't afraid to ask the question.

Emilia hadn't shed a single tear over the course of these terrible months. Not one. But now, as she sat back down, one fell down her cheek. It slowly slipped onto her neck, and was absorbed by the cotton of her T-shirt. It was the first tear of that horrendously long in-between time, the chasm between the before and the after.

'Because my mother always took me to the sea. It was her favourite place,' she admitted, staring into space as if she wasn't there. 'She'd rent an umbrella and a beach hut at Bagno Amore for the three of us, back when we were happy. The only relief I have now, the only good thing in

my life, is the thought that she never had to know what
I did after.'

I knocked at 9 p.m. with a bag full of books.

She answered immediately, as if she had been waiting
behind the door, barefoot and in her pyjamas. She half
hid behind the door, standing on tiptoes – maybe to appear
taller – and smiled. But as soon as she looked down and
saw the books she asked angrily, 'What did you bring
them for?'

I hesitated on the doorstep. The wind that blows on
November nights is so indifferent to us, to our feelings,
as if it comes from the frozen belly of the mountains. It
ruffled my beard and the hair I hadn't cut for months.
My stomach was in knots; I hadn't managed to eat anything
for dinner.

'I wouldn't know what to say to you without them,' I
responded. 'I'm not good at talking about myself. I'm not
good at making things up either. So if it's OK with you,
I'll read you something. Otherwise I'll go home to bed.'

'Sorry, you're right.'

She opened the door wide, stood to one side to let me
in and I stooped, for the first time in decades, into Iole's
kitchen.

All the houses in Valle are tiny and have low ceilings,
short beds and small furniture because they were built
long ago, for a generation very different to ours. She and
I were clearly the wrong size, in the wrong time. I felt her
watching me from the corner she had remained in.

I wandered like a fidgety giant around that Lilliputian room, not knowing where to look. Her pyjamas were very thin and I shyly averted my eyes from her shoulders, her slender neck, her collarbones which pushed through her top. I fixed my gaze to the walls to keep myself anchored. I recognised the unchanged arrangement of oven gloves on the sink, the copper pots on the sideboard, the holey chestnut-roasting pan.

'Your grandmother – or perhaps it was your aunt since she didn't have children . . .' I thought out loud, 'would always invite me in to eat roasted chestnuts.'

'That wasn't my aunt,' she hurried to clarify. 'I never met the previous owner.'

And I had no reason to suspect that she was lying: why should she be? Even if she had kept everything, doilies included, that the 'previous owner' had. I took the books out of my bag and laid them out on the table.

'Non-fiction, novels, poetry. You can choose.'

She walked over reluctantly and forced herself to consider them. I was aware of my discomfort growing in the silence as she decided. To break it, I asked her: 'What did books ever do to you?'

'They remind me of a person it hurts me to remember.'

She was sincere. But I wasn't yet capable of distinguishing her revelations from her lies, the past from the present, the sweetness of her freckled face from the darkness that lay behind her eyes. I just thought about how it hurt me too to remember certain people, but it was for this exact reason that I clung desperately to any object, place, or habit that had once belonged to them.

'Do you live in that flowerpot across the road?' Her tone was brusque suddenly. 'With the embroidered curtains?'

I nodded.

'And do you live there on your own? Or with your mother? Sorry. Your wife?'

'On my own,' I responded in a mumble.

She squeezed her eyes into slits, scrutinising me as if this detail had made me suddenly more interesting.

I felt electricity in the air, like on a summer afternoon before a storm, when the sky darkens, all the birds fly away, the animals hide, and you know that out of that void an inferno is about to explode.

Why was I there? Why, when I had withdrawn completely from the world? When I had burnt the telephone book with the numbers of my school and university friends, and cut off every significant relationship, and stopped phoning my sister? Why had I accepted this proposition from a stranger?

'Have you chosen?' I asked.

She looked down again at the titles, stroked one of the covers with her fingertip. 'They're all the same to me. You decide.'

I grabbed a title at random, not looking, because now I was in a rush to conclude this business and get out of there unscathed.

She led the way, swaying almost imperceptibly as she climbed the stairs, slowly shifting the muscles and tendons inside those white cotton pyjamas with little red hearts that exposed her underwear. Her body had a chimeric quality – a child, a fully-grown woman; defenceless, threatening. I tried not to scrutinise it but at the same time I interrogated it: what has brought you here?

Then we left the glow of the electric light and slipped into a well of darkness.

'Wait there,' she said, waving a hand in my direction.

I listened to the sound of her bare feet moving somewhere to my left, treading on the worm-eaten boards of cherry wood, making the same creaking my own did every night when I went to bed, injuring the silence of Sassaia. I heard the scratch of a match, the sizzle of flame. I turned in that direction and saw her room, now unveiled by the glow of five candles.

It was the same as mine, as Basilio's, as anyone else's who had ever lived in that lost village. Worn-out flowery wallpaper, heavy old walnut furniture and the smell of damp wood. But here, hung on one wall, there glimmered a row of canvases painted with such intense colour that they looked alive. I was astonished. They were glimpses of Sassaia, but the brushstrokes were energetic and free – certainly not the style of any average local painter.

She placed the candle holder on the chest of drawers and slipped quickly under the covers.

'You can sit there,' she pointed at an upholstered chair far from the bed, 'and move that horrible doll. I need to get rid of all this old crap.'

My legs were too long and my body too big for the chair, but I tried to wedge myself in between the arms by sitting sideways. I opened the book at a random page. My hands were shaking and I hoped she didn't notice. I did, however, see that she'd left the shutters open.

'Do you want me to close them?' I was about to get up, but she lurched upright with an alarm that shocked me.

'No no! Leave them like that.'

'Doesn't the sun bother you in the morning? It comes up on this side.'

'On the contrary,' she said, lying down again and pulling the sheets up to her chin. 'I finally get to sleep for a couple of hours when the light comes in. If only I could keep the candles lit . . . But my dad says it's too dangerous, and I can no longer believe in this myth of the electrician.'

'How old are you?' I couldn't help asking.

'Because I'm scared of the dark?' She laughed. 'I'll tell you if you tell me first.'

'I'm thirty-six.'

'You look at least ten years older!'

I wasn't offended. Actually, seeing her face suddenly amused, her cheeks taking on some colour and her neat white rows of teeth revealed in a disarming smile made me smile too. I stopped quickly, though, because the laughter hadn't reached her eyes. They were still and helpless, submerged in an unknowable abyss.

'I'm thirty-one. But you tell me I look twenty-one, OK?'

'OK, it's true.'

'And now,' she closed her eyes, 'begin, please.'

I cleared my throat and concentrated. Then, as if I were at school between the high walls of the old building in

Alma, in front of a small and innocent audience, in full voice I recited:

Come love let us sit together
In the cramped kitchen breathing kerosene.

There's fuel enough to forget the weather,
The knife is ours and the bread is clean.

Come love let us play the game
Of what to take and when to run,

Of come with me and come what may
And holding hands to hold off the sun.

'I don't like it.'

'It's Mandelstam . . .'

'Never heard of him.'

'Russian poet, one of the greatest of the twentieth century. He died in a gulag in Siberia.'

She raised her green eyes to the ceiling. 'Ah, he was inside!' She smiled. 'I like him better now. Read another one.'

I continued, wedged into the armchair, in a voice that, due to some absurd emotion, broke in a way it never had in front of my students. It hardened and got stuck, defeated by certain passages:

I see the moon, un-breathing,
a sky dead as canvas:
your world, strange and sickening,
I welcome, Emptiness!

She couldn't seem to handle these verses either.

'Do you know anyone who needs staff?' She propped herself up with her elbow on the pillow and placed her head on the palm of her thin-fingered hand. 'I need to find myself a job ASAP.'

'A job, around here?' I almost laughed. 'Ever since the Seventies nobody's done anything here but leave.'

'Is there not even a little trattoria I could work at? An older woman who needs a hand around the house? I'll do anything, even cleaning cowsheds. My father won't let me stay here if I don't get a job.'

'Why do you want to be here so much? There's no one here, you're young . . .'

'You're young too.'

She got out of bed and went and opened the window. Cold air filled the room and I shivered. She didn't. She leaned on the windowsill, pulled her red hair from one side of her face and lit a cigarette against the darkness.

I wondered where she came from. Her accent wasn't from Piedmont, or from anywhere else I could identify; she kept the shutters open at night; at the age of thirty-one she needed someone to read her to sleep. I was devoured by the desire to know, but, at the same time, instinct told me not to probe.

I got up as if we had finished and it was time to go.

She continued: 'Anyway, it's not true that there's nobody here. You're here.'

I could see her cigarette glowing each time she inhaled.

I stayed standing with Mandelstam's *Eighty Poems* in my hand, searching for a way to say goodbye, but I couldn't find it. In the half-light of the candles, she insisted on staring at me as she smoked. And something about her reminded me of the outline I'd seen on that first evening, dancing.

'What experience do you have? What did you study?'

She smiled in a wilfully crafty, seductive way – more like a middle-school girl than a woman of thirty.

'What qualifications do you think I have?'

'I have no idea.'

'High school certificate? Professional qualifications? Or do I seem too stupid for that?'

'I'm not judging anyone.'

'Wow, do you want a medal?'

She leaned out to throw her cigarette butt into the alley and closed the window. Instead of going back to the bed she walked towards me. I could smell her. And feel the heat that her body emanated through the fabric of her clothes. And her heart in the silence. And mine.

'I graduated in fine art,' she said, moving closer and removing almost all the space between us.

'Well,' I replied to break the spell we had fallen under, 'I might know someone . . . Did you do all of those paintings?' I gestured towards the canvases. She nodded as if she no longer cared about finding work, or anything for that matter. 'They're wonderful,' I told her sincerely. 'Basilio has been a house painter forever, but he's good,' I continued, grinding on. 'He could've become an artist if his parents had had the money to send him to Turin . . .' I was tempted to step backwards, to hide behind the wall of words. 'He doesn't just paint, he restores, decorates – he's even been asked to work on the frescoes in the churches of Valle, as well as the one in Alma and some other towns too. But he's too old to manage alone . . . He's the only other resident of Sassaia, along with us two.'

As soon as I said 'us two', she kissed me; pulling my shoulders down with both her hands, forcing my mouth open with such hunger that I couldn't put up any resistance.

She pushed me over to the bed. I didn't want it, and I didn't want anything else. It was the first thought that had crossed my mind when she said, 'Come to my house this evening and talk'. Undressing her, touching her. It had been her first thought too, she confessed months later.

For the rest of that evening we said nothing to one another. Words would have been impossible for either of us. Numbing ourselves against each other's bodies was almost a liberation. I felt all of my isolation and hers holding on to and annihilating one another in turn, on that single bed that smelled of long-closed rooms, of forest, of memories. We were the only glow of light in the mountains.

It was the thing she had been wanting for years: to fuck a man. And I, to fuck a woman I felt something for. We had stumbled upon each other. She would've done it with whoever had lived opposite, and I with any girl who had come to die where I was buried.

But now we were alive. And I was in love with her without knowing anything about her. And if I had continued not knowing, life would have been a perfect place. Like that night.

6

HAVING MIRACULOUSLY FOUND A bar of signal, the telephone burst into life. The room was bathed in light, the half-open window bringing in the smell of stone and mountain streams on the breeze as Emilia lay on the bed chewing her nails.

When she saw that it was Marta and not her father, she squeezed both her thumbs on the green circle, as if she still had the old Alcatel from Year 5 with the rubber keys, the one that became an 'exhibit' and was never given back.

'I was about to call you, I swear,' she burst out.

'I need to tell you something.'

Emilia chose not to notice the sombre tone of Marta's voice. 'Wait, me first. I have *unbelievable* news.'

'I'm all ears.'

'I lost my virginity!' She shouted it as if she was at a protest with a megaphone in her hand. Marta remained cold.

'Fucking hell. What is it, your fifth day there?' She returned to her usual teasing, cheerful tone. 'Anyway, sorry to remind you, but it's hardly like you were an innocent little virgin . . .'

'My hymen was intact, until last night.'

'Fair enough. Who is he, what's he called?'

Emilia burst out laughing. 'I have no idea!'

'I've always said it,' Marta was invigorated, 'even when nobody believed me, and you wouldn't listen to me either. I've always said you were a winner.' She put her reason for phoning to one side and let herself run. 'Do you remember that day in the yard? When I interrupted the match for you?'

'How could I forget it?'

'You were sat there on that little wall, legs dangling down . . . what a picture! When I was made to volunteer at the old people's home, some of them were lobotomised, and they always reminded me of you in that period. I said to you: "Baby, you have a fire, don't waste it." And indeed you haven't!'

Emilia smiled, sinking her head into the pillow and closing her eyes to remember more clearly. Nothing was as gratifying as Marta's approval, and so few moments of her life were as sweet, in hindsight, as that day in August 2001 when their friendship began.

She could still recall, through the depths of time, the pounding of her heart.

It was five in the afternoon and tons of cicadas were jammed onto the branches of trees, buzzing like mad.

Bologna, on the other side of the barbed-wire fence, looked like a post-apocalyptic wasteland. The buildings they could see all had their shutters down and their balconies cleared. No sounds of cars came from the streets. Just a muggy emptiness dripping over everything.

On this side, however, in the imposing yard, they were all present. Noisy, sweaty, half-naked. There were no summer holidays from this place. They played volleyball, endlessly, because there was nothing else to do in the summer when time melted along with the asphalt. It was so hot that sometimes the girls went into the vegetable garden they were cultivating for their gardening course, unreeled the hosepipe, turned the water on and squirted it at each other in turn, soaking their clothes and hair. They took it too far, of course, and were scolded. Happiness? *Verboten!*

Their slender bodies pulsated under the sun. They were so radiant inside their horrible adolescence. If they scored a point, they smacked each other's bums, kissed on the lips in front of everyone – but secretly, in the bathrooms, or at night, once the TVs were turned off, things got rough. And when they scored a point, they went wild – no, ballistic. Emilia had never heard certain swear words before; she learnt them all there. After a mistake they slapped one another, pulled each other's hair. They were such a spectacle; if only someone had been able to see them over that wall, admire them without knowing who they were, where they were, the lives they had come from. They were so beautiful, so alive. They wore jeans they'd ripped perfectly to reveal half a buttock, tank tops rolled up to just under their bras and held tight with an elastic band. All of them except for Emilia, who sat to one side on a wall. Every so often she woke from her trance and squinted at them. She was astounded by how gracefully they skipped under the net, clobbered the other team with shocking rage, by the fact that they were *girls*. Normal ones, not that different from the ones who, in that same moment, were playing beach volleyball in Rimini, Riccione, Punta Marina, armed with parents standing at the side of the court or boyfriends they'd later rub up against in the cabins.

With time she would become a veteran and, despite her laziness, and more for the sense of being in a team than for love of the sport, also a passable volleyball player. But at that point she'd been there about a month and a half and was confined to the wall that enclosed the vegetable garden, at a distance from the pitch.

Everyone in that walled courtyard, in which the sky was a bordered rectangle rather than an infinite thing, was diseased. But Emilia was convinced that she was the one with the most serious illness, the most purulent wound. If in her life before she was already the favoured target of bullies, now, in this horrific nightmare, she was like that Greek hero, injured and damned, abandoned on a rock in the middle of the sea, dazed by the sun and dried out by the heat. What was his name again? Philoctetes.

Since being marooned here, she hadn't once tried to talk or pass the ball to any of the other castaways. And they had held back from looking too closely at her void, because according to the rules of the place, which worked the opposite way to how things worked outside, the more wounds you had, the worthier you were of respect. But she didn't yet know the rules; she thought they were disgusted by her and that was that.

That day, after a teammate had been hurt badly enough to have to leave the pitch, Marta looked around and, instead of calling up one of the girls who was waiting patiently at the side, she decided, for some unfathomable reason, that she wanted Emilia.

The other players broke into a chorus of protest, but Marta cared little what other people thought, and she strode through the mugginess towards Emilia. She stood with her hands on her hips, her majestic shadow enveloping the new girl.

'My name is Marta Vargas,' she introduced herself, needlessly. 'I've been here two years and I have another eight ahead of me.' Translated: I am an unrivalled, indisputable authority, and as a rule, others come to me, not me to them.

Emilia, full of anxiety medication, had tried to bring her into focus through the fog she was imprisoned in and which, when she succeeded, was left pierced by the black, almost blue, hair that shone down Marta's back. And by her dark eyes that, as Emilia would discover later, she had inherited from her Vietnamese mother. And by her catwalk height of one metre seventy-seven, her athletic legs, perky breasts, ferocious smile. She looked just like Sailor Mars, Emilia thought, before looking down again.

Marta didn't seem to appreciate this. As the others continued to protest, impatient to start the game up again, she had snarled at her not 'you have a fire', but 'get up off your arse and come and play, you're not the princess of the wall'. Then, since Emilia had dared to keep her eyes cast down and her legs dangling, Marta grabbed her chin with her nails and gripped it so hard she left marks.

'No one begs here. No one waits, doing fuck all, to be saved. In case you didn't understand, princesses don't exist. We're all dickheads, bitches and queens in the same way.'

'Hello? Heidi? Are you there? I asked you what the guy does! Does he earn much? This is crucial information.'

The Marta of now, like the queen of back then, shook her back to life.

'I didn't ask . . .'

'What the fuck, did you not talk at all? You just jumped on him and pulled his pants down? Good girl, that's how you do it.'

'No, he actually read me some poetry.'

'Umm . . .' This detail was disappointing to Marta. 'You can't survive off poetry.'

'Meh, maybe he's a shepherd. He has a beard . . .'

'Christ, Emilia, a sheep-herding poet? Just no. You need to find a businessman, an engineer, a lawyer. If he writes and you paint, it's over; you might even be the one who ends up supporting him! But is he clean? Or does he have a record?'

They both giggled.

They were two adults now. They were no longer playing volleyball; the days of timetables, fingering in the toilets and having to be sedated to get through Christmas were over. They no longer belonged to that place. They were survivors; and yet, they didn't belong anywhere else.

'I don't think he'd be capable of taking a wallet someone dropped on the street,' Emilia responded.

'OK, well, fuck him then, but don't fall in love. And now I'm sorry but I have to give you some bad news.'

Emilia got up from the bed and sighed. 'Today? Really?'

'Myriam's brother called me.'

The line faltered and Emilia had to go to the window to get back in range. 'I don't want to know.'

'She's dead.'

Emilia stood there staring at the high sky that was an infinite thing, yes, but had already gone back to being distant and unreachable, like it had been in the yard.

'The funeral is tomorrow afternoon, in Piacenza.' Marta hesitated. 'If you can get to Milan in the morning, we can go together.'

'Do we have to see each other again at a funeral?' Emilia felt her cheeks getting hot. 'After all this fucking time, at Myriam's funeral? Are you taking the piss? We always promised we'd meet for dinner at a Michelin-starred restaurant, at the biggest rave in Europe, on the Costa Smeralda, and now you're suggesting a fucking funeral?'

'Come on, Emilia, we pissed, studied, sang, cried together for . . . how many years?'

'We mostly slapped each other.'

'She killed herself, Emi.'

'Coward.'

'She didn't get help from anyone. They all left her alone. They took her little girl away because she ran away from the residential community again and kept shooting up . . . And in response she pumped so much of the stuff into her veins that she could have died twice.'

It wasn't an irrational thing to do, Emilia thought. If any one of them were to read their own story from the beginning, paying particular attention to the most important chapter, then what Myriam had done would have seemed the logical conclusion to all of them.

'I made a vow to myself a long time ago that I would never set foot in a cemetery again in my life. I won't go to my father's funeral, I've already told him. And I'm sorry for Myriam. She was a bitch, but I'm sorry . . .' Emilia's voice cracked, 'especially for that little girl. But it's too easy to do what she did.'

They fell silent, each of them hanging on to the other's breath, their phones resting against their ears, listening to the emptiness of Milan merging with the emptiness of Sassaia. They were both remembering their old room. The four identical beds, perfectly made up. Myriam slept next to Afifa, Marta next to Emilia. Keeping watch over their sleepless nights, pinned to the wall in a strategic position, was Brad Pitt in skintight jeans, rebaptised 'The Angel of Masturbation'. And then there was Luke Perry, sullen, and Brandon from *Beverly Hills 90210* with that floppy hair that was no longer trendy down on earth. But the four of them had been left behind, on a separate asteroid, and while up there, adrift, they found, challenged and loved one another. Sizing each other up with suspicion at the beginning, bombarding each other with verbal arrows. But they ended up sharing everything: G-strings, pads, kisses, fears, maths and philosophy notes, desires.

'I shouldn't have asked you to come. It's too soon for you.' Marta's voice cracked too. 'But you have to do me a favour: when you see a nice view, up there in the mountains, give her a wave. Because I'm certain she's gone to heaven. It doesn't matter what people think, we're all going. We've sweated for it. And fuck you if you ever pull anything like that, OK? Keep fucking the nameless guy, earn some money and enjoy this shitty life as much as you can because I want to see you again. Then, I promise, I'll take you out to dinner, on me. But you *stay in line*, as Frau Direktorin used to say.'

She put the phone down because she was crying, and crying in front of the others was something you didn't do. The old rules still counted:

1. Don't cry.
2. Don't slander.
3. Keep your word.
4. Don't rat on family.

These were the fundamentals of their education. Emilia repeated them in her head to stop herself from falling.

At eleven o'clock I went into the woods because I couldn't stand waiting any longer. For what? For her to wake up and come and find me? For her to knock on my door? Why would she?

I took my gardening gloves, hat and net bag. I pulled on my boots and put two slices of bread and cheese in my knapsack for lunch because I wanted to be out for as long as possible.

I was certain she wouldn't want to see me again, that she already regretted it: no way would such an uninhibited and sexy woman settle for a caveman, a 'poor bachelor' as I was known in the town.

A man around here marries as soon as possible, at twenty. He impregnates his wife, becomes a severe father, works hard twelve hours a day moving cattle and stones, and when he finishes goes to the Samurai to drink and play cards with the other men. He doesn't read poetry, he doesn't fuck strangers in their thirties on the first night of knowing them. And, if this place doesn't suit him, he leaves – like almost all my own friends had.

I went up the escarpment of Monte Cresto through piles of dead leaves that came up to my calves. It was a strange November, so warm that the animals were still out, not yet preparing for hibernation, the birds were perched all over the tree branches, disoriented insects buzzed around slowly, and there was an ocean of light between the trees, the chestnuts glistening on the sea floor.

I bent down and started to pick them up, separating the intact ones from the rotten ones, the ones full of holes, with the same intuition I had as a boy when everyone in Sassaia poured into the woods before the winter froze us inside for months. The best nuts, the biggest and hardest, I didn't put in the net with the others, but in my pocket. It was a task I should've done the evening of November 2ⁿᵈ, but she had plunged into my life and made me forget.

I did notice a little bloodstain on the bedsheet. Who would've thought? She was the first woman on whose face I'd seen pleasure. Who had guided me into her as she desired, who had said indecent words and hadn't hidden anything from me, except . . .

Except where she came from; why she was here; her name.

I had fled like a thief as soon as the sun slipped into the room. Without daring to look at her, without leaving a note. I just got dressed as quickly as possible, tried not to make those goddamn wooden floorboards creak, repeating to myself over and over that nothing irreparable had happened, nothing of significance. And I continued to repeat it to myself now, without really believing it.

There were just crevices, ravines and cliff edges. No path, no clearing. But I knew those woods better than I knew myself and I didn't get lost. On the contrary, I knew exactly where to go. Like a bolt from the blue, I felt I needed to go to a place I hadn't been back to for years. It was where the partisans hid during the war, before they were found and slaughtered. And where Brother Dolcino and Margherita are said to have fallen in love, before they were burnt alive. Where the courageous, the heretics, the witches met: *our* secret place.

It was just a ruin, really. Hidden in the dense forest in a corner the sun never touched. When I got there, I dropped my knapsack and bag of chestnuts on the ground and lay down on my back, my arms spread wide among the leaves. I stared for a long time at a comma of sky indented by the tips of the beech trees, frozen in the phony summer that bubbled around me.

Then I found the courage to close my eyes and listen again to the chorus of voices from when we were children.

Some were calling from outside the ruin, alarmed, tentative – and among these I distinguished my own whining: 'Vale, come out! Where are you? Vale!' Others resounded from inside, on reconnaissance, looking for the partisans' guns, the witches' cauldrons, led by the boldest voice of all: my sister's.

Valle was still populated then. There were few of us children, maybe twenty-odd across all the hamlets, but we knew everyone and we grew up together. In the summer we'd go out in the morning, with bread and cheese in our knapsacks, and not come home until evening, tired and hungry. We were never looked for or reprimanded. The only rule was, don't die – at the bottom of a crevice, torn to pieces in the dark. But we moved like wolves in packs and watched each other's backs. In our shorts, calves scarred by brambles and pockets equipped with penknives. Valeria had a switchblade: she could carve branches into blowguns and spears, and she liked to etch her initials into bark to mark her territory. She had her own company; she didn't want me clinging on to her. But I followed her regardless, attached myself like a tick to her friends, who were six or seven years older than me. She was the one who first ventured into this building that might have once been a hayloft, or a shelter for sheep, or a place to store chestnuts. She burst in with a stick and drove away the bats, terrorising them, and imparted orders to the boys. She was the boss, the conductor, the witch of the woods.

And I stayed outside, with the cowards. Frail, scrawny, ugly. I was already a little swot who could read, write and count at five years old, but she, eleven, was a prodigy of beauty, of vitality, of such resourcefulness that she had no need for books or grades. Everyone in Valle was in love with her, and I more than anyone else. Because she was free and fearless, because she shone. And I had the same blood as her! Nothing could have pulled us apart – of that much I was certain. We were like granite, slate, mountains.

And yet, things went the way they went.

And after, she was no longer free or beautiful. After, I watched her harden, fall silent, dry up.

I had never betrayed her, I realised, astonished, until yesterday.

As I lay on my back among the leaves in front of the secret place of our childhood, torn to my marrow between forgetting the night spent with the stranger whose name I didn't know and running breathlessly to her; between forgetting Valeria and deciding to finally look for her; down there, in Sassaia, in Iole's creaking house, the stranger wandered restlessly, wrapped in a dressing gown. She realised she had run out of clean underwear and bedsheets, and it dawned on her that a much bigger challenge than the lack of a television awaited her: the lack of a washing machine.

I didn't see her as she went continuously to the window to see if I was home. I didn't spy on her as she sunk into a soft and formless Saturday, smoking cigarette after cigarette, insulting an old roommate out loud: 'What a bitch, you could have at least said goodbye. You could've got my number from Marta and told me, "I'm so fed up of not being able to sleep, that now I'm going to sleep forever." I would've understood. I would've sent you a kiss. I would've said: "Think of your daughter, for God's sake, don't be a twat."'

I was sure she had judged me as a silent lover – stiff, mediocre – and discarded me. But she, with her hair wet and arms covered in cuts she had inflicted on herself straight after her shower, had at some point dug out her A4 block of paper and her pencil case. She was tired of managing her pain with a disposable razor blade. She sat down in the kitchen, lit her umpteenth Winston Blue and, with a grey soft lead pencil, attacked the blank page.

'Words are useless,' she explained to me later, 'but drawing isn't.' A straight line, a curve, a circle, are faithful to things, respectful of their limits, of the painful things you can't see under the surface: drawings aren't fixated on definitions.

'I haven't even asked you your name,' she said to the sheet then as she traced, blurred, blackened.

Anyway, what would your name tell me about you? We are not our names, our surnames, our relationships, written up in differing amounts of detail by psychiatrists, social workers, consultants, she thought.

We are chiaroscuro.

Pits of darkness from which come, sometimes, chance slices of light. And I was good; she could see it immediately. I was angry, barricaded into myself like a tangle of thorns, but I was good. Unlike her.

I headed home as the sun was setting. I peeked at the house opposite: the lights were out; it looked like no one was in. When I got to my door, I stepped on something that made a familiar sound. I looked down and saw it was a sheet of paper rolled into a ball, like one my pupils might throw to each other with the answers on. My heart immediately began to disobey me again.

I could have ignored it. My head said it was fair to remain faithful to the past; the future was just a vague, useless fantasy. But I picked it up anyway.

I went into the house. I closed the door behind me. I pinned myself against the wall in a part of the room where I was sure I couldn't be seen. Then, in the residue of light that remained of the day, I unfolded the sheet.

It was a portrait – clear, precise. It was of an old man with his face hidden behind a beard and framed by shaggy hair, his forehead crumpled, infinite sadness clotted in his defenceless, childlike eyes.

It was me. I recognised myself in a way I had never recognised myself before.

She had understood: I was a happy child, then I became an old man overnight, and in between there was nothing.

In the bottom right-hand corner was written:

Sassaia, 7th November 2015
For you, from Emilia

7

'WOMEN ARE NOT VIOLENT. According to recent research into the cerebral cortex, they have a superior capacity with respect to men in processing suffering, anger and frustration. And this would explain, at least in part, why only 4.2 per cent of the Italian prison population is female.'

This fact made them split their sides laughing.

'Wahey, girls!' Giada shouted. 'We are the exception: the crème de la crème!'

'They're saying our cerebral cortex is retarded like men's,' Yasmina dissented. 'Personally I feel offended.'

'Me too,' Myriam interjected, slamming her hands down on the desk. 'I didn't wash up here for being like a man: men drove me into here!'

'Oh yeah! She said it!' A liberatory shout.

Pandolfi, the poor Italian teacher who had brought the article in with God knows what edifying intention, tried to bring things under control but it was fruitless; the fire had already been started. 'We are not men, for fuck's sake! We are the OPPOSITE of men. Who are the arseholes who wrote this?' 'Just because we didn't swallow it down and take it on the chin like other women, we're brain-dead, are we?' 'Listen to these motherfuckers!' They were on the verge of a revolt.

As always, Marta brought the discussion to a close with a concluding statement: 'What refined methods of processing pain, humiliation and grief are they talking about? When someone wants to rape you and beat you black and blue, the slaps, scratches and kicks in the balls they get back are called *gender equality*.'

Pandolfi stood up and implored everyone to calm down. What had she been thinking? It was the worst lesson of her life. She was a kind of lay sister with redemptive fantasies, but her students put pins on her chair, drew dicks on her register, and had no idea what to do with the redemption she had in mind.

But in the end, the 4.2 per cent story turned out to be popular. It made the girls feel special. From then on, in moments of depression, they'd point at one another and proudly say, 'Hey, remember – you're the 4.2 percent, you are.' 'Hold your head high, you exceptional woman.'

In that place, generally speaking, things functioned without much cultural, linguistic or artistic mediation. When she arrived, Yasmina barely knew fifty words of Italian. Afifa was born and raised in Italy, but was so outraged – quite rightly – that she hadn't been given citizenship, and that she was constantly called '*la negra*', 'banana muncher' and 'monkey', that she hated everything and everyone and mostly vented her rage by furiously pulling other people's hair out.

If one of the girls received some bad news, she wouldn't write it out in her diary or sublimate it in a drawing of rainbows and unicorns, and she wouldn't turn the other cheek or assume the contrite and patient expression of the Virgin Mary. At the hint of a false statement, a badly-judged joke, she'd spring into action like a hyena, and the violence was pure, brutal, female.

You could direct it at others, or you could direct it at yourself: it didn't make much difference. The fact was, Emilia would try to explain to Rita at some point in their journey, that when you were suffering to death, you wanted to die. To annihilate yourself, your interlocutor, everything around you. Raze it all to the ground and make it as simple as possible.

'Why?'

'Because physical pain is a solution to other kinds of pain.'

'Is that why you keep cutting yourself?'

'When you're drowning, you don't have time. If your lungs are full of water, it's not like you can just stay there . . . You're desperate, for fuck's sake. You just want to make everything silent and come back to the surface, to shut up the unbearable noise in your head and try not to fall into the hole in the middle of your chest where your heart's supposed to be.'

'So you cut yourself.'

'Yes. And I feel my body come to life again. Which is the only thing that keeps me holding on to the world.'

'So now you want to stay here, holding on?'

It was 2006. Spring. Emilia was twenty-one years old.

'I want to keep doing university.'

'For your father? Or for yourself?'

'Mainly for my father. And for Vargas: it was her who persuaded me to study. And for the others, the younger ones, because I want to be a role model for them like Marta and Myriam have been for me.'

'And what are you doing for yourself?'

'I don't exist.'

Rita arched her gull-wing eyebrows, drawn on in black pencil. 'You're here, in front of me.'

'I am what you see me as. I am the daughter my father sees. The poor specimen of a human that professors see when they come to do my oral exams. I'm a friend to some, a bitch to others. But whatever I do, I remain Emilia Innocenti, don't I? There's no way to escape from the photos or the newspaper headlines. And so everything I do, I do for the others. And for me, I cut myself.'

Rita took a deep inward breath. 'Do you think it's possible to live beyond Emilia Innocenti? I mean, do you think you can be a different person from the one other people see? From the one other people remember? Do you think you contain, inside that body, someone who deserves something?'

Emilia reflected at length, with total sincerity. And then she responded, with certainty: 'No.'

'What are you doing?' she shouted out of her window to me as I was making space between the flowerpots on the windowsill.

It was ten in the evening. Sassaia was pitch black. The light that was on in my kitchen and the light that was on in her kitchen glowed in perfect symmetry.

'I'm putting a handful of chestnuts out for the dead,' I responded.

'The dead?' Emilia crinkled her mouth in disgust. 'Pah!'

She was smoking, wearing jeans and a bra. I glanced at her without daring to look at her face while I fussed with my cyclamens, cutting off their yellow leaves and watering them. She straddled the windowsill, her legs hanging down on either side like a femme fatale. Her dark areolae and her even darker nipples could be seen through her white bra.

'What do you mean, "for the dead"?'

I could tell the topic troubled her. She kept her head tossed back against the window frame, her wavy red hair falling down her back. She took her cigarette out of her mouth and tapped the ash into the alley and it was so narrow, so cold, that I could see the goosebumps on her scratched and scarred arms.

'Tradition dictates,' I explained, 'that in these days of November, having gathered chestnuts, we leave the best ones out for the deceased.'

'"Tradition dictates"?' She looked at me, perplexed. '"Deceased"? What planet are you from?'

She was still inhaling. She brought a knee up to her chest and hugged it, perhaps to warm herself up. She left the other leg hanging from the windowsill, childish and provocative. Her weapons of seduction seemed like they were borrowed from a Nineties TV series.

'I never believed in that shit,' she continued. 'I never even left salt under the Christmas tree for the reindeer when I was little . . . But, just in case,' she was serious now, 'do me a favour and put a chestnut out for Myriam.'

I nodded. I bent down over my net bag.

'She doesn't deserve it,' she clarified. 'But I'm a lady and I don't hold grudges.'

She observed me, making sure I added one more chestnut to the little porcelain plate. Then she stuck her head out into the alleyway, raised her head to the starry sky looming over us both and shouted out loud: 'Myriam, I'm leaving you a chestnut, OK? For all the times you nicked my fags, my Intimissimi thongs, my issues of *Cioè* magazine. Try and look after yourself up there, wherever the hell you are!'

She went back to leaning on the window frame and looked at me, satisfied, waiting for a reaction. But I didn't know what to say, what to do. Whether to quickly close the window or not close it again for the entire night.

'You haven't said anything about my drawing,' she reproached me.

'It's very good . . .'

'*Good* means fuck all.'

I moved the little plate to the right and left, put it in front of me as if it could protect me. 'It's just I've never been drawn before . . .' I tried, sincerely. 'You caught me off guard.'

'Like last night?' She smiled, too explicit.

I didn't want to end up in that mess. Because she was a mess. I was looking at the cuts on her arms and it was obvious she had done them to herself. I joined the dots: she was clearly unwell. And it didn't matter how much sex she offered me. I was allowed to make a mistake once and then go and get on with my life . . . but the second time would be my fault.

'I've got to get up early tomorrow,' I said. 'I must say goodnight.'

She hardened. 'Tomorrow is Sunday – where do you have to be?' She threw her cigarette butt into the alley in disdain. 'So this is how girls get dumped after a one-night stand. Forgive me, it's never happened to me before.'

I hated myself. 'I didn't mean that . . .'

She jumped down from the windowsill in an athletic manoeuvre, insolently closed the window and tugged the curtain across.

And I stood there like an idiot with the chestnuts for my dead and for hers.

I closed my own window and took a pan from the sideboard because I hadn't had dinner yet. I put it on top of the fire and broke three eggs into it. I cut some slices of Toma cheese and melted it over the yolks. I poured myself two glasses of wine and gulped them down one after the other. I wolfed down the eggs in the oafish way I'd seen shepherds do in the thick fog of the valley in winter, absorbed in a solitude only experienced by those who live solely in the company of animals. I brushed my teeth. I turned out all the lights and went upstairs.

Her window was still lit.

I got into bed fully clothed. Like her, I left the shutters open. My heart was beating in the dark in sync with the distant toll of the bell down in Alma.

I should've been planning my lessons for the day after tomorrow. A chart to teach the youngest children the *sh* sound – 'shutter', 'shadow', 'shame' – and one to teach the older ones what a verb is: an action that breaks a stasis, a state of immobility, of death pulling us towards it. What a noun is and what a proper noun is, and why only the latter requires a capital letter.

'Emilia.' I don't know how many times I repeated it in my head.

Because, even if there are many people who have it, on this whole planet that name designates only you. Yes, you're a self-harmer; yes, you need someone with you to help you sleep. But you won't be repeated, you won't happen another time.

I got up and ran down the stairs. Then outside, and I kept running until I knocked at her door, the sound of my knuckles reverberating into the mountains.

Emilia made me wait this time. Made me pay.

And I wanted, so, so much, to make this mistake.

She opened the door, annoyed, still in her jeans and bra.

'My name is Bruno,' I told her, breathless.

'I don't give a shit what your name is.'

I went inside and closed the door behind me. I closed my eyes and kissed her, filling my hands with her hair, my mouth with her saliva, unhooking her white bra to feel her breasts, to feel her heart.

She let me kiss her. Then she detached from me and started slapping me, with all the strength she had. And I took every slap, watching her as she beat me: she was so furious, so pale and absent. She started punching my chest, my abdomen, my sides. She was so thin; I was a boulder in comparison.

We just had to keep words out of our story, I thought. Keep the past out of our nights. With that pact, I would keep coming back.

'I'll always come back,' I told her. 'Every night that you need it.'

She wasn't hurting me. She was just surrendering her darkest parts.

Eventually her fists softened, and she let her hands fall beside her hips. And I held her with my whole body, as if I had finally found a new home. The old stone houses, the owls, and the woods listened to our breathing.

'I promise you,' I reassured her.

8

We were meeting at a quarter to eleven in front of the church in Alma. I got there late, flustered, lugging my leather briefcase laden with books and lined paper. I was worried about Martino Fiume, who had done nothing all morning but irritate his classmates – a sure sign that his father had come home drunk the night before and raised his hand to him. And then Patrizia had kept me in the staffroom for twenty long minutes – in the name of some bureaucratic nonsense that I hate, and to which she dedicates infinite amounts of energy – flirting, putting her arm around my shoulders, suffocating me with her saccharine perfume, and I, as always, had been incapable of fighting back. Torture.

When I saw Emilia standing on the steps, however, I forgot all about Martino and his father, the 'sh' sounds, the nouns and verbs, even Patrizia and her stupid forms. Emilia looked so out of place in the Alma piazza with her torn jeans, her tasselled leather jacket, and her tight red jumper with the anarchist symbol on the front. Not at all appropriate for a job interview (even if it was just with Basilio). Seeing her there with her hair tied in a ponytail, wearing three kilos of lipstick and blowing Hubba Bubba,

I couldn't help thinking, amused but serious, that that was my girl.

She heard my footsteps and turned instantly. She was about to smile but stopped herself. 'Hello,' she said. I stopped at a distance and responded even more coldly. 'Good day, let me accompany you.'

The piazza was deserted. Bar Samurai was on the opposite side and its door was closed, as was Rosa's shop and the post office. Nobody could have heard our exchange. Nobody was at their windows or on their balconies. Alma was the largest village in Valle and it felt like its 903 inhabitants had been extinct for centuries. But I knew they were there, and that they would soon spot us, and fastidiously observe us, eviscerate us from behind the shutters, the cracks, the curtains. I knew that immediately afterwards they would set to work, sharpening their specialised skills in uncovering sordid affairs, unmasking us, giving a precise name to the suspicious appearance of Mr Peraldo alongside the alcoholic *foreigner*. For this reason, I had carefully prepared Emilia for our first public meeting, like you prepare a lover who's been invited to the same party as your wife. And it didn't matter that I wasn't married and neither, as far as I knew, was she; that we were more than of age and free to do as we wished. That was the theory. In practice, outside of Sassaia, we were not free in the slightest.

I led the way. Emilia followed me, not giving anything away. I was hoping that the church, for the sole fact of being church, would ward off any gossip in advance. We exchanged a quick glance before going in, then, as if we hardly knew one another, as if we hadn't spent every single night together for the last ten days, we slipped through the side door, into the folds of a thick velvet curtain where I stole a quick kiss, in disdain of the gossipmongers, the zealots, those who believe they hold the truth in their pockets. Love can be as little as disobedience.

Inside, the shade was frigid and thick: a black aquarium except for the bright lights that lit the inner wall which Basilio, sitting on top of a high scaffold, was working on.

He was so absorbed that he didn't notice us at first. (Also, his hearing was beginning to leave him). Emilia stiffened when she saw the frescoed wall depicting the *Last Judgement.* She suddenly lost all the enthusiasm she had expressed on the phone to her father – I had over-heard one of their calls when she was walking in the alley while I was repotting some cyclamens, deliberately slowly – for this unexpected opportunity to use what she had studied.

I called out to Basilio. He finished applying rice paper soaked in distilled water to the blackened wing of a blond-haired angel and, very slowly, turned towards us. He didn't say hello, he didn't smile, he didn't even nod his head. I had explained to Emilia that it wouldn't be easy to get to know him. He was a profoundly private, introverted, timid man; one who had never wanted to work with anyone before and if now, after a week of my ceaseless insistence, he had been convinced to give her a try, it was only because his body was weary and he had three years to go until he retired.

Struggling down from the scaffold, he brought his small hunched and fragile frame to stand in front of us. He raised his glassy gaze up to Emilia's face and observed her carefully through the lenses of his old glasses. His icy blue eyes, lucid and flickering, were proof that somewhere inside that pile of tired bones, there still resided a brilliant soul.

There was a momentary hint of surprise on his face. I noticed it but gave it no weight.

'This is Basilio Raimondi, Valle's most renowned and celebrated artist,' I said as he shook his head in disapproval of the flattery. 'And this is Emilia, the person I told you about, who did the pencil drawing. Emilia . . .' I realised I didn't know her surname. '. . . has a degree in Fine Art,' I finished.

'Do you know how to restore a fresco?' Basilio asked her straight away.

Emilia took a moment to respond. I had never seen her so pale. She fiddled with her nails, pulling off little bits of skin. Finally she nodded. 'Yes, I took two exams in restoration.'

'This is a humble church of the late fourteenth century,' Basilio explained, 'in a small, out-of-the-way village that, in its heyday, boasted 2,130 inhabitants. Along the river, a little further down, is where they burned Margherita Boninsegna alive, so you get the picture; it's always been a valley of witches, heretics, rebels. Which might be why, despite our characteristic modesty, we have such a marvellous *Last Judgement* as this. It's no Giotto, but . . . look at it.'

Emilia made the effort to do so and immediately looked down again.

Basilio, unlike everyone else of his generation, always spoke in impeccable Italian, which was because he didn't have friends and didn't spend time with anyone. Instead – and this was a secret I had discovered by chance – he read voraciously, drawing upon the old library that a Freemason, grateful for how he had frescoed his house, had bequeathed him.

'Do you think you can do it?' he asked Emilia. 'Make this *Judgement* legible again? There are parts, as you can see' – he pointed them out to her – 'the inferno and the devil in particular, which have been eaten away by lamp-black and salt efflorescence.'

'Is this all there is to restore?'

Basilio was surprised by the question, as was I. It was an entire wall – nothing 'all there is' about it.

'There's also a wooden Black Madonna to repaint.'

'Then, if it's OK, I'd like to start the test with that,' she told him. 'After that, if you decide to take me on, I'll help you with the fresco.'

'Where do you come from?'

I shuddered. It was such a simple question, yet I had never found the courage to ask it. I turned to look at her and saw her clearly, almost imperceptibly, shudder too.

'From Le Marche,' she replied, 'a small town in the province of Pesaro and Urbino.'

Instinct told me she was lying.

'Where did you study?'

Emilia regained some colour. 'At the University of Bologna,' she announced proudly.

Basilio strained his lips into a sad smile. 'I don't have a degree myself. But I would have loved to study. And to visit Bologna and Urbino, which I've seen only in paintings.'

The furthest he had ever been was Turin, where he had started university full of pride and aspiration – he was at risk of becoming the first graduate in the history of Sassaia – but after less than a year, his family's money ran out and nobody else had wanted to finance him, so he had had to come home and paint ceilings white for a living.

It was so painful for me to see myself reflected in what that man had given up that I couldn't stop myself from saying out loud, as childish as it sounded, 'Even without a degree, Basilio, everyone here knows how talented you are. Otherwise they wouldn't trust you to restore churches like this one, and shrines, and villas.'

His mute response wasn't much of a consolation, a weary expression carved into his tired, wrinkly face, half-covered by a long and curly beard – like my own, but white. He flicked away my words as if they were flies and turned to Emilia: 'None of that matters now. I'm past it. But you're young and I want to see what they taught you in Bologna.'

I watched them move away into the darkness of the left aisle. He was walking over to the statue of the Black Madonna and she was following him, calm, closer than before. *Like a little nun*, I was surprised to find myself thinking in the dark church that was once filled to the rafters and was now being repaired for I don't know who.

I was amazed by the gentleness that Basilio, usually so coarse and closed-off, had shown her. And by her unease in the company of this poor old man, which contradicted her provocative outfit and Hubba Bubba, chewed at a slower and slower pace, then secretly spat out – I couldn't have not noticed – tucked into a receipt, and stuffed into her pocket.

I intuited that, in some secret way, they recognised one another. As if they weren't just two people I knew – him for decades and her for a fortnight – but also two strangers inaccessible to me.

'What time shall I come and pick her up?' I shouted to Basilio.

He made a sign for me to be quiet with his finger on his lips, to remind me that we were, after all, in a church, and its priest was the town's biggest gossip. He spread one hand wide and placed the other thumb over his palm to respond: six o'clock.

He had already understood that there was something going on between Emilia and me. There was no need to hide it from him. I knew he wouldn't say anything to anyone.

Before leaving, I whispered into the dark: 'Good luck, Emilia.'

My impression would later turn out to be true: Basilio had recognised her. He was the only one who did. And for this reason he had already decided to keep her near him, regardless of her restoration skills: because he always did the opposite of what everyone else did.

That lunchtime, having left her alone for the morning with the Black Madonna and Child, he shared his bread and cheese, fruit and water with Emilia, who hadn't realised she needed to bring a packed lunch. They sat at the top of the scaffold because it was unseemly to eat anywhere else. In Basilio's opinion, it didn't matter whether you were a believer or not; if in doubt, God was to be obliged.

'You've done an excellent job with the crown and the veil,' he told her.

'Thank you,' she responded, silently chewing and keeping her eyes cast down.

'You'll have to excuse me if I'm a bit grouchy sometimes, I'm not used to having someone else around. Except for chickens, geese and canaries.'

Emilia swallowed, took a sip of water from Basilio's canteen and, purposefully turning her back on the *Judgement*, said: 'I hope not to get in your way. I want to be useful. I really care about this job . . . it's always been my dream. At least,' she thought aloud, 'since I started dreaming again.'

Basilio listened carefully, observing her discreetly. He knew perfectly well who he had in front of him. Emilia, on the other hand, didn't suspect that he knew, otherwise she would've immediately got up and run as far away as she could.

Though she didn't say it, she remembered him too. They were just muddled fragments from her childhood that she wouldn't have been able to put in order. Her aunt had always talked admiringly of 'the painter', and he had been at their house a few times, for a coffee or to drop off some eggs. Emilia had forgotten his name, but not his face; not those eyes that, despite the etchings of suffering and tiredness on their lids, still emanated an extraordinary light.

Basilio didn't ask her any more questions, and didn't make her uneasy by alluding to any detail of the past. They talked about the history of that little village church, about the sculptor who had carved the Madonna and Child from a trunk of oak, about the minor artists who had devoted themselves to the portrait of Christ and the saints, and the shame of not being able to find out the identity of the anonymous creator of the *Judgement* fresco, which stood out a mile from all the other works. Such a beauty and no mention of him or – why not – her, in any book or document. Wasn't it unfair?

'Perhaps not,' Emilia responded, 'perhaps who we are and what we do aren't the same thing.' She looked up and added: 'Like Caravaggio, for example.'

'You're right.' Basilio nodded. Their eyes met for a moment. 'Art is always an attempt at light, a mere scrap compared to the darkness there is in life.'

When their break was over, before returning to work, he said: 'I'm sorry I can't pay you much.'

Emilia smiled because this meant she had been hired. 'Sassaia isn't very expensive. And it's enough that my father knows I'm managing to look after myself.'

Basilio remembered Riccardo perfectly. He had thought often of him over the years. He had prayed for him, and for Emilia.

They each returned to their own work. The Black Madonna was an extremely well-done copy of the one in Oropa. She was dressed in gold, with a golden veil and golden hair. Even her child had golden curls, and smiled with the same radiant detachment towards the pitiful affairs of humans.

Repainting her instilled a sort of painful peace in Emilia. The Madonna's dark origins put her at ease; she was said to embody the night from which comes the dawn. Part of Emilia would have liked to be the child she held in her arms, safe forever. A creature just created; clean, blameless. Suspended from the earth in a bubble of unshakeable love.

Emilia's childhood had been a little paradise, which made her violent expulsion from it all the more heartbreaking.

She was working with her whole self to blend the colour, intensify it, searching for the exact tone the Madonna had been given when she was new, which time had inexorably ruined, faded, betrayed. She wanted Basilio to be proud of her work, to take her on permanently. She wanted this start: this house, this half-boyfriend, this job. This threadbare and abandoned place – in spite of the predictions of her father, Rita and Venturi – was showering her with gifts. As if she was a queen, as if she deserved them.

The exam on Giotto's *Last Judgement* was the only one Emilia hadn't passed at university. She had ended up giving in and switching to a different module. She'd gone nowhere near Michelangelo's *Judgement*. She would rather die than set foot in the Sistine Chapel or the Scrovegni: she was sure of it. In Bologna, in San Petronio Basilica, during the only guided tour she had ever been allowed, when she noticed Giovanni da Modena's giant fresco with the black Devil devouring the head of a man, she had become breathless and had to leave.

There were places Emilia couldn't return to. That she wouldn't return to even if it meant inflicting every violence on herself. Venturi had admitted it too:

There are holes you can't fill.
They'll always be there, dark and deep.
But, if you want, you can construct a life around them.
Like how grass grows at the edges of craters. Like how you can surround a well with pots of flowers.
Your life will always be a ring around this abyss.
Do you think you can accept that?

Rays of light pierced the shadows, heavy with dust and distant times. The church, though small and empty, dominated her with its judging silence. A memory suddenly passed through her mind. One of the many tightly gagged, restrained and straitjacketed ones that resided in the depths of her subconscious, where there was nothing but craters.

The smell of incense in the cathedral in Ravenna, the voice of the priest during the funeral, the mahogany coffin covered with white roses, her favourite flower. Emilia had felt minuscule. That day – January 2nd, 1998 – was when she began to disappear. Her body had remained, in the same way a headstone, a plaque or a framed photograph remain. But internally she had been emptied out. Inside her, nothing moved.

The Madonna's face was chipped on one cheek and under her right eye. As Emilia filled and sanded, half of her repeated to herself: *Let yourself start again, I beg you.* But the other half was frigid: *They'll suss you out, it's just a matter of time.*

An innocuous question like, 'Where are you from?' was all it took to turn her stomach. And when Basilio had asked: 'Where did you study?' she felt so relieved to be able to respond, for once, with the truth. She diligently pronounced: 'Alma Mater Studiorum, Bologna'. She only omitted one small detail – the 'branch' in which she had completed this nice degree. The so-called 'special' pathway that had led to her unimaginable 96 out of 110. And led to her father crying like a baby, out of joy for once.

Emilia was constantly engaged in the struggle of hiding her entire past behind her body. Only her body was tiny, and her past gigantic.

Bruno will find out the truth, she told herself, *and not want to see you anymore. Basilio will fire you. The residents of Alma will hunt you down with their pitchforks because that's justice. There is no place on this earth for you. You should be with the devils, clutched in their claws, burning in the flames.*

Afterwards, we paused in the antechamber, between the thick velvet curtain and the side door.

'How did it go?'

Emilia checked that Basilio was far enough away not to hear and, when she was sure, with a radiant smile I had never seen before, exclaimed: 'Really, really well!'

'Did he hire you?'

'He told me to come back tomorrow.'

Her happiness, I noticed, was thawing the most frozen part that remained inside me. 'I don't think Basilio has ever been so kind to someone,' I commented.

'It's called having a pussy, and it has that effect.' Emilia returned to her usual irreverence. 'You should know that.'

She was about to push the door open, but I stopped her.

'Let me remind you that we are about to step out onto the great stage of Alma, on which we are the principal attraction.'

Emilia looked up at the sky. 'I beg you, let's toss some crumbs of scandal out for these Bible-bashers.' She put a hand in my trousers.

'You don't know them.' I smiled. 'They've burnt many witches before. Do you want to be another one?'

'Absolutely.'

'Samurai will be full at this time, we'll end up in a densely packed lair of gossip . . .'

'And so be it!' Emilia snorted. 'Remind me what I have to do: go out first, and up onto Stra' dal Forche?'

I was about to repeat the shortcut, to explain to her again the enigmatic plan I had architected, and which to anyone who didn't live in Alma and the surroundings would sound paranoid. But here in the shadows, I saw a new

Emilia. Under her big-mouthed act, her defensive armour, her lifeless eyes, I glimpsed the young woman who had been pushed, for some obscure reason, to Sassaia. I saw that today, this woman had received some satisfaction.

'Let's leave together,' I said, changing the plan. 'We'll go out for dinner.'

She squinted her eyes as if I'd said: I'll take you to America.

'If you want to, that is. I just feel we should celebrate.'

Something in her eyes shifted. Like an infinitesimal shimmer from a galaxy a billion light years away, from a star that had certainly died some time ago, but which I could still catch sight of. And it gave me courage.

'They've already seen me stumble drunk out of the bar,' she reminded me. 'Your reputation will be ruined.'

I kissed her and responded: 'I couldn't care less.'

I had spent the last few hours sitting on a white rock next to the river, ranking the most alluring titles which might convince my thirteen students to read a goddamned book, coming up with strategies to make the idea of opening one seem relevant to a world like this, where all feelings were distorted and where you felt you had to hide yourself in order to be loved; where entire roads were abandoned, houses left empty, and where every corner reminds you that here, time has finished, and that whoever is still here is a loser. I intended to do whatever I could to make them understand that reading could free them from the enormous solitude of this place, and its meaningless laws.

The first law that needed to be dumped: don't trust strangers.

So I opened the door wide and we walked out of the church together in the full light of the sunset, with Bar Samurai packed full of people, some of whom turned only the top halves of their bodies to stare at us.

We should have been more careful, in hindsight. Kept loving one another in Sassaia, spied on only by the stones, beech trees and animals. We could have bought ourselves some time, perhaps. Or perhaps not, because that which must happen will happen, in spite of all the care taken to avoid it. So maybe we did the right thing to take that little morsel of happiness, all of it, for ourselves.

Writing it down now, it sounds like we walked out of the church hand in hand, arms around each other's waists, kissing passionately. In fact, all we did was cross the threshold at the same time, and walk side by side across the piazza, without touching, with no alarming gestures, proceeding in parallel. But our mere appearance was enough.

Walking past the windows of Samurai, I prayed silently: God, let Patrizia not be there, let her not see us. Even though up until that point I had only ever spoken to God in the form of an argument.

9

DEATH IN THE HOLIDAYS is a thing that doesn't happen, especially not to thirteen-year-old girls.

Emilia had only recently started her periods and was disoriented in her body. Her cheeks were pocked with spots and she missed her childhood; when she read aloud in class, it was as if the letters were piled up on top of each other, melting, but the teacher didn't understand and went on humiliating her in front of everyone. Emilia felt like the only sad girl in a happy world and now, as if that wasn't enough, she was also forced to listen to the words 'come on, dear, *you must* go on' said in such a grave tone, as if it was some pearl of wisdom, by unpleasant acquaintances – neighbours who had seen her grow up, yes, but what did their condolences really mean? They were saying all this while laden with shopping bags and bottles of Prosecco, their heads already at their New Year's feasts, anticipating the countdown on Radio 1, preoccupied with a future which, for her, had just become nothing.

Emilia and her father spent the final night of 1997 in the kitchen, completely alone. Sitting opposite one another in silence, avoiding each other's gaze, the table unset, the TV switched off, the sink full of dirty dishes.

They heard the first fireworks in the distance, fire-crackers set off by impatient teenagers who just couldn't wait until midnight. From the gardens of the houses around them, from the illuminated front windows, arrived torrents of laughter, gusts of music at maximum volume then suddenly turned down, perhaps out of fear, perhaps because someone remembered the misfortune of the Innocenti family.

Emilia, in reality, heard nothing. She just listened, inside herself, to the irreversible collapse of her right ventricle, left ventricle, aorta. She stared at the marble slab of the table and saw her classmates as if in a magic mirror.

They'll already be dressed up by now, she thought. *They'll have put on their velvet headbands, Swarovski hair slides, high-heeled shoes. Then, once out of their parents' cars, they'll have added another layer of makeup to the one their mums allowed. They'll run their pocket combs through their hair one last time, straighten their bracelets, their little rings, the sheer tights they're not used to wearing under their short skirts. Finally, arriving at the small bar they had collectively hired for the occasion, with speakers pumping out 'What is Love?' and bottles of Sprite neatly lined up to conceal the vodka, they'll make their triumphant entrance in front of the boys.*

It would have been her first party without parental supervision. But instead, she was at home, with Papa, contemplating the end of her adolescence before it had even begun.

You were supposed to be telling me not to put on too much lipstick, Emilia reproached her. *You were supposed to lend me your bra, drive me to the party giving me advice on how to respond to those bitches Sofia and Vanessa who always leave me out, who call me 'carrot head'. You were supposed to show me how to walk in high heels, to smoke a cigarette, yes: without inhaling. You were supposed to exhaust yourself telling me to do my homework when I don't want to, or because I prefer looking at the video games at the library when you'd so love for me to read instead. You were supposed to explain how contraceptives work, the Pascoli poem I don't understand. But instead, you died.*

At a certain point her father got up. It must have been nine or ten o'clock, but in reality time had disappeared, and in its place had spread a lunar desert in which there was no gravity, no day or night, no life.

Her father held himself up with effort and determination. He leaned on the table with both hands and looked at her.

They would move forward with frozen food and ready meals for years. That night, like every night to come, neither of them would even attempt to sleep without a pill. People say that when someone's ill, you have the opportunity to get used to it, to find a reason for it. That you see the person you love become so unwell, so unrecognisable, that in the end you just want to let them go.

But what reason was there? Emilia wanted to reply. What getting used to? She would've kept her there, on the anti-decubitus bed, forever. Even at thirty-nine kilos, even though she was gross, with three hairs on her head, stunned by the morphine, she would've stayed forever her mother.

She was selfish, a spoiled only child. But you try going on with your life *after*.

If she could've, Emilia would have clung on to her pile of bones, her withering thirty-seven-year-old skin, until the bitter end. She would have claimed that exhausted and skeletal version of her mother for herself until the right moment arrived. Or, until she was a hundred. A hundred and ten. When, with a bit of luck, they could even have died together, just a few hours or days apart. Her mother was no longer able to feed herself independently, she could hardly breathe, but you can't compare the two things. You couldn't compare being able to stroke her skin, squeeze her warm hand, tell her how school went with never being able to do that again.

So her father had stood up, leaned on the table with both hands, looked her in the eye, breaking her flow of thought that went uninterrupted from the morphine drip to Sonia and Vanessa with glitter on their eyelids, from the phone call to the funeral directors to the kisses her classmates would be having that night without her, the disco music in the background, as if death and getting off, the tumour and the noise of the speakers, were the exact same thing.

He said: 'Emilia, we have to eat.'

He was thin, his eyes sunken and swollen.

'We have to make some pasta.'

With his days-long beard, hair suddenly white, completely in pieces. But commanding and categorical.

'It's you and me now. And we have to be enough.'

*

When I raised the garage door at the edge of Alma and revealed the beaten-up red Seat Ibiza, Emilia burst out laughing. 'How many centuries old is it?'

She walked over to the bonnet, looked at it with amusement, pushed her index finger into the crust of dust and drew a giant penis.

'Go on, say it,' I provoked her. 'Marta wouldn't approve.'

'Oh, Marta would throw up all over it! She would never get in anything less than a Mercedes, waxed and polished.'

I dug out a little vacuum cleaner that had been lying unused for years with a pile of other motoring tools: the kind of tools over which I had always favoured Giacomo Leopardi. I started suctioning dead flies off the seats, crumbs left from long-forgotten days out, cobwebs. When the inside looked acceptable to me, I checked the oil, the water, the tyre pressure, and finally invited her to get in.

'After you! I'll even let you drive, if you want.'

'No, no.' Emilia turned red. She hurried to get into the passenger side, put on her sunglasses and immediately changed the subject: 'It's too clean, it's blinding me. Like new, just like in the Seventies.'

'Eighties,' I corrected her.

I turned the key in the ignition not knowing what to expect. The last time I used it was more than a year before, to go and see Gisella at Motel Le Piane. The thought filled me with sadness.

With half a tank of petrol, I reasoned, we might be able to get out of the province, and then past Turin, into the

Piedmont I had only ever passed through in the summer, as a boy, to go to the sea in Liguria.

The old banger came to life and miraculously got out of the garage. Sliding down the country road, picking up speed on the descent, it launched us into the world.

Emilia rolled down the window even though it was cold; November had decided to do its thing, by this point. I pushed my foot down on the accelerator as if we were being tailed, while she held her head out of the window to feel the wind in her ears, her hair whipping her face. Life hitting us.

I thought again of Marta: the only hint I had at my disposal to help reconstruct Emilia's story. We were catching our breath in the candlelit room as if it was the thirteenth century when that name first came out. And I had pounced on it with a hunger I didn't know I had.

This is how it went: Emilia had asked me what I did for work and I had responded, very calmly, that I taught Italian in a primary school. To which she had a noteworthy reaction: one of surprise, almost alarm. Shaking her head, she commented: 'Oh God, as if I'm fucking a teacher . . .'

'What's strange about that?'

'It's pathetic.' She covered her face with both her hands. 'Marta will be disgusted with me when she finds out.'

'Who's Marta?'

Emilia never named anyone in her life, except for her father every so often. It seemed like she'd had no life at all before her arrival in Sassaia. I sat up with my legs crossed to listen as carefully as I could. She uncovered her face and with extreme gravity responded: 'A friend of mine from boarding school.'

It wasn't that I didn't wonder who still sent their children to boarding school in the Nineties or Noughties. It was just that Marta was more important.

'She has extremely high standards,' Emilia continued with pride. 'She lives in Milan, in a hundred-metre-square apartment, in a very chic part of the city. She's a researcher, you know? She works for a pharmaceutical company. She only goes out with managers and directors, and at dinner she always pays because she's a free woman and a feminist.'

'Don't tell her, then, that you're going out with a teacher. Make me a . . . I don't know . . . a university professor!'

She was scandalised. 'Lie to Marta? We've taken an oath. We cut our fingertips and mixed our blood in the toilets. You don't go back on that.'

'And what kind of boyfriend would she like for you, this Marta?'

'Well . . .' she reflected, 'someone rugged, very masculine. Loaded, but also cultured. With a degree in something serious: science, or maths. A manager.'

I burst into laughter in a way that hadn't happened in maybe twenty years.

'You'll never find a manager in Sassaia or Alma. But rugged men with calloused hands and holey vests, who smell like a cowshed? Take your pick.'

A strange thing happened then. It was as if Emilia had gone. Her gaze was elsewhere, she coiled a lock of hair around her fingers and whispered: 'She used to read me their essays before going to sleep.'

But when I asked who she was talking about, she shook her head with embarrassment. 'Oh, nothing.'

I thought back to this episode and, again, to the response she had given Basilio: Le Marche. What did I have? Nothing. The only time I'd seen her father, on the balcony with the mattress and sheets, he had looked to me like a rich man. The boarding school could have been one of those American-style campuses where wealthy families sent their children to study. Maybe there was a campus like that in Pesaro or Urbino. Maybe I should have looked on the internet.

As we drove, the country road slithered through the woods, plummeting down to the river on one side, then petering out between the black mountains in the distance.

'Where are you taking me?' she asked, ruffled, winding the window back up.

'*Come with me and come what may,*' I responded, '*holding hands to hold off the sun.*'

'Mandelstam.' She smiled.

I turned to look at her: her freckles, her thin cracked lips that would struggle to withstand the winter, her opaque and impenetrable eyes, like embers. Could I love her without knowing who she was?

When we got to the junction, I remained still at the stop sign for a long time, even though the road was empty.

I had begun to suspect – not all the time, but certainly sometimes – that Emilia was lying to me. I didn't understand why she had hidden such an unimportant detail as not having a driving licence.

My intention was to turn left, towards a bar in the valley I'd heard good things about but had never been to. I wanted us to have something new, something that was just ours, as if we had only just been born.

But at the last minute, like a kamikaze plane, I turned in the other direction.

The restaurant was called Cervo Verde. It stood perched on a hilltop in Donato, at the edge of the province in a much sunnier valley than ours, carved out by a much less turbulent river.

When I got to the entrance, my stomach dropped. The last time I had crossed that threshold, it was for lunch on a Sunday in early August. Twenty-five years had passed.

Emilia wasn't decisive about entering either. She stood there staring at the door as if waiting for someone to open it. But I couldn't decipher that detail: I didn't have the necessary knowledge. Her indecision defeated mine and I pushed down the handle.

Sometimes time is merciless, other times it's miraculous.

If I thought about what had happened to my Valle — towns that at the beginning of the Sixties had thousands of inhabitants and now had just tens — my heart paused. Sassaia was populated by thirty-five families at the time of the world-famous stonecutters and masons. The area just a little further down from Alma prospered from the numerous hat factories, woollen mills and hemp farms. When I was a child, there were so many open shops, holidays for every patron saint, noisy bars overflowing with people until late at night, bakeries, markets. Then it was as if a plague came and emptied the houses and bars, the restaurants and piazzas. As if time became an avalanche and, rolling down from the top of the mountains, silenced every voice.

Here, though, at the Cervo Verde, time had conserved and protected every detail. Horns still hung from the walls; stuffed owls and partridges with glass eyes stared back at you, stunned; black and white photos full of men in hats and women in headscarves harked back to a time when this land was rich and nobody would ever have imagined that one day their grandchildren would flee en masse. Even the tables seemed to be dressed with the same tablecloths, adorned with the same rustic carved-wood centrepieces as they had been decades ago.

But, since today wasn't a Sunday in August 1990, but rather a Wednesday or Thursday in November 2015, there was nobody in the dining room which overlooked the Alps. Just Emilia, who wandered dreamily between the tables, stroking the cutlery and napkins.

'You can't imagine how long it's been since I was last in a restaurant.'

'Me too,' I admitted.

She looked up at me. 'But you're sad, I can tell.'

I stood still, uncomfortable, not knowing how to respond. Unlike her, I couldn't lie.

An old woman in an apron with her hair in a bun came out of the kitchens to welcome us and ask where we would like to sit. Emilia picked a square table by a window that framed the Mombarone. We sat down opposite one another while the woman lit a small candle and I felt my hands trembling. I started to sweat.

Self-sabotage, it's called. When you want to get out of the rut you're in and finally allow yourself a normal activity like taking a girl out to dinner, but at the same time you want to punish yourself for the mere act of trying. So, of all the places you could go, you choose the one you fear the most.

Emilia read the menu, which was typical of the area, with enthusiasm: polenta with venison, polenta with Alpine cheese, or polenta with cheese and butter. And I tried to focus my attention on her, on her beautiful smile, on the present moment, but my gaze kept falling off to one side, as if pulled by a magnet towards the past and a long table made up for a big, noisy, happy family. And as Emilia ordered a bottle of house wine and polenta with Alpine cheese for both of us, I watched the cheers, the paper fans, the laughter of that Sunday, playing in front of my eyes like an amateur short film, and felt an intense pressure bearing down on my lungs.

'How many girlfriends have you had?'

I was brought back to the here and now with a jolt. 'Why do you ask?' I realised that our glasses were full of wine. 'Is the number important?'

'Fuck yes! It's fundamental. Go on, tell me.' Emilia raised her glass. 'The truth, please.'

'Zero,' I admitted, clinking my glass with hers. 'I have had zero girlfriends.'

She shook her head, incredulous. 'In thirty-six years, nothing?'

'Just rare, sporadic, sad nights. Which started at a late age.'

'You've never been in love? You've never lived with someone? You've never introduced a girl to your family?'

This last question was particularly painful.

I clearly saw the relief on her face as I answered, 'No, none of that.'

We downed our drinks. The wine helped bring me back to the surface.

'And you?' I asked.

Emilia took a deep breath and puffed out her chest. She leaned back in her chair and sighed. 'Oh, I've had a *shit ton* of guys. I've fucked men in the toilets of the Imperiale and the Cocoricò in Riccione. But I've also had proper relationships, like two, three years long. One even lasted five years – with Emanuele, the love of my life.' She didn't look me in the eye as she was saying these things. She smiled to herself, as if in a trance. 'We lived together at university. He even asked me to marry him . . . But I wasn't ready.'

Of all her words, instinctively, one stuck: Riccione.

The polenta arrived. Emilia's face lit up. I didn't know if it was the wine, the restaurant, or the successful trial shift with Basilio, but she was definitely cheerful. I, on the other hand, felt like I had a weight tied to my ankles, and beneath the table there was a lake, deep and black, waiting to pull me under – which was encouraging me to take all that unhoped-for, unmerited, unexpected happiness, and set fire to it.

'Why did you move from Le Marche to Sassaia?' I couldn't stop myself. With seriousness, with violence, with desperation: 'Or rather, why from Riccione to Sassaia?'

At that, Emilia's face turned completely dark.

She finished chewing and then swallowed, put her fork down, and looked me in the eye with an intensity that, without a doubt, was hatred.

'Interrogations don't work with me. You need to know that.' She wiped the corners of her mouth with her napkin. 'And if you're going to be a jerk, I'm going to finish eating, get up, take your car, and leave. Even if I don't have a licence and don't know the roads – fuck it, I'll still do it and leave you here.'

Her transformation terrified me.

'Have I asked you why you brought me here when this place clearly hurts you so much? Did I ask you who or what it reminded you of? Did I rub salt in your wound? No, because I'm not a dickhead.'

'Sorry.'

I suddenly took her hand across the tablecloth and squeezed it.

I closed my eyes. I could feel tears running down my cheeks, and I couldn't do anything to stop them.

She must have been shocked because, after a moment's hesitation, she squeezed my hand back, in between the glasses and the breadbasket. I couldn't see her expression but I heard her voice become sweet: 'You're nicely fucked-up too, eh?'

I felt myself crumble. And her hand holding mine.

'Listen, let's eat. Let's not let this delicious polenta go cold. You know what Rita, another boarding school friend, always said to me? That you have to start again somewhere. And I didn't believe her, I didn't want to, but I was forced to. So, out of all the places in the world, I picked Sassaia because it's the most beautiful. It's like . . .' she reflected for a moment, 'a stone uterus. You're safe, innocent, warm like in a nativity scene, When the world outside is freezing and cruel.'

I opened my eyes again and looked at her through my tears with a feeling that, without a doubt – even if she had lied to me since the start, even if I still didn't know the price of it – was love.

'Don't ask me anything else,' she concluded. 'We can remain at the border, OK? Never crossing it.'

By the time the whole class turned up at the funeral, tidy and dressed in black, Emilia no longer had a heart.

From the first pew (the one reserved for close family) she turned to the back of the room and saw a crowd of people whose names her mother didn't even know. She sized them up one by one, the boys from her class, and especially the girls, who now had boobs, waists and bums whereas she was still flat as an ironing board. She guessed that, behind every downcast gaze and forced silence, their thoughts were flickering back and forth between the New Year's party she wasn't at, the peach vodka they'd downed in one, the daze after the first round of a spliff, that thing that *Cioè* magazine aseptically called *petting* but really meant trying to have sex without the courage to go the whole way.

They were there, on a straight line that ran seamlessly into their lives ahead. And she was here, at a dead end. Her horizon now ended with the coffin of her mother, who was called Cecilia and loved Richard Ford and Daniel Pennac novels and the poems of Umberto Saba. Who was thirty-seven years old, who taught Italian at the Ungaretti primary school in Ravenna, and who had always preferred the sea to the mountains.

She liked getting a tan, going as far out as she could on a pedalo to watch the big umbrellas on the beach become tiny coloured spots – 'Look, Emilia, it's Lilliput!' – and having lunch at the restaurant with sand still in her swimming costume. But, more than anything else, she liked going back to school in September and seeing her pupils, listening to them talk about their holidays, correcting the diaries she had set them as summer homework along with 'wild and free reading'.

Her mother was a good person, who had never done anything – anything at all – bad.

She had stocked the school library out of her own pocket, given free tutoring to children from poorer neighbourhoods who were struggling. When life struck her with the miscarriage of Emilia's little brother – an episode she remembered perfectly, even if she was only five at the time – her mother had spent a couple of days crying in bed, and then, instead of being angry, signed up to a volunteering programme that entertained children who were recovering on the paediatric ward.

As the priest droned on about the mysterious workings of the Lord, which are always right and as they should be, all Emilia could think was that her mother's funny expressions, her habit of taking the jackets off her books and leaving them spread around the house, her way of probing Emilia about possible little boyfriends with nothing more than a raised eyebrow, were now in the past.

From now on Emilia would come home from school, humiliated as usual by her Italian teacher, by Vanessa and Sofia who pulled down her knickers in the toilets – 'Who's fucking you, carrot head? You're disgusting!' – and would no longer find her mother reading in the living room.

She'd no longer be able to cry, curled up with her head on her mother's chest. She'd no longer hear her say, 'They're weak, that's why they're saying hurtful things. Strong people are always generous.' Instead, as she opened the front door to the house, she'd be met with a chasm. A deafening, gaping crater, which still smelled of the clothes in her tidy wardrobe, her perfumes lined up on the bathroom shelf, her novels filling the entire living room bookshelf and that neither Emilia nor her father would ever touch again.

When they brought the coffin out of the church, Emilia could no longer see her classmates, nor her teachers, nor her relatives, nor the sky, nor the earth. When they put the coffin inside a recess high up in the monumental cemetery of Ravenna, and then started to block it in, with that definitive sound of cement and trowel, Emilia could no longer breathe, no longer hold herself up, and she collapsed like a sack of potatoes.

When she got home, she punched in her mother's phone number and listened to the voice saying: 'The number you have dialled is not currently available'. She would keep on punching it in, that number, every day, obsessively. She would keep on phoning to hear, instead of the usual 'Hello, my love', an anonymous voice saying, 'The number you have dialled . . .'

It's not true that after, you keep moving forward.

After, there are consequences.

And the first one, the most significant one in Emilia's life, was a voiceless, implacable rage.

10

WE GOT BACK TO Sassaia late that night, confused and shaken by the words said at the restaurant, which continued to bore into us like the carpenter bees that weasel their way into little cracks in the shutters and buzz and dig until the shutters are hollow.

The cold had fallen suddenly like an axe. The damp of the forest penetrated our bones. We used our torches to open up a path through the densest parts, where the dark bubbled with danger. We shouldn't have dressed so lightly; we shouldn't have done many things. And yet. 'Shouldn't have' isn't how you move on.

Halfway up the track, between the small roadside shrine and the giant boulders, I stopped and grabbed Emilia's hand. I wanted to ask her with my whole self: tell me who you are. But I couldn't, because then she would ask the same of me.

So I kissed her, fiercely, in a way that discharged all my frustration. Emilia trembled under her tasselled leather jacket, but she didn't push me away. It was as if we were always on the verge of losing one another, overshadowed by the threat of a memory, a question, the people we had been and who, together, we no longer were.

We switched off our torches, pushed ourselves against a chestnut tree and ended up among its roots, tangled between leaves, stones and frozen earth. The moon was almost full and its light rippled like a brook through the branches. In the distance, Alma's church bell rang out to signal one of those early, indeterminate hours in which nothing was yet finished and nothing yet begun. We had goosebumps on our skin, scratched by the brambles. As we kneaded our bodies one into the other, I said to myself that I could go in now, into the partisans' hideout. That I'd no longer be scared, of either the bats or the unexploded bullets. That for her I'd go and see what the darkness was made of, what smell it had. Even without my sister.

'We're ridiculous,' Emilia said eventually, her hair full of leaves. 'Fucking in the woods is something teenagers do when their parents are at home, not people in their thirties who could be warm indoors.'

'I skipped being a teenager. But I'm recouping it now, with you.'

I saw that she was on the verge of saying something important in response, but then seemed to have second thoughts, so we switched our torches back on and started walking again. Emilia went ahead and kept up the pace to keep warm, despite her tiredness. She was beginning to take ownership of Stra' dal Forche. It had already become her home, I thought. When we arrived at the sign that said SASSAIA she turned to look at me and smiled. 'Who'd have thought?' she said. 'I should thank him really, that Aldo guy, for not having brought me the TV.'

We could be happy, I took the risk of thinking.

'But if it's this cold in November, fuck me,' she rubbed her arms and kept walking as fast as she could, 'what is it like in January? I can't feel my fingers or toes.'

'In January we'll do nothing but shovel snow, break ice, fill the wood burner and use up our supplies. Speaking of which, by the way, we should start stocking up soon. We could get snowed in a lot.'

'I can already hear my father revelling.' She imitated his voice: '"Told you so, silly girl!"'

In the alleyways illuminated by the moon, between the silent, abandoned houses, through the squares so tiny they didn't have official names, only ones in the local dialect like *Surtun*, *Busc* and *Stela*, we walked with our arms wrapped around one another. I too could feel the winter arriving, smell the wind that rolled down from the mountaintops. But for the first time, I realised, I would go into the town to do the big apocalypse shop, buy wood in industrial quantities from Rivetti, and wait in front of the stove for the storms to pass, not alone but with her.

Arriving between the doors of our two houses, I asked her: 'Do you want to sleep at mine?'

Emilia was surprised, as if she'd never contemplated the possibility. As if my house was a coffin, a cave, a closed and inaccessible museum. In some ways it was.

'OK,' she replied, more out of the urgent need to get warm than of authentic conviction.

I shivered as I was turning the key, but not from the cold. Nobody, except for me and Valeria, had been into that house for so many years I'd lost count. I pressed the switch and the light came on, revealing, in its raw and naked form, my life.

Which was a desert. A tidy exhibition of artefacts: a butter churner, an egg basket I no longer used, a crown of flowers woven and left to dry, testimony to a childhood day out, and numerous mugs and cups that belonged to people whose tone of voice, or smile, I could no longer remember. But only I saw this mausoleum. Emilia was too cold and tired.

'I'm scared I'll catch a fever,' she said, her teeth chattering.

I looked at her. Her lips were purple.

'I can't not go to work tomorrow, it's my second day. I can't let Basilio down.'

'Don't worry,' I told her, 'come with me.'

I led her upstairs, into my room, and lit the weak table lamp I usually read by. I threw some wood into the fireplace and made Emilia sit down on the armchair next to it. I put a thick wool blanket around her shoulders.

'Wait here.'

I went back downstairs and put some water on the stove, making sure to do each task in the exact way Valeria used to when I got sick, then went back up with a cup of steaming nettle tea. Emilia, cloaked in the blanket, was almost asleep. I gave her the scorching mug and put a hand on her forehead. 'You've only got a slight fever; you'll feel better in the morning.'

I didn't close the shutters; I didn't turn out the light. I didn't dare say it out loud, but I had started to want it again – the future.

When Emilia had finished her tea I led her to the bathroom and helped her take her clothes off even though she was exhausted and the winter was already eating away at her bones. I ran the water in the shower until it was hot and I promised her the cold would be over soon, she just had to trust. She wilted against the tiles. I picked up the sponge and the shower gel and washed away the debris of leaves and soil from her body.

'Too much excitement today,' she said, looking down with shame.

I wrapped her in my dressing gown. I dried her hair with the hairdryer. I gave her a pair of my pyjamas and a painkiller and tucked her into my bed, curled up on the side no one had ever slept in.

'Why are you doing all this for me?' she asked in a tiny voice, as she closed her eyes under the covers.

'Because.'

I had never said it to anyone before.

But Emilia understood my silence and opened her fever-bright eyes wide. With panic in her voice she almost shouted: 'You can't!'

I stayed sitting next to her on the edge of the bed.

'You can't,' she repeated. It was an admonishment. She squeezed my hand so that I wouldn't leave, so that I'd immediately take back the words I hadn't said. 'You don't know me, you don't know.'

'These ten days with you,' I told her, 'have been worth a thousand times more than the ten years that came before. I don't care if you just want to have fun, or don't want commitment, or just need company and I'm the only person around. I don't need reciprocation, I don't want to hold you down, I don't want anything. I'm just happy you're here.'

Emilia let go of my hand, staring at me in a desperate stupor.

'I don't deserve it,' she said.

'Me neither,' I responded as I stood up. 'But go to sleep now, because we have to be up in six hours.'

'When we got sick, we had to go into isolation so we wouldn't give it to the others,' she mumbled, 'and I missed my mum's hugs. I'm not used to the cold. I'm not used to all this.' And, before sinking her head into the pillow, she added: 'I've missed so many winters I forgot what they were like.'

I left the room. I turned out all the lights downstairs, then upstairs, apart from our lamp. I got into the shower myself and, when I got out, dripping wet in the dressing gown she had used not long before, I looked at myself in the fogged-up mirror. It was one or two in the morning, but I didn't care. Tomorrow at school my pupils would be flabbergasted, but I didn't care about that either. First I grabbed the scissors, then the razor. Chunks of beard fell into the sink like an animal shedding its winter coat. Chunks of armour; of my mask.

When I was cleanly shaven, I saw a different man in the mirror. He wasn't a complete stranger, though: I had kept him silent inside of me all that time, prohibited him from every form of happiness. Enough.

I got into my bed which, for the first time, wasn't freezing or desolate or only mine. I lay down on my side in the same position as Emilia. I reached out a hand to feel her forehead: the fever was already gone. I wouldn't allow any of the past to come and disturb us.

Patrizia had been at Bar Samurai when Emilia and I left the church and crossed the piazza. She was sitting with her friends at a table next to the window and, like the rest of the town, had seen us.

When I turned up at school the next day, with the couple of hours' sleep I'd had showing clearly on my face, deep bags under my eyes and, most significantly, no beard, she was crossing the corridor in the opposite direction. First she slowed down, surprised. Then she shot daggers of hate in my direction. Finally she walked on without even a nod.

We have been working together since 2005. I had been back living in Sassaia for a year – one of the worst in memory. She had just got divorced. At the beginning, we had two other colleagues who made our relationship easier. But after not very long, thanks to a drastic shrinking of pupil numbers, just the two of us remained, and things immediately took a complicated turn. She felt lonely, and for her, loneliness was a thing of many unmanageable tentacles, whereas I felt I was absolutely fine alone and didn't want to be the solution to her emptiness.

I had never done anything to encourage her interest, nor to offend her. The time she had sneakily tried to kiss me in the staffroom, I had pushed her away as delicately as I could and before hightailing it out of there as fast as possible, even said sorry.

On the other hand, Patrizia had never seen me with anyone else. Gisella lived thirty-five kilometres away from Alma and nobody would ever have suspected that, of all people I, the reserved and austere Mr Peraldo, would take part in such an activity. As far as Patrizia knew, I could easily have been gay. I hoped she thought so. I could see her fragility and it made me sad to hurt her. I tried to get along with her, to greet her outbursts with kindness, even if I didn't like her way of teaching, even if I didn't like her. A reserved friendship was all I could offer her.

That morning, her heels echoed scornfully under the nineteenth-century ceilings of the school as if they wanted to walk all over me rather than the worn-out black and white tiles. I immediately understood that something terrible must have happened inside her, but, in all honesty, I just didn't care.

When I went into the classroom, my thirteen pupils were so busy chatting and swapping Pokémon cards that they barely noticed me. I called them to quieten down and when they had eventually all settled at their desks with their eyes to the front, a granite silence fell over the classroom.

I observed their squinting, incredulous little eyes, and I was so changed, not only in appearance, that I burst out laughing. 'OK, children, it was just a beard.'

They were still perplexed.

'I'm not an imposter, it's still me: Mr Peraldo. And I can finally reveal my age to you: I'm thirty-six.'

They started to smile, showing the gaps between their milk teeth, first timidly, then with more confidence. They were used to running around among decrepit old men and the idea of having such a young teacher probably made them feel a bit cool.

'That doesn't mean we're not doing our lessons like usual. Today the younger ones are learning the "sh" sound and the older ones are doing verbs. Are you happy with that?'

'Nooooo!' they called out in unison.

'Come on, put those cards away and take out your notebooks.'

I opened the register and did the brief roll-call in that enormous school with a view of the river. The same one I had attended, as had Valeria and various generations of the Peraldo family before us, and where now only the stragglers were left. Then I got up and went to the board: 'When we put *s* and *h* together we get a new sound: *sh*,' I wrote, pronouncing '*shutter, shadow, shame*', and hearing them repeat the words in their sweet voices.

Why on earth, I wondered, should I have kept my promises to become a famous university professor, to teach at the Sorbonne or in Berlin? To give up those sweet voices?

For once, that morning, I didn't feel like a failure.

Later on, during breaktime, I went into the staffroom and found Patrizia with a takeaway espresso from Piero on a coaster from the Samurai. I broke the silence in an unusually cheerful voice: 'Good morning, Patrizia!'

She didn't reply. She continued to sip her coffee and stare out of the window at the children in the playground running and climbing, sweating with their jackets open, their scarves dangling in the cold that, on that sunless day, turned their breath into clouds of condensation.

She was so tense her hands were shaking. But I was so happy that, paradoxically, I insisted that she be too.

'Martino got all his verbs right,' I told her proudly. 'I don't know if it's because his father didn't come home drunk last night, or because he's realised he doesn't want to fail anymore, or just because he's on good form today. But he's like a different person.'

'*You* are a different person.'

She put her cup down on the table. Without looking at me, she rummaged in her bag agitatedly. She pulled out her phone and started typing uncontrollably, and then hurried out of the room.

A pinging made me jump. It was coming from my leather briefcase. It was my phone: an object I was so unfamiliar with I almost always left it switched off or on silent. Still, the only person I truly cared about hadn't called me for years, and the last texts she sent me were so terse they were more like telegrams. Vodafone wrote sometimes. Or call centres phoned. It was a pain.

But that morning my life had changed: there was another person close to my heart who could've been calling, texting, feeling the need to tell me something. We had exchanged numbers over breakfast. 'Shit, we're like properly going out now,' Emilia had commented. Like me, she didn't know her number off by heart. 'I changed it not long ago,' she lied. And now I was hoping that, on a break from restoring the Black Madonna or the *Last Judgement*, she had felt the desire to write to me.

I grabbed the phone and looked.

But the message wasn't from Emilia.

It was from Patrizia.

EVIDENTLY I am not enough for you. Not thin enough, not alcoholic enough, not enough of a bitch. I didn't think you were the kind of guy who used prostitutes. You have disappointed me IRREPARABLY.

I felt a surge of hatred. For the word 'prostitutes' above all.

I was an altar boy when I was young. One part of me felt forced to be good: to suck it up, to try and understand, to turn the other cheek. I should delegate the description of Patrizia to this part of me. I should start by saying that I don't intend to judge her, not now or later, because I know all too well that the weaker we are, the more we hurt people.

But right now I just want to say 'fuck it' and have no pity. The capitalised adverbs alone say a lot about her. Like her fake nails, which she struggled to keep intact: they kept breaking, the polish flaking off, her fingers like clumsy claws.

At the time of these events, Patrizia was forty-five. After the end of her late and brief marriage, she moved to Alma to be closer to her ageing mother; but maybe she just wanted an excuse to hide away. As will become clear, Valle is perfect for hiding away fugitives.

She was perennially on a diet, drinking only coffee with sweetener, replacing lunch with protein bars, but then at five she'd go to the Samurai and gorge herself on spritz and crisps, and never manage to lose weight. She often started conversations that focused on the discreet, temporary presence of some very rare incomer with: 'I'm not racist, but . . .' Some mornings she walked into the school in a cloud of hairspray, bound in short, skintight, low-necked dresses that said *look at me*. Other mornings she'd crawl along close to the walls in oversized jumpers and long dark skirts whose only purpose was to cover: *don't look at me*. I knew she had a Facebook page she was very active on, but I, not knowing anything about social media, had no idea what kind of stuff she posted there, who she voted for – although I could imagine – or what TV programmes she followed with bated breath: mostly true crime, probably. She had tried to convince me to get a profile so we could chat: 'It's fun to exchange messages, and it would make you feel less inhibited.' She had asked me to go out: 'A quick coffee?' 'A little dinner?' And I had drunk the odd coffee with her, but I'd always found an excuse for the dinners. Every time I caught a glimpse of her at the Samurai with a man, her legs crossed and bandaged in fishnet tights, permanently energetic, I hoped she had found the one for her. But it would only ever be a few months until she was single again. She hated maths. She didn't like children. Alma felt tight on her. She was a gossip. She was fragile. She was angry.

Reading her message that morning, I intuited something I didn't want to see – stealthily, somewhere in the distance, the price that was to be paid for all the unprecedented happiness that had overcome me began to take shape.

That same evening, in fact, as Emilia and I were fucking with the fervour of the fifteen-year-olds we never were, Patrizia began her investigations on Google.

11

We had only had two loves, before. One for me and one for Emilia. Even if it feels like a stretch to call them loves.

To show how two people in their thirties could throw themselves into a relationship with such poor preparation, it might be useful to give you an idea of how little experience we'd each accumulated before we met – and how twisted and superficial that experience had been.

There was the famous Emanuele who she had lived with and who had asked her to marry him, and of whom I was supposed, in theory, to be jealous. It's worth telling the true story that Emilia, constrained by certain events, told me later on. A story that I can only tell in her words, recalling them as faithfully as I can, with her nervous way of speaking in fits and starts, always defiant and on the defensive. It should've been clear from the start, but a person in love doesn't ever want to *see*.

'The college – let me call it that for a bit longer – was an ex-convent. Cosmic irony – can you say that for this kind of thing? From the fifteenth or sixteenth century, I can't remember now.

'It had these really high barrel-vaulted ceilings, and huge windows that all looked out – imagine – onto apartment buildings and balconies: normal apartments where normal people lived. And some people said this was a positive thing, because that way we could feel like we were part of the city, rather than outcasts, rejects. Bullshit. We had the lives of others thrust right in front of our eyes, under our noses, and we weren't allowed to live like that ourselves. It drove us crazy. Even if sometimes, I admit, seeing families gathered around a table, or two old people watching the TV, made me feel a kind of tenderness; as if those strangers were keeping me company too.

'Anyway, the big window in our secondary classroom looked straight out onto the first floor of a building, into an apartment where we could see everything even down to the soap in the shower. And in 2002, or maybe it was 2003, this picket-fence family moved in, with the young mum, handsome dad, the two- or three-year-old little sister with her hair always in bunches or plaits, and the total dreamboat older brother.

'He was also a jerk. But I can only see that now. At the time I didn't want to know. It was April or May, and whenever he was home alone he wandered round in his underwear with the windows open. He was about our age and in the mornings he'd leave for school on his scooter with his rucksack. He'd come home for lunch and when his parents weren't there he'd do topless press-ups, push-ups and lunges on the balcony. He was really buff, with gel in his hair. He knew who we were, and that we were watching him.

'Imagine how much the situation must have turned him on. Imagine what we were like. Whenever the teacher left us, even for a minute, we would all press ourselves up against the window. Whoever could whistle would stick her fingers in her mouth, and we'd shout, "Bravo!", "What's in your package?", "Bet you're super well-hung!". At the beginning he would smile and blow us kisses. Then, once he got more confident, he showed us how he'd lick us out with his tongue.

'He was our great forbidden love. A collective love that, in the end, had just one victim, and that was me. Because I was the biggest sucker.

'We never saw boys, and he was a big deal – so hot, super sporty . . . who knows how many girlfriends he had. If he had brought one home – and we would have sniffed it out immediately – I think we would've started a riot. But he was never that much of a jerk.

'We named him "the Neighbour". The middle-school girls and even the foreign girls from Italian literacy class made endless excuses to come into our classroom to see him. In those months, magically, we all wanted to do every workshop, every afternoon course, always finding excuses to go and study there, only there . . . we even read! But in the mornings we couldn't even get out of bed, since he was at school, snogging the girls from his class in the toilets. All these small changes in our behaviour made the army suspicious, but we were good at concealing things. We could've all got a diploma in acting.

'We were sixteen, seventeen, eighteen: think of our hormones. And he would just chill there on his balcony with his muscly arms, his cheeky grin, the gelled quiff that flopped over his eyes. He would blow us a kiss goodbye as he went off for football training, or to meet his mates in the piazza to smoke weed, or to hole up with his girl-friend. And all of us were sent to our single beds.

'I won't tell you what we did in those single beds. The Neighbour made us all wet our knickers. They insisted that we become nuns, that we sublimate everything. But how could you forbid us, at that age, from continuously thinking about sex? There were some of us who had never even heard the word "sublimate". Others had kids outside, born when they were fourteen. And then there were the losers like me, who hadn't even lost my virginity in time.

'I'm not ashamed to say I fell in love. It had never happened to me before. I had only tongue-kissed a boy with braces, who I didn't even like, in a beach hut when I was in Year 9. It was gross. Emanuele looked – to me – like Justin Timberlake, and he was there, he was real; he could see me, notice me and, paradoxically, because of the place I was in, find me interesting in a way nobody outside ever had. I had always been "carrot head", "Spotty the dog", "poor little orphan" or "loser", and now I was a fully-fledged *bad girl*. So I took my chances.

'Marta wanted nothing to do with it. She wanted to punch him. "You're taking shit from a privileged wanker," she'd say. "His arse gets to stay in the warm with his little mummy and daddy doing everything for him, paying for everything for him. He lives in the centre of town and has a brand-new scooter, he's fucking all the posh little girls he wants and then he comes home and has a quick wank over you, over us, to help him fall asleep. He's treating us like charity cases – how the fuck can you not hate him?"

'I just couldn't. Because I too, unlike Marta and nearly all the others in there, came from a wealthy family like Emanuele's, and I had once had a cool scooter, a nice house, a gym membership, and my every whim satisfied by Daddy. But, also unlike almost everyone else, I didn't have a scrap of experience in matters of love and sex. I think everyone except me had already had sex. Many even had boyfriends who they wrote to and phoned up and who were waiting for them outside – cheating on them, yes, but it was better than nothing.

'I wanted something too: a miserable little scrap of normal life. I had my period; my mood swings; hormones in abundance. The Neighbour was everything that the convent didn't have – and I wanted him . . .'

'Maybe because I was the most desperate, it was my idea to write to him.

'A stupid little note, at first. Like: "I wanna give you a blow-job, what's your name? We all finger ourselves every night thinking of you." The other girls whistled, clapped, spurred me on. "Throw in a 'suck', a 'swallow'. . ."

At this memory Emilia let out a beautiful laugh, so full of tenderness for herself and her companions that she managed, despite the night of no return we had fallen into, to move me to tenderness too.

'Anyway, I wrote this note, I screwed it up into a ball like I did with your picture, and then the real challenge began. Because you try passing a note between two grates and landing it on the balcony opposite. We weren't javelin throwers. At best we played darts. It was a shitshow. Plus we had to do it all in a hurry so the army wouldn't get suspicious, and it had to be when he was on the balcony alone, because if not his mother might have picked it up. Imagine the scenes!

'I don't know how many times the first note bounced off the grates. Then it fell into the street. We wrote another one and it fell again. We all tried: me, Afifa, Myriam, Yasmina. Not Marta because she refused to "stoop so low". She was in a class war against the Neighbour.

'Getting the correspondence started required some intense training, but then . . . he wrote back!

'You should have seen his throw. A formidable aim. He landed it on the first try, so sure of himself. I'd love to know what became of him, what job he has, whether he has children.

'Anyway. On the first note he sent us, he wrote: "My name's Emanuele, and you? You're my wet dream. Tell me how I can get in there and pleasure you". We went out of our minds. We started screaming as if we were at a Backstreet Boys concert, and we accidentally tore that precious piece of paper because we passed it between our excited hands so much. A distraction, *thank the Lord*!

'After that first exchange, we started to really have fun and we got better and better at folding up the pieces of paper into aerodynamic shapes. I would like to know what became of them, those pornographic little notes: which of us managed to capture them, to take them home. But maybe they ended up in the bin. Because who would be so stupid as to take a souvenir home from the college? Apart from me, obviously. I kept all of his letters to me, and I still reread them sometimes.

'I never thought about running away. Out of everyone I was the only daddy's girl – zero criminal mentality, zero street smarts. I was a dead girl walking. I just wanted to keep on the straight and narrow and suffer. But Emanuele offered me a drop of life, and it turned me upside down. To the point that I then started dreaming, seriously, of running away to him.

'As a group we wrote obscene things, to which he responded even more obscenely. But alone I wrote that I loved him, implored him to wait for me, I made absurd plans for how we could snatch ourselves even a kiss. And he, in his little notes addressed *4 EMI*, played along. He wrote that he had noticed me straight away, that I was the most beautiful, the sexiest. I don't know now whether to call him nasty or naive. He didn't realise, I guess, that he was playing with the feelings of a convict. But nothing is ever just one thing, there's always more to it. And so, yes, he was playing with fire, but he was also giving me relief.

He reminded me what it meant to wake up in the morning with a reason not to kill myself.

'He had the internet at his disposal and a modest quantity of porn, and we didn't. We were at risk of becoming repetitive in our four or five threadbare fantasies, always lesbian in tone, since that was our thing. A little group of bean flickers was formed, with me at the head, living for that sex via passed note. And then there were the proper people, like Marta, who stood next to the window one day and said: "Can't you ask him for cigarettes? Ask your sexy Emanuele for cigarettes. You're giving yourselves away for free. That is not a thing. Stop getting used and start using him!"

'She was right. There were some girls in the group with a past in prostitution, but, you know, love makes you foolish, even when it's abstinent. So those who in their previous lives would charge a thousand euros for a weekend were suddenly pulled back from the imbecility and took the reins of the business. "Yes, let's write that if he wants to continue he has to throw us some weed. Otherwise, he can go fuck himself." "Oh, we're not like his little high school bitches, we're professionals."

'"We're queens," Marta encouraged, "*que-eens*. The 4.2 per cent of the nation. We are a rarity, a delicacy." She kissed the tips of her fingers. "Value yourselves, respect yourselves. Exercise a little feminism, for God's sake."

'Although she later graduated in molecular biology and became a pharmaceutical chemist, she should've gone into politics. Speeches, debates, that was her bread and butter. She could've started the revolution.

'Hot Emanuele started throwing us packs of Lucky Strikes. "Well, when you have an allowance . . ." Marta commented caustically. Then he moved on to bits of pot wrapped in tinfoil, on the condition that we showed him something concrete – tits, arses – through the window bars. He too had business savvy. I remember sometimes he would throw us an already-rolled joint to let us lick the saliva he had stuck it with – the most physical contact we could dream of.

'But for me, unfortunately, a film had started in my head.

'A film where he could fall in love too. Where he could wait for me. Where in a few years, when I had my first leave permits, we would run away and get married abroad, with some false documents that – given my new acquaintances – I would easily be able to procure. I had lost all clarity and dignity. And who knows what he did with my letters, whether he read them out to his classmates to show off. Who knows if he knew what I had done. I don't think so. He wasn't smart enough to find out.

'However, it was a paradise that couldn't last. In fact, they had already sussed us out. The army was biding their time, just waiting for the right moment.

'Then, on an afternoon in June, my black month, the time came.

'At 2:45, punctual as death, Frau Direktorin plunged into the room while we were in the act of committing the crime.

'And she busted our arses.

'Epically. Gigantically. I can still remember it now.

'All of Bologna heard her booming voice.

'Marta's face turned white as a sheet.

'Frau Direktorin was one of the good ones, by the way. She loved us, and we loved her. But when she was angry the walls shook.

'She put us all in detention. No more leave permits, no more reductions in sentence, no extra phone calls. She immediately wrote and sent a warning and then, with no mercy, had the windows covered with a fine metal mesh, with such tiny holes that only air could pass through, not even a mosquito. She was ruthless.

'And, naturally, she sent a letter on headed paper to Emanuele's family too. His picket-fence parents must have seriously chewed him out because we didn't see him for a long time. His blinds were always down and only his little sister and her South American babysitter went out onto the balcony. Then they left for the holidays – lucky them – and the apartment remained closed behind shutters for a week – just like us, who now only went to the classroom to goof around, do our nails and play cards, because the adventure was over. And when the lovely little family returned in September, my personal Justin Timberlake did let us see him again, yes, but never condescended to look in our direction. We didn't exist for him anymore, just like we didn't exist for the rest of the world.

'I kept writing to him in my diary. Promising I'd give him my virginity under the slice of the portico that I could see from my room. Planning escapes to Spain, Brazil and, why not, Sassaia. But in the meantime, in college, we returned to our usual routines. In the bloom of youth, with our tight butts, endless desire, hard nipples. And boys couldn't get anywhere near us. What a waste.

'It's inhumane, isn't it? There is no right to sexuality, of course. Imagine going and saying that to one of those people who shout, "Throw away the key!" Try telling one of them that we were sixteen, seventeen years old, and we just wanted to fuck, to fall in love. Their veins would get so big their necks would explode, those people. Those people who don't know, who have never come to visit us, never got to know us. Who have no idea.

'The truth is that each of us had a reactive, wide-open body. If you were lesbian, it could be paradise every so often. If you weren't, you could try it. Either way, there was a form of affection. So maybe my only love before you wasn't Emanuele, but Marta. Because we helped each other and we touched each other. We warmed each other's hearts, and the shells that contained them.'

My only love before, on the other hand, was Gisella. But I don't have the strength to tell that story now.

12

THE FIRST SNOW WAS just a dusting on the slate roof tiles, on the naked branches of beech and chestnut trees, in the cracks of shade between the houses of Sassaia, where it stubbornly persisted, thin and hard like glass.

Emilia was constantly slipping over. One wipeout after another, she said, and she laughed, she really laughed. That light coating didn't just satisfy her, it illuminated her. She bundled herself up in two vests, a thermal top, a fleece, a puffer jacket and a pair of waterproof trousers and rolled down the steep slope under the viewpoint into the mush of fallen leaves, over the brown stains where slivers of sun had melted the snow, screaming like a madwoman.

I watched her from the top wearing just a wool jumper with the sleeves rolled up. When she got to the end of the clearing and hit the tree stumps with her back or chest, she'd get up, scramble back up the hill, and start again; untired like a child. 'Come on!' she shouted. 'Loosen up, you doddering old codger!' And I smiled, but I didn't loosen up.

I should write that we were happy. Because it's the truth. In those cold and precarious days, with me at school teaching adjectives and her in the church, five hundred metres away, wearing Iole's woollen overcoat under her ski jacket, repainting the cherubs.

We were happy one Friday afternoon, out in the Seat doing the shopping at Centre Gross – a suburban area at the bottom of the valley with warehouses and shopping centres – almost like a normal couple. Emilia was pushing the trolley, puzzled by the fact that the snacks she liked as a child were no longer produced, and bemused by the new snacks that had replaced them. I, on the other hand, gathered up flour, polenta and tins of tomatoes, and swallowed all my questions, like *When was the last time you went shopping?* I didn't skimp on sugar and other non-perishable ingredients that we would later have to drag, sweating and swearing, up Stra' dal Forche in the freezing cold.

We were happy in front of the stove in the evenings, sinking our spoons into pasta soup, drinking too much wine and ending up passing out on the sofa without even making it upstairs to the bedroom. The Sundays gathering wood in the forest, followed by Monday mornings with my alarm going off at six in either my room or hers, frozen like a cave with the ashes lying in the chimney, the glass covered in condensation and the two of us under the covers, each immersed in the warmth of the other, legs entangled, her bottom pressed into my stomach, clinging on to this life raft.

We were happy, yes, in that fistful of weeks in which I managed not to ask her anything. But there was a woodworm boring away at my insides. And I knew that time was a bastard.

The second snow, indeed, didn't take long to come. It fell at night, secretly, one Saturday in mid-December. When Emilia woke up in my bed in the morning, late because neither of us had to go to work, I heard her exclaim: 'Bruno! It's all white outside!'

I had just opened my eyes. She turned towards me, her face pale and streaked with the milky light that filtered through the curtain. 'It's all, all of it – really all of it – *completely* white.'

I was used to it; she wasn't. When it snowed heavily, Sassaia no longer existed. It became a lack, a void pressed onto the side of a mountain, and we could pretend to be detached from the world, were free to do whatever we liked. 'Well, no one can see us,' had become Emilia's favourite sentence. Stealing a kiss in the alley, peeing halfway up the mule track, pulling my trousers down against a chestnut tree.

Only, that morning she added, 'I had never been here before, in winter.'

She mumbled it without realising, struck by the now edgeless world that had turned white outside.

For a moment – just one – I saw, as if in a vision, a girl with frizzy red hair tamed into two plaits. A handful of freckles on each cheek. Denim dungarees. Standing in the piazza, holding Iole's hand, who, unlike the girl, was crystal clear in my memory. Iole was talking with the other women, saying something about this niece of hers. Maybe it was the Feast of the Assumption – the church was open. Iole had various relatives dispersed around Italy who came to visit in the summer and stayed for a week or two, played in the town, mixed with us.

Could it be possible that I had met Emilia before?

The question chilled me in my bed, froze me to the point that I could no longer move my arms and legs, or breathe. She, meanwhile, leaped out of bed to get dressed. When I joined her in the kitchen, my heart heavy and my throat closed, she didn't even want breakfast. She was pulling on her gloves, scarf and hat. She wasn't hanging around. Wonder had turned into chaos and frenzy. Before I had a chance to compare her thirty-one-year-old face with that fleeting fragment of memory, she had already pushed open the door and thrown herself from the step, arms flung wide in angel flight, into a metre of snow.

I banished what I was sure was a trick of memory. I filled the big moka pot and cut some bread. The snowy silence of Sassaia was like a chasm that cleared the acoustic nerve: the perfect sound of nothing, only shattered, that morning, by Emilia's laughter. She had such ferocious enthusiasm that you couldn't help but wonder why a restaurant, a supermarket, a bottle of wine, or a snowfall had such an exceptional effect on a person of her age. The noise was such that after a while, Basilio turned up in his rubber boots and felt hat, holding a stick, to check that everything was OK.

Emilia was throwing snowballs at my windows and shouting: 'Come on out if you're brave enough!' It made me happy when she played the fool. I was already incapable of sleeping without her, eating dinner without her, I even managed to feel her absence while teaching, during the only hours we spent apart. But that sentence – *I had never been here before, comma, in winter* – had begun to dig away at some place inside of me, the weakest point, and started to lower the temperature, darken the light, sour the taste of the blackberry jam I'd made in the summer.

The snowballs stopped. I heard Emilia's voice apologising: 'Did I wake you?' And then Basilio's saying, 'Fat chance! I'm up at five every morning.'

I looked out of the front door. It was strange to see them together, all bundled up with the snow reaching their knees. I asked if they wanted coffee. Basilio said yes and came in from the cold. Emilia was torn; she knew she had to maintain a certain level of decency in front of him. But it was he who said, 'Go and have fun'. And she, as if she expected no less, fell over again and again, rolling in an alleyway, jumping off a wall, sliding down a set of steps. We stood there absorbed in watching her for a moment, then Basilio planted his stick and we went inside.

The coffee was ready. I put the moka pot on an oven mitt in the middle of the table. Basilio took off his boots and jacket and sat down. We drank in silence listening to her running and singing: the only sound in the whiteness.

'She's brought you a bit of life, eh?' he said, putting down his cup and nodding his head towards the window.

I felt my cheeks turn hot. 'Don't tell anyone, please.'

'Who do you think I'm going to tell?' He smiled.

We weren't friends. We just shared a gigantic solitude in the shape of Sassaia. He was the only remaining inhabitant of this place before I returned, or escaped, from Turin. I remember that one of my first evenings here – I hadn't even unpacked my cases and, when I wasn't going up and down the valley like a madman, I spent whole days in bed with the shutters closed, my eyes wide open in the dark, my head between my hands – he had knocked at the door so loudly and with such insistence that after about twenty minutes of knocking I had to give in.

He knew my whole story. He said, 'Choose a different place, Bruno.' I had thought he didn't want me getting under his feet, but actually it was only me who was worried about that. I responded, 'I don't have a different place.'

He didn't give up. 'Pick up an atlas. Close your eyes and open a page at random. It could be Paris, Cuba, Japan. The world is endless, as are the opportunities you still have.'

I told him to piss off. 'So why aren't you out there taking all these opportunities?' I was in such a pitiful state that I had no shame, not even about disrespecting an elder.

'I've missed the boat. But you're still young.'

I shouted in his face: 'Would you rather I killed myself?' And he walked away shaking his head, saddened as if I were his son.

Ten years later, he was looking at me with a satisfaction I had never seen on him before.

'You were right,' he continued after a while, with his usual long gaps between words. 'She's talented, she works hard.'

'I'm glad.'

'We'll be able to bring Alma Church back to life, then Novella which is in ruins, and also Donato, my favourite.'

A sarcastic laugh came out of my mouth. 'Won't it be too much church for Emilia? She seems completely allergic to religion.'

Basilio suddenly looked serious, almost grave. 'Nobody knows God better than she does.'

He got up. Pulled his boots back on, his jacket, his hat. He walked out without even thanking me for the coffee. Leaving me alone on my usual chair, with the certainty that I was the only one who didn't know.

'Papa, you don't understand.'

'Are you snowed in? I've seen the weather reports.'

Emilia bit the index finger of her glove to pull it off and hold the phone better. 'Yeah, and it's paradise. It's like being inside a cloud, you walk and you don't know where you're going. Anyway,' she retorted, 'if I'm snowed in, so is my boss.'

'Very canny of you.' Riccardo's tone changed from worried to amused. 'As it's snowing and you have nothing to do, if I were you I'd be making the most of that drip of an internet connection to look for something less precarious . . . for the new year.'

Emilia's good humour dissipated. She was phoning him for once, being a good daughter. Sitting on a pile of snow at the edge of the woods, in a spot where her phone had four bars of signal, she immediately lost her patience.

'You're never happy. I'm a conservator, that's an unbelievably cool job. What more do you want?'

'A permanent contract, a job that gives you something
in terms of career progression and a pension.'

'You didn't even want me to come up here! And now
you're talking about pensions? What is this? What the hell
are you talking about? When we're done with the churches,
we'll start with the big houses. House painters earn a ton
of money.'

'Am I allowed to say that this wasn't what I hoped
for you?'

A magpie suddenly took flight from the top of a pine,
creating a green tear in the uniform whiteness.

'You've got some cheek.' Emilia stamped on her glove and
kicked it away. 'Less than two months ago I was in a shithole
above Pianoro, with no bank account, no phone, no documents . . . Frankly, even if I was milking cows it would be
impressive, but I have a job, doing the thing I studied.'

'Should I treat you like a street urchin then? You want
me to be happy with any kind of step forward because
it's better than before?'

'Yes sir.'

'Well, I know you're worth more than being a painter's
assistant.'

Emilia had a flashback to her father at visits: the most
elegant, the most educated, the most well-kempt person
there. An alien.

There was this room painted in pastel colours – yellow
and pink – with a flourish of flowers and butterflies in

the corners, like a nursery. There were four blue tables, also infantile, and four wooden seats around each one for visitors, maximum three at a time.

Her father looked like Richard Gere in the wrong film. He hitched up his cashmere trousers as he sat down, showing his Scottish knitted blue socks and polished shoes. He was a shining bust on the other side of the table which became greyer, older and more tired with each year, because time is, indeed, a bastard. Anyway, Riccardo Innocenti was still there, oblivious to the height of the obstacles, his glass half full of the microscopic residue of good left in his daughter and her *future*.

Emilia remembered his motivational speeches, his verve, his granite optimism that even turned the heads of the patched-up families on other tables. Mothers veiled in flowery headscarves, fathers with paint- or plaster-splattered trousers, sisters and brothers with fake designer jeans and worn-out trainers. Parents who told her companions to eat more because they looked too skinny, or to try to go back to school to get their 8th grade certificate, or to hold on because they had a little brother waiting back at home – 'He really misses you, he's always asking after you'. Or a child – 'He lost another tooth, he's got a sweet little gap'. Or saying things like 'they've given us a council house', 'we've got those hair straighteners you wanted on credit: you'll find them on your bed as soon as you're out', or 'they've locked your uncle up in the Dozza, what an injustice, for just thirty grams'. Emilia envied them, the recipients of this news, while her father incited her to send her drawings to an art magazine, to think about her degree, and she just wanted to say, 'Can't you see where the hell I am?'

Riccardo could see where she was, yes, but it was as if he didn't see that her situation was the end of her life, eternity and beyond. He brought her a stack of paperbacks every time (hardcovers, with which she could easily have blinded herself or someone else, were strictly *verboten*): things like Buzzati, Cassola, Eric Fromm – *The Fear of Freedom*, come on! – which she systematically 'donated' to the little 'college library' for the use of people like Marta, who had nobody come and visit her apart from her lawyer and could do nothing but suck it up and read.

'Maybe you haven't yet accepted the fact that your only daughter won't have a career, won't get married, won't give you grandchildren and that, if she survives this shithole of a place, that alone will be an enormous success. Speaking of which,' she felt the need to push it further, 'have you heard Myriam has killed herself?'

Her father stayed silent for a long moment. Emilia thought she had done it, defeated him.

'I'm really sorry about Myriam,' Riccardo said sincerely. 'I didn't know. I'll send a telegram and some flowers to her family today.' But then he started up again because that's how he was – invincible. 'I remind you that Marta lives in Milan and has a very impressive job.'

'Don't start with the comparisons.'

'It's not about comparisons, but examples. Your job is just fine as a starting point, don't get me wrong. But what

I'm trying to say is don't get complacent. Don't lose sight of the horizon, of what your life *still* has to offer.'

It was incredible how determined parents could be to not see their children as they were. It was pathetic, their will not to give up, to insist that their child was an extension of their own dreams rather than nothing but wild, ruinous fragments.

Her father was a famous architect; a respectable man, held in high esteem in Italy and abroad. This point was hammered home in the newspapers. The journalists loved rummaging around in the bullshit of destiny: a man of such prestige, and look at the child he ended up with.

'Do you know what? I won't phone you again.'

'You need to learn to accept encouragement and constructive criticism.'

'Piss off. I just wanted to tell you that there's a ton of snow here, and that it's beautiful, and that I'm getting my own back for that time it snowed in Bolo and they didn't let us out into the courtyard, not even to touch it. Because we didn't have the right *equipment*, because we would *get sick*.' Emilia aped the voice of a guard she hated. 'We watched it from the window, salivating, raging, until it melted, then they let us out. And now I'm being repaid with interest,' she used Marta's favourite expression, 'and you're breaking my balls.'

Riccardo laughed. 'That's my job, darling.'

Emilia jumped down from the pile of snow, her bum soaking wet in spite of her waterproof trousers, and couldn't help laughing with him.

They were able to laugh together in circumstances where another father and another daughter would've been at the end of their tether. That was their secret strength: they could reach rock bottom, cry, and, their faces wet with tears, make each other laugh. 'You know what? Instead of digging further and further downwards, we could try a lateral tunnel and see where it takes us,' he had said on the day after she was sentenced.

'When exactly are you coming?' Emilia asked.

'I should make it for the 23rd, the morning of the 24th at the latest. But do you think I'll manage to get up the mule track?'

'We'll shovel it, don't worry.'

'Who? You and Basilio? I thought he was an old man with arthritis?'

'There's another person who lives here too . . .' Emilia admitted, 'in Sassaia.'

Her voice changed imperceptibly, embarrassed, hardened. Riccardo understood straight away.

'You didn't mention it . . . A fellow?'

Emilia swallowed her words. 'More or less.'

'Remember that you have a right to a normal life now.'

We had accumulated so many sheets that needed washing that, snow or no snow, it needed to be done that weekend. I was pushing them into a big basket – the *cistún* that had belonged to my grandmother – when Emilia came back inside, nervous, perhaps worried. She slammed the door and tossed her phone onto the table. She flopped down, wet, on the sofa.

'What's happened?'

'Nothing.' She pointed, irritated, at the basket: 'Surely you don't want to do laundry in this weather?'

'Yes, before it starts snowing again.'

'You're sick.'

She had gone too far away for me to be able to hear anything – I had tried opening the window a crack – but it was clear her change of mood had something to do with the phone call.

'Does nobody have a washing machine up here?' she asked with resentment. 'Is it possible?'

'Some of the people who come from Turin or Milan in the summer have had one put in,' I responded calmly.

'And why can't we buy one? Are you so disgusted by modernity? God, you really are an old man, inside and out.'

I tried to maintain my self-control, keeping my voice low and calm to neutralise her current of rage.

'I'll take you to buy one, if you want.' I pulled the basket onto my back. 'You just have to times the delivery costs to the power of three. Unless you want to hire a pair of mules.'

Emilia yanked off her scarf, her jacket and her snow boots then snarled at me, 'Do you have one, a father?'

I left. I grabbed my hammer from the hook to smash the sheet of ice that I was sure would have formed on the surface of the water at the washhouse, and kicked the snow aside as I walked along the alleyway.

That's how it worked, with Emilia. One minute she was gleeful, tender, sensual, licentious; and the next there seemed to be so much hate in her body it was as if she wanted to raze the entire planet to the ground, you included.

I struck the water and the ice cracked in spokes. I submerged a month and a half of sheets, mine and hers, into the freezing water. A month and a half of sex every sacrosanct night without knowing anything meaningful about one another. Observing objects, habits and customs from our previous lives that no matter how hard we tried, were unreachable.

It was hard. Suppressing innocuous questions like 'where were you born?'. Suspecting that each of her responses was a cover. When I found myself with the better Emilia, I convinced myself it was all OK. But when she behaved like a first-class jerk I wanted nothing more than to stick my hand in her bag, pull out her wallet and read her identity card: surname, date of birth, place of residence.

It was December 19th and our happiness was extremely fragile.

With my stick, I pulled out a pillowcase and then pushed it down again, as if I wanted to drown it.

At a certain point Emilia emerged from the whiteness of the snow. She approached me as I soaped and rinsed, placing her boots in the footprints I had left and walking towards me with a smile on her face, repentant. She stuck her head into the washhouse. 'What a perfect house husband I've found myself.'

'I don't know if I can do this, Emilia.'

'Do what?' She smiled stubbornly even though my face was dark.

'Just fuck and nothing else.'

She sat down on the moss-covered stone wall and caressed it with her bare, red fingers, her nails painted electric blue.

'Sorry. It was a conversation with my dad. Nothing to do with you.'

I continued to soap, rub, rinse – and not look at her.

'It's just that he's coming in a few days, until New Year's Eve, and it's making me anxious. Living together as adults, using the same bathroom. I don't even know where to put him, and what to do about you ... I'll have to rappel down knotted sheets from the window.' She laughed. 'And then Christmas. Christmas destroys me.'

'Tell me about it.'

Comma, in winter.

Maybe it was Christmas that made me fall into anger and depression, too. Or maybe I realised that, despite our feelings and the furious shared will to do so, we wouldn't be able to live like this for long, illegal immigrants in the present. Like two people without families, without histories.

'Let's play a game.' I let go of the sheets and looked at her. 'I'm going to tell you something about me now, something true, and you, in exchange, have to tell me something about you. OK?'

Her gaze immediately clouded over, the smile disappeared from her lips. But my tone was unusually aggressive, unwilling to tolerate any attempt at escape. So Emilia put her arrogance to one side and nodded yes.

'The answer is no,' I started, 'I don't have a father. Or a mother. As you'll have noticed, nobody calls me, nobody pops round, I don't have the problem of deciding whether to introduce you or hide you away.'

I put my cold-cracked hands on the washbasin. I looked into her eyes, into the impenetrability I had begun to hate.

'I've told this story twice in my whole life. Once in a police station and once in court.' I saw her twitch. 'I'd rather shoot myself in the mouth than stumble my way through it again.'

The sky was still and white, indistinguishable from the earth. Every so often I glimpsed a chimney, a balustrade, a gable. Short and broken lines that, hanging mid-air, no longer had any meaning.

'But for a measly crumb of your truth, Emilia, I'm willing to tell you mine.'

13

'It was in the papers and on TV for a while. A TV crew even came to Sassaia once, which was unheard of. The journalist was really glamorous, with this billowing hair. I don't know how she managed to get up Stra' dal Forche in high heels. Maybe she brought a change of shoes. I also don't know why she was so impressed. She wanted to interview me and my sister; she was really insistent. Her cameraman was a metalhead who wore an AC/DC T-shirt and obeyed her every instruction. They took up position in front of the house and waited until after sunset. Sharks.' I took a breath. 'There was a cable car. Three mountains from here, fifteen kilometres by road. A cable car that was opened in 1952 to connect the Sanctuary of San Giuseppe with a glacier lake and a refuge at the top of Monte Stella.

'My parents were mad about the mountains.' I took another breath. 'There wasn't a single Sunday or holiday when we didn't go up some heap of stones or other in our hiking boots, butter and anchovy sandwiches in our backpacks. My father said you needed to get above the trees to start to understand. That the sky needed to weigh on your head. That the rocks were millions of years old and climbing them helped put your problems into perspective.

'My parents were two simple people: a stonemason and a housewife. They hadn't studied. The fact that I was doing so well at school at first astonished them, then convinced them that the future might reward us. But we were such a normal family. We weren't envied or admired; we didn't bother anyone, we didn't stand out. I was a fraud, as would be revealed later. We weren't rich. My parents argued but loved each other. In the grand scheme of things, whether or not we existed changed absolutely nothing. And yet,' I took my hands off the wall and turned away from the part of the mountain that was sunk in white, 'I can promise you we were happy.'

You couldn't see Monte Stella from Sassaia, not even from the top of Cresto, not even on the clearest of days: a gift of geographical compassion. But I knew, every day, every instant, that it was there. It was. Unmovable, like all mountains.

'On Sunday August 26th, 1990, at 8:35 in the morning, we bought our tickets and got into the queue behind another little group of people to go up on the cable car. There was a café just near the base where we had been having a second breakfast of coffee and croissants. I can even tell you what flavours they were: plain for my sister, chocolate for me. We all got into the cabin. Note, it was *all* of us. First the little group of strangers with a blond boy, who I'd discover afterwards was five-year-old Thomas from Busto Arsizio; then my father and my mother, my sister and me; and finally an older couple.'

I could relive these two minutes for eternity.

'My mother was wearing a little green cap with a peak, her ponytail pulled through the hole above the adjustable strap, which made her look young and carefree. My father had the camera around his neck and was playing with the zoom lens. They moved forwards towards the front window to get the best view. Nobody else got on after the old couple. It was the end of the season so there weren't many people around. My father and mother had their arms around each other's waists, enclosed in a moment of intimacy. I didn't have a single hair on my cheeks or chin, and I was clumsy and moody. My sister was winding me up, saying my socks were a biohazard. The lift operators looked bored in their little office, repeating the same actions and gestures as all the other days, years, decades. My mother turned towards me at a certain point. Without detaching from my dad, she put a hand on my shoulder, as if to check I was there. Or to reaffirm that she was there, and that she continued to love me even if I had become this strange man-child with a gruff voice and a new shyness. She stroked one of my cheeks. I pulled away, embarrassed. She started to laugh. It was the most precious moment of my life, but I didn't know it.

'We were all there, waiting. The cable car operators checked to see no one else was coming. There were eleven of us and the cabin could hold thirty. Then Valeria hit her forehead with the palm of her hand and shouted, "Oh no! I left my rucksack in the café toilet!"'

I turned towards Emilia: she was still there. Suddenly calm, her eyes like two stalactites pointing at me. I assured myself that the washhouse was also still there, and the sheets. That Sassaia was still empty of all its inhabitants and that it was still 2015.

'It's absurd, if you think about it. A rucksack. The little rucksack of a girl, containing some oh-so-important little letters from her boyfriend, pads, maybe a little ring from an Easter egg as a token of love.

'I huffed and moaned, "Ugh that's so typical of you." Mum said, "Run and get it, quickly! You can get the next lift." She turned to me. She was wearing a red T-shirt, denim shorts, she was my mother: nobody could have loved me more than her. 'You go with her, go on! That way you can come up together on the 9 o'clock." Valeria ran off. I followed her against my will, just because my mother had told me to. My sister was six years older than me and didn't need accompanying. But I obeyed because I was obedient. I could have protested, said, "It's her rucksack, she left it, her problem."

'It's not a big deal, if you think about it, a rucksack.

'Valeria was running and I walked sulkily behind her. Our relationship had been different for a while: I was practically mute. She was seventeen and had a boyfriend. I was irritated by their kisses and by my own body. She was always in the bathroom with the door locked and her secrets were getting on my nerves, all the more so on that day. That Sunday. When she didn't even want to come with us because she wanted to see her boyfriend. And who knows what it was that was so important in that rucksack. I wondered whether she had her period.

I was thinking about the strange things that happened in my underpants. I was asking myself these stupid questions as the cabin was departing. Valeria went into the café, and I was neither on this side of childhood nor the other.

'I got to the garden of the café and waited outside. I turned and I saw the cable car going up. I saw my parents still holding each other and looking. No longer at the mountains, but at us. At me. They were waving.'

Twenty-five years had passed and I still couldn't cry.

Couldn't understand.

Couldn't accept.

'After ten metres I saw the cabin fall.'

Today, as I write, I know that Emilia lost her mother to breast cancer when she was thirteen: the same age, more or less, that I became an orphan. She hadn't yet told me that snowy morning at the washhouse, but in some way I had known it from the very first moment I met her. The point is that, around the time you go to middle school, you have to detach yourself from your parents, resize them, criticise them, see them for what they are: two people of many, who happened upon you. But if you lose them at that age, it's impossible to ever detach yourself from them. Impossible to resize them. Impossible to grow.

Emilia looked at me with such attentive eyes and didn't dare come closer.

I knew it too: those who survive are untouchable. The pain forms a kind of force field.

She remained standing in front of me, on the other side of the washhouse, and waited patiently, with real interest, for the rest of the story. I was struck by the fact she didn't seem disturbed or upset. But I was too absorbed in myself in that moment to worry about why.

'I asked myself why,' I continued, 'every single day. I didn't see my sister when she came out of the café, I just heard her behind my back, saying, "Got it!", relieved nobody had stolen her violet rucksack. I was paralyzed in front of the empty space between the broken cable and the earth covered in glass. My body had already understood what my mind hadn't: it was empty and silent like a crater. Valeria hadn't realised, not yet. 'Hey, move it, what are you doing?' I felt her chest push against my back, her breath on my neck which at a certain point started to get lighter, thinner, as if she too were dying. With them. With me. People were shouting, running from all directions, calling the police, ambulances. Not us.

'We were inert matter, standing at the edge in a non-space, a non-time. We stayed planted to this spot of grass like two lampposts, breathing together slowly. For minutes, hours, who can say. I just know that at some point we were uprooted from there and taken to the hospital.

'It was all over the papers and TV news for a few weeks. The world had discovered that there was a place called Sassaia and that it contained two orphans who had miraculously survived the Monte Stella cable car disaster by some stroke of fate. But Sassaia didn't want its story told. Everyone dodged the microphones and huddled around our house, protecting us from sharks and busybodies. They brought us food, cleaned the house, made sure that we were sleeping, that we were washing, that we were eating and drinking. Then other accidents happened, other news, and our story became boring. Absurd things happen everywhere, all the time: disasters, catastrophes, plane crashes, earthquakes, motorway pile-ups. Ours was one of many.'

Emilia nodded, as if she understood perfectly.

'We remained alone, Valeria and I. We were terrified of the freedom. We were no longer kids like the others, but rather the two passengers who got off the cursed cable car just in time to dodge death. Survival is a curse. But I won't tell you about afterwards. Nobody is ever interested in that.

'I'll just say this: Valeria left her boyfriend and threw away the rucksack with his letters and ring. Every time we silently looked at the other's face, we saw it: guilt. The house was suddenly enormous for just the two of us. She stuck it out until I was eighteen, then she left.'

I looked down and stopped talking.

The white sheets were swimming and swelling like jellyfish under the waterspout. There was no sun. White light poured out across the whole sky. There was no way of knowing if it was half past eleven or two in the afternoon.

My time broke that morning. From then on, I just pretended to be alive. Through the highs and lows, the long depressive periods and brief interludes of illusion. The unspeakable is never the moment itself, the overwhelming instant. It's the long, blank, inexorable *after*.

I have thought every day that it would've been better, a million times better, to die all together in that cable car. None of the four of us would have complained or asked for more. We would have been crushed together, our bones, lungs and hearts mixed up, as if we'd become a single person on impact. It would've been a happy ending. And I wouldn't have given a damn about dying at eleven years old. I had been happy a bunch of times: in the woods, at Christmas, at school. We had done nothing bad. Nothing to deserve being separated like that, clean down the middle, two in the cemetery and two at home. It was hell, after.

'It was hell,' I said to Emilia now. 'Until you came, like a bolt from the blue, and gave me cause to question for the first time in twenty-five years whether maybe, despite everything, life might still be worth living.'

I was crying now.

Emilia took a step towards me, then another. She reached a hand towards my cheek to dry it.

My lips shook as I implored her: 'Please don't tell me you found Sassaia on the internet, that you only chose it because the rent was the lowest in all of Italy. Nobody just comes here. Everyone comes back. Tell me who you are.'

Emilia froze and dropped her hand.

She closed her eyes and responded: 'I can't.'

'After all I've just told you?' I stretched my arms out to the sides. 'Why are you so stubborn?'

When she opened them again, her grey-green eyes were no longer impenetrable. They were lit up; a battle was underway under the surface.

She said: 'You have no guilt. None at all.' Standing still, half a metre away from me, she added: 'But now I can see that innocence is also a burden.'

I didn't understand. I saw only her constant evasions, and I was exasperated. 'As children, in the piazza. Did you and I never meet? Answer me.'

She looked at me and remained silent.

'Have you been here before, in the summer? Were you related to Iole?'

Her eyes were locked on mine. I was sure that her silence was a yes, but I wanted her lips to come apart, her voice to admit it. I needed it. But her lips remained sealed, her voice mute.

'We can't be together,' I concluded. 'If you know my story and I don't know yours, it means we can't be together.'

I grabbed the sheets, wrung them out so hard that the skin on my knuckles opened, and stuffed them into the basket.

I heaved it onto my shoulders and headed towards home. It had started to snow again. The wet sheets weighed about a hundred kilos. They would take at least a week to dry in the attic. Then I'd fold them up and put them away, and I'd force myself not to look to see whether the lights were on or off in the house opposite. Then, Sassaia could no longer be my hiding place.

I felt her hug me.

Her hands thrust under my jacket from behind my back, her nails digging into my skin.

'This isn't for what you just told me. It's for what you are now.'

I struggled to turn around and look at her. The snow was dusting our shoulders, our hair, our eyelashes. My pride was stupid, and Emilia was determined.

'You are not that cable car,' she said. 'Like I am not what I did. I will tell you,' she nodded, 'I know I have to tell you. I just need a bit more time. Wait for me, please.' Then she struck my heart with a tiny punch: 'But we are not our traumas. We are not defined by what we have committed or suffered. The past is not where we are right now. We are somewhere else. I didn't know that until today. You told me what you thought was *everything*. You explained why you're alone, why you live in Sassaia, but that's only *one part*,' she concluded. 'Another part has already started. The truth,' she smiled, 'changes too.'

14

'Tell me about Angela.'

Emilia stopped breathing.

Out of all the names in the world, that was the only one that couldn't be spoken. Like the character in Manzoni's *The Betrothed*, the one with all the power.

'It's been three years.'

It was as if a block of granite had struck her straight in the chest. *Tell me about* was a phrase she could no longer stomach. She wasn't only expected to *repay*, but also to *recount*. And the second verb was decidedly worse than the first.

'You can tell me anything. A physical detail, or an anecdote. The important thing is that we start to *extract her* from the silence.'

Emilia had broken into a cold sweat. Like at night, when her period was coming and her body became icy and feverish. She, like everybody else, had two lives. The speakable was just the innocuous tip of the iceberg; the unspeakable was who she was.

Venturi smiled patiently. Emilia had never clicked with her because, unlike Rita, she wore pretentious frameless glasses and white, cream or ivory ironed shirts, with pearl jewellery to match: little glimmers, never trashy. Her composed way of sitting – back straight, legs crossed, pen between her fingers – incarnated the very concept of a woman who had mastery over herself; a balanced woman who had learned to tame her femininity and thus made you feel all wrong. She seemed like pure reason where they were a bundle of nerves. And her job was to stick needles into their deepest parts.

'I can't.'

'You have to. You will never be free, even when you're out of here, until you confront this topic.'

A laugh resounded from Emilia's rotten heart, that unmistakable laugh of protest: *I'm not a topic, you bitch! I'm the Unnameable!*

Emilia crushed the packet of cigarettes which, unlike in Rita's office, she wasn't allowed to smoke. But *the topic* was so fragile and potentially lethal that Venturi proposed, as an exceptional case, that they went outside together.

It was 2004. The light was clear and the temperature pleasant; it could have been April or September. It was impossible to remember the months, which had no value on this side of the big walled courtyard, and nor did the seasons. For the residents, only light and dark meant anything. The school year and the holidays. Because other people working meant there were appointments, activities, distractions, sometimes effectively filling the minutes and the hours. Other people being on holiday, however, meant a total void stretching out under their feet, ready to swallow and annihilate.

They went outside. Some of the ground floor windows were open, and 'Toxic' by Britney Spears was flowing out of one of them, as if from the bedroom of a normal girl. But it was ten in the morning and all the normal girls were at school, while they, at the convent, went to lessons on and off for a few hours a day, or workshops in cooking or sewing or sometimes carpentry, a hangover from when this delightful building was for men. Who knows what that was like... One of the guards had a boyfriend who was also a guard, but for the boys. 'They set their beds on fire from morning 'til night,' she told them. 'They just fight all the time, it's one big brawl. They're overflowing with testosterone.' And the girls, who had little testosterone but no shortage of rage, devastated families and inauspicious diagnoses, listened to those stories and dreamed of a co-ed convent, where they could convert their cells into love nests, have secret dates in the library, stuff tender notes filled with spelling mistakes under the doors; their sentence would practically be a marriage preparation course. Then, of course, they'd be motivated to change!

Emilia and Venturi crossed the courtyard slowly. Walking side by side, Emilia realised how short her psychologist, no longer barricaded behind her extremely tidy desk, had become. Was it possible? Or had Emilia perhaps got taller? How many centimetres had she grown in captivity without realising?

Her father was constantly supplying her with clothes: fleeces, dungarees, T-shirts, comfortable and unpretentious things. It's not like it was a fashion show in there. But they were all garments of quality, with the brand name always on display, because you still had to demand respect in those corridors, maintain a certain status, maybe even arouse a little bit of fear – use the power that wearing certain brands gave you over those who had only ever had the fake versions.

Papa worked out what sizes she needed, even in underwear, and Emilia passed on the things she grew out of to the others, who couldn't wait, who went wild for them, who were already delighting in the fantasy of getting out and going back to their neighbourhoods with a pair of Armani jeans. They tried them on in front of the mirrors that hung above the sinks in the bathroom, climbing up onto the toilet seats to get a full-length view. It was always a party when Emilia handed out her clothes. There were some girls who literally didn't have socks, or only ones that were full of holes. Some of the teachers would take their socks home to mend them, and one time a fifteen-year-old girl replied distractedly to one of the teachers as she handed them back, good as new, 'Thank you, Mum.'

Throw away the key! Throw away the key!
What do those people out there know?
Is it really your fault? If you're fifteen years old?

Emilia and Venturi got to the little wall that surrounded the vegetable garden. It smelled of mallow, rosemary and sage. Venturi looked at the aromatic plants that had, for once, been diligently planted, watered and fed. The vegetables would soon be harvested and cooked. Emilia would've preferred animals, to tell the truth: baby goats or soft, curly little lambs. But there was no budget for pet therapy, of course. There wasn't even enough to pay for the staff needed to run the place normally.

They didn't sit down. They stood and listened to Britney Spears in the barbed heart of Bologna.

'Do you think you can describe her to me? Even just one detail? Her hair, say, or her eyes?'

The rectangle of sky high above their heads was a bright uniform blue with just a few clotted-cream clouds sailing along.

'Blue,' Emilia said, taking a drag on her cigarette. 'Like this sky.'

She was tired of hearing *tell me about* . . . Because it's not true that if you don't talk about something out loud, it doesn't exist. It exists more. It exists so much that you breathe with a single lung because the other one is squashed, your throat is obstructed, your heart is a hole. But saying it out loud means extracting a bullet so well buried that it is now part of your body, that tissue has grown around it and it has grown nerves. Extracting it is akin to dying.

'Her hair wasn't much. Dark blonde, fine, flat. She didn't like it and always had it tied up. Her eyes, on the other hand,' she inhaled again, 'they weren't easy to forget.'

She took a pause, surprised. The words were trickling out like blood from a picked scab, and she was unable to stop them. She imagined Venturi's beaming, satisfied face, but she didn't want to turn around.

They listened to Britney in 2001, too. They would spend entire afternoons watching MTV, smoking secret joints, or playing *Resident Evil* on the PlayStation. They should have been studying, but Emilia never wanted to, and anyway, the Unnameable only needed to work for half an hour each night to pass.

'She had this *perfect* family,' she continued. 'A white terraced house that wasn't that different from mine, but fuller: full of furniture and voices. Her father worked in a bank, and her mother stayed at home, was always there.' She sucked on the filter as it burned between her fingers. 'She also had a dog – a Labrador like the one in the toilet paper adverts – and a big brother, who was fit. Her mum took her to dance classes or out shopping, laid her clothes out on the bed every morning before school with matching shoes, and her kitchen always smelled of pancakes and eggs sizzling on the stove.'

Britney Spears was still singing, and now all the girls on the ground floor had joined her, shouting in a sort of English mixed with Arabic, Romanian and Italian. They had probably taken their clothes off, climbed up on the beds and were jumping and swaying, forgetting where they were and the lives that had brought them there.

'Were you envious of her?'

No, I was trying to have a thing with her brother. Her mother had always saved me a warm pancake when I knocked

*for them both on the way to school on our scooters. I wanted
to swap places with her.*

But she didn't say that to Venturi. She let the glowing
filter burn her fingertips, feeling no pain. All that rottenness had come out and she felt lighter.

Then she said goodbye to the shrink and went to dance
with the others. The heavy doors were always open in the
daytime. And the guard would let her pass even if she wasn't
a ground floor resident; by now the whole place was her
kingdom. The younger ones welcomed her like a queen,
because this was what she had become: a veteran, like Marta.
The little Romanian and North African girls with olive skin
and big shining eyes would be gone again in a few months;
home or, if they didn't have one, into community housing.
While she and Marta and the other very rare Italians would
stay there for years, like celebrities and legends, within those
zealously repainted fifteenth-century walls and monastic little
cells cleaned to the point where you could lick the floor.

They all poured out into the corridor – some dressed,
some in their knickers. Emilia danced with her eyes closed,
swinging her hips and rubbing up against the others' bums,
stretching her arms into the air as if she was trying to grab
something in the sky. And then, when Britney had finished,
that song came on.

The song of the summer of 2001: 'L'Amour Toujours'
by Gigi D'Agostino.

What can I say? Calling it cheesy would be an understatement. The music blared out, *tunz tunz tunz,* as if it

were a Saturday night in the provinces. It flooded the entire Riviera like fog over the Adriatic in the morning. It had the most beautiful words . . .

Emilia sang along, imagining she was in one of the huge nightclubs she hadn't managed to go to in time, just like she hadn't managed to lose her virginity to the Unnameable's brother in time, or fall in love in time, or live like everyone else that summer that smashed her life – and her soul – into pieces forever. She sang, crying and jumping and whipping her hair.

Until the guard decided, 'That's enough, you've played enough at *discoteca* now.' And started rattling his huge brass keys against the metal doors, producing a sound that immediately hushed their voices, turned their bodies limp, silenced the music.

The sound that none of them would ever forget, like you never forget your mother's voice, the beat of her heart in your belly.

15

THE MORNING OF DECEMBER 24th, the sky was cloudy and heavy with snow, and humidity rose off the river, numbing the bones.

Emilia stamped her feet and blew warm air onto her gloved hands. She was waiting for him under the 'P' of the little car park in Alma, the same place they had parked when she arrived on November 2nd.

In less than two months, so many things had happened: the kinds of things that happen in the outside world. She was wondering whether he would find her different, if he'd see the new feelings that were stirring in her. She saw the nose of his Volvo pop out from around the final hairpin bend and her heart started beating like a stone bursting to life.

Riccardo smiled at her through the windscreen, handsome like an old actor and impatient to get parked. Emilia's eyes were shining and her throat was sore, but she was excited. She had always obsessed over the part of the family that wasn't there, over the empty seat between her and her father, but as he got out of the car in his pinstriped suit, silk handkerchief folded in his pocket, she realised that if she had made it here, to the future, it was because he had never stopped loving her.

'Emi!' He reached out towards her.

Emilia ran into his arms.

Everything passes. And, if it can't pass, it changes.

'What's happened to your voice?' Riccardo held her by the shoulders to check her over.

'I've just got a cold. In Bologna the thermostat was always at a thousand, whereas here I've only got a stove and a fireplace to heat the whole house.'

'In Bologna' was their diplomatic way to allude to the past.

'Do you have paracetamol? Have you registered with a doctor?'

Emilia furrowed her eyebrows as if he had never taught her the basics. Riccardo shook his head and was about to start with his usual advice, but it was Christmas Eve; they could give themselves a day off. He hurried to pull on his coat and swap his shiny leather shoes for a pair of waterproof hiking boots. He opened the boot to reveal a panettone and a bottle of fizz, but suddenly changed his mind. 'Take me to see the church, first.'

Emilia's pale cheeks turned hot. She wasn't expecting a surprise test. She blew her flaky nose to buy herself some time.

'What is it? Are you embarrassed?'

'As if!' She was terrified that, standing in front of the Black Madonna or, worse, the group of the damned in the *Last Judgement* that she had forced herself to work on, he would think: is this it?

They walked through the village, huddled close together to keep warm. Banks of dirty snow flanked the pavements. Grey smoke rose from the chimneys, the only sign that the mountain village was inhabited. The river carved away into the silence, clashing into white boulders with its suffocated roar. Her father wanted to know all about Basilio, about the techniques they were using, the age of the church. Emilia responded in a low voice and kept looking around cautiously.

She was a resident of Sassaia now, but for the inhabitants of Alma she was still a 'foreign body'. Worse: 'the outsider who's sleeping with the teacher', 'the alcoholic from God knows where', 'leading that good man Peraldo astray' and, by the laws of contagion, the innocent little children he taught too. So, as Riccardo assailed her with his enthusiasm, she hunched up her shoulders. His questions came to her as if from afar, on a broken line, and in the meantime she glanced furtively at the windows, the doors, the dark corners of the old village that were riddled with snakes.

Bruno – 'the saint' – accompanied her to the church every day before going to school, then came and picked her up at the end of the day as if she were a child. And at his side half of her felt free and half felt like a whore.

While inside she was thinking: If only you knew . . .

The Christmas Eve mass was underway, but Riccardo made to go in anyway and so Emilia had to follow him. The priest was preaching diligently to his flock, who had all come out for the occasion. At their entrance, he paused and observed them. Someone turned in their pew, someone else whispered something. The priest resumed with Genesis.

Cain said to his brother Abel, 'Let's go out into the fields!'

The little old ladies, all bundled up, sank back into their coats. The men, felt caps in their hands, returned to listening (or napping) in the damp darkness. But, in the back row, one head of black hair didn't turn back around obediently towards the altar.

She kept looking at them both, brazen. Her perm was so dark and intricate that she looked like Medusa. She had harpooned her gaze on the bodies of the intruders and was staring now, searching with X-ray vision. Her eyes narrowed, glowing and excited at the sight of her helpless prey, as if behind the corneas a magical intuition had just been ignited.

Emilia didn't know her; had no idea about her sleepless nights consumed by the blue light of the computer screen as she interrogated it doggedly, like a fortune-teller with a crystal ball. That in the hateful hours of two or three in the morning, she'd demand answers from Google, send inappropriate messages on Facebook, stalk profiles of distant relatives and long-gone ex-residents of Sassaia who, for the most part, didn't respond. But she was never discouraged: she refined her search on the surnames, burrowing away in genealogy websites. She had all the time in the world. Her frustration was just fuel for the fire as she sniffed, nosed and scratched away at posts and comments, hunting out useful clues.

She wasn't stupid. She had put on weight again, and could be considered an 'unfuckable dog' or an 'elephant', like she had found written on the walls of the teachers' bathroom, almost certainly by that ex-pupil whom she had failed twice. But she was intelligent. And intelligence was all that mattered. In this vile world that uses women and then disposes of them, fucks them and then betrays them, she had learned to defend herself. To trust nothing but herself and her own instincts. And right now, her instincts were telling her that this girl with witch-red hair, who had sneaked in there, where everyone else's life was ending and nobody's beginning, *definitely* had a secret. A dirty, thorny secret. A husband, or some obscene photos, or maybe even an addiction!

But as Emilia passed behind her, she couldn't hear the convulsive thoughts whirling around in the head of the Medusa, nor could she imagine her incessant research, squeezing the last breath out of her faltering internet connection. She lived in terror that someone might take it upon themselves to investigate – but she thought that someone could only be me, the person concerned. Basilio didn't seem like the type. And who else would have good enough reason to?

Emilia and her father reached the painting of the *Judgement*, which was still semi-concealed by the scaffold. A trickle of grey light filtered weakly through the glass.

Riccardo stayed silent for a long time, staring at the wall. Eventually he nodded proudly. 'Well! I didn't believe it.'

Emilia felt a pang of joy. She knew she had worked hard on her little group of the damned, that she had helped them re-emerge from the darkness in all their gaudy desperation, but her father's recognition beat every other satisfaction hands down. Of course, she wasn't entirely responsible. Basilio had guided her with excellent suggestions; from above, sitting between winged cherubs and basted in divine light, he had encouraged her – nodding like her father was now – to keep going, to polish again, to remove the scale and residue until she reached, what, purity?

Remember who you are, she told herself.

The congregation was reciting the Lord's Prayer behind them now. Their irritation seemed to seep out from the clashing chorus of their prayer towards those two rude people who hadn't prayed, hadn't received communion, and were now standing there pointing and commenting as if they were in a museum.

Riccardo lingered over tiny details. He complimented her, surprised and happy, while she couldn't help but think of her mother's distant face on the other side of the living room table, her muscles tense, jaw tight, when Emilia was in Year 2 or 3 of primary school. It was clear by that point that even the speech therapist couldn't resolve it.

Emilia's mother listened to her read – or rather stutter, stumble and tumble over the words – during the still, hazy afternoons with the television turned off in the terrible silence of their house, which was nestled in a neighbourhood of identical houses where the affluent people of Ravenna hid themselves away. Her mother forced a smile to mask the torture she was undergoing inside. Their daughter, their only daughter. What a disappointment.

Emilia remembered her father getting home at eight in the evening and dinner never being ready, because she and her mother were still sitting at the living room table, textbooks wide open. Emilia's mother was a teacher, she knew how you had to be with children: don't lose patience, don't shout, don't get exasperated. But the girl in front of her wasn't just any child; she was her daughter, and she wasn't getting better. She struggled in maths too: seven times two, what does seven times two make? So obvious, like saying the night is dark and the day, light. But her daughter didn't respond. She was retreating. 'How can you not know it? How can you not understand?' And those obstinate, angry questions sent Emilia into a crisis. Numbers and words merged together in an indistinguishable, incomprehensible magma, into which she too melted, with a single thought cutting through: even a woman like my mum, who volunteers, whom everyone loves and respects – even she eventually loses patience with me.

Indeed, after all those hours resisting and battling, Cecilia's smile collapsed and her frustration and disappointment came out in torrents. *You came from me, for God's sake! From me and your father. How can you have come out so badly?*

She didn't actually say these words. But that was what she was thinking; unsaid, between the lines, the implicit thing that would dominate Emilia's life as she remained stunned, inert like a broken doll that needed to be thrown out. Until her father the architect came home from his studio with a package of fresh cappelletti filled pasta, gave them both a kiss and said: 'That's enough now. She hasn't learned yet? She will.'

When they walked up Stra' dal Forche together for the second time, all the roots in the forest of chestnut trees were buried in the snow, and the naked branches above their heads were tangled in a dense and wiry mesh. Her father was pulling the wheelie suitcase with evident effort, and Emilia had to force herself to slow down so that he could keep up as she carried two bags full of provisions among which – she couldn't help noticing – there was a wrapped tray of filled pasta.

'Of course you're steaming up here like a train now,' he told her, out of breath. They hadn't even got to the roadside shrine yet.

'Give me that suitcase,' she responded. 'I do this twice a day, five days a week. And my calves,' she teased, 'haven't even turned to rubber!'

Riccardo wouldn't let her take the case, saying, 'I'm not that old yet.'

Emilia wondered whether he had anyone in Ravenna – a friend who had in some way taken the place of her mum in that enormous empty house, at least at the weekends, at least for dinner now and then. For the first time, she dared to formulate the thought in her head, even if she couldn't find the courage to ask him.

He, on the other hand, fully intended to ask her the same question. They proceeded in silence for a while on the snow-shined pebbles, crunching over the salt thrown down by Emilia and me at the end of entire Sundays spent shovelling. And my name was in the air, perceptible between them. Father was waiting for the right moment. Daughter was already considering how to hand him the information. A bit of practice, of gradualness, would've done them both good: a couple of little boyfriends at high school to pave the way. But they hadn't had the opportunity.

'So.' Riccardo came out with it. 'When am I going to meet him?'

Emilia's pace quickened.

During the convent years, after the disappointment of Emanuele, she let herself sink into a fantasy: that one day she would meet a boy like her, who had grown up in the same rooms, with the same schedule, the same background noise of huge keys like Hades' around the neck of Cerberus, and they would've understood one another immediately with no need for explanations: the shutters would stay open and the television would stay on all night.

It wasn't an unquantified fantasy: most of her companions' boyfriends had been in and out of similar places as if they were enthusiasts. When they were on the phone, they would discuss articles of the penal code with such precision and ease that they could have easily got a law degree. Giada, 8th grade diploma, was often correcting the lawyer. Afifa knew the law of this country better than any 'blood citizen' – and anyway, there was no joking about blood in a place like that. As for Marta, she was undecided for a long time between molecular biology and law. The fact that her story would be the Redemption Story was already a done deal, she just needed to decide on how she was going to get there. In the end she chose the molecules: they were more reliable than the law. 'Anyway, frankly I've already done my fair share of trials.'

Her father was letting her walk ahead. And, as they got gradually closer to Sassaia, Emilia found clarity again. The paranoia that stalked her from every angle in Alma here dimmed to the point of disappearing. The tree trunks and the rocks, the cliffs and the silence – that gigantic silence that for years she had never been able to listen to, swamped by the shouting, the chatting, the television, the walkie-talkies, the keys – made her feel new again.

She hadn't found a boy like her, but rather a perfect innocent, a victim. That's how things went. Life doesn't ask for permission, doesn't let you make plans. No, life loves to take you for a ride.

Emilia stopped walking: she could no longer hear her father's footsteps. She put down the bags that held the Christmas Eve dinner and Christmas Day lunch under the middle-of-nowhere sign that read SASSAIA FRAZ. DI ALMA. Then she sat down on a rock that was jutting out, and thought.

Did she have to introduce us? Even if we weren't officially together yet and might not ever be? Because girlfriends and boyfriends need to know everything about one another, or at least a minimum of their birthplace and surname.

But she had told me hers was 'Morelli', which she'd stolen from Rita. And while she was committing that theft, she thought how much she hated Italian bureaucracy for not allowing her to change her surname. 'Don't you understand?' she had shouted. 'That if I write "Emilia Innocenti" on my door, I'll never live a normal life?' 'And what,' the bespectacled, imperturbably grey face of bureaucracy had responded, 'kind of a normal life do you expect to live?'

Bruno will never accept it, she reasoned. As she waited for her father at the top of the mule track, her thoughts returned to the Sunday we had spent listening to the radio in Iole's kitchen. The radio said a mother had left her 18-month-old daughter to die of hunger and thirst. She had gone out to fuck her boyfriend for six days and six nights, and the little girl was left alone in her cot, lying in her own faeces, eating the foam in her pillow in a desperate attempt to save herself from her wretched abandonment.

'She needs the electric chair,' Emilia clearly remembered me saying, on impulse, stopping stirring the sauce on the stove and looking up at her. 'I'm not in favour of the death penalty, but in some cases it's the only reasonable option.'

Emilia had felt her stomach collapse. She wanted to vomit, but she couldn't say anything, just nodded and continued to press the backs of the gnocchi with a fork.

The radio added details. The presenters in the studio consulted top psychologists: *The mechanisms of the psyche. Dissociation. The mother had been abandoned by her own mother.* They were looking for an explanation. But there isn't an explanation. *If someone is a monster, they are a monster.* What more do we need to know? *Are you trying to justify it? Really? Disgusting! Justify the little Ravenna girl? She girl is a monster!*

She ran into the bathroom. Bent over the toilet bowl, she swore to herself: I will never tell him. And if the price of being with him is to pretend that I am not me, I'll pay it willingly. In the meantime I had turned the radio off, and went and knocked on the door, unaware: 'Are you OK, Emilia?'. No, I'm rotten. Bruno is a good person, she was saying to herself, he doesn't belong to the army of people who shout *Throw away the key.* Yet even he had said *the electric chair.* Naturally, his parents were killed. It was involuntary manslaughter, of course, but he's the offended party.

And she? She was the vomit in the toilet.

Her father emerged, trudging, cashmere coat unbuttoned, forehead beading with sweat. When he reached her, he put the suitcase down and eased himself onto the protrusion of rock next to her.

He admitted, 'I'm getting old.'

Emilia looked at the white path in front of them, and imagined all the life that breathed quietly under the ground. The animals sleeping in their holes. The hidden eggs. Time coiled up in a warm, invisible cave.

'Do you have a girlfriend?' she asked, not looking at him. 'Someone who knows the whole story, and is with you anyway?'

Riccardo hesitated and ran a hand through his hair. Then he responded: 'Yes.'

'Since when?'

'Three years ago, but we knew each other from before. I wouldn't call her a girlfriend as such, at my age. We call ourselves *companions*.'

'Is she from Ravenna?'

'Yes.'

'And she knew everything?'

Her father sighed, as if that wasn't the point. The sky was so low it came through the trees and overflowed, humid and frozen.

'Have you ever talked about it?' Emilia insisted.

Her father placed both his hands on his knees, as if preparing to confront a subject much bigger than himself, a challenge he'd failed before it began. And yet it needed confronting.

'Or perhaps you manage to be together without ever talking about it?' Emilia turned to him with her sad green eyes which only moved slightly, like the putrid surface of a pond rippling with some new and unexpected form of life. 'Is it possible, in your opinion?'

'You can't live like that.'

Her father moved his hand from his own knee to hers, and squeezed it gently.

'Listen, Pa, this boy knows nothing. And he doesn't need to know anything. Anyway, he's not a boy, he's older than me. He wouldn't understand, he wouldn't accept it. I know he wouldn't.'

'Emilia.' He father started again.

Can you talk of guilt when you're sixteen years old?
Is guilt the same in adults and adolescents?
But if the adolescent is not yet an adult, who is acting within their guilt?

'You've paid,' he said calmly, 'remember that. You've finished your journey. If you really like this person, when you feel like it, you'll tell him how you ended up here, and why. And he, if he really knows you, will see you just how I see you.' His eyes were full of tears. 'I'm very proud of you, Emilia.'

16

As I was opening the front door, struck by a dark blade of cold, I couldn't help thinking of Basilio at home alone.

I knew what kind of day he was having. For the last fifteen Christmases I had cut wood, shovelled snow, cleaned out the stove, and eaten lunch and dinner in silence like every other winter's day; with the only difference being that I secretly hoped it would go quicker. Sure, living in Sassaia helped things along: no strings of lights, no Midnight Mass full of families, no festive decorations on the houses, no reflections of flickering trees in the windows. But even if it was just me and Basilio up there, burrowed into that clump of frozen stones, that day was not like *every other winter's day*.

As I rummaged in my wardrobe for my smartest shirt, I struggled to believe the invitation was real. I wasn't invited to the lunch – that would've been too much – but to the more neutral afternoon.

It was five to four, pitch black, and the thermometer outside was saying it was less than three degrees: it was time. And although I had been ready for hours, having patted some aftershave on my cheeks that I think I'd had since I was a teenager, wearing a pair of blue corduroy trousers and my only pair of leather shoes, bought for my graduation and never worn again – even with all that armour, as I crossed the alleyway, I felt naked.

I had woken up anxious. The absence of Emilia on the other side of the bed unsettled me. I'd had dinner without her the night before but I wasn't hungry. I'd forced down a bowl of soup, surprised by how, over the course of a couple of months, my old, well-worn solitude had become so unbearable. It was the idea of meeting her father, perhaps, that was bothering me most. Of finding myself in the presence of the past that she was so stubbornly keeping from me.

Arriving at their door, I was about to knock. But I suddenly heard them laughing behind the warm glow of the window and immediately dropped my arm, and hid behind the doorframe.

The silence of Sassaia was even vaster in winter. Every distraction had been removed: the birdsong, the rustling of the wind through the leaves, the stubborn buzzing of insects. The only thing you could hear, amidst the leafless forests and stillness of the mountains, was time: sitting on the world like a giant. And it was pierced, now, by their two cheerful and sarcastic voices, which seeped through the walls along with the warmth of the fire.

They were talking about politics. I heard Emilia reeling off a list of foreign names and ranting: 'Imagine if they could vote too, how great would that be? That's why they don't want to give my friends citizenship.' Her father had a much lower voice so I couldn't hear his response. I could distinguish only his outline through the curtain, nodding yes. They were sitting close together, conspiratorial. Whatever the word 'family' meant, seeing those two together at Christmas in the warmth of the old stone house made it pretty clear.

I knocked twice and their voices halted.

It took a minute before Emilia came and let me in, visibly embarrassed. But I was even more so. I spent a ridiculously long time bashing my shoes on the doormat, letting the cold whirl into the room as Emilia shivered and didn't have the guts to look at me. Her father got up from the table to come and shake my hand, smiling and friendly. He was the same man I had seen putting the mattress out in the sun on the front balcony. The same elegance, the same ways of a man of the city. But now, looking at his face properly under the unscrupulous light of the lamps, I was sure I'd seen him before. I mean, before last November 2nd. A long time before. And this certainty closed my throat up just as I was trying to utter a hello.

'Riccardo, nice to meet you.'

His handshake was vigorous but not violent: he didn't need to stake out any kind of hierarchy. When he let go of my hand, I found enough enterprising spirit to pull out of the inside pocket of my jacket the bottle of walnut liqueur I'd had steeping in the cellar and hand it to Emilia, who grabbed it as if she hardly knew me. Then I took off my jacket and looked around to find a place to put it, as if I didn't know my way around that kitchen where she and I had done, literally, everything.

We sat down. Me opposite Riccardo, and Emilia in the middle. The table had been cleared, so that just a few crumbs and a jug of water remained from their lunch. Emilia was biting her nail, I seemed to have lost my voice, and Riccardo observed us, amused. He stretched his arms out to the sides and said, 'I wouldn't mind trying a snifter of that *nocino.*'

He went confidently over to the sideboard and took out three crystal glasses. He knew the house very well, I thought. Emilia and I looked at one another. Her index finger was bleeding where she'd pulled a little strip of skin off with her teeth. We both felt a desperate need to drink.

Riccardo put the glasses down in the middle of the table and filled each of them to the brim.

'You can tell it's good,' he commented, 'from the colour.'

He had nothing of the classic jealous Italian father about him. In fact, he was sensing our tension and trying his best to put us at ease. He was the kind of person who always endeavours, no matter who he has in front of him, to put everyone at ease. I thought that, with a father like that, Emilia couldn't have been through anything too bad in her life. Other than the death of her mother, I mean. She couldn't have been a drug addict: the most likely conclusion I had come to. And she couldn't have been a teenage mum and given her child up – another, less convincing hypothesis. With a father like that, I thought, her life before Sassaia surely couldn't scare me off.

'Bravo,' he nodded, tasting my liqueur, 'the walnut really comes through.'

'There are so many chestnut and beech trees around here,' I managed to muster, 'but if you head in the direction of Piaro and down into the valley from there, you can find some walnuts.'

'Near the river, right? I know where you mean.'

I looked up at Emilia just in time to see her dart him a look. But he seemed so calm. He changed the subject with ease. 'Emilia tells me you work at the school in Alma. Do you have many pupils?'

And I, deep down, was like him: making others uncomfortable made me uncomfortable. I didn't need to ask how he knew where I meant. It was Christmas; the last thing I wanted to do was make Emilia feel awkward. I had promised I'd wait for her.

'Thirteen this year, across all the age groups. It's a mixed class.'

'A bit like the olden days, eh? It must be fascinating running a school like that, in such a small town. It being such an important place for the children, but also for the community.'

I thought of Patrizia and a bitter smile escaped my lips. 'Almost all of them have the internet now. School bores them. They already know they want to get out of here as soon as possible. Only one is sure he'll stay – he wants to be a shepherd like his father, which means he doesn't even need to learn standard Italian.'

Riccardo was listening with interest, his legs crossed and sipping slowly from the little glass in his hand. Emilia had downed hers in one, and was already pouring a second. I noted that the liquor was warming her cheeks: the freckly pink colour of them was lovely.

'I'm sure it must be a real challenge to make children care about spelling, with all these games and videos in their pockets. Especially in a place like this, with no cinema, no library.'

I had showered with too much bodywash and now, instead of my own smell, I could smell Scots pine. The neck of my shirt, done up to the top button, felt tight. It wasn't me, being dressed up like that. Yet the stove emanated a delicious warmth, the blue chequered tablecloth reminded me of home, and the *nocino* that was melting Emilia's nerves was also melting mine.

'One morning we saw a deer,' I heard myself saying. 'On the bank of the river that our classroom looks out onto. Martino Fiume, the pupil I was telling you about, the one who wants to be a shepherd, saw it first and called everyone over to the window. It was majestic. It had this huge, imposing pair of horns. And its coat, its face: regal. It was so close that we could see into its peaceful yellow eyes. It was like an apparition, a messenger. As if the king of our valley had come down from the woods to tell us something.' I finished my second glass and put it down. 'The children all then wrote in their essays, each in their own words, that it had been a magical and unforgettable experience. The deer is a difficult animal to catch sight of, it's almost as if it doesn't exist. And yet it was more real than anything else.'

Emilia jerked up all of a sudden. She ran over to a drawer, opened it and returned with a piece of paper and a pencil.

'Describe it to me again,' she said. She moved a bit of the tablecloth away so she could put the rough paper on the wood and started to trace, darken, blend, in a trance. I understood that this was her way of managing the situation, so I chose the most precise adjectives I could, starting with the horns: dark, knotty, wide, scratched, worn down by time, by bad weather, by battles, fearsome, solemn.

Riccardo watched her, enamoured. And I watched her in the same way. Hunched over, her hair covering her face, her hand quick. She was left-handed, I noted. Her gift flowed out of her through her fingers. We no longer spoke, me or her father, so as not to disturb her until she was finished, until she lifted the sheet of paper up and showed us the exact image of the deer that my pupils and I had seen one morning in late April.

I couldn't stop myself from asking her: 'When did you discover you had this talent?'

An innocuous question, I thought. But her face turned dark, like it often did, with a lethal abruptness. The ecstatic expression of creativity immediately left her. She was back to being disenchanted Emilia, on the defensive. But she didn't want to lie in front of her father.

'Late.'

Her father, for the first time, looked down.

'At high school . . .' She grimaced. 'I went to classical high school, but I wasn't very good. Then I *changed schools*, and then . . . One day I didn't know what to do, I was next to a window, I had a notepad and a pencil. I was bored. There was this horizon of rooftops and hills. And it happened.'

I held on to the deer. I took the sheet between my hands and looked at it, astounded. It was alive, its face coming out of the paper and staring at me.

Riccardo got up again. To thaw the frozen silence that Emilia's words had provoked, he opened the fridge, took out a bottle of sparkling wine and said, 'We were waiting for you to do the toast.'

I put Emilia's drawing back down and looked around me. There was no Christmas tree. There was no nativity scene or butcher's broom centrepiece on the table, nor red candles on crowns of pine needles sprayed white. There were no painted pine cones or salt dough angels. It was a dark winter's afternoon with a terrible weather forecast overnight.

On previous Christmases, Basilio and I had never sought each other out. We had gravitated along the same orbit in solitude, like Emilia and I had before we met. It was fine like that, really; to bring our silences together would've been worse. But today was different. Riccardo was about to unwrap the panettone. Emilia had broken the vacuum of Sassaia, forever. We were about to celebrate, like every other more or less Christian family on the planet.

'Excuse me,' I said, 'this isn't my house. But would either of you mind terribly if I went to call on Basilio?'

'Of course not!' they responded in unison, as if they desired the same, but hadn't dared propose the idea.

So I put on my jacket and headed outside. I switched on my torch. In the dark, in the snow, wearing those leather shoes with the silver buckle, so unsuitable for the loose stones underfoot. I was running. Thinking back to my sister and I on Christmas Eve, leaving milk and biscuits out on the kitchen windowsill for Father Christmas. One time Valeria had added a fake lipstick for Mary, and I a slingshot for the Baby Jesus. Even if we were already a bit too old, in some way we still believed that Christmas could prove the existence of the extraordinary.

Nothing changed, absolutely nothing. Lunch was the same as always, and there were obviously no toasts; alcohol wasn't even to be dreamed of. On two or three of the years they were given a slice of pudding, when Governor Ruggeri was there, who was a divorced father – maybe that's why he came to bring them a panettone and, with quite some audacity, wish them all a merry Christmas.

There were always very few of them there at Christmas. The majority managed to get themselves some kind of permit, even if it was just for six hours, or four, just enough time to get home, eat lunch, digest it and turn around again. But what would you choose? It was the chance to hug your family again, open some presents, drink a glass of wine – or better, get completely hammered – maybe smoke a joint in the haven of your old room.

The veterans, and the newbies who had only been there a few months but had chosen the wrong people to peck at, just sat there with their pricks in their hands. Metaphorically, of course. And it was pure depression. Absolute dejection: the whole world was celebrating the sacred joy of having a home, a family, of believing more or less in the Lord or human goodness, while you had neither a house nor a family nor a faith, and definitely no human goodness.

The convent was half-empty: everyone – to come back to the same point – had someone to share a steaming dish of tortellini with. Just a few representatives of the army were forced to clock in, pissed off because obviously no one wants to work Christmas. And it's not like that place was a hospital, where people go in an emergency through no fault of their own. Everything was entirely their fault, and they were ruining Christmas for everyone else.

Marta spent the whole day filing her nails, plucking out hairs, applying all sorts of DIY masks to her face and hair – a slop of egg and sage and other stuff she'd helped herself to from the kitchen. It was still a day of celebration, wasn't it? So she, who had never been to a spa in her life, was playing beautician. She lay on the bed wearing a bathrobe, as if from the windows she could see the Dolomites or something. She sighed and rearranged the slices of potato that were shrinking the bags under her eyes. She turned to Emilia and Myriam, who didn't even want to turn the TV on – it was all just Christmas films! – and said: 'It's almost silent, do you hear it? How wonderful . . . you should kiss your hands and thank Christ or someone, rather than hanging your faces like that. Every bloody Christmas of my life, my father had an irresistible desire to kill my mother. Like he actually woke up with that idea in his head. He would look at the Christmas tree, hurl up his hangover from the night before, then roll up his sleeves over his hairy forearms. And right on time,' she told it as if it was a joke, 'before – or preferably during – lunch, knives would be thrown, and plates would rain down from the sky. One time an open bag of flour was flung through the air, like the napalm in *Apocalypse Now*. Eventually the neighbours would call their mates at the police station, who were still digesting their lasagne and had to write up the same old report again . . . Girls,' her toes flitted through the air, shimmering with nail polish, 'Christmases in here are a dream!'

After the death of her mother, Marta didn't have anyone waiting for her outside, so it was natural that she spoke like this. Myriam, however, had a little girl less than two years old, who had been put in the care of her grandparents and probably wouldn't even recognise Myriam when she got home. She was a mess at Christmas. She spent the evening of the 24th in the infirmary and got herself something strong that would make her sleep, and then addle her brains for most of the 25th.

For Emilia, the first Christmas in the convent was tough. She had been there six months. She was getting used to it, but the first Christmas inside is always 'the first Christmas inside'. She moped about a bit after the wake-up alarm, then tried to go back to sleep halfway through the morning in order to miss the others gleefully getting ready for their day release, enduring lunch in the canteen with the other glum holdovers – those with no relatives or with serious sentences, all with no appetite but plenty of bitter comments, the longing to slap someone palpable in the air. And then Emilia stopped resisting and went back to her room, opened the back of the remote control, and swallowed a battery.

Marta caught her at the last minute and shouted: 'What the fuck are you doing? You idiot!' She screamed for the guards to come immediately: 'This brainless fuckwit has eaten a battery!' The army was immediately told. An explosion of walkie-talkies ensued. Frau Direktorin was called on the phone: she was raging. Emilia watched the hustle and bustle in a state of stupor, as if she was in a film she had accidentally walked into, entitled *The Battery*. And in the meantime, 'a fucking battery' was repeated from one room to the next, from floor to floor. All the while Marta threw a barrage of insults at her: 'That's not what we do, Emilia, you're a fuckhead. You pathetic wretch.' Emilia didn't look at anyone, she didn't see anything. She murmured to herself with desperation and relief: 'Now I'm going to die'.

'Oh no you're not! They'll pump your stomach. Or they'll quarter you, which would do you some good! Retard.' Marta was angrier than Frau Direktorin. 'It's the adults who do this kind of fucked-up stuff, not us.'

The ambulance arrived. They took her away on a stretcher – Marta shouting, 'Have a merry Christmas in

Sant'Orsola Hospital, magical idiot!' – and transferred her to the hospital, sirens blaring, with two furious officers in tow. The doctors in A&E – also furious – gave her an X-ray. Her father, who like her was completely new to this situation – to call it unbelievable would be an understatement – came as fast as he could from Ravenna to Bologna. He still hadn't come to terms with what had happened six months earlier, and now his daughter had swallowed a battery. He was a wreck of a man, destroyed beyond words. Wasn't all that had happened enough? No, she had to eat a battery too. And what had he done wrong to deserve a daughter like this? Who was, quite literally, a catastrophe. If only she hadn't been conceived, hadn't been brought into the world, his life would've been peaceful, would've been *normal.*

They let him visit her briefly. Emilia was lying on the bed, fresh from an endoscopy, with such intense nausea that she could feel it in her hair and the tips of her toes, still in a daze from the sedation. But the sight of her father's face was the real punishment. The real death that she had wanted to inflict upon herself, perhaps. Because Emilia no longer knew what she wanted. To live and to die had become synonymous, two verbs merged into one. Her father walked over to the bed and looked at her. Then he collapsed, like a sandcastle.

He burst into tears, hiccupping, snot pouring out of his nose like a child. It was a devastating spectacle for her. Because that man was good. He was a pillar of strength, understanding and dignity, and up until that moment he had tried, knowing not what resources he was drawing on, to hold it together. He had kept himself busy so as not to give up hope. He had glued himself to the phone, driven all night, spared no expense on lawyers, experts, consultants. God was whipping his back, and he got back up again and offered his front too. But the battery was too much. The triple-A of the remote control had burst his banks.

Riccardo said nothing to her, didn't even sit on the edge of the bed. He ascertained that his disaster of a daughter was still alive, and he cried and cried and cried. Then, when he was done, he bent over to give her a kiss on the forehead, and left.

That Christmas Day of 2001 Emilia swore she would never make her father cry again. And she conceded that Marta was right: the convent was better than the hospital.

I came back again with Basilio. His light, bright eyes seemed to tremble in surprise behind the fogged-up lenses of his glasses, or perhaps it was a deeper sentiment: gratitude.

'It was so last-minute,' he said apologetically, 'I could only bring this.' It was a box of *torcetti* butter cookies.

'Oh you needn't have! Let's not be formal, not today,' Riccardo responded. And since they already knew one another and had done, superficially, for a long time, super-ficially they made real eye contact when they shook hands. Then, having no desire to pretend, nor to bother Emilia and me, they added no more.

It had started to snow again outside. I could tell that Emilia had drunk more of the liquor; her body had softened, melted to the point of resting on my knees and staying there a while, even in front of the others. We stroked one another's cheeks and hands. Now the introductions had happened, and hadn't gone badly, all things considered, we both started thinking about how we could sneak back to my house later on.

'Your father will pretend not to notice,' I whispered.

'But the Madonna's going to come down,' she said laughing, meaning the snow. 'And you'll have to help me abseil down from the window . . .'

'Come on, stop touching me.'

Riccardo and Basilio pretended not to notice. They were talking about the weather and the very real risk of being stuck up here until the new year.

'It's not a certainty,' Basilio said. 'Bruno can clear the whole track in a morning. When do you need to get back by?'

'Well,' Riccardo smiled as he unwrapped the panettone, 'it depends how things go. I wouldn't want to get in the way . . .'

Then all four of us sat down around the table, each with a glass full of fizzy wine and a slice of panettone on one of Iole's little porcelain plates. Riccardo raised his glass and looked into his daughter's eyes: 'Well, cheers! Merry Christmas!'

'Merry Christmas!' Basilio and I responded, his voice raspy with emotion.

Emilia said nothing. As the glasses clinked over the table, she didn't look at me or Basilio; she just looked, with profundity, at her father.

Over the years, she got used to the Christmases. She'd lie down on the bed next to Marta, naked under her bathrobe, to have some beauty treatments in the convent-spa with a view of the brick wall and barbed wire. And then, after some time – a long time – she started to benefit from the famous permits, and her father started coming to pick her up like a child at the school gates. They would go first to McDonald's or Burger King to have a quick lunch alongside those who, due to work or religion, weren't celebrating Christmas. They would eat a burger and then leave, to enjoy the only gift Emilia desired: a walk. Preferably in the hills, to Villa Spada or Villa Ghigi; in the sun, the rain, the mist, the snow, she didn't care. She just wanted to feel the soft dirt squishing under her feet. All that sky above, opening up so wide that it enveloped her, making her head spin. In the convent, in some ways, it was like being in her mother's belly: tight, embracing, safe from the immense threat of the world. You suffered in there, you suffocated. But the truth you weren't allowed to admit was that it also felt good, because your problems – the ones that brought you there – stayed outside the walls.

Now, finally the only woman among men, with the glow of the alcohol warming her neck and earlobes, Emilia thought that this Christmas in Sassaia was as wonderful as the ones she'd had as a girl, when her mother would stroke her head on the sofa in front of a Disney film.

She couldn't help wondering if Riccardo was also thinking about the battery. Whether he was comparing this Christmas with that one.

They had worked hard in the meantime. They had been good. Everything could've been destroyed so easily, but that morning, before Bruno arrived, she had pleaded with her father. And Riccardo had sighed: 'Do not ask me to pretend our surname is *Morelli* in front of Bruno, please.'

'Of course not! Just don't say anything!'

'You do need to tell him at some point though.'

'Papa . . .'

'You need to get it straight in your mind . . .'

'Yes, I will, with time.'

'Not too much time. It'll only get worse the longer you leave it. You can't take that poor boy for a ride.'

'I'm not taking him for a ride! I'm protecting him.'

It was getting late. I held Emilia's hand in mine, concealed under the table. We were all talking of happy things. The snow was falling in big flakes and wrapping Sassaia in a cold blanket, with only one light lit, only one room warm.

When I got home that night, for the first time in years, I had the courage to think about phoning my sister.

17

Five days later, the sun came out.

I accompanied Riccardo down Stra' dal Forche (I'd lent him my old knee-high boots) with a shovel over my shoulder to clear the worst bits. I waved him off in Alma piazza without a word, but with a sincere smile. Then I marched back up the hill.

When I met her at home, Emilia was already naked. Smelling of sweat, I collapsed on top of her as the snow melted around us and Sassaia, once again all ours, dripped from the rooftops, the branches, the thorns of the brambles. It was almost midday when, melted in a puddle of light, we became the exact same thing.

Afterwards, we remained lying on the bed in silence, holding hands, finally free from the commitments of work and family. The sky was so blue, inflamed by the cold: as if the universe had just been forged, and no other man or woman existed on this earth.

'I have a proposal,' she said in an unusually high and ingratiating voice. 'Only if you want, obviously. Only if you don't think it's totally weird.'

I turned to look at her: every one of her freckles crackled in the light.

'Shall we go dancing tomorrow night?'

I burst out laughing, then, when I saw she was serious, furrowed my brow: 'What do you mean?'

'Dancing!' She gave me a little push. 'Dancing!' She stood up on the unmade bed and flung herself about in the sunlight, in front of the window through which nobody, not even the hibernating animals, could see her. 'In the club!'

'But I'm almost thirty-seven . . .' I smiled. 'I didn't even go to the club when I was the right age.'

'All the more reason to go now! There is no right age.'

'There is,' I nodded wisely, 'there absolutely is. There aren't any clubs around here anyway.'

'But let's look on . . . what's it called?' She struggled to find the word. 'Google! We'll search it on there, the club.'

'Don't ask me to do something like that. Anyway, tomorrow,' I realised, 'is New Year's Eve, it'll be chaos.'

'Exactly.' Emilia stopped jumping. 'I don't want to think tomorrow, or remember.' She was serious, her eyes clouded over like the heavy waters of a swamp.

Fireworks never went off in Sassaia. The little fire-crackers that my pupils lit in Alma filtered faintly up through the woods. It was the ideal place to spend any festivity. There were no big dinners or noisy happy families to make you feel like a failure.

'We'll be fine here. If you want, I'll go down to the city and buy you a bottle of Dom Pérignon.'

'It's not about that,' she said stubbornly.

'So what is it about?'

Punctually, the Mask of Great Omissions formed on her face. Half smile, half blush, and minimal movements on the stagnant surface of her murky green eyes.

'I'm begging you.' She fell onto me. Highly predictable diversion tactics. She bit my earlobe and whispered, 'I beg you, grant me this gift.'

I wanted to laugh. Because of her tickling and reaching her hand down between my legs.

'OK.' I turned her over onto the mattress and pinned her down, making her pay the price for this favour. I could already picture myself: a clumsy mammoth struck by the strobe lights, immobile as a mountain in a moving sea of people young enough to be my children. And she, expert of the nightclubs where she had probably spent a thousand wild nights in her obscure youth, would leave me stranded. I'd lose her in the jumble of bodies.

'You're asking a huge sacrifice of me, you know that? At least swear you won't leave me alone in a place like that.'

Emilia unlocked herself from my arms. She stared at me with a devastating expression. Her eyes shone as if she were about to cry. But it wasn't possible, was it – crying over a nightclub?

When the tear really did fall down her cheek, it took all I had not to see it.

We had a late lunch, dishevelled and in a mess. The kitchen was an icebox, so we pulled the table closer to the stove; Emilia in her underwear with a fleece and a pair of knee-length socks, me in a vest, with my wool trousers and other pieces of clothing strewn around. We put together polenta and Maccagno cheese with the leftovers from Christmas, and drank some *nocino*. It must have been three o'clock by this point, but the sun was still strong outside. After all those days of storms and darkness when the houses of Sassaia sank into the clouds, heavy and furious with snow, the valley was now a bay of light, a calm miracle.

So we didn't even clear the table before pulling on our snowsuits to go out before it was too late. The mountains' icy tips looked so imposing, as if they had grown during the bad weather. The rays of sun blinded us as we threw snowballs in the woods. And I, dazed, drunk, chased her and hid in ambush behind tree trunks.

We should never leave these woods, I thought. *We should quit our jobs and never again set foot even in Alma; plant ourselves a vegetable garden, get ourselves some chickens, live like my great-grandparents did, dependent on chestnuts and polenta and cease all contact with civilisation and history.*

Instead, coming back inside, I let her pull my arm. 'Come on, come on! Get your phone out!' I sat down at the table obediently, pushing the glasses and dirty plates to one side. I set to searching for a nightclub on Google while Emilia goaded me.

Since I was a mountain boy without a washing machine, radiator, TV or microwave, I wasn't good at using the internet either; I was slow and she was getting restless, insulting me, telling me I was all fingers and thumbs. I told her: 'You do it, then.' She grabbed my phone impatiently, but then looked bewildered too. She was five years younger than me, and certainly more of a city person – even if the city in question differed each time I enquired: Bologna, Rimini, Pesaro, Urbino . . . Yet she pushed on the screen with her index finger as if she was having her fingerprints taken. A deluge of information and reviews popped up, and Emilia gave me the phone back, overwhelmed, embarrassed. 'You choose'.

The nightclub, the internet, Le Marche and Emilia-Romagna merging into a single region: these were all alarm bells. But I, in the most resolute way, did not want to hear them.

'Tartana,' I concluded. 'Fifty-two minutes, 47.8 kilometres. That could work.'

'Hello? Valeria?'

'Who's speaking?'

As I'd exhumed her number and listened to the line ringing, I'd regressed into a hollow space in time when we were still six and twelve, walking home loaded up with treasures – pine cones, mushrooms, a grasshopper in a jar with holes in the lid – from one of our expeditions up Monte Cresto, then collapsed in unison after dinner, on twin beds separated only by a bedside table.

'Who's speaking?'

The lamp was on because I was still scared of the dark. The smell of creeping pine still hung in our nostrils. The whispered voices of our parents in the kitchen.

'Hello? Is this a prank?'

'Valeria, it's me, Bruno.'

Silence.

The silence that comes with an ugly discovery.

Those two children were dead now. We were thirty-six and forty-two, and we no longer knew anything about each other.

'Who's calling you at this time? Come on, we're leaving!' I heard an irritated male voice say in the background. And straight away hers responding, docile: 'One second, I'm coming!' Finally to me, not docile at all: 'Has something happened?'

'No. I just wanted to wish you a happy New Year.'

'Are you taking the piss?'

Her voice had taken on a strange timbre. She had evidently deleted my number from her address book.

'Have you been drinking? Are you drunk?'

I had got home not long before, and the kitchen was freezing because the stove had been cold for hours. There were ghosts everywhere and Valeria wasn't wrong: if I hadn't drunk all that sparkling wine and *nocino*, I might not have been so reckless.

'I was just celebrating, like everyone else. And I wanted to know how you were.'

Silence again.

Again, the insistent male voice in the background.

'Maybe you can tell him you're on the phone to your brother?'

'I'm coming!' she called to him. Then, quieter, 'He doesn't know you exist.'

So what does he know? Does he know about the cable car?

'It's not a good time, Bruno. If there's nothing serious, let's talk another time.'

Serious.

The trial was in 1991. The same year Valeria graduated in Education – with a very low grade, because after all, there was no longer anyone to bring a school report home to.

She found work in the city as a supermarket cashier. The Witch of the Woods; the captain of all expeditions to the partisans' hideout, wielding her stick with the flint point in the dark. Now, she would catch the bus down in Alma at six in the morning, with her hair greasy, nails bitten, no makeup. And she'd come home on the bus at six in the evening, as tired as she was when she left, apathetic and silent. While she was gone, I'd make my lunch by myself, do my homework by myself, take care of the laundry by myself. Only at dinner did we sit down together at the table and utter very few words. She punished herself by never going out with anyone – her violet rucksack had been burned in the back garden. She chastised herself by wearing only men's clothes, oversized and scruffy, our father's work clothes usually – we hadn't thrown away anything of our parents', not even their socks. And when I finally turned eighteen and she was no longer legally obliged to look after me, she quit her job and left. As if there was no other option.

'Where do you live now?'

'In Ostia.'

Which to me might as well have been Singapore, Sydney, Honolulu.

'And what are you doing in Ostia?'

'I'm a lifeguard in the summer. In winter, I do odd jobs.'

'Since when can you swim?'

'Sorry, Bruno. You think you can pick up the phone after this long and get into my business?'

'Time doesn't change the fact that we're actually pretty close relatives.'

'And you're still holing yourself away up there, in that stone shitheap?'

She hadn't stopped being my sister straight away. Every so often, in the early years when she still lived in Milan, she came back. Never for Christmas, never in summer, but every November 2nd she'd turn up at the cemetery gates.

She wore a miniskirt. Fishnet tights, black knee-high boots she'd never learned to walk properly in, with heels so high they looked like stilts, a studded leather jacket, and a bra you could see through her sheer top. Her face was stained with makeup, her hair shaved on one side and green or bright pink on the other. It was a shock for me the first time I saw her again. As if the other place she had gone to was a realm of extraordinary transformation.

'You have no idea how much life there is out there, in the world,' she had said to me once while balancing at the top of the stepladder, organising a bunch of white viburnum next to our mother's smiling face mounted in the oval of the plaque dated 1954 – 1990. And I had thought: isn't Sassaia part of the world?

She was working in a night-time establishment. A transgressive place, 'where everyone does whatever they want: smoking joints, having threesomes . . .' She smiled, allusive.

'And what do you do, in this place?'

She came down the stepladder, moved it about ten centimetres along and then, climbing up towards our father with a brand-new candle and another viburnum, winked at me. 'Poisoned cocktails.'

I was now in my final year of secondary school and was the only boy in a class of fifteen girls, each one more of a swot than the next. But the biggest swot was me. Because all of them, since they lived closer to school and didn't lose the hours that I lost on a rural bus and then up a mule track, arrived home and had someone to talk to, to argue with, to watch TV with. I trekked up Stra' dal Forche with my rucksack full of books and, when I arrived, found nobody. No TV, no radio. Just absolute solitude, emptiness – enormous freedom I had no idea what to do with. I would immediately slam a heavy book down on the table, just to make some noise, and set to underlining it so as not to see, not to remember. I ate dinner in the company of the Second World War, *Oedipus Rex*, the sonnets of Ugo Foscolo. What could I know about the nightclubs of Milan? Of threesomes? I was already living like a hermit.

We divided up the compensation money into two separate accounts, two separate lives. Only the anniversary united us.

'Yes, I still live in *our* house. And I didn't call you to interfere, but to reconnect.'

'Any reason?'

'I've got a girlfriend.'

It just came out; it wasn't my intention. But Valeria laughed. A beautiful laugh that immediately, instantaneously, broke my heart.

In a suddenly surprised and happy tone of voice, she said: 'No way! Are you getting married?'

'No, no wedding.'

'Ah.' She didn't like that.

The male voice interrupted again in that part of the universe where she lives, Ostia, around – I went to check straight after – 700 kilometres from Sassaia.

'Do you still have to get ready? Who the hell are you talking to?'

'No one. I'm coming in a sec.'

'A sec'? I had never heard her say that before.

I tried to imagine the face of that man – her boyfriend? – and what kind of house they must live in. And whether in that house they smoked crack, or whether children had been born there. Life was truly a merciless thing if you could go from being the Witch of the Woods to this nomad who had changed jobs and cities God knows how many times.

Whoever had neglected to maintain that cable had ended up compromising our souls in the process. And there was no way, there would never be a way, to repair them.

Or maybe there was?

'Vale? Are you still there?'

'I'm here.'

'Can we be in touch every so often?'

'Was it your girlfriend who made you want a family again? She's not pregnant, is she?'

'No, she isn't. But can we stay in touch?'

'I have to go, goodbye.'

Before hanging up, in an extremely quiet voice, she added: 'I think so, yes.'

18

A BIG WAREHOUSE IN the middle of rice fields. Its neon sign beckoned across the flat farmland like a lightbulb to moths, a feeble snare jostled between closed factories, abandoned houses and, a little way ahead, the motorway toll booth, or the edge of the universe.

Here it was; the Tartana. A reinforced concrete parallelepiped, at once new and old. The promised land, which Emilia was drinking in from a distance, chomping at the bit in the passenger seat as we crawled along the dirt track in a slow procession of headlights.

She was burning with anticipation as she pointed, pressing her finger against the windscreen as if trying to touch it as I drove, in low spirits, ignorant. I parked the car, still knowing nothing. In the wide-open plain of frosty grass, amidst dozens of other cars sinking into the petrol blue of the night, two boys were vomiting into a drainage channel, and it wasn't yet half past ten.

It was painful to watch as Emilia walked eagerly towards the party in her best clothes: a denim miniskirt with a pair of leggings underneath (Rosa didn't sell tights), an aquamarine top that showed her belly button, her usual jacket and Dr. Martens, red lipstick, glittery eyelids.

'Oh what I wouldn't give for a pair of heels!' she had implored in front of the mirror before we left. But her fairy godmother hadn't intervened, and she'd remained Cinderella in rags. She dragged me by the arm towards the entrance, her ignorant, wooden, bear prince, in the same chequered flannel shirt and corduroy trousers that I wore to go mushrooming.

We settled into the queue of shiny girls and floppy-haired boys, free but for the strict instructions from their parents to be outside at three or four in the morning, punctual and sober. We were aliens. But the teenagers didn't even see us, we were transparent to them, like all adults: the embodiment of an end they never wanted to meet. I noticed that Emilia had lost her euphoria suddenly, like usual. She was staring at the girls with a dark, hateful look in her eyes.

'Look, *they* all have high heels,' she whispered, to me or to herself. 'Look how much of Mummy's makeup they've caked on.'

I didn't like this version of her. Her sullen tone of voice. Her dark laughter. Her nonsensical envy.

We were old and out of place. My heart felt heavy at the idea of going inside. And then something happened.

Emilia suddenly lost her patience, grabbed my hand and jumped a large chunk of the queue. There was straight away a chorus of protest to which she calmly responded: 'Good little children! I have a special invitation. My friend and I are on the guest list.' They, though not happy, were placated. But from the crowd rose a crystalline female voice that shouted, 'Whore!'

Emilia spun around like a hawk. She picked her out immediately. She smiled, transformed. Her face scared me, and the sixteen-year-old in question and her friends must have felt the same way, because they turned white and silent, taking a step backwards.

Emilia went over to them, completely at ease. Her gaze glacial, eyes putrefied green. She isolated the blonde one, grabbed her by the collar of her jacket, spat in her face and then said, loud enough for them all to hear: 'If you mess with me, I'll cut those piece-of-shit heels right off you.' She sprang out the blade of a penknife, a dark impulse that came from – where? 'Or I can go straight for the neck.'

There, as that scene played out, it was all as clear as the crispest mountain morning. I should have understood there and then that her preprogrammed propensity for threats and carefully calibrated violence could only be the result of a certain, very specific apprenticeship.

'A woman cannot call another woman a whore,' she whispered to the girl who was now in tears. 'Have you ever thought about what it means? Or do you just parrot everything you hear, like a stupid little girl? Playing the same game as the men who have been screwing us over since forever?' She pushed her away. 'You've got some studying to do, little bitch.'

She closed the penknife and put it back in her pocket. She lit a cigarette as she walked back over to me. She inhaled with a terrifyingly angelic expression on her face. Perhaps she was thinking that if Marta had been stationed somewhere to witness the scene, she would jump out now with a round of applause: that's how you do it, girl! Lessons in style *and* in feminism!

Respect, girls, respect is the most important thing.

I was disturbed.

Crushed.

They let us pass. The compact mass of frightened teenagers opened into two wings to let us through to the metal door.

I paid for two tickets with shaking hands as she quickly finished her Winston and put it out on the ground, crushing it with her foot.

'I know. It was too much.'

We were sitting on stools and leaning on the bar with our elbows, sipping watered-down Negronis in plastic cups.

She was seriously regretful now, and worried. As I would learn some time later, getting into a spat had been a really stupid thing to do. *Imagine if they'd phoned the police! Imagine if they'd asked for my documents and the blonde one had pressed charges!*

She drank, and rubbed a hand over her face to dry the sweat.

I didn't look at her.

'It's just you can't call another woman a whore. It makes me nuts when that happens. Do you think a woman would really turn to prostitution if she had an alternative? If she'd been brought up in a different world? I mean . . .' She was talking fast, shouting to be heard over the booming sound of *tunz tunz tunz.* 'There might be some women who are prostitutes out of choice. But they're a minority. And anyway, you have to think about whether that choice is really a free one. Why would you allow an ugly old slobbering stranger with a beer belly, who's probably dirty and smelly, to enter your body if you could avoid it? Would you risk becoming pregnant because a bastard wants to use you the same way he uses a urinal to piss in? No – you just can't call another woman a whore.'

'What were you doing with a knife in your pocket?'

I made myself turn around to look at her face, her mask.

'It's small, it's practically harmless. But I was taught it's good to carry one.'

'Who taught you that, your father?'

Emilia bit her lip. Then she turned back to her cup: 'I'm sorry, really. I understand it was too much. I made a scene . . . I used to study acting – well, I went to an acting class. Maybe that's why I was so convincing, eh?' She tried to laugh. 'Oh, you're boring when you play the little saint.'

I felt alone, drastically alone, at the edge of a dancefloor swarming, as predicted, with spotty, excitable, inexperienced teenagers bathed in the mechanical strobes of blue, green and orange lights. At the decks, an ageing provincial DJ named Kevin was warming up the crowd by shouting, 'Put your hands in the air!', 'Put your arms in the air!', 'Put your drinks in the air!'. The speakers blasted out songs I'd never heard, all the same. And I was sitting next to this perfect stranger with a knife in her pocket.

This thirty-one-year-old bully.

Not even on the most squalid nights of my life, not even when, not long back from Turin, I drove the Seat Ibiza like an outlaw over this same plain, between these same rice fields, with Gisella sat next to me. Not even on those nights did I feel so betrayed.

'I'm sorry again.'

'Are we going to spend our whole lives like this? With you saying sorry, reassuring me, and then revealing again straight afterwards that you're not normal? That you're completely off your head? That one day you were born in Bologna, the next in Pesaro, the next in Riccione? And me silent, because I have to wait for you? Why do I have to believe you? Why do I have to be a total moron?'

I got up from the bar. Emilia tried to stop me.

'I'm going to get my jacket. I'll wait for you outside.'

'Please.'

'Calm down, I won't leave you here. Take your time. If you manage to find someone of age, take him to the toilets like you used to do.'

I was disgusted, and so determined that Emilia released her grip and let me go. Enough. I had to end it immediately, before 2015 became 2016. I had served my purpose: I'd brought her to the nightclub, put her to sleep without a TV, kept her entertained in an abandoned village.

I passed my raffle ticket to the cloakroom attendant and got back my mushroom jacket. And as I turned around I couldn't stop myself searching for her one more time on that sad dancefloor, under those vulgar lights in the middle of the crowd, undulating like a Tagada ride at the fair.

I spotted her, raising her arms in the air as DJ Kevin ordered. With her eyes closed. Her hair down. Her head tipped back. The only adult, with her bare belly and muddy Dr. Martens on her feet. In ecstasy.

I waited outside along with half a dozen parents, two cars rocking rhythmically with their windows fogged up, and a group of metalheads passing around a joint.

Sitting on the bonnet of the Seat Ibiza, I didn't feel cold. I didn't feel anything. I was just waiting to take her home, like a taxi driver. And then – why not? – I'd pack my case and head to Ostia.

Valeria would never have let herself be degraded so easily. When she was the Witch of the Woods she went around with the same penknife in her pocket as Emilia. Perhaps, I thought, it was me who had overreacted? 'Whore' was a cowardly, odious word. But was Emilia justified? Valeria had never threatened anyone.

You couldn't even see the moon down there; no stars, no mountains. I'd become an orphan again just like before she arrived and, what's more, I was burdened by that feeling I didn't dare name. That I didn't want to feel, but yet I felt, alongside the anger, rage and disappointment. A feeling that made me insecure, that should've been the purpose of a life, so they said, its best part. Instead it was an affliction that corroded me, my identity, at the root, and annihilated it.

The countdown erupted over that desolate shred of farmland. Midnight exploded with a roar from the concrete parallelepiped. DJ Kevin blessed the New Year: 'Welcome to 2016!' The future had just begun, and I felt driven down, into the darkest darkness of the partisans' hideout.

Emilia emerged, sweaty, with no coat. She practically sprinted towards the Seat. She stopped, breathless, in front of me. She'd have a chill the next day, I knew it.

She bent over with her hands on her knees. The bare section of her stomach was covered in goosebumps, her hair stuck to her forehead.

'My mother died on December 31st, 1997,' she said, breathing heavily. 'My class had organised a party and I was the only one who didn't go. They never invited me again afterwards. I'd missed the boat forever. I was born in Ravenna. When I feel excluded, when I feel different or like the least cool one, something goes off inside me. I know, it's scary. Don't think I haven't worked on it. They diagnosed me with an anger problem. They diagnosed me with a ton of disorders and defects, and I swear I have tried, I've confronted them. Don't doom me to failure if I relapse once in a while, please. I've never been to a nightclub. This is the first time in my whole life. And now I'm asking you to come back inside and dance with me. Just one song. Then we can leave.'

'Dance on your own.'

'No.'

'I don't know when you're lying and when you're telling the truth.'

'I just told you the truth! The truth you so desperately want!'

I was at the end of my tether. It was late. Ravenna – she was coming to tell me this now? Why? It's just a city.

I got down from the bonnet and went to open the side door. Fuck the future; there was only the past. Life was all a past that you couldn't change or modify or salvage.

'You want another truth?' she shouted. 'You want it?'

I kept one hand on the door and the other on the roof of the Seat.

'I'm not interested anymore,' I lied.

'I'll tell you anyway: I love you.'

She spat it into my face, like she had spat at the girl earlier. She stared at me, trembling.

Nobody had ever said that to me before.

I had never said it either.

I picked her up and carried her back inside, growling, 'Just one song.'

Which turned out not to be *one* song, but *the* song.

The big song of 2000, or maybe 2001. One of those summer earworms that don't stop assailing you, in every café, from every radio station, from June to September, then that's it. After that, only small-town festivals and extremely rural nightclubs remain stuck in time. Because it's nostalgic, because it gives people back their lost youth.

The song was so famous that even I knew it: 'L'Amour Toujours' by Gigi D'Agostino.

On the dancefloor, the teenagers were already drunk and tired. And when DJ Kevin, who must have been about my age, put on that track, none of them knew the chorus, apart from me and Emilia who, brimming with wonder, looked into my eyes. She took my hands and started to laugh and jump, enthusiastically repeating: 'I don't believe it! I can't believe it! It's a sign!'

She wanted me to let go, to think of nothing, the way she was doing, to not remember or demand anything of ourselves, of our broken existence.

She wanted me to close my eyes like she had, and throw my head back, and let my body go to the music that we hadn't danced to when it was the right time.

She wanted us to shine together in the sad heart of that night, pierced every so often by a blue or green light, and sing with whatever breath we had left.

And I obeyed her, because that feeling was stronger than everything else.

Than dignity, than anger, than any idea or opinion.

It echoed around my head, melted warmly into my veins: I love you.

I knew something, yet I knew nothing. Only that, even if this was our last dance, I had to dance. If this was our last moment, I had to live it. Everything ended; the future was inevitable. So I kissed her with everything I had.

19

Inevitable.

Like the tax collector, like the officer who puts a ticket on your car, like the gravedigger.

In the teachers' room on Thursday January 7th, 2016 at 10:30, her eyes darting with satisfied glee, Patrizia slammed a creased printout from the internet onto my desk.

She couldn't even manage to wait until the end of the morning, knowing full well that I wouldn't be capable of breathing, let alone teaching, after this. But how could she hold it in any longer? So keen was her hunger to see me crack. So many hours of investigative work lay behind this sensational discovery. So strong her desire to reach the orgasm as soon as possible: to be right, to have won.

'I'm sure you already know,' she hissed in an ingratiating voice, 'she *must* have already told you. But just look how sweet she is in this photo, your little girlfriend.'

I picked the piece of paper up, pretending to be annoyed; I straightened out the creases with disdain; and I surrendered.

As I struggled to decipher the title of this article from the archives of the *Corriere della Sera* dated June 24th, 2001, my vision turned foggy and my head started to spin, and I could no longer comprehend the Italian language, or what day it was, or what year, or who I was.

'Oh come on, don't tell me she hasn't told you any of this!'

Ecstatic.

Triumphant.

As my strength crumbled away, the ground collapsed beneath my feet and my heart froze over, she cooed in my ear: 'Pretty big trouble the little redhead got herself into, huh?'

Whenever I pass her, even now, she hardly acknowledges me and strides onwards, quickening her step, looking down, cheeks red. Sometimes I turn to look at her. And I want to stop her and ask: how long did it last, your happiness? An afternoon? A couple of days? Was it worth it?

That Thursday January 7th, though, we were next to one another in the teachers' room. It was cloudy, it was the day after Epiphany, the day they say *takes all the holidays away*, electricians up ladders dismantling the Christmas lights. And I was stunned, pummelled to a pulp by one word in the title that my heart still refuses to write, to this day. And by that photo.

Because the image was clear and devastating in its simplicity. My ears started to screech with the blunt, roaring sound of nothing that spread deeper down, to my arteries, my right ventricle and left ventricle, my pulmonary alveoli. Like when the cable snapped and the cabin dropped to the ground and smashed into fragments so tiny it was impossible, afterwards, to put most of the bodies back together: I heard nothing. Everything went dark. It felt like one of those dreams where you never stop falling.

Patrizia tried to caress me with her fingernail.

I jerked out of the way, horrified.

With my last shred of rational thought, I managed to assemble a plea: 'Please, don't go spreading this around. And cover me for the next two hours.' Then I put the sheet in my pocket and ran out at breakneck speed through the woods. But even running as fast as I could uphill with my eyes closed, I couldn't leave it behind, couldn't not see it. The black and white, badly printed rectangle.

Emilia was in the centre, partially pixellated, but undeniably her. Lost and bewildered like the blonde girl she had threatened on New Year's. Hair tied up, wearing trainers and a white T-shirt. Eyes blanked out to protect her identity, but I knew how empty they could become.

Emilia, being led away in handcuffs by the police.

PART TWO

5,264 Days

20

Who knows if souls get older. If they maintain the voice they always had and their typical teenage ways of calling things 'da bomb' or saying 'chillax'. If they remember and feel anger. Or if they let it all go.

Emilia was applying rice paper to Satan's snout, staring at it with a surly, absent gaze. Wearing her jacket indoors and fingerless wool gloves, her breath visible in the air, a July afternoon many years ago came to mind when she and Marta had had a fight. It was over the immortality of the soul.

In the light of the lamp, she pushed the pads of her fingers into the distilled water compress to try and rescue the blue of the horns, the yellow-green of the legs of the doomed man who thrashed around in Satan's jaws, the black of the claws that were crushing the Devil's next naked and desperate meal; even if, in theory, you should arrive in Hell already dead and bodiless.

Meanwhile, Basilio was observing her from the Paradise that he had almost finished restoring. The saints were lined up and Christ was seated, ready to issue his sentence.

'If we keep going at this rate, we'll be done within the week.'

Emilia looked up at him: 'I won't like it, you know.'

Basilio nodded. 'Me neither, but there's an interesting Danse Macabre in the Donato chapel, and the Pietà is remarkable. But it won't compare . . .' And he waved his arm towards the wall.

It was the only wall that was lit up on that grey January day. The holidays were over and the church had sunk back into its dusty abyss, in the depths of which glowed some frail candles still burning from the offerings. Emilia had been avoiding this job for as long as she could, and today, under her shirt, her heart thrashed against her chest. It was stupid if she thought about it: they had watched, in their cell, all the episodes of *A Day in the Courthouse*, they'd even punished themselves with *The Silence of the Lambs*, doing impressions of Hannibal Lecter. But that fresco wasn't about actors or other people: it was about her.

She had just turned seventeen when her judgement began. They had had to provide her with a table of all the various roles and functions and a schedule of the legal process, because she knew absolutely nothing. She had no idea what a district judge, magistrate or public prosecutor was. Judges were so grown-up – omnipotent, like Christ and the saints. They had the power to decide, literally, who she was, and how many years they would take from her life.

Until now, after almost fifteen of them, she found herself working with dedication and care on these painted bodies, rotten with guilt.

Would they be forgiven, one day?

Would she too get to become a soul?

It was fresh air time, which in the summer was from 5 to 7 p.m. because of the heat. It was 2005 or 2006. The walkie-talkies announced in unison: 'The girls are on their way down!'

They laid out their towels on the bare concrete of the walled courtyard. All four of them were wearing skimpy bikinis, flip-flops and sunglasses. They were armed with old detergent bottles filled with water to spray themselves with. 'Shame there's no hot guys here to enjoy our butts.' But how many squats, lunges and stretches did they do every day to keep them firm anyway, in vain?

'Innocenti, let's see what you've got.' Marta opened one of Emilia's notebooks aggressively – she got nasty when there was something to interrogate.

Afifa and Myriam were lying on their stomachs to tan their buttocks and already had their eyes closed. 'What is this exam on?' one of them asked.

Emilia replied grandly, 'Visions of death and the power of time.'

'Uuh!' They were all struck down. Even Marta, according to whom death – they had discussed it before – was just a question of cells kicking the bucket, followed by the dark chemical reactions of decomposition.

But 'the power of time' was a cool phrase, so cool it was impossible not to suspect that there was something else in their destiny, something other than putrefying guts and decaying bones.

'The soul according to Plato,' Marta read aloud. 'Go on.'

The youngest girls were playing volleyball. The army was watching them sweat and chat. Some rap music in English trickled from a window on the first floor. Afifa had just finished high school; Myriam was retaking, after various changes and transfers, and was determined to finish. Emilia and Marta were attending university. Lying there on the red-hot concrete in their G-strings with their books, they indisputably represented, in the history of that place, the Example to Follow.

'So,' Emilia began.

'You can't start with *so*.'

'Oh you're such a ball-breaker, Vargas! *So*, in *Phaedo*, one of Plato's dialogues about the soul, Socrates desires death because it liberates the soul from the body, which is a cage limited by vices, whereas after death the soul can access its ideal condition: the truth of being.'

It was not even a distant possibility, until a few years earlier, that metaphysics was something that could be discussed in the shade of the barbed wire fence. Emilia had once eavesdropped on a conversation in an office adjacent to Frau Direktorin's: 'You really have to be a loser to end up here. Those poor girls almost make you want to cry.' Right, so there were two options: *Throw away the key!* Or: *Poor Girls. No astrophysics, no chemistry, no philosophy.*

Anyway, Emilia had stuffed her visual arts timetable with pretentious modules on ancient philosophy, bioethics and other things that were judged as 'at the limit' by Vilma, her tutor: 'Do you really need to be probing death, the soul and the afterlife all the time?' And now she was proceeding like a freight train with a description of the soul that, according to Plato, 'is the part of us that is like an idea. Which means it can't be corrupted.'

'So it is always good?' Myriam was struck by this possibility. 'No matter what happens to our bodies?'

'It doesn't exactly say that . . . Plato compares the soul to a chariot.'

'A chariot?'

'Like a cart. Pulled by two horses with wings. One is white and represents the intellect. The other is black and represents irrational instincts. And then there's the Auriga . . .' Myriam looked confused again, and Afifa was asleep. 'A sort of driver, who represents the reason that governs light and dark.'

'A fair amount of bullshit,' Marta commented, checking against the notes. 'But I'd say this time you get a higher mark than 21.'

'Oh, but it's Plato!'

'We're going to become worms, Emi, not glimmering paragons of the truth of being.'

'I prefer to think that the soul exists.' Emilia dug her heels in. 'And that we all have one.'

Marta's face changed. 'All of us?' It was never advisable to dig your heels in with her when she had *that* tone of voice, and she sat in *that* position, with *that* look on her face. 'Really, Innocenti? You'd like it if *certain people* became radiant souls? Perhaps looking down and listening to us right now?'

Emilia held her gaze. 'Yes, I would like that.'

Marta got up, pounced on her and slapped her hard. 'I do not want to ever meet the soul of that man! Do you understand? He didn't have a soul.'

But Emilia defended herself. 'What are we doing here, if after everything we're all just gonna be worms?' She grabbed Marta's beautiful blue-black hair and pulled it as hard as she could. Because this wasn't philosophy: it was living flesh.

'There's fuck all after this, Emi.'

'We're paying for nothing, then?'

'Do you seriously want to believe in God?'

They were twenty and they were fighting like the little girls who had just arrived, squeezing each other's wrists, pinching each other's tits through their bikinis. Afifa and Myriam had walked away: you didn't interfere with other people's shit. The army, however, did intervene, promptly and looking rather fed up; shutting down a fight in that heat was horrible work.

They sent them to Frau Direktorin, who slammed her fist onto the board, her patience exhausted. 'If you continue like this I'll send one of you to Rome and the other to Prontremoli!' She put them in isolation for five days as punishment, time to meditate on their actions. But before they had managed to forcibly remove their bodies, before they were confined to solitude, Emilia had just had time to whisper to Marta, her face wet with tears: 'I *need* the soul to exist. Do you understand? Because I *have* to see her again one day.'

Even if she knew that it wouldn't happen. Even if she was repenting now, she knew that Hell couldn't be empty and Heaven full.

For the simple reason that victims and executioners must never ever, not even at the end of time, meet again.

I am required to do something now: to reconstruct the events of that day from the viewpoint of Emilia. Even if that means looking at myself from the outside and feeling hatred towards what I see. It won't be a painless report, but I owe it to her, at least in writing, to re-establish a bit of justice.

It was three o'clock. Emilia was hurrying to finish applying the rice paper before putting her tools away.

In the middle of winter, night fell at four o'clock and Basilio would finish early. They turned off the lamps, came down from the scaffold, said goodbye and see you tomorrow at nine. And, like every afternoon, Emilia left first, impatient.

It hadn't been easy for me to stick around after Tartana. She had had to cough up some details for me. The white house in Ravenna. Her mother who taught Italian and found her daughter to be her worst student. Her various problems, cognitive and relational, which became expensive sessions with a speech therapist, a psychologist, a music therapist. But she was extremely careful to stop at the beginning of June 2001.

I always sat on the steps to wait for her, usually with a book in my hands and a felt hat pulled over my curly hair, a woollen cloak draped over my shoulders, my leather briefcase full of assignments to mark. But that day I wasn't there.

Emilia shivered. The body always knows what the brain doesn't want to. *He's been held up*, she thought, *the boiler's broken, a pipe's frozen, a tree's fallen on the road* – despite the fact that I had never been late before. She lit a cigarette and inhaled until her lungs burned.

Basilio came out. 'Where's Bruno? Has he come down with something?'

'No, no. He's coming.'

'Do you want to walk up with me?'

'I'd prefer to wait for him.'

'As you wish. See you tomorrow.'

'See you tomorrow!'

Emilia watched Basilio head slowly into the low clouds that kept Alma frozen. He was hunched over, unstable on his old legs and careful not to trip on the loose cobbles. She wondered how he had the strength, twice a day, to walk Stra' dal Forche – and why.

It was twenty past three. Emilia pulled her phone out of her pocket to check whether I'd texted. Nothing. But it was unusual for me to resort to using my phone; it would have to be a matter of life or death. The fact that there were no messages meant she didn't need to worry.

She sat down on the step, pulling her jacket around her. She let herself be watched by the patrons of the Samurai who dared look at her from the glowing windows, as if she was still a novelty. She lit another Winston. She thought again of Marta, of her graduation: the first in the entire history of that place. They had put on a little party – alcohol *verboten* – and Marta had squeezed both of Emilia's hands in hers, her black eyes gleaming with satisfaction. In the bathroom, before going out to meet the applause, she said: 'I've won, Emily, I'm happy. I've settled all my debts. Just one more year and I'm free.'

Those phrases – 'I've won', 'I'm happy', 'I'm free' – stuck in her mind.

When it was her turn to graduate, the second in the history of that place, she felt no joy. On the contrary, she felt like she had reached the end of the line. Despite the fact that her father was moved to tears, and that Frau Direktorin had organised a similar party for her, with Coca-Cola and Fanta, and was repeating: 'I'm proud of you, Innocenti. I'm so proud.' Despite the fact that Venturi, Rita and her secondary school teachers had all been there, and she had gone to the trouble of smiling at all of them, on that day of joy all that came into sharp focus was a void.

Emilia spotted her, standing against the back wall at the vanishing point of all the raised hands, in the deafening silence under all the hurrahs: the outline of a person that was no longer here. And it wasn't her mother. She was holding a mojito in a plastic cup with a black straw. Her blue eyes shone, and her mouth was tensed into a grimace: 'What's all this for?'

The bell rang four times.

I still hadn't arrived.

Perhaps, she realised, the price of love was the truth. And she really was searching for the words. The words to tell me *what fucked-up thing I did*. But it wasn't as easy as I thought.

It isn't like if you add up the death of your mother, the dyslexia and the bullying, you get an explanation.
I know.
We are not a chain of causes and effects. We don't work like gravity, rain or times tables.
I know, Rita.
If you take us apart, you'll be sure to find some inner workings missing.

The sky had turned black. The streetlamps made pockets of condensation suspended in the air. Even the people in the Samurai had got fed up of watching her.

Emilia raised her eyes towards the clock tower: it was 4:47 p.m.

It was clear that I wasn't coming.

She went back up the hill alone, with the torch.

Her beam of light revealed a tree trunk; a branch broken by the weight of the snow; a pointy bit of rock; the roadside shrine with the Black Madonna inside.

The forest at night-time, in January, was deserted. *The worst suffering you can inflict on a human being isn't burning*, thought Emilia – *it isn't cutting, isn't pain. It's solitude: no face to recognise yourself in, no voice to remind you that yes, you too are a person.* That was how she found herself after the arrest, in a bare room with a single bed.

She felt the cold inside her bones, and further in, perhaps where her soul really resided. She was worried, yet calm. Having a fair amount of experience of disasters, she kept up her pace. She prayed, yes, because she believed a bit in God. *Dear God, let Bruno not have slipped on the ice and broken a leg or his head. But he's too much of an expert. How many winters has he spent up here, alone? Dear God, let him not have had a heart attack or an aneurism. But it's impossible: he's too young.* What else could happen in Sassaia?

She walked on, her boots trampling the hard snow, following our old, superimposed footprints, hers and mine indistinguishable from one another's. She held back her anxiety – and her breath – as she sweated under the lining of her jacket. She felt the tension in her body: the badness that was like a hole in reality, generating whirlpools, friction, undercurrents. *I'll find him there repairing a pipe,* she told herself, *or fixing a wonky roof tile. God, let nothing bad have happened.*

When she got to Sassaia, her heart could no longer sustain her.

She reached the alleyway.

And when she saw me there, intact, sitting on the steps leading up to my house and illuminated by the harsh light of the outside lamp, she was so happy and relieved that she felt she might explode.

She ran towards me.

'You scared me!' she shouted, laughing. 'I'm going to hit you!'

She moved to kiss me, to squeeze me, but I retracted. A bodily movement that said 'don't touch me'. Horrified – that is the right word. Emilia knew it because many people before me had looked at her the exact same way.

I was holding the piece of paper that Patrizia had given me, which was crumpled in my hands.

'What's happened?'

I hate myself for it now, because I am no longer that blind person.

I threw the piece of paper at her.

Emilia bent down to the ground where it had fallen and picked it up.

She looked, but she didn't need to read.

'Why, Bruno?'

My legs were jelly, my chest collapsed, my bladder needing to be emptied.

'Why did you search?'

I squeezed my hands into fists. My body was rigid and tense with disdain, tears falling silently down to my chin.

'You're a monster.'

I had the courage to say it, to spit what everyone spits in the heat of the moment, when faced with certain news, ashamed of myself, yet shouting. Because what else can you do when you're freaked out and you can't think straight, but try to protect yourself?

Emilia closed her eyes.

'You allowed me to fall in love with you without knowing anything about you.'

She held the paper in her hands. She didn't throw it away, didn't stamp on it, didn't set fire to it with her lighter. Because that sheet of paper was still, despite everything, part of her story.

She tried to tell me: 'This isn't all I am.'

But I didn't want to hear it.

I couldn't.

Like the many good people, or perhaps just normal people, who had sat in the seats of the saints and the blessed during her own particular judgement, at Bologna Juvenile Court, Via del Pratello 36. When she was forced to speak, they didn't hear.

But fifteen years has passed now – fourteen and a half, to be precise.

She reopened her eyes and tried to tell me again: 'If you'll listen to me . . .'

I turned to go inside.

If I could go back now, I swear I wouldn't behave like I did.

She was destroyed, defenceless, and I didn't want to look into the eyes of the woman I loved and feel pity. I wanted to stamp my feet like an impotent child; to just remove the obstacle in front of me.

Before I slammed the door in her face, I shouted with all the hatred I had in my body, 'Get out of Sassaia.'

But she stayed there in the old snow.

'Get out, for God's sake, get out!' as if I had the right. 'I don't ever want to see you again!'

And she stood there in the street, like a lifeless thing.

She looked down at the sheet of paper she was still holding in her hands. It was the first time she'd read an article about herself from beginning to end. She had come up here where it was less than ten degrees, her fingertips numb from the cold, and stood in the glow of the only light switched on for miles, not to save herself but to find herself inexorably in the same place.

She read it and thought that she would like to have a soul. That way when she died she could finally be free, and reach someplace that was neither heaven nor hell. Just a place, a simple place, nameless, but with a viewpoint from which the small and faded Earth was only just distinguishable.

She would immediately recognise her mother up there. And Emilia would pull her into herself with arms that weren't arms, kiss her with lips that weren't lips. And then her mother would say quietly, sweetly: 'She's over there, go and have a chat.'

She'd point. And nobody would have bodies or twisted-ness anymore. Just goodness to cling on to.

21

EMILIA OBEYED MY ORDER.

She ran into her house and turned on all the lights, not even stopping to take her coat off. She pulled her duffel bag down from the top of the wardrobe and stuffed in the essentials: knickers, socks, jumpers, A4 paper, pencils. She had five minutes, no more. She changed the batteries in her torch, grabbed the bag and her rucksack, and turned off all the lights. She shut the door and locked it, before leaving the key under the doormat.

Goodbye, Sassaia.

She began to run downhill in the dark, at breakneck speed, like that time she missed the bus – but that wouldn't happen this evening. She fell and hit her knee on a rock, felt a stinging pain on her temple and blood running down it. But there was no time. She got back up and started to run again. The torch shook in her hand and transfixed pieces of the forest. She tripped again, desperate, and got up, her trousers covered in mud, hair full of twigs. *Be grateful you had these two months. You didn't deserve them.*

She emerged from the stone steps between the bar and the grocery shop. It was 5:47 p.m. The bus had just arrived and she got on, breathing heavily. She didn't have a ticket.

When she pulled out all the money she had in her purse, the driver said, 'I only need two euros.' But she was no longer capable of counting.

The bus was empty. She dropped down on a seat in the back row. She didn't want to see the four streetlamps of Alma, the glowing windows of the Samurai and Rosa's, the clock tower and the school disappearing. She closed her eyes, thinking, *they'll all already know.*

After two bends in the road she felt her phone vibrate, making her jump in her seat. She hoped that it was me, that I at least wanted to hear her version of the story. She pounced on her rucksack and opened it with trembling hands, but couldn't find the phone, so she emptied all its contents out onto the seat next to her. Between the wallet, pouches, sanitary pads and penknife, she saw that it was her dad.

Emilia sank back into her seat, letting the phone ring. When it went quiet, she picked up the knife. This was why she always carried it with her. She lifted the sleeves of her jacket and fleece and pressed a deep, vertical cut along her whole forearm. The pain calmed her like a Rohypnol melted under her tongue. Then she gathered her scattered belongings and put them all back in the bag and pulled the hood of her jacket up over her head.

After three or four stops, people started to get on. They looked at her and then immediately looked away, giving her a wide berth as they moved to sit elsewhere. Nobody wants badness near them in case it might be contagious. After all, she was wearing jeans with blood all over the knees, and one sleeve stained the same colour. Someone would call the police, for sure. It was a question of minutes, seconds. What did she have to lose?

Five thousand, two hundred and sixty-four days busting her arse for a future that didn't exist. Or rather: existed, but didn't want her. It had just chased her away.

Get out of Sassaia.

Would she ever forget the image of my face, swollen with hate and disgust, shouting those words?

And she loved me.

They arrived at the station at 7:20 p.m. She stood looking at the departures board in her dirty clothes, her bag slung over her shoulder, upset but alert. Two trains: one to Turin and one to Milan. The one to Milan was leaving in a quarter of an hour from platform 2. She went over to the machine and bought a ticket. Then she went into the bar and bought the last stale sandwich and a can of beer, along with a pack of Winston Blues. That was all her money gone.

She ate the sandwich as she dragged herself along platform 2, and smoked as she waited with the last people on the planet, all washed up on that platform like cuttlefish bones. She was among family again.

When the train stopped in front of Emilia, a long serpent covered in graffiti, clattering through the fog, it seemed to welcome her. Its row of little glowing windows promised not an illusion but an escape in the form of a tired local train, with dirty toilets and a thin layer of grease on the windows. Emilia got on, walked through a couple of carriages and found a seat.

That's when she phoned.

We hold on to the good and restart from there. My arse.

When Marta picked up, her breath warm in Emilia's ear, Emilia said: 'If they asked me now, in this precise moment, if I wanted to go back inside – to the army, to Frau in a bad mood, to alarms at seven, handed-out meals in the canteen, brass keys turning in the locks and making all that noise, the toilet where we used to go and study at three in the morning so we wouldn't wake the others, remember? And Venturi driving us crazy – though she was quite helpful in the end – and seeing Rita and her backcombed hair twice a week, and Pandolfi who got us through high school, the two hours of fresh air time playing volleyball, the laughs, even Myriam killing herself . . . I would immediately say yes, yes, yes!'

'What the fuck's happened?'

Emilia banged her head hard against the glass.

None of the people in that second-class carriage flinched; the dealers, the prostitutes. They'd seen it all before.

'Freedom is a shitshow.'

'What the fuck has happened, Emilia?'

'Freedom to hurt myself? To hurt other people? Thanks, but no thanks.'

'Are you going to tell me what's happened or not?'

'That bastard went and looked me up online.'

Silence on the other end of the phone.

'I don't know how he did it. I didn't even tell him my surname. He could've waited for me to tell him.'

'Where are you now?'

'I'm on the train, coming to yours.'

'When do you get here?'

'I don't know. I didn't look.'

'Tell me where you got on, at what time, and I'll find out.'

Emilia stared at her reflection in the window. At that time of night all the normal families were together, eating dinner in their warm houses; couples were making love; friends were lingering over a final bit of intimacy around little tables in bars. But those were the nice lives of others that took place on another planet. This one, whatever planet this train was on, was completely black and empty. She could no longer see outside. Just inside. And the inside was a dirty mess like her. A reject. *We hold on to the good.* Even Rita had lied.

'You get into Central Station at 9:03. I'll wait for you on the platform, but make yourself look decent. I can't take you out to dinner looking like a jailbird.'

They both burst into desperate laughter.

I had watched from behind the curtain as she left, hiding in the shade of my bedroom, before going down to the kitchen. I filled up a pan of water and laid the table as I waited for it to boil.

I wasn't proud of myself, but the fact was this: I had no more words, just a silent block of anger. In the hours

I'd waited for her to come back from the church, I had done nothing but cry, screw up the article, walk around the village a hundred times unable to stop, think, breathe. It was like banging up against the same memories, again and again.

In 1991, when I went into the courtroom to testify, my eyes immediately sought them out, but they didn't look back at me. They adjusted their glasses, read their documents, turned their watches around on their wrists: they seemed so preoccupied. They had no idea what it meant to take a life and dig a crater inside it, to desiccate it, until it was completely barren. And yet that was exactly what they'd done.

The boy in the cable car died holding on to his grandparents. We knew that from the position of the bone fragments. His parents, who had survived, were sitting not far from me and Valeria in the courtroom, clutching a stuffed rabbit.

You could tell – from our faces, our unkempt clothing, our nervous tics, the bags under our eyes, the way we were clearly dragging ourselves through survival – that all of us were dead in that courtroom. All of us except them: the guilty, who failed to conceal their boredom as they listened to our stories, disengaged, fixing a bit of hair. They were clinging on to their own lives. They wanted the sentence to be short. Never mind if nine people were dead and many more only alive in appearance. They had saved money. Maintenance is costly, after all. My parents had died at forty years old for one fewer item on the invoice. Valeria would become dependent on SSRIs because of frugality. I would end up a hermit on the top of a crag for the sake of a few euros. And none of us, least of all that small blond boy named Thomas, had done anything wrong.

I had watched Emilia tucking the keys under the doormat, running away with her duffel bag on her shoulder and the torch in her shaky hand, and I had felt hatred.

Now, as I laid out the tablecloth, as I put down a single plate, a single glass, a single napkin, a single set of cutlery, I felt the resentment rising in my body.

The relatives of the victims are hardly ever shown in the news. Or, if they are, it's minimal. Nobody wants to see their pain. We're not as interesting as the killers, but we're too alive to be sanctified. We're condemned to live on the edge of an abyss, in the exact same world where they, the murderers, get to breathe, think, watch TV, eat, maybe even laugh, joke, make love.

We accepted the money because our uncle forced us to. Because the two of us were a girl who had just come of age and a boy who had a whole life ahead of him. 'You'll need it for university, your bills, your shopping. Your parents would've wanted it, no question.' So we took it. We never talked about it, never named it, but tacitly decided to use it only for what was absolutely necessary. No nice thing should be bought with that money. No holidays, no colourful fleeces, no CDs, no flowers. Only driving lessons, Valeria's rent in Milan at the beginning and later my own when I was at university in Turin, petrol for the Seat Ibiza and supplies for the winter.

After five years, the murderers were out and we were still trapped. Incapable of living a normal life, of having normal relationships; Valeria, who had never held down a job or a man, who never managed to stay sober, and me, who had gone back to Sassaia to hide away and serve my sentence fully.

If it was God who put Emilia in front of my house, he was cruel.

As she watched the imposing steel arches and heard the unrelenting loudspeaker announcements, Emilia felt the big world looming over her.

She followed the flow of everybody else, all marching in the same direction. The train had been almost empty when it left but stop after stop over the course of the journey, it had filled with people, who were now all pleased to have reached their destination.

Not Emilia. She was sweaty and smelly. She could feel her greasy hair and dirty hands. It was much warmer down here, but she was still dressed for Sassaia. She unzipped her jacket, loosened her scarf to reveal her old holey and bloodstained fleece and worn-out work jeans. They had promised each other a night out at the Cocoricò, the Imperiale, the Billionaire. Instead, she was at the end of the line.

Emilia stopped about a metre away from her.

The last time they had seen each other was on Marta's twenty-fifth birthday. It was nine in the morning; they had finished breakfast and gone back up to their cell, and

Emilia had helped Marta pack her case for her transfer to adult prison.

They couldn't say goodbye. They only pressed their lips together, briefly, and then Marta left. She crossed the second-floor corridor as everyone shouted and protested and vowed to set fire to their beds. The army all had shining eyes because 'you become fond of the girls in the end – how could you not?'. Frau shut herself away in her office for the rest of the day and refused to see anyone; she was definitely crying. Emilia wedged her face through the bars to watch the prison van take Marta away and, her heart broken, whispered, 'Goodbye'.

Over eight years ago.

Now there they were, standing in front of each other. *The living present*, as Leopardi writes in my favourite poem. The crowd flowed out, leaving only the two of them on Platform 3 of the west concourse, slowly recognising each other, repairing time, in the crude light of the lamps, the skirts of Romani women swishing and the tracks full of rubbish, a pizza place still open up ahead.

Marta was wearing heels which made her even taller than usual – thin stilettos, half covered by soft dark brown leather – and a cream coat tied at the waist with a wide-brimmed hat in the same colour. You would never, ever have guessed who she was or where she came from.

Emilia didn't dare move, not wanting to sully her friend.

Marta had become a woman. Expensive clothes; a made-up face that didn't betray any emotion. But her dark black eyes were still the same.

'Magical Emi.'

Emilia smiled.

'Look what love's done to you.'

'You, on the other hand, are still a queen.'

Marta stepped forward, closing the gap. She grabbed Emilia and squeezed her as hard as she could. As if Emilia was exactly what she had been looking for. As if she could recreate the feeling of dragging their two desks into the toilets while the others slept so that they could stay attached to one another the night before their exams. The feeling of their fingertips touching, their blood mixing.

Emilia buried her face in Marta's Sailor Mars hair and filled her nostrils with her coconut shampoo, the same scent that used to fill their cell after a shower.

22

UNTIL 1999, NOBODY HAD ever graduated from high school at the Bologna Institute for Female Young Offenders, due to the simple fact that the school didn't exist.

There were literacy courses for the foreign girls and work preparation courses for anyone who had finished middle school. And who gave a shit if they were all of obligatory school age; the general opinion was that you never came back up from certain lows. It was enough to eliminate most of the spelling mistakes in your Italian and be able to use the subjunctive clause every so often when the goal was a frying station at a fast-food chain or a cleaning job. The highest ambition: that they didn't go back to shoplifting, dealing, robbing, fighting and, in the most serious cases, killing.

Then, in the spring of 1999, two things happened that would change everything: the appointment to director of the peculiar, learned Italian poetry enthusiast, Frau Direktorin; and the transfer from Nisida of the young, unmanageable inmate and cause of countless disciplinary measures, Marta Vargas.

Legend has it that the first time Frau and Vargas met in the director's office, it went like this:

Frau: 'Don't give me problems, Vargas, because I can get extremely angry.'

Vargas: 'Don't worry, Frau.'

Frau: 'I'll repeat myself: I don't want a single burnt sheet in here.'

Vargas: 'Chill out, Frau.'

The next day, the army had had to run into Marta's cell with an extinguisher. After just a couple of days in isolation she was called into Frau's office again.

'Vargas, I know you're angry. But right now I am angrier.'

'I'm sorry, Frau. It's nothing personal.'

'What shall we do? We have many long years ahead of us.'

'You tell me, Frau. I didn't want to be transferred to Bologna. How the hell is my mother gonna visit me now? Who will pay for her travel expenses?'

'And who was a headache at Nisida? Who got themselves this transfer?'

Vargas raised her shoulders, ruminating on her chipped black fingernails. She was so poor she had arrived with just one change of clothing and no coat. She had been lent that nail varnish by an inmate at Nisida: she wouldn't be able to touch it up again.

Frau relaxed back in her chair, drumming her fingers on the imposing desk, the President of the Republic hanging in full view behind her. 'Have you ever considered studying?'

Vargas looked up, insolent. 'Studying what?'

'Manzoni! Plato! Petrarch!'

'Never heard of them.'

'You're seventeen, you've finished middle school. You have to do high school, Vargas.'

'High school?' Vargas exploded into a laugh so loud you could hear it in all the offices on the ground floor. 'I used to watch the high school kids walk by the window with their designer backpacks, lip gloss, Converse on their feet and a stick up their arse. But there's no stick anywhere near my arse, that's for sure.'

'Vargas, we have to change this language.'

'Frau, you can't change the past.'

'Vargas, I will bring high school to you, in September, and you will enrol and you will graduate. If you don't study, I'll shove you back in isolation for a month and you'll need Galileo's telescope to see a leave permit.' She smiled wickedly. 'And then maybe, since we're here, I'll bring university to you too. We won't set any limits. Anyway, how many years do you have left? Nine? Ten? Don't throw them away, make the most of them. You become a doctor, and I take you out of isolation.'

That's how the revolution started: with a threat.

Frau Direktorin was an incurable romantic: she believed in it – in restorative justice, in redemption through culture. And she wasn't wrong about Vargas: she was the ideal candidate for her project. Frau was clear that she wasn't after some utopia, just the right to study. Vargas was smart – no attention deficit, hyperactive or otherwise. She was hungry, she was furious. Her report from Nisida spoke of 'assiduous frequenting of the institutional library', even if it was between bed sheet pyres and attempts to escape.

Legend has it that that morning in April, Vargas challenged Frau as she got up from the chair. 'If you manage it, to bring me high school in jail . . .'

And the very next day Frau Direktorin turned up at the state education department like a battering ram and busted the minister's balls. She was attached to the phone for weeks, stubborn, shouting, swearing, unstoppable. Until, not a high school (let's not exaggerate), but the professional hospitality education institute, Artusi, opened a branch in the female young offenders' institution, changing the destiny not of all the girls, but of some of them, forever.

And how can we redeem them, otherwise?
Without history, without Pascoli, Manzoni, Dante?
'You were not made to live as brutes'!
Go, go forth and study!

Emilia and Marta emerged from the grand atrium of Milano Centrale into the night. In Piazza Duca D'Aosta they paused for a moment, dazzled by the Hotel Gallia, the Pirellone, all the lights. They were both thinking the same thing: they had never been in the world together like this after nine at night.

'You look like a hobo. I can't take you out to dinner.'

'I'm not hungry anyway.'

'Listen to me.' Marta's gaze cut through her. 'I'll put you up, I'll help you. But you have to get yourself back on track.'

Emilia laughed. 'You sound like Frau.'

'Of course I do – we speak once a fortnight.' Marta started walking towards the taxi stand. 'She always asks after you.'

Emilia was floored. She thought that Marta, aside from memories, had cut all ties with the institute like she had. A long time had passed. Both of them, as if struck by a fairy-tale curse, had had to leave the convent on the day they turned twenty-five. They had both finished their time at the adult prison and then in residential rehab, moving progressively towards a semblance of a normal life. But the institute remained the place of their youth.

'What do you mean, *you speak*? Do you call her or does she call you? Why didn't you tell me before?'

Marta offered to take Emilia's duffel bag and somehow managed to look graceful carrying it, even though it was filthy and gross. 'I wanted to tell you face to face,' she said, not stopping. 'You've gone white.'

'Well, we're outside, but it feels as if we're still in there.'

Marta stopped again and smiled. 'And that surprises you?'

They were about to cross the road to the line of white taxis waiting there, when three boys intercepted them. The oldest couldn't have been more than twenty-three, with his designer baseball cap and pretentious watch on display. He looked at Marta and gave a long whistle.

'Ciao bellissima.'

Instinctively, neither Marta nor Emilia moved out of the way. They didn't step back. They didn't walk faster.

They observed the boys, instead, with the utmost attention.

The other two – shorter than the first – nudged one another, giggling.

'Ciao,' Marta responded, serious.

A fantasy, no less. Just an old fantasy they'd joked about in the shade of the main courtyard.

'Where are you off to so quickly?'

Beautiful strays, all three of them. But especially him: bomber jacket and ripped jeans, Gucci bumbag defiantly on view. Shining eyes hiding under long lashes. Coffee hair, big hands. A maltreated, unpredictable, capricious god, with the record of his crimes written all over his face.

'Do you want to get a drink?' he insisted, still addressing Marta. Emilia wasn't in a state to attract anyone.

He reached his hand out towards her cheek, but Marta dropped the duffel bag and blocked his wrist with a precise movement.

'You don't want to do that,' she said.

'Oh!' The god whistled again and with his free arm stopped his friends, who had been about to intervene. 'What's your name? I'm already in love.'

They both recognised the accent, the same as Afifa's.

'I'm Marta, she's Emilia. I'll warn you: we've done over ten years.' She clarified, 'Each.'

Emilia looked for Marta's eyes. How could she just blab their sentence, like it was nothing, to someone she'd just met? She would never be able to do that, not even under torture, not even to someone she loved.

Marta seemed so calm, so at ease. She kept the boy still, her hand lingering on his wrist, the one without the watch, standing so close it looked like she wanted to smell his skin.

'And you, Tunisi?' she asked him. 'What's your name?'

Tunisi smiled. He and Marta were practically holding hands.

'Habib. And that's Rami and Luca.'

'How do you get by?' Marta asked, out of the blue.

'Why that question?' Habib darkened; impetuous now, on the defensive. 'We're mechanics, we were born in Italy.'

Marta let his arm go. 'Mechanics don't go around in a Gucci bumbag and a decent fake Rolex.'

'She's a copper,' one of the two boys said.

Marta sighed. 'Nisida, Bologna Juvenile, then Dozza. And you, Habib? What luxury hotels have you stayed in?'

It was as if she had been doing this forever: seducing boys outside the station.

He admitted, 'I did a spell in Beccaria.'

'Oh, I always know one when I see one.' Marta winked at Emilia, who was speechless. She had suddenly gone from the mountain of omission and lies in Sassaia, the continual anxiety of hiding everything, to this Milanese night in which they were chatting about the past with perfect strangers, without embarrassment or shame.

'Have your friends done a spell or two as well?' Marta continued. It was a rhetorical question: the best friends of inmates are always from inside. Habib nodded before returning to his goal. 'Shall we get a drink?'

'Not this evening. My friend is shattered. And the bars I like wouldn't let you in anyway.'

All three of them protested bitterly.

'You have to study first.' Marta said it with a new, almost maternal tone of voice that Emilia had never heard before. 'Get yourselves a degree in economics or law, then you can get married to someone like me.'

'You haven't been inside.'

'I have. I just used my time well.'

'You're pissing me off, cougar.'

'Oh, I quite like you. Give me your number, maybe I'll call you.'

Habib stepped backwards, stunned.

Marta retrieved a pen from her bag, passed it to him and put the back of her hand out towards him. 'Write it here.'

'Why did you do that?' Emilia asked once they were in the taxi.

'What were you telling me before, on the phone? That you missed prison? Well, so do I.' Marta looked out of the window. 'Do you remember when we used to fantasise about them putting the women and men together? That all those damned boys would come to the convent?'

'I've had my heart broken. I don't feel like having fun.'

'Even if I let you have Habib?'

'He's got curly brown hair; he'd just remind me of him.'

'But did you see how beautiful he was? Young, pure. You don't have to explain anything, you don't have to hide anything, you just fuck and it's all clean. If you're lucky, you get a whiff of the cell still on his skin.'

Emilia stayed silent for a while. The taxi slipped between sumptuous apartment buildings, discount stores, fast-food chains with lights in the window saying 'open', even at that time. Then she said to Marta: 'You can't do this.'

'Can't do what?'

'Live out a seventeen-year-old's fantasy at thirty.'

'I take them to a hotel, my dear. Never home, of course.'

'And you pay?'

'Always. I'm basically buying them. And they like it.'

The taxi driver, who had been pretending not to listen, glanced at Marta in the rear-view mirror.

'He was, like, ten years younger than us.'

'Exactly. I'm not interested in the older ones. They remind me of my father.'

Emilia couldn't stop herself. 'Why did he search for me?'

'Because they always search, Emily. They sniff out the silences, the hesitations, the inconsistencies. And they just can't respect the boundary; they have to cross it, because they believe they have the right to, even though they're only burning themselves. They find something in the papers – don't even get me started on the papers – and they fly into a panic.' Marta smiled. 'That's why I pick guys up at the train station.'

The night was lit almost like daytime; continuously traversed, devoured. Emilia couldn't help missing the woods.

'The colleagues I've been out with all presented like tough guys, muscles perfected in the gym, but the only violence they'd ever seen was on Netflix. They had everything easy: school, career, a little family. They'd never been to the cemetery, never needed to think about the fact that you die in this world. But Habib has slept in the station, you can tell.' She kissed the phone number he had written on her skin in biro. 'He has had to swim to avoid drowning, has risked killing and being killed. He's hungry, and he'll have sex with me because of it.' She leaned forward to point out a shortcut. 'I prefer going this way, thanks.' Then she returned to stretching out on her seat, opening her designer leather bag. 'My colleagues never made me come.'

The taxi driver hadn't said a word the whole time. When he got out and opened the door, Marta passed him her credit card. As he put it into the reader, both girls were aware of the bulge in his trousers. Marta signed the receipt. He kept looking at her for a long time, stubbornly, as she got out and walked to the grand wooden door. Before going inside, Marta stared him directly in the face and shot him a nasty smile. Beauty was her curse. But she knew that now, she was used to it, and she stared him down with the hate that, like her beauty, had never left her.

Finally, since he didn't understand, she flattened her hand, brought it to her neck, and mimed the cut of a blade over the jugular.

The taxi driver got back in the car and drove away.

When Emilia first arrived at the convent, the school was already well underway, albeit with half the hours of normal schools, and no special educational needs teachers despite the need for them. The classrooms were overseen by the army, who kept the doors locked, and the girls were constantly smoking and tapping ash onto the floor. The patience of the teachers was worthy of sainthood; they explained over and over again the same declarative subordinate proposition, the same Punic War, the same maths equation. But what did it matter? At least there was a school.

In October of 2001, Emilia sat down at a desk alongside Vargas, Myriam, a Romanian girl and a ridiculously blonde Slav. Pandolfi, the Italian and history teacher, gave her a warm welcome, telling the others enthusiastically, 'Our new classmate has come from classical high school!'

The ridiculously blonde girl turned up her nose. The other one grimaced in disgust. Myriam, who had always been a bitch, pretended to vomit. Clearly none of them liked her highborn origins. But her charge was known. Word got around quickly in there. The second someone new came in, everyone already knew the why and the how and would play at guessing the length of their sentence. In Emilia's case, the TV news had practically boomed into every cell: 'Oh, this one will be on your team in volleyball tomorrow!' So yes, Emilia might have been dressed in too much designer clothing, might have had a wealthy family behind her, but her crime was hefty, and she inspired fear and respect. And indeed, that day, Vargas had given Myriam a slap around the neck to remind her how things worked in there. And the other two had understood.

Emilia didn't breathe, she just tortured a corner of her lined notebook. Then Pandolfi violently slammed down the Italian literature textbook in front of her, bringing back the rules of school where the rules of jail were prevailing.

'Giuseppe Ungaretti,' she announced vehemently. '*Morning*'.

Vargas and the Romanian girl already had cigarettes in their mouths, sprawled out in a way that would've been enough to warrant a note in the register at Emilia's last school. Myriam was drawing a huge unicorn in her notebook. Emilia found the courage to look up and observe the scene, and couldn't believe what she saw.

She had been hurled from a class in which she was always the last, the worst, constantly at risk of failing, to one in which she could excel. Vargas, seeming to intuit her thoughts, smiled as she blew smoke in the direction of Pandolfi's face. The teacher kept reading out loud, undaunted: '*I'm illuminated with immensity*'.

'Jesus, is it over already?' 'Is that all it is?'

Despite the comments, she continued, 'But listen: *I'm illuminated*, pause, *with immensity*'. And she went on with more: *We are as / in autumn / on branches / the leaves*, and then more: *in this poem / that nothing / remains to me / of an inexhaustible secret.* Myriam scratched her bum, while the other two let that twentieth-century Italian settle in some part of their brains and their destinies. Beyond the bars, a bright sunny day clamoured in Bologna. Almost four months had passed since her arrest and Emilia thought for the first time that maybe, *maybe*, she wasn't in hell.

Now, fifteen years later, she and Marta got into a wooden lift with a wrought-iron door. The mirror reflected the image of two opposites: one a beauty, one disgusting, one elegant, one a hobo. But it was only appearance. Deep down their hearts were the same.

The lift came to a halt at the third floor and Marta led Emilia along the corridor. The apartment was from the early 1900s, with Liberty decor that Emilia recognised and silently relished. On the tag above the bell of the door at the end was written VARGAS. Fair, thought Emilia.

Marta's story had caused an uproar. Between the front-page news and the evening TV shows, debates fired up among those who knew nothing about the realities of a life in the margins, but always had something to say about it. She'd caused a scandal, for sure, but nothing compared to Innocenti's story. Because unlike Innocenti, Vargas had a justification, a solid motive.

Vargas opened the door wide for Innocenti and turned on the light, revealing a living room crammed with books from floor to ceiling, a flat-screen TV as big as a cinema screen and, in the middle, a white leather sofa that at least five people could fit on.

'Fuck me,' commented Emilia.

'Go and have a shower.' Marta helped her take off her jacket, scarf and fleece and put them straight in the washing machine. 'The bathroom is there. Clean towels are in the cupboard next to the sink.'

The white-tiled bathroom was warm and cosy – nothing like the icebox in Iole's house. Emilia got undressed and sat on the toilet seat. She moved the blind to look out of the window, but there were no mountains, no moon, no stars.

Marta walked in precisely at the moment Emilia, naked, was wiping herself with toilet paper. They exchanged looks with an embarrassment they wouldn't have felt in Bologna: they were too old now to pee together.

Marta saw the cuts, old and new, on Emilia's arms. She said nothing, but took a bottle of disinfectant from the cupboard and placed it on the sink where Emilia couldn't miss it. Emilia started to realise that, despite the strength of certain memories, time continued to exist, manoeuvring covertly, and ruined everything.

She got into the shower quickly. Marta stayed sitting on the floor nearby, in her knickers. A minute passed that way, divided by the glass and the years gone by. While she lathered up with the sponge, Emilia said: 'You must earn loads to be able to pay for a place like this.'

'This was always it, wasn't it? Freedom.'

'You must be proud.'

She heard Marta sigh. Although she was getting cold, she didn't turn the water back on so she could listen to her friend's silence instead.

'Sometimes I think I'd like to have a daughter just so I could pay for her piano lessons,' Marta said in her new voice, the same one she used with Habib outside the station. 'To pay for her to do synchronised swimming, gymnastics, theatre classes. Never volleyball. If I had a daughter, all this money would make sense. I could admire her onstage at the end-of-year show, sit in the stalls and proudly watch the little girl I could never be. When I was ten, I already knew all about hand jobs, blow jobs, anal sex. But she would only have to worry about singing and playing. About shining. And I would shine through her.'

Emilia switched on the water again and turned the temperature up. She put her head under it, closing her eyes. She still hadn't cried since I had shoved that sheet of paper in her face. And now, in the secret of the water, she wanted to.

'It's a shitty subject,' she said when she got out of the shower.

Marta handed her a towel.

'I don't think I'll have children, don't worry. I wouldn't want to inflict a father on anyone.'

Emilia would've liked to say that not all fathers were equal, that there were wonderful ones too. But from what pulpit: privilege?

Emilia would've liked to say that she had gone to dance lessons, and music, and swimming, but had never emitted so much as a flicker of light that could make her parents proud.

The past didn't matter anymore. They were in a bathroom again, at night, alone. Emilia sat down on the floor on the mat opposite her friend, her hair dripping down her face.

'When I realised I was in love with Bruno, I asked myself, what if I get pregnant? Or if we stay together, and then he wants a child? How do I tell him? That no child would deserve my suffering?'

A tear sparkled between two of her eyelashes, held like frost between blades of grass.

'My father has already paid, and he had nothing to do with it.'

Marta took her hands, squeezed them and shook her head hard. But Emilia nodded, certain: 'My story ends with me.'

23

Silence had returned to Sassaia, dense like a cloak of cloud. I had taken up the habit of walking alone in the frozen forest again, and I was on my way home. It was dark; it must have been about five. How many days had passed? It must only have been three or four, but it felt like years. In the narrow alleyways between the empty houses near the washhouse, I stopped suddenly and pointed the torch.

I saw her again. Clear as day. Vomiting.

She was pulling herself up out of the water having washed herself and was looking at me.

I heard her ask me again to help her get to sleep that evening.

I ran home as fast as I could, locking the door behind me.

After dinner there was a knock on the door. It could only have been one person, but I jumped all the same. I put down the plate I was washing and went to open the door.

Basilio didn't even take his jacket off. 'What's happened?'

I turned my back to him and returned to washing my plate.

I heard him pull out a chair and sit down.

'Do you want a coffee? Something else?'

'I want to know where Emilia is.'

I turned off the tap. 'I don't know.' I put the plate down again, aware that I had been washing it over and over, and went to sit down across the table from Basilio. 'But she's left.'

'Why?'

'Because I know who she is. And I don't want anything to do with it.'

'Did she tell you herself?'

'Patrizia Rocellati.'

Basilio slammed his fist down on the table uncharacteristically. 'That jealous witch.'

'You knew.' My voice was full of resentment. 'I was the only fool who didn't.'

Basilio took off his glasses and put them into his jacket pocket, rubbing his eyes.

'I think that's why Iole died. She was in shock. She couldn't believe it; she loved that niece of hers. She only talked to mc about it, the news didn't spread up here. Too distant a relative, and it had already been a few years since they last visited by the time Emilia's mother got sick. Nobody in Sassaia or in Alma put two and two together. I mean, we don't even have television.'

'She always denied that she even knew Iole.'

'She wanted to protect you.'

'Please.'

'I saw her, the way she would leave the church to meet you. The way she talked about you. I don't know if I've ever been in love, I don't remember anymore. But I know it when I see it, when it happens to others.'

'I was the wrong person.'

'You were or you are?'

I looked at him. 'Leave me alone.'

'That woman carries hell inside. Nobody will ever take that away. And yet, in spite of it all, she fell in love.' He stood up. 'The two of you brought this place back to life. Who are you to condemn her to another sentence? She's already been judged, Bruno, sent down, and she served her time.' He put his glasses back on. 'None of us contains only one person.'

I remained seated. 'I can't do it.'

'I'm not saying it's easy. I'm just saying you were happy.'

'But how can you get married, have children, plan a life with a person like that?'

'*Emilia*, not "a person like that".'

'OK. But how do you do that?'

Basilio headed towards the door.

'When did you start thinking this way? That there's only one kind of life: marriage, children? Since when have you been so fixed on being like everyone else?' He stood still for a second, lost in thought. Then he just said: 'It's a shame the *Judgement* of Alma will remain unfinished. I can't go on without her.'

When he closed the door I covered my face with my hands. My beard had grown back; solitude only took a short time to return, the way weeds did, or an infestation of insects. I forced myself to go to school. To make food.

To keep the house tidy. I couldn't speak to or look at Patrizia, though. I had only managed, in an extreme sacrifice, to implore her once more to please not tell anyone, especially now Emilia had left – there was no need to rub salt in the wound. But she didn't seem particularly surprised by the news. She just nodded, neither satisfied nor relieved. She had already destroyed everything; the rest didn't matter.

I, on the other hand, had stopped sleeping. I stayed awake until late at night, drinking and torturing myself. The idea had even popped into my head of phoning Gisella so we could smoke ourselves dumb together, and fuck.

That evening I finished an entire bottle of génépy, then, at two or three in the morning, stone drunk, I went outside and crossed the alley. I bent down, lifted her doormat and picked up the key. She had left it there for me, I was sure. She had known I was watching her as she hid it. She wanted me to do what I was about to do.

I turned the key in the lock and went inside. The kitchen was freezing. I turned on the light. It was a mess. She had been in a rush and had left tracks everywhere. A hairbrush on the sink with two red hairs caught in it. A glass on the table half full of water, with her cocoa butter fingerprint on the edge. Her hiking boots.

I went upstairs and into the bedroom lit by a dribble of moonlight. I walked over to the bedside table, took a match, struck it and lit all five of the candles. Then I moved the doll and wedged myself into the armchair. I took Mandelstam out of the inside pocket of my jacket, opened it at random and read out loud, adjusting the pauses and looking stubbornly over at the empty bed:

Can't snooze among strangers –
Only death, and this little stool, for company.

I let the silence bury those verses. Then I got up. I took off my trousers and threw myself onto the bed. I took myself in my hand. And sobbing, for the first time, I told her I loved her. And that she mustn't come back. That I wanted her. But that I didn't have the strength.

After the orgasm I fell asleep there, fully clothed under two blankets. It was three or four degrees in the room at most. I buried my face in what remained of her smell.

'And so, what are you?'

They responded in chorus, together, sure of themselves: 'Inmates.'

'Oh no, my dears.' Pandolfi shook her head, smiling like someone who's seen it all before. 'You are students.'

'What the fuck, Miss?' they protested, like their pride had been damaged.

'This is a school, and you are its attendees.'

'There are bars, don't you see? And anyway, outside we'll always be ex-convicts.'

'I am paid by the Minister for Education, not the Minister for Justice.'

All that trouble for Dante, for the XXVI canto of the *Inferno*, the one with *You were not made to live as brutes but to follow virtue and knowledge* that Frau wanted to have painted on the walls in the corridors.

'But Miss, even if we call ourselves students from now on . . . it's not like calling something by a different name changes what it is.'

'That's where you're wrong!'

Pandolfi was fired up that morning: 'She must've gone out with a guy', '. . . or she's had a joint'. They were all smoking one cigarette after the other, sluggish, because what else can you do in prison? Lavish little smirks and obscene comments on that good-natured woman who had got it into her head to make them study in prison, even when others had done everything they could to dissuade her. There was nobody who hadn't said: 'You won't do it'.

In the meantime, from the corridors came the usual screeching of the walkie-talkies: 'so-and-so's coming up', 'so-and-so's arriving', 'so-and-so's at a visit', 'they're all going out for fresh air'. Keys turned and doors slammed. Britney Spears or Christina Aguilera or whoever it was whined out of one cell, and from another seeped the sound of a too-loud TV playing a repeat of a dating show. While all that chaos – the shouting, the keys, the doors, the walkie-talkie, ceaseless – was going on under every vault of the convent, Pandolfi took the bull by the horns.

'You want to be called inmates? Fine. But you have to call yourselves students too, because you are also that. And are you daughters, or not? And friends, or enemies? Girlfriends, some of you. Mothers, others. People with dreams of becoming models, chefs, singers, volleyball players. You're sporty, or arty, some of you are even readers. You're a hundred, a thousand words! But the most important of all of them remains,' she pronounced clearly, in a very loud voice, '*students*.'

She stood up and began to walk around the little classroom with its whiteboard, map of the world and yellow, green and blue desks like in primary school. But it was prison, and there was no denying that. They were 'young inmates', because that's what was written on all the signs in the corridors: 'Notice to young offenders'. They were convicts. Branded. Stamped. Decreed. Always and forever.

'*Students* is a word that contains a movement, a transition. *Students* is a word that carries you out of jail. Not just that, but it also changes what you have in your head, the ways you think about yourselves. The ways you've been brought up. The ways others have watched and judged you – as if people could either just be 'right' or 'wrong' for their whole lives! Change is in our nature. Language,' – her eyes lit up – 'brings the first possibility of change. Because yes: if you call yourselves something different, you can *be* something different.'

Marta had opened her mouth to contradict Pandolfi, but had second thoughts. She lit yet another cigarette. Maybe that was the moment she decided to become that one case in a million that Frau would one day present with great pomp to the ministry.

In the classroom, the girls had all gone silent. Pandolfi launched headlong back into Dante and the foolish lunatic

Ulysses who didn't want to take it easy, mind his own business, make money, bring water to his mill, find himself a woman, set fire to his shitheap of an island. He wanted to know. To go. To be something other than what he'd been told he was.

Verse after verse, phrase after phrase, Pandolfi led her lovely class of ragamuffins, which was continuously changing as inmates came and went, sixteen-year-olds who were fresh to reading and writing and twenty-year-olds with no more than a middle school certificate, the overwhelming majority of whom had special educational needs or disabilities, all dedicated smokers. She didn't leave anyone behind and patiently led the class over the Pillars of Hercules to their diploma.

Marta's alarm went off at 6:30 a.m. on Monday. Spooning in the double bed, they woke and got up immediately, the same way they had done for so long.

Emilia made breakfast. She had already learned where the cups and cutlery were, and the juicer. They had coffee together in silence. It was strange now that the weekend was over and Marta had to go back to work, resume her routine in which Emilia was a perfect stranger. Neither of them really knew how to act.

As Marta put her makeup on, Emilia made the bed and hoovered. She noticed a glass ring on the dresser and went to find the polish and a cloth.

'Leave it be . . .' Marta said as she threaded her feet into a pair of red stilettos.

'I don't want to just scrounge off you – at least let me clean.'

Marta grabbed her bag, and gave Emilia a serious look from the doorway. 'Eat. There's stuff in the fridge and you've got your hospitality certificate so I'm sure you can cook. The computer's over there, you can look for some ideas of things to see in Milan. Head out, go for a walk. I'll leave the keys here and a hundred euros, OK? Buy yourself something nice.' Emilia listened to her uneasily, the hoover in her hand. Marta wasn't finished with her commands: 'I'll be back at seven. Call me if there's anything you need. Ah . . .' she was about to finish, but at the last minute she turned back with a nasty smile. 'And we need to decide what to do with Habib . . .'

She closed the door and disappeared for real. Outside, into that unknown and too-big city. Emilia was alone in the empty apartment, still in her pyjamas, clutching the hoover. She put it down and finished her cold cup of coffee, before pulling on her clean, nice-smelling jacket and going out onto the balcony to smoke.

She looked at Milan. It meant absolutely nothing to her. The high-rise buildings, the Sky and Intimissimi billboards stretching above the rooftops. A solitary poplar tree in the middle of a roundabout. Cars, cars, cars. *What do I do now?*

She saw the scaffolding in front of her eyes, Basilio turning towards the left side door to check whether she had arrived yet. But she wasn't going to. She couldn't. That life there, that long-debated, daring, risky plan was over, and no other plan awaited her.

That weekend she and Marta had only gone out once, to buy groceries. The rest of the time they stayed at home, locked in like in their old cell, on the sofa eating rubbish in front of the TV. Getting drunk and talking. Drinking all of the alcohol they weren't allowed at the time. Telling each other all there was to tell of the years they had spent apart, without even permission to phone each other at the start – only letters, like it was the nineteenth century, or like they were in two different trenches in one of the World Wars.

'Wasn't it romantic, though?' Emilia said.

'Uh, your handwriting was terrible, I could barely read it.'

'Yes, but the things we told each other in those letters? They were everything.'

'Did you keep them?'

'Of course. I even kept the little notes from the Neighbour!'

When Emilia was still at young offenders and Marta at the adult prison, and then when Emilia moved to the adults and Marta had been released, they wrote at least once a week – sometimes entire A4 sheets, sometimes just two lines, but the important thing was for the other one to feel their presence, even if, in Emilia's case, the words sometimes ran together, or were misspelt or just plain wrong, which Marta hated.

Then, when Emilia moved into community, they could phone. With obstructed breath, deafening pauses, the voice of one breaking the heart of the other. Marta had a mobile at this point, even if it was a decade later than normal people. Emilia, however, was still attached to the landline connected by the community calling cards. Eight years apart, then three days clinging on to one another, woven together, inseparable. In overalls, like old times. The world outside, now available, didn't interest either of them.

Emilia was smoking now, her elbows resting on the balustrade of the balcony. She imagined me cleaning the house; my coat wrapped around me up Stra' dal Forche; at the counter in Rosa's buying bread; in the school playground watching over my little pupils who could do no wrong. And she immediately extinguished those images, closing her eyes to erase them.

Then her phone rang in the living room for the hundredth time. She threw her cigarette down into the traffic below, went back inside and resigned herself to answering. 'Hi, Pa.'

'Emilia, I haven't been able to get hold of you for three days. That is not OK.'

He was angry.

'Don't worry, I'm in Milan with Marta.'

'In Milan?'

He was worried.

'It was her birthday yesterday,' she lied.

'What about your job?'

'We've almost finished so Basilio gave me a week off.'

'Oh.' She hadn't convinced him. 'How is Marta?'

'She's great.'

'And you?'

'Fine, thanks.'

'Your voice sounds strange.'

'Pa, really. I'm doing great. Milan is so cool.'

'When do you head back?'

She couldn't respond.

'Emi, are you there? I wanted to tell you that Aldo has found an electrician. He can come and put up a satellite dish next week whenever it suits you.'

Emilia stared at a random point in the sky, which was opaque, heavy, its smoggy haze pushing down on the rooftops. Here and there a chimney pot emerged, an antenna, an air vent. No horizon.

What does it mean *to die?* she wondered.

The heart stops, OK. The neurons cease transmitting messages; the brain turns off. But what do you actually *experience?* Pain? What do you think as you die? What do you remember, what do you see? Is there something that comforts you? That you can hold on to? Because *you* couldn't be *just a body.*

'I don't want a TV anymore.'

'Are you joking?'

'No,' Emilia confirmed abruptly, 'I don't need one anymore.'

24

Gisella and I were introduced by a mutual friend, a guy from the equally empty village next to Sassaia who had built a marijuana greenhouse sheltered by the woods behind his house.

In abandonment you're freer to transgress; to be reborn or even end up losing yourself. In 2004 my objective was the latter as I fled Turin in the middle of the night. I filled the boot of the Seat with books and the few items of clothing that hung in my student wardrobe without saying goodbye to my housemates, without cancelling my contract for the house we were renting, without finishing my PhD. This string of withouts in tow, I drove at full pelt away from the city lights, away from the future and towards my dark mountains.

When I arrived, the Sassaia house was sunk in dust. I stared at the framed photo in the entrance hall for a long time: my mother, my father, Valeria and I on Monte Casto, on a Sunday hike. All four of us were smiling, rucksacks on our backs and walking sticks in our hands. Valeria had a flower between her teeth. Wherever I went, I would always come back and bump straight into this.

I took it down and put it in the attic. Unable to sleep, I waited until the sun was high in the sky and called Sebastiano, the only one of the old group who didn't have children, or a wife or girlfriend. The only one who hadn't moved to Turin or Milan to seek out a more decent job than being a drug dealer and cultivator of, he specified, an 'organic and mafia-free' product. That evening we met at his house, which you could call a restructured ruin, and smoked ourselves into oblivion. I fell into a state of unconsciousness that was all I had desired. I emerged from it painfully, hours or days later, lying on the ground with a dog licking my face. And I keenly felt the angst of being alive.

Twenty-five, and I didn't know what to do with myself. I didn't want to seek out new horizons only for the money to run out, after which I'd die in Sassaia of hunger or cold, or else I'd survive only on chestnuts and rot away, wrapped in old blankets.

The boxes from Turin would remain in the boot for a whole year, during which time Sebastiano and I would do nothing but get stoned at my house or his, stumbling down alleyways so deserted that nobody could judge us or save us. We soon started complementing the joints with ketamine and LSD, washing them down with génépy. We vomited in the snow. We listened to black metal at a volume high enough to chase away the sea of forest animals that surrounded us. We talked shit, slurring our words. We cooked panfuls of polenta that we gulped down at any hour, preyed on by the munchies. If we went out at all, it was to drink in some godforsaken bar in Valle, surrounded by old men playing cards, who would greet us lazily with, 'Here come the twits.' Two perfect nihilists, with one difference: Sebastiano sometimes wanted to fuck. And I didn't.

Rather than staying alone, I would go down to the valley with him in the Seat Ibiza, to Le Piane Hotel, and that was where I met Gisella. She was lying on a small sofa, laughing, latched onto a guy who was pouring Prosecco partly into her glass and partly down her cleavage. It was the middle of winter, but she was wearing a pair of fishnet tights under a ridiculously short black leather miniskirt. I was struck by her wonky teeth and her face, thin like a young girl's although she must have been almost forty. You couldn't really call her beautiful, no. Beaten to a pulp by life, yes. But her laughter was so genuine it warmed what was left of my heart.

Sebastiano and I waited as she disappeared with the guy and then came back, and finally we bought her a drink at Le Piane bar, which gleamed in the middle of the frozen rice fields, the fog so thick you couldn't see more than a few steps in front of you. It looked like the underworld. In that otherworldly place we became familiar, joking like old schoolmates, as if there was no money involved.

Sebastiano had been a client of hers for years and supplied her with marijuana. In those months I had been draining the compensation money on drugs and petrol. The idea of working in a school, of teaching the alphabet and correcting punctuation written by a small hand grasping a pencil hadn't yet passed through the antechambers of my brain. But I knew that I wouldn't spend the cable car money on a prostitute: that was the line I wouldn't cross.

So I waited downstairs in the lobby, that time. Sitting on a threadbare armchair, lost in my own void. I reached out towards the plywood table in front of me and picked up the sports pages, *TV Times* and *Gossip*, flicking through them while Sebastiano and Gisella did their stuff in a room upstairs. And I thought about how this proximity to others having sex, their slightly chaotic companionship, could be enough for me.

They wandered along the Navigli, holding each other tight against the cold; Marta at ease in her heels, Emilia, who had so desired to wear them, now having to cling to her friend's arm to avoid falling over.

'It's nice here, isn't it?'

Emilia nodded, but she felt uneasy. Not only because of the patent leather stilettos and elegant black bodycon dress Marta had lent her, but also because of all the people filling the bars and restaurants, waiting outside for a table, laughing without a care in the world. She observed them, those couples, those groups who looked like they were enjoying life, feeling that still, at thirty-one years old, she and they didn't belong in the same world.

'Do you remember Vilma?' Marta asked her.

'Of course I do.' They had both had her as a youth worker.

'Sometimes memories come back to me . . . Little things, but they feel, I don't know . . . *significant*,' said Marta.

'Like?'

They stopped on a bridge, hugging their too-light coats around them. The wind lashed at their faces, which were so heavily made-up they looked like masks.

'Like one time I stopped at a book stall in Montagnola Park. I was on my way back from volunteering at the old people's home. God, I loved them, those little old folks.' She smiled. 'They knew where I came from and yet they still called me their "favourite granddaughter". Maybe because they didn't have the internet.' She winked.

She rummaged in her bag in search of the Camel Lights. She put one between Emilia's lips, the other between her own and lit them both.

'Anyway, the book stall. I saw this book, a paperback. A famous one, that even you who don't read would've heard of: *Crime and Punishment*. I was obviously curious. I could hear that Vilma was calling me, and I knew I couldn't stand there thinking about it and get back late. What is it they always said?' Marta blew the smoke out and mimicked a baritone voice: '"You have to show remorse. You have to show awareness." – the magistrate, the lawyer, all of them pontificating on repentance. So I, who had just five euros, bought myself Dostoyevsky.'

They started walking again because it was too cold to stand around. The canals were still and black as the night-life raged happily all around, in waves, in the great sea of the night.

Emilia knew that Marta wasn't capable of remorse, not deep down. They had confided in each other once when they were alone clearing tables in the canteen. Emilia was seventeen then, Marta twenty. Two brief stories, full of holes. Especially Emilia's, which took only three words. But friendship required that specific confession: you can't not say why you're in prison, and anyway, it was hardly a secret.

But it was the very things that everyone else knew that were, for them, *the unspeakable things*; to say 'I' next to certain verbs sounded unreal. They went and pricked their fingertips with the razor blade they'd hidden under the mattress straight afterwards. That was when Marta confided, 'I hate myself. But I'm happy to have saved my mother'. They never spoke about it again. Not even when Marta's mother died of cancer, just like Emilia's had, and Marta wasn't given permission to go to the funeral so as to '*maintain propriety*' and avoid any tension. Not even when it had become clear that in this world nothing could be saved.

'I started reading *Crime and Punishment* and fuck me, I was absorbed. I was unbelievably absorbed. I didn't sleep because I just had to keep reading.'

'You'd spend the night with any book, you.'

'No, Emi, this one was different. Something was happening to me that in real life could never happen to me: I was falling in love. I mean, not just turned on, fully falling in love with Raskolnikov. He understood me, I understood him. If he had been real, I would've waited for him outside his jail until the day I died. Then, just as I'm getting to the best bit, Vilma bursts into the cell. 'What are you reading?' She went nuts when she saw what it was – "Oh this is no good for you!" – and confiscated it. Do you get what I'm saying?'

Emilia paused on a little wall to undo her shoes – she couldn't handle the heels anymore – laughing because that's just how Vilma was: overprotective.

'Like,' Marta shook her head, 'I'm inside for murder, and you take Dostoyevsky off me?'

'She wanted to protect us.'

'Yes, but from ourselves? From our own crimes?'

Emilia turned around, tossed her cigarette butt and stared at the reflection of the lamplights trembling on the dense petrol-black water. The word 'murder' had fallen between them, like any other word. But of course, it wasn't.

Marta had said it like it was a fact of life, because it *was* a fact of life. But it wasn't one that fitted into the normal sequence of events, just one thing amidst many. It was a kind of sinkhole for the future to cave into.

'They knew us for everything else,' Emilia said. 'They saw us in our pyjamas, reading our books, cooking . . . They loved us. For the rest of us, I mean; not for the bad stuff.'

It was moving to think about them now, under the big night sky of Milan. Rita, Venturi, but also Frau, Pandolfi and some of the guards they were fond of, who used to cheer them up when they were struggling to get out of bed in the morning. Vilma, too – she seemed like a classic old spinster, but she put so much effort in. She was obsessed with the garden and adored taking them out there, teaching them how to plant a bulb and water it, as if all that gardening could cleanse them and make them innocent again. And maybe it worked for the others, the ones who were inside for dealing or shoplifting. But for them?

Marta was also staring at the lights rippling on the surface of the water in the wind; all that unmovable blackness underneath. She finished her cigarette and checked the time: they were late, but making them wait had been a calculated move.

'I went into a bookshop, like, my second day of freedom,' she crouched down to help Emilia put her shoes on again, 'and I bought another copy of *Crime and Punishment*. The most beautiful, most expensive edition I could find, with a hard cover and such pointy corners that if we'd had this book inside we'd probably have used them to cut our throats. I read it three times in a row, my Raskolnikov.' She took Emilia's arm and pulled her into the night: 'Right, let's see if Habib's up to it . . .'

At Porta Ticinese, the view of the Darsena docks reminded Emilia of the port in Ravenna and her stomach turned. Habib and his new, older-looking friend were waiting at the entrance to the bar, looking very smart. Emilia had no desire to flirt, absolutely none. But Marta was walking with long strides, untying her coat to show her neckline as she headed towards a reserved table, her tight trousers showing off her stupendous body that had been abused so obscenely as a child.

Some people have it – that strength – and Marta was one of them. A sort of ferocious attachment to life that meant that whatever happened while you were alive, even the most horrendous, most irreparable things, you had to live, to go on. Like Ulysses.

I was driving in the fog again, along the main road that ran straight through the fields which I now knew led not only to Le Piane, but also, after another ten or so kilometres, to the Tartana.

Emilia was sitting in the empty seat next to me. Her absence never left me. She asked again, enraged, 'Why? You think a woman would sell her body if she had a choice?'

I found a single free spot in the car park and drove in. It being a Friday night, the bar was full and even the hotel lobby felt lively. I got to reception, handed over my ID and went up the stairs to the third floor, room 52.

When I knocked, I was overcome by a heavy tiredness, as if driving there, back to the past, had been a swim across the ocean. Then Gisella opened the door, smiling at me with her overlapping teeth, and I saw myself again in her bruised and welcoming face.

'You look so sad,' she said.

I took off my jacket and collapsed onto the bed. This room had always been our room. The blinds lowered and mosquito net taut, both in the insect-infested summers and in freezing and desolate winters like this one. A little table with two glasses and a bottle, the windowless bathroom with the fan, the quilt that smelled of moths. Here, in full view, was my one relationship before Emilia.

See? I imagined saying to her now. *I kept secrets from you too.*

On the ceiling I projected her disgusted face as she curled her lip and lit yet another cigarette. *This is worse than my story about Emanuele. Marta would not approve.*

But think how clumsy I would've been with you, I replied, *if I hadn't had Gisella. We would still be stuck on Mandelstam.*

I heard Gisella's voice calling me back here, into the present, asking me what had happened. I gave myself a shake. 'Tell me about you first, Gise. How's your son?'

'He's in high school now!' she announced proudly as she poured us both a drink. 'We're getting on much better with his new foster family, and I think he might even be learning to forgive me.' She sat down close to me and passed me a glass. 'How long has it been since we last met?'

'Over a year, I think.' I pulled myself up and drank a long sip of mellow red wine, which warmed my body. I looked at her. 'I'm glad you're doing well.'

'So what's this mess you've got yourself into?'

'An enormous one.'

'It can't be that enormous! Compared to when I met you, you're a flower. No more red eyes, no more smell of weed . . .'

'I fell in love with the wrong person.'

'Ouch.' She poured more wine into our already empty glasses. 'Married?'

I laughed. 'Infinitely worse.'

'Addict? Degenerate mother? Whore?'

I nudged her shoulder with mine. 'Stop it.'

'I'm a beautician now, on a permanent contract, and I'm three years clean.'

'I know.'

'So, what's wrong with this girl?'

Between lost souls there's always a recognition, without the fear of judgement. I had always told Gisella everything, but I couldn't even think about saying that word now.

I got up and started walking around the room. Could I hope to resolve something by substituting one body with another? I distractedly picked up the remote control and turned on the small television: something I had never done before.

'She had some issues with the justice system.'

Channel 1, Channel 2, Channel 3. I stopped flicking at a shopping channel; I needed the background noise.

'But who hasn't made mistakes?' Gisella asked, not at all shocked.

'There are mistakes and *mistakes*.'

Sebastiano had done a night in prison once too. However hard he'd tried to conceal his evening there, there was always a Patrizia Rocellati around ready to identify the cracks in others.

But Emilia's story was different. The story of Emilia *Innocenti*. Whose surname was a tragic stroke of irony, like in the works of Aeschylus and Sophocles in which Fate is always there to mock and remind you that you're only a human being, only a breath.

I searched, naturally – everything there was to search. I turned the internet upside down and then went to the regional library to leaf through the newspapers from June, July and August 2001, pulling them out one by one from an archive so dusty it actually smelled of oblivion. I reconstructed the extremely short timelines of the investigation and arrest followed by the long and wearying trial, and then I had to stop. Because when it came to what happened after, there was silence.

Reading those articles was like having someone stand in front of you with a scalpel, opening your chest at an exasperatingly slow pace and doing open heart surgery with no anaesthesia. Because from those short articles, always accompanied by the same pixellated photo of her in the handcuffs, emerged a very disturbed girl, the kind of freak who one instinctively turned away from, ran away from shouting *monster!* – a deranged person who could never be forgiven, not even by God. And yet, as I lingered over the details retold with morbid pleasure by each journalist, I found her an inch away from me, in my arms. I saw her laughing, getting excited like that time in the washhouse in the snow, telling me she loved me outside the nightclub, and getting up after having fainted that first day at the viewpoint, with the terrified eyes of a deer. I could feel the heat of her living body, the good nature of an animal. While the sadistic surgeon was cutting me in half, I couldn't believe that the Emilia Innocenti of the articles and the one I had met were *the same person.*

'So? Should I distract you from her, or not?'

On the TV, a faded Wanna Marchi lookalike was pontificating about a tacky necklace, a Milan phone number running across the bottom of the screen. Gisella took both of my hands in hers and we stood in the middle of the room, suspended and insecure like my first time; the time I came alone, without Sebastiano, and put fifty euros on the bedside table for her to take away the burden, one among many, of being a virgin incapable of surrendering to life.

On the highway, as I had fled Turin at 150 kilometres an hour, the maximum I could push the Seat to; reopening my father's garage on the edge of Alma and sighing because I still missed his voice, missed being able to hug him; climbing up Stra' dal Forche as the sun was coming up and its pink light returned to me my unscathed island of stones among the chestnuts, my failure, my definitive entrapment in the wound, I was convinced that nobody in the world would ever be able to fix me.

But I was wrong.

'Gise,' I said, 'can we just sit and chat?'

Between November 2nd, 2015 and January 7th, 2016, I became whole again.

'I'll pay you for the bother.'

Gisella shook her head. 'You don't pay for friendship. And anyway,' her face bloomed into a new smile, 'I have choices now.'

25

June 2000, THE SUMMER Gigi D'Agostino and Ricky Martin boomed from every radio in every café, bar and beach club on the Riviera. The girls got on their scooters at two in the afternoon when the sun was at its highest point and rode in their thin, floaty sarongs to the sea.

Going to the beach without their parents' permission joined them together, right down to the marrow. On those escapades, continuously overtaking one another and beeping their horns, they became indistinguishable.

It was only a brief moment: the time it took to run the length of the highway and get to the pine woods with the wind in their hair. Once they'd reached their destination, the law of nature returned to rule.

They'd put their rucksacks down on the sand and get undressed, and the differences between their bikini-clad bodies separated them clearly. Curvy and skinny, developed and flat-chested. Essentially, Miss Beach and Carrot Head. One had many friends and boyfriends and a wonderful family, and one had none of those things. She had a father who was often away for work, a big empty house, and a heart dark in cavernous solitude.

She didn't get why the other girl was hanging out with her. Out of pity? Because they were neighbours? Their relationship had been marked by an essential ambiguity ever since the blonde princess moved with her whole picket-fence family into the house next door and had charitably, generously, invited the motherless child who was dawdling around her garden to play PlayStation.

The ambiguity was this: that they weren't proper friends, but they spent every afternoon together. That at home, they'd sit intertwined on her bed, bent over her brother's smutty magazines, brimming with complicity, yet in front of others Emilia had to keep her distance and wait on the reserves bench. So every time they arrived at the beach, there was always a jumble of all their classmates' towels together, their bodies stretched out and interlaced, and then there was Emilia's towel and Emilia's body over to one side. Isolated, excluded. Depending on the day, sometimes her body was mocked, sometimes tolerated, sometimes misled. Emilia's soul was never taken into consideration.

Carrot head. Who would ever fuck you? Ironing board. Poor motherless girl. The underdeveloped one. A couple of beach clubs down was Bagno Amore, where her mother no longer occupied the first sunbed in the second row, and could no longer turn to check Emilia hadn't hurt herself, wasn't being hurt.

There had been one day that summer, her first and last *free* summer, when the two of them arrived and the group wasn't there. They had got the wrong day, and the strip of wild coast between the beach clubs was full of families with their chaotically arranged umbrellas and cooler bags, but no classmates.

They laid their towels out all the same, the other girl profoundly disappointed, Emilia enthusiastic about the unexpected opportunity to be alone, just the two of them outside without the weight of the ceiling above their heads, and without the herd. She had always liked the sensation of having space, sky, horizon. They went in the water and swam together. But the idyll didn't last long. They were immediately approached by two grown-ups.

Two tourists; men. Who were heading, naturally, towards the other girl. The other girl had always desired to be fawned over, to be pursued.

They moved to the bar, their bikini bottoms wet against the plastic seats. The two grown-ups bought them a Cornetto each and proposed a *special, artistic thing*. 'Because did you know we're artists? We exhibit all over Europe.' Emilia immediately felt like dying. The other girl licked her ice cream, behaving like a worldly woman at fifteen, saying yes, yes, yes to the special and *artistic* thing.

So they walked together into the pine woods. Going all the way in until they reached the deep, dense, hidden part. There would be 'a surprise' the wolves had said, 'a present'. Emilia wanted to turn around and run away, but the other girl was annoyed and dragged her: 'You're a sissy. What do you think's gonna happen? There are two of us.' Two roses with a thorn each to defend themselves. And the tourists – in their forties, double their height, double their weight – asked, smiling, 'Aren't you scared?'

They convinced the girls to undo their bikini tops. They arranged them into a pose, adjusting their bodies into a suggestive composition on a half-rotten wooden picnic table, the hands of one resting on the wet bikini bottoms of the other. Then one of the men, the one with the beard, pulled out a piece of paper and pencil from his rucksack. And he drew them, clutching one another, bare-chested. The other guy told them to stay still in that position, and touched them lightly to arrange them better. Their nipples, groins, belly buttons, feet. The touching was disgusting, exciting and horrendous all at the same time.

Nothing else happened. Time passed and everything was consumed by stillness and imagination. Finally, the artist, as he defined himself, showed them his drawing. A detailed soft pencil sketch, and whether it was mediocre or brilliant the Emilia of then couldn't have said, but the Emilia of today, albeit through the fog of memory, judged it as fiercely remarkable – despite the tricky fact that those two men were nothing more than two wolves.

'So are you gifting it to us?' the other girl asked, brazen. He smiled again, his teeth blackened with smoke: 'Oh, no! This is a memory that you are gifting to us. Open your hands'. He thrust a twenty thousand lira banknote into each of their palms, which was more or less equivalent to their weekly pocket money. Emilia thought it was all all right, as long as they now left them alone. What they decided to do with that drawing afterwards didn't matter. What mattered was just that they didn't take their bikini bottoms off, that they didn't make them get down on their knees, kiss them, or who knows what else.

Yet she felt dirty, sullied all the same. As if through that bare-chested drawing paid for with forty thousand lira, those two men had stolen something from them, something intimate, something important. It was a disgusting, nauseating afternoon. And Emilia repressed it for years.

'Emi, are you there? Are you dreaming?'

'Is it a nice dream? Are we in it too?'

And then this evening, suddenly, maybe due to the fact of them being two girls and two guys, strangers yet already intimate, it erupted into her mind like a geyser. And she froze.

It was 1 a.m. They weren't properly drunk, but were certainly uninhibited, Marta and Habib especially. Emilia and Mohamed kept to the discreet role of 'chaperones'. The bar was still full, and you had to shout to be heard. Every so often someone glanced at them, curious, maybe because two (young) North African men and two (less young) Italian women were considered a noteworthy sight.

Habib's dark eyes shone with defiance. 'I just don't believe it,' he said to Marta, 'that you went from jail to . . . What did you call it? Anti-tumour drugs?'

Marta stretched across, her whole bust on the table, in an aggressive gesture.

'I'm not saying you're a liar. But, where were you? In a luxury young offenders?'

'No, it was a shithole.'

Habib looked at his companion and shook his head. 'I tried to study myself. I enrolled at the mechanics' technical college. But then they put me in a cell with this bastard who never washed and beat me up. I'd walk into the canteen and there would immediately be tension between us and the Chinese guys. There was a period when there were forty-two of us, and capacity was thirty-one, so we were always fighting, getting a new charge every day. I went in with a two-year sentence and came out having done three, pill popping, cutting, my life finished. And then I called my mother, and she'd got diabetes from the stress. And it was my fault. And then I just wanted to sleep and to smoke, and not to think.' His face was dark now. He seemed to have aged a hundred years as he recounted these things. 'Far from giving me an education, all prison did for me was raise my pain threshold.'

Marta looked up at him, amazed: you didn't expect certain phrases to come out of the mouth of certain big shots. But when you've suffered like a dog and your heart has been deeply excavated, it's complex. Emilia too stared at him in silence, and thought that he wasn't wrong. When you were in jail, the problems outside became enormous and you just swayed like a reed in the wind, powerless. There were the nice breezes, especially in springtime when the warmth arrived, the daylight hours got longer, and you were convinced you could do it, that you could change at least some small things. Then you didn't skip lessons, and insults and forks didn't fly across the canteen because you knew you would get to go back outside afterwards, you would get to see your father smiling at the next visit, you could overlook the bags under his eyes and the new wrinkles.

But then, like an axe, depression fell. Especially near Christmas, when a panettone advert could bring you to your knees. Or when a guard came to tell you your brother was in the hospital, or your mother or grandmother was dead. When at visiting time you saw your father in pieces, trying to hide it, and you knew you were responsible. Then it was as if the darkness swallowed you up, as if the cell no longer had doors or windows and was tightening around you, a rotten and poisoned placenta. The fireproof mattresses started to burn. You'd beg for pills in the infirmary. You'd cut your arms, you'd turn up at school once a week forty minutes late, because why would you want to get out of bed? When it was dark and cold outside, and scabies was going round inside. And the other people inside weren't all friends, there were also bitches, people who tormented you, whose faces you would've liked to smash. And it's not like you could say, 'I'm going out for a walk now to calm myself down'. No, you had to stay there, every hour, every day, your nerves on fire. Everything on fire.

What did the people outside know, Emilia thought looking at them, the ones sitting at the other tables? Yet now, she thought, she was outside too.

'It was a shithole,' Marta repeated after ordering the fourth or fifth bottle of wine, 'but it had its good points. High school, university: who would ever have gone to them outside? Certainly not me.'

'Why not?' Mohamed laughed. 'Did your parents not send you to school with a boot up your arse?'

'No.'

'I still remember my father's belt,' Habib intervened. 'Luckily he was put away in San Vittore.'

'Him in San Vittore, you in Beccaria,' Marta commented, 'that's called "the Cycle of the Defeated", and it never ends.'

Neither Mohamed nor Habib seemed like people who had read Verga, but they were smart and understood the concept.

Emilia checked her phone under the table. Nothing: no calls, no messages. Sassaia, she realised, was beginning to fade. Like a minuscule star in a distant galaxy. A barely perceptible glow, that was perhaps already extinguished, that perhaps never existed.

Why aren't I like you? she thought for the millionth time, looking at Marta who moved her hair out of her face, smoothing it down, preparing herself.

'Do you want to hear a story?'

Because everyone had one. And you could start from the top, write new chapters, turn the plot upside down, intensify the twists. But you couldn't rewrite old chapters – or delete them.

'There was once a girl . . . Let's call her Sonia.'

The bar was starting to empty out, and the background noise was diminishing.

'She was born in a town with 12,000 inhabitants, in a dry, flat place 120 kilometres from the sea, where no one had ever taken her. She saw the sea for the first time when she was seventeen, from the prison van. And then, for a brief period, from Nisida.' She smiled, as if it were still in front of her eyes.

'What a spectacle to wake up to Procida enveloped in mist, to see the waves and the seagulls . . .' Emilia felt Marta squeeze her hand under the table.

'But let's go back to the start. She lived in this shithole of a place, Sonia, so far up the arse of nowhere that it was already, in itself, a prison. There was only one nice thing in her childhood: a library, next to the school. It was practically deserted, frequented only by old people, but she liked it because there she wasn't surrounded by stupid classmates who had no problems. And nobody watched her in the bathroom like they did at home. It was like an escape.' She smiled again, and her eyes welled up. 'An escape from her life.

'The hours would pass there without her noticing. Until it got dark, until her mother got off her cleaning shift at the hospital and she could go home without the risk of being alone. She liked crime novels and science books. It was silent in the library: nobody shouted, nobody swore, nobody wanted to pull her knickers down or force her to give their friends a blow job. And so little Sonia did well at school. Her teachers noticed her bruises and told social services, and Sonia waited for them. She thought they would be able to save her and her mother. But since that place was so deep in the arsehole of nowhere, with just one shut-down factory, full of bitter, unemployed people and no fairy godmother like in the storybooks, social services never came. Just the perv remained.'

Emilia looked at the faces of Habib and Mohamed, serious and a bit pale. She knew the story, but they were listening to it for the first time and were struggling to keep drinking. They clutched their glasses in their hands before putting them down again without taking a sip.

There were fewer and fewer people in the room, more and more silence and attention around them. It was like being in court during the trial: the first time Marta had ever felt heard. Important.

'Sonia *always* went to school, never missed a day, because she knew that as soon as she set foot inside, she was safe. She hated the summer and Christmas holidays with her whole being, but September always arrived and brought liberation with it.

'Until *someone* decided that, with the end of middle school, Sonia's life could end. She had studied enough for a girl, and no one would come looking if she was kept home at fourteen. So Sonia, who lived in a fetid, crumbling apartment that was ironically right opposite the scientific high school, observed her ex-classmates every morning at eight as they walked in, all smiles and rucksacks. And she felt an enormous sense of injustice. But what is truly unfair? The cause or the consequence?

'If you want to know how I did it, Habib, how I studied in prison,' Marta looked up towards a waiter, one of the many who were now free, and ordered the last bottle of the evening, 'I'm telling you that as soon as I had an opportunity, the first real opportunity of my life, I grabbed it.'

The bar was closing. When the time came to pay, Habib took a roll of money wrapped in an elastic band out of his pocket, but Marta was emphatic: 'Please, put that away.'

They staggered out, shaken and silent. It was snowing lightly outside but it wasn't settling; it melted on contact with the tarmac, their coats, their hair. They walked to the Darsena docks. None of the four of them wanted to go home, not when there was still the sound of scooters and life all around them.

Then Habib, who was the youngest and bravest, grabbed Marta by the shoulders and gave her a long – a really long – kiss.

Mohamed took a bit of weed from his pocket and rolled a joint which they then passed around, joking and laughing. That kiss had somehow marked a full stop, and they had started again.

'What shall we do?' Habib asked, taking Marta's hand. 'Don't you two want to go to bed?'

Marta looked around until she saw a lay-by with a single taxi, its green light on, awaiting them. She ran towards it in her heels, beckoning them to follow her. Emilia took off her shoes and ran in the same direction, her tights getting soaked.

All four of them got in, and the destination Marta asked for surprised none of them. Now they were out, they couldn't afford to miss anything, ever again.

Once in the hotel, they handed over their ID and went up to the third floor. Then they split off into couples: Marta disappeared down the corridor to the left, her arm around Habib, Emilia and Mohamed to the right. But first she turned to look at her friend: premeditation as an aggravating factor even though she had been granted mitigating circumstances for the abuse she had suffered. And now she was kissing this boy she'd just met with such zeal it looked like they were in love. It looked like he loved her, in spite of everything.

She wondered: Why can't you, Bruno? Why can't you look at me and see *everything else*? Love me *in spite of*?

She and Mohamed had been silent for the entire evening, and now they found themselves in the same room with a bed in the centre.

Emilia went over to the window, pulled back the curtain and, lighting a cigarette, said immediately: 'I'm sorry, but I can't do anything.'

Mohamed sat down on the edge of the bed and he too lit a cigarette. 'Why not?'

'Because I'm already in love. Unfortunately.'

He nodded. He went over to her and leaned on the opposite side of the window frame. 'I have a wife in Tunisia, but I don't really know her. I was forced to marry her.'

They both looked out at the night. The moon emerging from behind a wall of clouds. The empty streets, closed curtains, no light except for the streetlamps. Suddenly, between the puddles of melted snow, Emilia saw two scooters speed by. A blue Phantom and a yellow SR, ridden by two girls in light sundresses and helmets covered in writing and stickers. She felt the cool of the pine grove on her skin, the carpet of soft needles under the rubber of her flip-flops.

Maybe that drawing still existed, she realised, somewhere on the earth. She and her entwined, bare-chested and languid, still existed. Maybe someone possessed that proof, had kept it. But proof of what?

She suddenly turned towards Mohamed. On an impulse, she took his hand and squeezed it.

'You Muslims, do you believe in the soul?'

26

The weeks passed idly. January became February; different names for the same cold. Winter in Sassaia is a time that wears so thin it's barely perceptible: a membrane. The heart beats slowly as if in hibernation. The hours of daylight are barely long enough to get the essential tasks done – going to and returning from work, getting food and wood – before darkness falls, heavy as a blanket of bricks. The cold pierces every bone with every gust of wind. The snow is hard, an old, imprisoning crust. The world shrinks down to the size of the warm fire in the stove.

I was alone again, but it wasn't like other winters. And this was the problem: when you've been happy, it's very difficult once you're not anymore.

I dragged myself around in a restless and resentful torpor, accumulating empty wine bottles outside the front door. I didn't read, I didn't clean. I didn't communicate with anyone who was over twelve.

Valeria had stopped responding to me again, and certainly hadn't called me back. Basilio greeted me reluctantly without slowing down to chat – he blamed me for the unfinished church. Every time I went down to Alma, everyone stared at me with a sharp, insistent gaze that said: 'Where's the redhead?'. They had a dark hunger to know, but didn't dare ask. 'What, you miss her now?' I wanted to shout.

Patrizia was going out with a guy from a nearby town now, *a married man*, everyone was careful to specify. She had new things to think about, or perhaps seeing me in ruins was enough for her. At school we didn't make eye contact, just communicated the essentials via email.

She was about to hit me with a moderate blow, but in these weeks I couldn't have imagined it. I was too busy brutalising myself. If it weren't for my pupils, my thirteen children in the abandoned valley, I would've stopped going into town altogether. Teaching spelling was the only life jacket keeping me afloat: 'Heart, hurt . . . There's no F in "enough".'

'Why?' they asked.

'There's no reason.'

'But what are the rules?'

'Language is a living thing; it doesn't always follow the rules. What was incorrect fifty years ago is correct now. We no longer call women *the fairer sex* because a woman's beauty is no longer considered her most important quality. The smartphone you all love so much is now in the dictionary. Some words die, others are born. It depends on their use, and on time.'

They looked at me, perplexed. 'So what do we do? If there are so many exceptions?'

'What do we do?' I found myself smiling despite myself. 'We make mistakes.'

I must have picked my phone up a hundred times. Calling her was out of the question. But where was she, how was she? I was drowning in wanting to know.

Ciao Emilia.

I tried writing a message and immediately deleted it.

I'm sorry. Are you OK?

But she was right: when you need words, they're never there.

This happened in mid-January, but at the end of the month I gave up and turned the phone off for good. Listening to its stubborn silence was too much, as if the silence of Sassaia, the forests, the mountains and myself, wasn't enough. I once again became the Bear, sealed in his cave. But while the weekdays rolled by, albeit like boulders, Saturday and Sunday were an unmoveable mass.

That's how one weekend, at dawn, I crossed the alleyway in my pyjamas, bent down to the doormat, took the key to the front door and, desperate, on an empty stomach, started sweeping Emilia's floors. Then, not satisfied, I cleaned the windows and dusted the shelves. I brought the duvets and the mattress out onto the balcony to air, plastered some cracks in the kitchen, repaired a little leak in the sink. Eight uninterrupted hours later Iole's old house had never been so clean.

I spent the following Saturday on the attic. I pushed the remains of unfixable furniture into binbags along with the broken bedside lamp and piles of mouldy newspapers. I pulled the thick cobwebs down from the ceiling. I was methodical, focused, feeling this visceral urge to clean, to purify. When there wasn't a speck of dust left, I tackled the garden. It was a jungle, the brambles climbing well above the top of the rusty fencing. I intuited from the peak of Cresto and Camino that the view from there would be exceptional, but neglect was concealing the horizon. I remembered Iole's roses, the pear tree in the middle, maybe a plum tree, but it was impossible to distinguish anything in that mess.

I armed myself with thick gloves, knee-high boots and shears, and neglected my own house to resuscitate hers. I launched myself into nettles the size of shrubs and sheared, attacked and trampled. It gave me a morbid joy to pounce into the middle of that primordial jungle and bring the law back to it myself, with violence. And as I found the roses, the twisted trunk of the hundred-year-old pear, the plum tree – as I liberated the fence from climbing deadly nightshade and reopened the garden onto the Alps – I felt like crying, 'Wait till you see this, Emilia . . .'.

Finally, one Saturday, I took the Seat and went to the city and bought a modest forty-inch television. I carried it on my shoulders up Stra' dal Forche, sweating like a pig, until finally, exhausted, I put it up on the sideboard in her kitchen. OK, we still needed an antenna, but I gazed happily at the black screen nonetheless.

Emilia, when will you be back . . .?

Knowing that it wouldn't happen. Because it was me who chased her away.

And now, while my world was reduced again to the same minuscule point on Earth, Emilia's was broadening uncontrollably.

She visited the Pinacoteca di Brera gallery four times, standing for a good half an hour in front of Mantegna's *Lamentation of Christ*. She walked past Hayez's *The Kiss* without deigning to look at it: for her, love was now a stale and disappointing subject.

Death, however, was still one of her favourites. Like it had been in her university days, when the professors who came to the prison were sheepish around certain topics because they knew full well who she was. Yet Emilia was a river in full flow when it came to the subject of bodies, souls and the existence of evil. She didn't assimilate the technical language of philosophy; words like *ontology* or *metaphysics* sounded as alien to her as the lives of her old classmates who were going out dancing in Riccione. But she knew full well what evil was. Hannah Arendt was right, it was *banal*. It was a wretched business, endless and confusing, with no easy answers. And her only way to put it in order was to scrutinise, study and try to reproduce on a sheet of paper the expression of that lifeless Christ.

She visited a Bosch exhibition at the Gallerie d'Italia, and another on Caravaggio – her favourite painter – at Palazzo Reale. She had dedicated her degree thesis to him. From no other artist had such a powerful and visceral spark sprung. He knew what evil was. He had experienced it in his life – in the flesh, in the first person. How else could he have transformed it into that dense and enormous darkness, cut by that blinding, divine light? How could he have represented so rotten a fruit, doomed from the inside, never ceasing to die?

She didn't dislike churches, and could spend hours sitting on a pew in Sant'Ambrogio or the Duomo in contemplation. The world, that for fourteen years she had only seen in books, was now hitting her with its beauty, leaving her knocked out and breathless. At the weekend, she and Marta went shopping, lingering over thousands of items in the changing rooms – all the dresses that hardly ever arrived in prison, folded up in parcels sent by relatives – then they met Habib and Mohamed for dinner. Who Marta, incidentally, had started to invite round to the apartment.

So as not to burden her friend financially, Emilia found a job in a fast-food restaurant. Her colleagues were all younger, second-generation immigrants, and she turned sizzling hamburgers from six in the evening until two in the morning. In the middle of the night she came home stinking of fat, and continued to smell even after a shower. Marta put up with it for a week, after which she told her, 'I respect all jobs, as you know. Even illegal ones if there's no alternative. But you didn't get a degree in fine art to tip sacks of frozen chips into rapeseed oil.'

'I don't have big ambitions. And it's not like Milan is gushing with opportunities for a fine art graduate!'

'You have to have ambitions. Did you put your CV in the right places? In all those museums you go to, private schools ... I don't know ...'

'Exactly, you don't know. The world is full of artists frying chips.'

'I know that I don't want to deal with your smell of chip fat anymore. So now,' she picked up her phone, 'I'm taking it into my own hands.'

Everything in life was solvable for Marta, because she felt she had already given enough of herself to the unsolvable. Over the course of a few days she found Emilia a little part-time fixed-term contract, which paid slightly better than the fast-food place. Emilia didn't appreciate it – on the contrary:

'What the fuck were you thinking?'

'How about thanking me, and off you go.'

'I had a hot colleague! There was life in there, and now you're sending me to work in a coffin!'

Marta burst out laughing. 'Are you serious? Don't you dare make me look bad in front of Signora Emma.'

They didn't talk for days. Marta was not open to discussing it further. She was the golden eagle, the lion, the black panther, while Emilia was an antelope, a gazelle, a raccoon.

So she quit the fast-food job, and at the beginning of February started her new life: four hours a day, from 8:30 until 12:30, in a tiny neighbourhood bookshop that was the saddest and dustiest she'd ever seen. The owner was in a wheelchair, which was the only reason she needed a hand in those five square metres of boredom crammed to the ceiling. Unfortunately Marta, the eternal exception, had weaselled her way into Signora Emma's otherwise septua-genarian-plus client base, and practically financed the hovel through her purchases of crime novels, nineteenth-century Russian classics and political philosophy books. For months there had been a scruffy, shakily handwritten sign in the window reading STAFF WANTED. And there was a reason no one had applied.

Emilia had a notoriously terrible relationship with books, but she gritted her teeth. Jail had been an excellent education in teeth-gritting: she had cleaned vomit-clogged toilets and floors covered in cigarette butts, endured fights, dramas, trials and media lynchings. Taking books out of cardboard boxes and putting them on the shelves wasn't the end of the world.

Her first priority was to placate her father. He had called her every day, angrier each time, ferociously asking her what her plans were, since 'a fast-food joint isn't a plan'. And 'where has Milan come from?'. And 'so after years of prattling on about it, Sassaia is suddenly of no interest to you?'. And 'this isn't how it works, Emilia'. And 'you need consistency in life. You need to work hard. You need a solid plan'. To which she had yelled, hysterical as usual, 'Why do I always need a plan? Can't I take it a day at a fucking time and see how it goes? We already know how it's going to go anyway, don't we? To shit!'

But her father was a bulldozer with built-in missiles. 'I'm coming to get you from Milan, Emilia, because you can't look after yourself! You don't know how to start something and finish it!' One evening Marta intervened, taking the phone out of Emilia's hand and putting it to her ear. 'Everything's under control, sir. This is Marta Vargas. I've found your daughter a respectable job in a small but excellently stocked independent bookshop. And independent bookshops, as you'll agree, are fundamental institutions, essential cultural outposts, a common good. If Emilia messes up, I'll buy her a one-way ticket to Ravenna.'

Riccardo was placated. He asked for photographic evidence and Marta provided it with sadistic glee. Images in which Emilia, among the shelves crowded with books, always had the same menacing expression: the same one as in her primary school photos.

But there was one perk. After clocking off, she had the whole afternoon to herself. She was free to sit on a bench with a slice of pizza for lunch or go down the steps to the metro and become engulfed, pulled along by the waves of the big, thrilling world. Everything was possible: stealing a lipstick from Coin department store, eating an artisanal gelato, mingling with the wealthy at an art gallery, sharing a joint with Mohamed at Parco Sempione.

She downloaded Facebook on her phone and so she was now on social media too. Under a false name: 'Magical Emi'. And she never posted a photo. But she found Afifa, Giada and Yasmina there. She put hearts under the photos of Yasmina with her son, of Giada in a nightclub or on the beaches of Elba. She chatted up guys in neighbourhood bars wearing fake designer clothes and men with foreign accents who put their shopping bags down on the pavement to have a rest.

She started to like Mohamed. They had even begun to tell one another stories – about prison and the activities they'd taken part in, about the time someone famous had come to meet the inmates, about the food in the canteen. Innocuous things, at the beginning, bashful attempts to share. But then, since they seemed to understand each other so well, they started speaking with more and more enthusiasm, laughing together, joking. It was liberating for Emilia to be able to say it out loud – 'young offenders' – without feeling the terror of being discovered and judged all over again. Mohamed had had the same school, the same adolescence. Well, almost; he had been inside for armed robbery. At Sempione, on what had now become their bench, he omitted no details when he told her about the balaclava, the pistol, the getaway on his scooter. Only at that point did Emilia find herself swallowing and digging her nails into the palms of her hands. No: she couldn't return the confession, she had to keep what she did quiet. Because even among ex-convicts, there are right crimes and wrong ones.

'You know,' she said to Marta one evening looking up from her phone, 'we only ever spend time with people who have been in prison.'

Marta looked up too, but from *War and Peace*. 'Because circles always get closed,' she explained gravely, 'and we still haven't closed ours.'

Emilia didn't get it.

'We have to go back.'

'Where?'

Marta stared at her through her metallic reading glasses. 'You know exactly where.'

Emilia shook her head violently, got up from the armchair and stood, disconcerted, as if she wanted to leave but didn't know which direction to go in. She burst out laughing: 'You're off your head.'

It was over these same days that the blow hit me straight in the face.

The morning of February 25th, during breaktime, I suddenly smelled burning. We had stayed inside because it was raining. The children were running wild up and down the corridor, in and out of the classrooms, all around the empty school, their voices bouncing around like inside the stomach of a mountain.

I tried to work out where the smell was coming from. Even Carlo, the caretaker, had come out of his office with a worried face. Both of us, amidst the shouts of the children, heard a subdued crackle of paper. We threw open the door of the teachers' room: the registers were going up in flames.

The alarm went off. Carlo grabbed the extinguishers while I counted the children. They'd always found it hilarious when we did practice fire drills. They didn't laugh this time, just grabbed their coats from their hooks and immediately got into single file, Diletta at the front, me at the back. Once we were outside and safely under the awning, I counted them. No Martino.

After ordering them not to leave the garden for any reason, I went back inside. The corridor was full of smoke now, but the fire had been tamed, and Carlo had called the police. The teachers' room was covered in a carpet of ash. I yelled 'Martino!' over and over again.

I went back into the classroom, looked under the children's desks, under mine. He had been at school that morning, I was sure: I had done the register. I kicked the others' rucksacks out of the way in search of his, and his wasn't there. 'Martino!' I threw open the doors of the boys' and girls' toilets. 'Martino!' For weeks he had been turning up at school one day in every four. He didn't hold on to a word I said, gazed out of the window, picked fights with the others, and all his notebooks were blank. I went outside again and asked in my most severe voice: 'Where is Martino?'

Eyes down, hands grasped, silence.

'Tell me where Martino is!' I shouted. 'Or you will all be held responsible and be failed and have to repeat the year!'

Diletta looked up, took a step forward and admitted, 'He ran away.'

'From school? Are you sure?'

'Yes, I saw him running from the window.' She burst into tears.

'Children, you're not grassing. You're helping your friend. It's fundamental that we find him immediately. Where is he?'

The rain was pouring down and the river was roaring. They all shook their heads, the smallest ones crying, the biggest excited.

'OK, then where do you think he is? Knowing him, where are the places he'd be most likely to hide away if he'd done something naughty?'

Again, a wall of silence.

'He could be afraid and hurt himself, he could get into even bigger trouble. Children, you have to help me.'

Luigi found the courage: 'There's a barn in the woods, above his house. He built a secret den there.'

'Thank you.' I instinctively reached out and rubbed his hair. 'Good, children. Today's homework, since the school is burning, is to read a book.'

'Noo!'

'I don't have a book!'

'Then read a newspaper, or a telephone book, or an old postcard! Oh, and write in your notebooks about the fear or joy or whatever other thing you've felt today.'

I didn't have time to wait for the parents and the police to arrive, so I left everyone in Carlo's care and also alerted Patrizia. I didn't have an umbrella, so I pulled up the hood of my jacket and started running as fast as I could towards the stone bridge. The river was furious. I crossed it and reached the other side of the valley, the one that was always in the shade. I ran through the cemetery without slowing down and up the narrow, potholed road that wound through the woods, so crushed by anxiety that

I didn't feel tired. I scrambled up the hill like lightning, my heart pumping like a piston. I understood what a worried parent must feel like, and it was hell.

Why did you do it? I asked him in my head. *Is this what you needed to do to get attention?* But in reality I was angry with myself: Why wasn't I paying attention? Why didn't I intervene? Why do I never get there in time?

This time, damn it, I couldn't fail.

After the last bend in the road, I saw the village of San Michele and a fistful of abandoned houses like mine. There was smoke coming from one chimney, and cows lowing in the shed next door. But I didn't stop, I didn't knock. I just trusted the children. I continued until the end of the houses and took the path into the woods. I was soaked, but I didn't feel cold. The rain, violent and obtuse, continued to drench me, but I'd be sheltered in the trees. I plunged into the muddy remains of the snow. I had been living as if in hibernation, my senses deadened by the cold, my thoughts rarefied, isolated, alcohol-soaked. But now I felt as if I'd been injected with pure adrenaline, alive and mad, in search of a child I hadn't known how to see, hadn't known how to speak to. And the forest seemed to never end, dark like the sky, angry and wet.

I'm praying, Emilia. Help me find him. Tell me he's here, that he hasn't got on the bus like you. Tell me he hasn't left. Tell me he hasn't thrown himself down some ravine.

When the beeches thinned out, a large clearing opened up and the rain got lighter. Across from me, I could see a stone ruin very similar to the partisans' hideout. Only there was smoke rising from one chimney.

I started running and praying again. I arrived, breathless, my legs no longer holding me up, opened what remained of a wooden door and found Martino there, sitting on an old mattress next to the fire, a cigarette hanging from his mouth and his dog curled up next to him.

He looked up, surprised. Then his face darkened. 'Who grassed?'

I closed the door. I took off my soaking wet jacket and sat down on the mattress next to him, covering myself in a filthy blanket.

Now I'd found him, and was certain he was alive, I could close my eyes and collapse.

'You'll fail me, right? I don't give a damn anyway.'

I was still getting my breath back.

Martino sucked his cigarette down to the filter, then put it out in an ashtray.

I looked around: other than the pallet we were sitting on, there was a decent supply of water, snacks and cigarettes. There was even a portable battery-powered stereo and a small number of *Tex Willer* comics.

'Are you planning on moving in, or what?' I asked.

Martino returned to staring at the fire. 'It's none of your business, sir.'

'It certainly is.'

'Will I go to juvie?'

I wanted to smile. 'You're too young.'

'Go ahead and fail me, I'm not going back to school anyway.'

'Martino, I'm afraid you don't get to choose. It's obligatory. The law says you have to go to school until you're sixteen, and you still have four years ahead of you.'

'Does the law count only for children?' he asked, contemptuous. 'Not for adults?'

The dog, whose name I knew was Misty from his homework assignments, buried his nose in Martino's lap, searching for a hand to stroke him. Martino kissed him on the head.

'Listen.' I looked at him and forced him to look at me. 'As far as I'm concerned, the fire was an accident. RIP to the old registers from the nineteenth century. The past can go fuck itself. But you need to explain to me, right here right now, in your own words and without lying, why you did it.'

He looked at the fire. He spent a long moment in silence. 'I didn't know where else to put my rage.'

Martino Fiume had straight black hair that came down to his shoulders because no one ever cut it. He got head lice very often. His fingernails were black, his clothes dirty. He was a neglected child, obviously not wanted. An only child with two parents who never turned up to parent meetings and had never opened the door to social workers. He was a person who had landed on Earth unwanted and uncared for. But he was intelligent, kind when he wanted to be, and what really mattered was that I cared about him very much.

I forced open his silence. 'Martino, I'm not your teacher now. We're not at school. I'm not interrogating you. I'm Bruno, and I want to understand, I want to help you. Please,' I took his hand, 'can you trust me?'

He pulled it away, frightened by the contact. He held on to his dog. Misty's eyes and his had the same abandonment etched into the depths of the pupils, the same sad sweetness.

'My mum's in the hospital.'

I also turned to look at the fire and let him speak, let him take all the time he needed.

'I tried to jump at his neck and strangle him, but he's so much bigger than me.' He lifted his fleece and vest and showed me a pizza-sized bruise on his stomach. 'I got this. But my mother came out worse. She stopped breathing; I thought she was dead at one point. He was stone drunk, like usual. He nearly killed her, then he pulled her up off the floor, threw her on the back seat of the car and drove. I thought we were going to fly off the road at every bend. He got to the hospital and told them, "My wife fell over."'

He got up to get some more logs. I didn't move.

'My father is strong. His hands are this big. You should see the way he pulls the calves out when the cows can't give birth. He puts a hand inside and just pulls it out, like it's nothing. He can smash a glass in his hand if he squeezes hard enough. He's done it a bunch of times. He's always pissed off with me and her. But why? What did we do? He broke God knows how many of her ribs and she, when

she woke up in hospital, just said, "I fell down a gorge."
I was raging.'

'You have to report him. I'll come with you.'

'Yeah,' he laughed, 'and then he'll actually kill us.'

'There's no alternative, Martino. Violent people go to
prison.' As I pronounced those words, I felt my heart
tremble. 'People like your father have to be stopped. You
can't pay the price for him; it's not your fault. It's his.'

Misty sniffed out a movement and started barking.
Martino, alarmed, hurried to the grey dusty window. But it
was nothing, maybe a fox. Then he lit another cigarette and
reached out towards a box I hadn't noticed before. Beer.

'Want one?'

'No, and don't think I condone you drinking and
smoking at twelve years old.'

'Hey, sir, this is my house and I do what I want.'

'This is not a house.' I got up. I was determined to act,
even if I didn't know how. 'This is a ruin and you can't
stay here. No child can live alone.'

'I'm not going back to my father's house.'

'No, definitely not. You'd just need to go in for ten
minutes, and I'll come with you. Get your schoolbooks,
your clothes, the things you need. You'll come and sleep
at my house tonight.'

Martino scrunched up his eyes again. I evidently just
kept surprising him.

'Come on, let's go,' I ordered. 'You need a shower and
a meal that isn't biscuits and beer.'

He kept staring at me.

'You can bring the dog,' I added. Then, since he still wasn't convinced, I reassured him: 'I'll talk to your father. I'll explain that you'll be with me until the situation is resolved. And then we'll go and see your mother and we'll resolve it. I promise.'

He got up. With slow and nervous movements he put some things in his rucksack. He put out the fire. He called the dog.

When we came out of the barn, the clearing glimmered with light. A crack had opened up in the wall of cloud that had covered the sky, and the sun was forcing its way through. The water shone between the branches, the grass, like a primordial language, clear and joyful.

Martino and I walked down the mountain in long strides as Misty trotted around us. There might be something I couldn't fix in me, but that didn't mean I couldn't fix it in someone else.

27

THEY SAT ACROSS FROM one another in first class, in the window seats. As Milano Centrale faded into the distance, two attendants came past with a drinks trolley and asked what they would like. It was only nine in the morning, but Marta asked for two mini bottles of Prosecco and two packets of crisps.

For a while they just looked out the window in silence. The flat valley that ran alongside them was monotonous, a frosty sheet broken up every so often by a farmhouse; a grain silo; a row of birches.

It wasn't an easy journey for either of them; they could each sense the other's tension.

'What's the first thing you want to do?' Marta asked in an attempt to defuse it.

'Smoke a joint in Piazza Verdi.'

'You're so boring. You're not eighteen anymore, magical Emi.'

They sipped their Prosecco from plastic cups, both retreating into the same memory.

Inmates meeting up outside during their leave permits was *Extremely Seriously Verboten*, let alone taking drugs together, but the two of them would set a time to meet in secret every time they could, in defiance of the magistrate, Frau, and the state penitentiary system that demanded a standard of compliance that no eighteen-year-old could ever live up to. At that age transgression is a physical necessity. And it's not like being a convict makes you a little saint; if anything, it's the exact opposite.

When she finally got her first leave permit, after years of imprisonment, Emilia had crossed the road, walked into the middle of Piazza San Francesco and fainted under the huge, boundless sky.

The boundaries remained, the schedules rigid and inflexible, and woe betide anyone who made a mistake. When you came back it wasn't to your parents, but to the guards who searched you, and if they found something Frau would send a report to the magistrate who would take away all your privileges.

Marta had to go to the old people's home and Emilia to the paediatric cardiology ward at Sant'Orsola hospital. Volunteering was supposed to instil *awareness* in them. And they were aware: of how old age dismantles you, of a hateful world that strikes innocent children down and forces them into a hospital bed. But they were still convicts. And eighteen-year-olds – well, Marta was twenty-one to be precise.

So they slipped away an hour early, armed with marvellously well-constructed excuses, and ran breathlessly towards the university campus where, at the corner between Via Petroni and Piazza Verdi, slumped on the ground with his long beard and black nails, they'd find their trusted dealer.

It was paradise to sprawl out, a blunt between their lips, in the covered entrance of the Teatro Comunale. If they got caught it would be an immediate transfer to adult prison. They mingled among university students, pretending to be the same as them – normal – while the weed made them tingle with wonder and gratitude for this bitch of a life they had landed on – all their own fault – and their eyelids became heavy, their throats dry, their hunger chemical.

They'd pretend they were free for twenty, twenty-five minutes max. Then the bell of San Giacomo would strike five o'clock and they'd shake themselves off. They'd jump to their feet and run, once again breathlessly, towards the convent, stuffing their mouths with handfuls of chewing gum, spraying deodorant on their fingers and hair. They pulled themselves together before entering the porter's lodge, even though it was difficult, really difficult. Because even if they forced themselves to think of horrible things – and that didn't take much effort – the giggle was there, at the bottom of their throats, and it fizzed and tickled. Especially during the search, when the guard checked their pockets, bags, knickers, repeating through gritted teeth: 'I ain't stupid, me . . .' But that weed, God it was good.

'Oh, because you never smoke with Habib,' Emilia smirked. '"I'm not in love", quote unquote, "I never fall in love".'

'It's called sex.'

'You're always texting.'

'He's enrolled in evening classes. I need to keep breathing down his neck.'

'You've decided to save him?'

Marta was offended. 'The goatherd made you bitter.'

'Schoolteacher. And I'm telling you, you would've liked him.'

'Seeing what he's reduced you to, I don't think so.'

'Then don't mention him anymore, please.' Emilia raised her voice. 'Just focus on your toyboy with the fake Rolex.'

The parents of two neat-haired, well-dressed children turned to look curiously at them from a few seats along, as did two German tourists in short sleeves. Only the Chinese businessmen on their laptops were too busy to notice.

Marta whispered to Emilia: 'Don't get us recognised, please.'

Emilia finished her packet of crisps. 'It's your fault. I didn't even want to come on this trip.'

They both turned to look at the countryside backed by that immense, indifferent, distant sky. It was like having a tooth pulled. Necessary, but painful.

Then the train started to slow down. And Bologna emerged.

Identical. Intact. With its red, yellow and orange houses all attached, its hills arched like the spines of big sleeping animals. The porticos, under which it had been so nice to shelter from the rain. And the two towers in the centre.

It was the same place they had arrived at in the prison van, decades before.

The city of punishment.
Of youth.
Of friendship.

As the heavy prison doors were opened, one after the other – a prison has many doors – Emilia, with her white sneakers and small face, looked like she'd landed on another planet.

She would never forget the intake office, handing in the gold bracelet her mother had given her for her confirmation and that she had never taken off. But now she had to part from it, as if she was removing her whole life, all the Emilias she had been, leaving – what? A mugshot and a digital fingerprint, like she was in a film. Only this wasn't a film, and a guard was really leading her along a corridor and up some stairs, through shouting and the noise of walkie-talkies and the stares of the other girls who had already seen her on the news.

Terrified, she walked into one of the isolation cells. She was fresh off the back of an arrest and an interrogation at the police headquarters that had lasted – how long? She had no idea. And then ninety-six hours in a holding cell, with hardly any food or water and no sleep at all, just falling every so often into a state of foggy half-wakefulness, at the end of which, she was denied bail.

She sat on the edge of the bed, repeating to herself in an endless litany *it's not true it's not true none of it is true.* With her knees together, heels together, her hands in her lap, she waited for someone to come and tell her it was all a bad dream, that she could go home now. To the white house in Ravenna, which had been searched from top to bottom.

She had been on a track, and now she had abruptly veered off and ended up in another world. And what had been in the middle? In the swerve, all thought had disappeared.

Every one of her nerves contracted as she breathed, absent yet wary, on alert like an animal being hunted from all sides. She wasn't hungry or thirsty; she was a knot of adrenaline. Reality was so dense and unreal that all she wanted was to lie down and sleep.

Maybe she did fall asleep. She imagined being able to, until after hours or days – time had retreated like a bear into a cave – she raised her eyes. Then she saw her: the girl in the cell opposite, studying her.

What is a person snatched from their school, their family, their home? Emilia still had that to learn, but the girl opposite her clearly didn't; she looked calm. She was wearing what looked like fourth-hand clothes, maybe taken from a skip. Her hard contours and detached facial expression reminded Emilia of the Romany lady who begged for money outside the Conad supermarket, and who Emilia avoided looking at whenever she passed her, accelerating her pace, embarrassed. But now she and this girl were together, in the same boat – with one difference. The other girl, it would turn out, had committed a ridiculously small crime in comparison with her own and therefore would be let out very soon.

'What's your name?' the girl asked.

Emilia was incapable of speaking.

'Are you the Ravenna girl?'

Even she knew.

'I've been here a while. It's not that bad. The director is nice, and the governor isn't too much of a ball-breaker.'

Emilia just kept staring at her, limp like a rag doll. The girl added: 'You can do sport, and drama. Oh, and the food isn't disgusting.'

Detention was like death: it made everyone the same. Pretty and ugly, educated and ignorant, wealthy and poor – even if, as she would soon discover, Emilia was the only wealthy one there.

When she finally reemerged from the fog of the anxiety meds – the doctor at the institute refused to keep prescribing them – Emilia gradually realised that the twelve or thirteen girls in the convent had nothing in common with the ones she had known *outside*.

From nursery school through to high school, in Emilia's classes there had never been a Moroccan, a Tunisian, a Romany, or a Slav; and not in her dance or piano classes either.

They all knew from the TV why she was there. So even in her immaculate white Adidas, Emilia was still the chief loser. And while outside, unbeknownst to her, the newspapers were describing her as a witch, inside they were half envious of her designer clothes and half sorry for her.

Like most girls her age, Emilia wasn't at all interested in politics. She had played hours of *Resident Evil*, watched Christina Aguilera videos on MTV and smoked joints in the school toilets, but her world ended there, in her house and her neighbourhood. For her, a poor person was an alien, an immigrant was someone who tried to sell you lighters and Romanies were the people who sat on their blankets outside supermarkets: they weren't fully-fledged people to her, just outlines without faces, stories or names. And now she had been plunged into the middle of them. Same canteen, same toilets, same school.

Her political education happened in one fell swoop.

Now, walking back up Via Marconi with Marta, Emilia contemplated the fact that Italian girls rarely went to jail – because they always had a family, a home, another option.

The only girls who ended up in prison were the ones so forsaken they'd never had a relative who could look after them or a broom closet to be punished in at home. Girls who'd never watched a Disney film at the cinema, never played *Fashion Designer.* So can you really blame them if at fourteen, needing some shoes, they steal them?

Emilia thought of Yasmina. When she was assigned to their cell, fourteen-and-a-half years old, Marta had looked up from an old paperback – a donated copy of Pavese or Moravia – and said bluntly, 'What the fuck are you doing here? This isn't a Barbie Dreamhouse.'

But Yasmina had never seen a Barbie, even if she looked a bit like one with her big black eyes, long curly hair, plump lips and amber skin. She knew a total of eight words of Italian, and when she carefully arranged her belongings on her bed, Emilia saw that she had fewer of them than she had words: just a nightie, three pairs of knickers and two pairs of socks. She didn't even have a toothbrush.

'Where are your parents?' Marta asked her in English.

'Under the sea.'

'And your boyfriend? You have a boyfriend?'

Yasmina shook her head violently. Her hardened eyes made her previous experience with boyfriends clear. She had been given a year and two months for the five or six chains she'd torn from the perfumed necks of classmates more fortunate than her. But taking the chains had just been a pretext: that girl had nowhere to sleep, no documents and no adult to feed her, dress her or take her to school.

Emilia would never forget her face at breakfast on finding a packet of Pan di Stelle biscuits in front of her. For weeks she couldn't get her head around the fact that it was possible to have a hot shower 'with shampoo' so often. She was more polite and kind than all the polite and kind girls Emilia had known outside and, when she started to attend the literacy course, she blossomed.

Now she had a job, a husband and a son. Emilia welled up just thinking about it.

'What are you doing?' Marta said. 'Are you crying already?'

It was a punch in the gut when they got to Piazza San Francesco. They looked at the big rose-shaped windows of the church that you could see the sky through, the children whizzing past on Micro Scooters, the gelateria:

everything was just as they'd left it. Emilia went to sit down on one of the benches because her legs couldn't hold her up.

Italian women never went to jail. It was impossible.

Unless.

Like Giada and Myriam, they had a drug addiction and were constantly running away from rehab.

Or.

Like Emilia and Marta, who had messed up big time.

So much so that there was no probation for them, no community sentence.

For eight years Emilia and Marta had watched the population of the young offenders change. They had become like the walls of the convent, a guaranteed presence for whoever got out and then got put back in again. They all knew that at Bologna Young Offenders they'd find a good canteen, the hospitality course, a nice courtyard, and Vargas and Innocenti.

The veterans, the big sisters – and that other title, the one that couldn't be said out loud.

'New chapter,' said Marta, forcing Emilia to get up.

They held hands and crossed the road. Diligent, grown-up, well-groomed: they had even gone to the hairdresser the day before. They were wearing their best coats, best trousers and tops, marking their distance from the girls they had been.

They turned slowly into the alleyway.

They looked up at the big iron gate, the insurmountable walls. They recognised the buildings one by one, the windows, the balconies opposite, including the Neighbour's, that had once formed their entire horizon.

Two flags flew next to the entrance: the Italian one and the European one, both slightly frayed and faded by the sun.

Marta's gaze lingered on those two pieces of fabric.

'You know what I think?' She turned to Emilia.

Emilia looked at her and, for the first time, saw her best friend cry.

'That this place shouldn't exist.'

Marta pulled a tissue from her bag and dabbed at her running mascara.

'Apart from the school, the friendships and nice moments that of course there were, a jail for minors is a contradiction in terms.'

Her anger returned.

'The vast majority of people who end up here shouldn't even be punished at all. For what? For the bad luck of having been born in a neighbourhood forgotten by God, or into families where slaps are thrown around like they mean nothing? If society brings you to the point of robbing, stealing, hitting, dealing, at fifteen, who's responsible for that?' She raised her voice. 'Where were schools and social services, where were Italy and Europe *before* the arrest? *After* is too easy.'

She turned to Emilia, the foundation on her face wet with tears, a fire in her eyes. 'Bars at the fucking windows? Keys and guards? How can you grow up like that? How can you hope to redeem yourself? Yasmina, Afifa, all of them: they should have taken them to the theatre, the cinema, entrusted them to better families, included them in that privileged world they had always been kept outside of. But instead they locked them in even more of a shithole and told them, 'You're the rejects.' In a *civil* society, they shouldn't have been arrested, they should've been reimbursed.'

Emilia looked down, her gaze anchored to the tarmac.

'I agree,' she said in a small voice, 'they should've reimbursed all of you. But what about me?' She shook her head. 'Not me.'

She thought that even if you dismantled the whole social structure and liberated it from all injustice and inequality, even if you healed it at the root, and it actually worked, evil always remains. Stubborn. Residual. Whittled down to a pinpoint, a single case. And she was proof of that.

Marta didn't respond; she was tired now. And there were some mysteries that even she didn't know how to resolve.

Together, they reached the entrance and rang the intercom. The door opened, like it had done so many times, only this time an unfamiliar officer answered, scrutinising them curiously. As if they could have been two youth workers, two teachers, two lawyers; two beautiful, free women in their thirties.

Goodness is stubborn too.

28

We returned to Sassaia from the hospital in the pitch black, exhausted, dragging behind us the remains of a heavy day.

Martino had tried his best not to cry, sitting on an uncomfortable seat next to the bed in which his mother was lying half-covered in bandages, like a piece of broken furniture. Adelaide was a bull-headed woman who I, with all the goodwill in the world, had tried to convince to report her husband. After three quarters of an hour, I got: 'It's none of your business, Mr Teacher.'

'But it is your son's business.'

'Martino is a big boy, he understands.'

'That violence is normal?'

'That his father is tired, and that family comes first.'

I got to my feet in the large neon-lit room, not knowing where to put my hands, my frustration, my nerves as the other patients observed us with a mixture of curiosity and pity.

'First before what, sorry? Before the gossip that will be spread in Valle whether you report him or not? Before the risk of being killed?'

Adelaide stared at me, lips sealed, fists clenched, as if to say: what the hell do you know?

'What is a family?' I asked her.

She smiled at me. 'You're the one who's been to school.'

Martino, meanwhile, was imploding. The 'boys don't cry' bullshit was evidently well-rooted in his brain – and why was I so fixated on removing it? On taking his existence into my own hands and fixing it? What did it have to do with me?

His mother was there, all bandaged up, on a drip. Her life was destroyed, yet she was defending the wreckage like a lion with a hard-won carcass.

'I can't tell you what a family is.' I took a deep breath. 'But I'm certain it isn't a place where you get beaten up. Where one person holds all the power and takes everything out on the weaker ones. Because that's the forest: a place where you always have to be on your guard, else you might get eaten. A family should be the opposite, shouldn't it? Sure, it was you who married that man, not me. What do I know about the complicated history behind it all? People should mind their own business. But I'm looking at you now, half-mangled, only alive by a hair. And I see Martino there, swollen with rage. And there's nothing in this family scene that looks normal to me, let alone fair.'

Anyway, we were exhausted, as I was saying, and dispirited. It was late: eight o'clock. Our steps echoed around the frozen houses of Sassaia. An avalanche of words, and at the end Adelaide had hardly said goodbye, just giving me a nod and Martino a dry kiss on the cheek. I had resolved nothing.

Misty pounced on us as soon as I opened the door; his joy and enthusiasm lifted our morale a bit.

'Right,' I ordered, 'shower time!'

Martino went upstairs without protest. He had become obedient in this house that wasn't his own. I washed my hands in the kitchen with the washing-up liquid, then thought about cobbling together a dinner.

It was Saturday evening, February 27th, and I hadn't touched a drop of wine since our unforeseen cohabitation began two days earlier. I uncorked a bottle now and glugged down half a glass before opening the cupboard: the usual polenta, to go with the usual Maccagno cheese and Swiss chard. I took it all out and started to busy myself. As I was cooking and laying the table for two, I heard Martino's footsteps, the sounds of him moving things, the jet of the shower, the roar of water in the pipes, and I couldn't help thinking that the house was alive again.

In a surge of lightness I grabbed the phone and turned it on for the first time in weeks. Misty wove through my legs, imploring me to give him a morsel. 'What do you want? Swiss chard? Nice try.' The phone made no sound: it might as well have been a wall tile. Not that I was hoping for a message or a missed call. Not that I would've admitted it.

Martino finished his shower and padded down the corridor in bare feet, soaking my carpet, making a mess. But it didn't bother me. I heard him open the door to his room – my parents' old one – plug in the hairdryer and dry his hair that was so in need of a tidy.

I had found it disturbing making up *that* bed, creating space for his clothes in the wardrobe where my mother's coats still hung, immersed in the smell of mothballs. I had found it disturbing getting the trunk of our childhood games and books down from the attic – Monopoly, Guess Who, Scrabble, Valeria's binoculars – and the collection of Salgari classics, which naturally Martino wasn't interested in.

We had established some schedules and rules: no running away from the house, radio off when it's time to go to sleep, hands washed before every meal and teeth brushed afterwards. We had also had to avoid the morbid curiosity of his classmates who saw us come and go from school together. It was all precarious, messed up, not exactly legal. And yet.

Martino came down smelling nice, his hair dry, and sat at the table just as the chard was done. He crinkled his nose when he saw it, but it wasn't like he was in any position to make demands. I filled a single dish so there was less to wash up. He started on the cheese. We ate in silence with our eyes lowered, in our slight shyness that didn't seem to be going anywhere. Between my beard and his hair, we looked like father and son. A crooked, savage pair of folk. He was amazed when I let him have a drop of wine. 'Only because it's Saturday evening,' I clarified.

The truth is that carrying my mother's cellophane-wrapped coats down to the chapel in Alma for the Caritas collection hadn't saddened me. The truth is that, as I came back up Stra' dal Forche, clear-headed and free, I was smiling.

After we finished, Martino cleared the table and I washed the dishes. This too was a division of labour established from the off to make things work. It was gone nine, but since there was no school the next day, I said, 'Go on, get Monopoly and we'll have a game.'

His face lit up. I poured myself another glass of wine. When he came back, we arranged the money and the pieces. As I passed him the dice, suddenly, unexpectedly, the sound of the phone cut the house in two.

I started. For a moment I remained sitting, incapable of reacting, of thinking, while Martino observed me in bewilderment and Misty licked the bottom of the pan. Then I got up, my heart beating out of my chest, and walked over to the sideboard. The screen emitted a stubborn light.

It wasn't Emilia.

'Hello.'

From a rectangle of night, through the curtain at the window, the moon emerged, full and white, illuminating the snow on the top of Monte Cresto.

Martino was trying to figure out a way to cheat; Misty, belly full, was asleep under the table.

'Hello, Bruno,' she said in that shrill, teasing tone I thought I'd never hear again. 'Well . . . happy birthday!'

I sat down again, suddenly.

'Don't tell me you forgot.'

I found my voice again: 'Yes.'

'You're thirty-seven years old, which means you're starting to get old not just inside but outside too. You need to celebrate.'

I felt my eyes welling up against my will. As Valeria rambled on about the weather in Ostia, the stormy sea, a building that had collapsed, my chin wobbled. I recognised the Witch of the Woods, her stick, her pea-shooter, her strength: she wasn't dead. I remembered her.

'I also wanted to tell you that I was with a piece of shit, but I left him. Valeria Peraldo is no longer interested in jealous men. I've started renting an apartment of my own. It's not a palace, just forty square metres, but if you're ever at a loose end for the holidays, like at Easter or in June when school finishes . . . If you fancy a trip to the sea, a change of scenery, there's a sofa bed for you here.'

What is a family? I couldn't tell you, Adelaide. I'm no expert. But.

I opened my mouth, dried out by tears.

A family is a cable, Adelaide.

A steel wire that holds you up, whatever happens. It stops you from losing yourself and dissolving because in that grip you know that you are loved.

'Thank you, Vale,' I uttered with what little breath I had, 'I think I might.'

I put the phone down, but insisted on keeping it in my hand, incapable of letting it go: it was still warm from our conversation. Martino was chomping at the bit to play, to build, to win.

I threw the dice after him, moved my piece on the board. Martino was already starting to build houses and hotels, invest money; I, not concentrating, couldn't keep up. I remained behind. I was going back.

To Turin. To the evening in which I'd slammed the Seat's boot down on my jumble of bags and boxes to come back here, call Sebastiano and, essentially, do everything in my power to die.

I hadn't thought since about what had happened. And now, between one throw of the dice and the next, it resurfaced in my mind all at once.

The tiny apartment in Via Po in my university years. My housemates brought girls back and I put earplugs in so I couldn't hear them, hunched over my desk studying.

I never went out. The world was an isosceles triangle formed by my rented room, the university faculty and the library. I never ventured beyond this perimeter, I never saw anyone. In fact, I had never even seen Turin.

It wasn't difficult to graduate early with top marks and proceed with my PhD. From the beginning I had been promised a teaching post and given glimpses of a radiant career. I was, after all, that little genius from Valle, wasn't I? It was my destiny to travel to conferences in Europe, have my work published. Only I was dead at the root, and I had no intention of saving myself – in fact quite the opposite.

One morning another PhD student who had just transferred from Florence asked for my notes with a smile, in a tone that suggested she wanted to be friends. I stood frozen, as if I'd been shot.

After I'd shared the notes, she asked if I wanted to study together in the library. I had gone unobserved for six years, but I seemed to still exist in spite of myself. And so, also in spite of myself, I began to wash and shave again. We transitioned from having a coffee standing by the machine in the faculty, to sitting down in a nearby café. I had never kissed with tongues, never touched a breast. One night I searched for porn films online in an attempt to understand how it was done.

I let myself be talked into a first date in a bar one evening. The three or four spritzes on an empty stomach helped. Afterwards, we walked along the river to Valentino Park. Alongside each other we were the trunk of a beech tree and a vibrant girl in her twenties with a Tuscan accent – who suddenly stopped and kissed me, the trunk. That's when I realised for the first time since August 26th, 1990, with some shock, that I had a body, alive with possibility.

Eventually, she invited me to a party, and I accepted. I had decided to at least give living a try. I bought myself a pair of jeans and new shirt specially. I rang the doorbell and could hear the music all the way down in the entrance hall. I went upstairs with the best intentions and found her there, at the door, flushed and drunk. Inside, the air was a blanket of smoke, empty beer and wine bottles everywhere.

I knew I was a frayed cable. And that if you don't finish what you've started before you die, there's no hope of being reborn.

But right now I was in a hurry. I was convinced that there would never be another girl. She grabbed my hand and pulled me into one of the rooms. I locked the door. The bedside lamp was on, the bed unmade as if others had just finished using it. After all, that was what I was there for, wasn't it? To not only be a son, a brother, an orphan. But to become *me*.

She lay down on the bed and undressed in front of me. I wanted her with my whole self. I wanted the tension, the erection, the loss of control. Instead, I tasted metal, under my tongue, under my sternum.

Corrosion happens in three phases, the expert had explained. Nucleation, almost undetectable. Propagation, which can and should be noticed in time. Then, irreparably, the final rupture.

I had gone through nucleation at high school, propagation at university. I had floated, far away, for all those years, in a blind rage at myself, at Valeria. What was there that was so damn important in that backpack? Little presents from your little boyfriend? Did you really trade our family in for a silly love story? Was that worth the opportunity to die together?

Life demanded a yes. Love. Opportunity. Sex. My PhD companion was taking off her jeans, her knickers, opening her legs. And instead of saying that yes out loud, I felt the twisted cables weaken until they snapped and I shattered into fragments. Instead of pushing back my shell. Instead of allowing myself enjoyment, I was stuck on November 2nd at the cemetery, year after year.

'Gotcha! Gotcha!' Martino was shouting at me with glee.

I looked at him now, like a moron.

Like someone who is finally beginning to understand.

'You have to pay me rent, sucker.'

That he's thrown so much time down the drain.

'You've only got one banknote left, I don't know if you realise.'

I realised that I wasn't so different from Adelaide. I too was convinced that, if you take a beating, it's because deep down you deserve it; that if evil knocks you down, it's your own fault.

But with Emilia, all it took was two poems.

Because life is alive, that's all. It wants to keep going, and it doesn't give a toss about the rest.

'Have you drunk too much?'

'No,' I shook my head, 'I'm extremely sober.'

I put the pieces back together. Martino had bled my wallet dry, practically thrashed me. I grabbed the dice.

'Good luck, dunce, it's your last chance!' he teased.

I threw the dice and landed on Jail.

He split his sides laughing. 'I won, I won! You don't have the cash for bail!'

I stared at that word: 'Jail'. Which in my head immediately translated to 'Emilia'. Had I really given up a future with her for her past? For my own past?

I looked up from my losing piece and Martino was radiant. Nothing is as spectacular as a radiant child.

'I want to tell you something,' I said, smiling.

'Yes, but I won.'

'You won, Martino. You are a champion. Nobody doubts it. But, for exactly that reason, I want to tell you this thing that maybe, one day, will be useful.'

'Only if you let me smoke.'

I sighed: it was all a trade-off, a compromise, a struggle.

'Only because it's the night of exceptions,' I consented. Then I reached out a hand: 'Give me one too.'

'You right now are seeing me like this, as the teacher. And you think I couldn't have become anything else. But teaching never crossed my mind, at least not teaching you guys at primary school. It was really the last thing I ever dreamed of.' I inhaled then breathed out the smoke. 'I lost both my parents when I was your age.'

Martino sat up erect in his seat, more interested than disturbed. 'The Monte Stella accident? I've heard people talking about it but I didn't believe it.'

I tapped the ash into a cup. 'Not *accident*. Let's call things what they are: *massacre*. But what I wanted to tell you is that at your age, I saw myself like my playing piece in Monopoly: fucked. My situation was so awful that, to cut a long story short, even though I gave all I had to studying, graduated and almost got my PhD, I then came back here and nearly killed myself with weed, alcohol and whatever other drugs I could get my hands on.'

Martino sharpened his gaze: I was becoming more and more interesting.

'I spent an entire year, Martino, *a year*, blackout drunk. I would open my eyes and the first thing I'd do was roll myself a joint and down an amaro. I couldn't stand even five minutes sober.'

I observed him: he was captivated. Children are attracted to badness because they don't have it themselves. They want to know it because they haven't touched it. And then what happens? How is it possible we corrupt everything with adolescence?

'One morning in May, I woke up on the riverbank rather than in my bed. Not knowing how I got there, or who I'd spent the night with. I was just an abandoned bicycle part, nothing more. I had a splitting headache, the light was hurting my eyes, the damp had soaked my clothes. I was disgusting. So disgusting that I told myself: now I'm going to die. I'll shoot something so strong into my veins that it'll send me to another world. And I had this terrible thought while the air smelled of flowers and there was the sound of jingling cowbells in the distance, and the mountains, the meadows and the sky were so full of sounds and colours that it was impossible to find a single emptiness.'

We put out our cigarettes at the same time. When we both looked up our eyes met.

'I had decided to die, absolutely decided. But then the bell rang and you all came outside for breaktime.' My heart swelled in my chest as I remembered it. 'Well, not you, the children before you, accompanied by a decrepit teacher you never met. That's when I realised I was outside Collodi, my old school. I pulled myself up, ashamed, all my bones creaking and hurting, and hid behind a birch tree. I looked at those children the way I looked at you when you won just now. They were playing hide-and-seek, football, chasing each other, rolling in the grass. And I thought a new thought: I thought that life hadn't only taken from me, not really. It had also given. Given loads. Beautiful days. Summers in the woods. Swims in that very river. Books I'd fallen in love with. It had given me love, so many times. And now it was my turn to give it back.'

It was bedtime. Martino was looking at me perplexed while Misty burrowed between his calves.

'All this to explain that, independently of the setbacks you've been handed, of the ugly things you've seen and heard, of the problems that are digging a hole inside you – and I know a lot about that hole, believe me – the truth is that neither you, nor I, nor anyone is truly fucked as long as we're alive. Especially not when you're twelve years old and have your whole life ahead of you.' I stared at him with a determination that started to frighten him. 'Promise me you won't do what I did and that you'll try your best to enjoy these years and all those to come.'

And, as I was saying it, I observed him nodding slightly evasively but thoughtfully. As I heard him upstairs brushing his teeth before bed, I felt also, clearly, this.

My cable, inside, was rebinding itself.

29

ON THE FAST TRAIN back, sitting opposite Marta who was sipping Prosecco as she leafed through the *Corriere della Sera* newspaper, Emilia felt a way she had felt very few times in her life: like she had a right to live in this world.

Opening the door to Frau's office again had been like a cannonball to the chest.

They had an appointment, so Frau should've been ready, prepared. Instead, when they materialised in front of her after all that time, she had to muster a superhuman strength to not cry. Her voice trembled as she asked, 'Is it really you? Vargas and Innocenti?' And the director almost collapsed on the desk under all the emotions that the inmates were absolutely forbidden to display.

But Emilia and Marta were no longer inmates. Realising that was another cannonball. They were adults, free citizens, elegantly dressed: no longer in those long overalls and fleeces that reeked of smoke, no more spots. Frau, on the other hand, had aged. She'd gained weight on her hips and her belly looked softer. She wasn't scary like she used to be. And even though the furniture, the floor, the bars on the windows in that room were the ones they remembered, they seemed different. Even the President of the Republic hanging on the wall had a new face.

Rita was right: everything – truly everything – changes.

'I don't believe it; how grown-up and beautiful you've become.' She got up, leaving her position of authority to walk awkwardly over and hug them. And they found themselves pressed tight against the soft, warm body of that woman, suffocating them with an affection that before would've been *verboten*. She was no longer Frau, but Gilda Pavulli, a person who among other things was also the director of a female young offenders' institution. As soon as she stepped back, she became once again the pugnacious, unstoppable leader and led them triumphantly from one office to the next. Rita wasn't there that morning. She hadn't been told they were coming and maybe, thought Emilia, that was for the best; it would've been too much. She would've had to apologise for never having phoned her.

Vilma had retired not long before but the governor, on the other hand, was still the same and he was moved too, though he tried to hide it. The majority of the guards and youth workers were new, but Gilda was generous with introductions, anecdotes, celebrations: 'These two! Oh, they drove me crazy! And now look at them! Graduated, reborn working women! I'm so proud!'

A light that Emilia and Marta remembered well streamed in through the big barred windows. Their eyes kept drifting to the courtyard where their adolescence had been consumed without ever coming to fruition. They could just about see the volleyball court and the ghosts of their throws and their smashes, their bodies lying out in that enclosed bit of air. Could you pay for a crime with your youth? Did time balance the accounts? They recognised the vegetable garden, dried out by the winter, and the walls where girls, no longer them, would go and sit from two until four in the afternoons, dangling their legs and throwing back their heads to feel the sun on their faces.

As Gilda chatted away, Emilia and Marta became more and more silent and uncertain. Was it really necessary to walk this corridor again, stop in front of the automated machine where every so often a guard had bought them a coffee too, next to the photocopier used to make signs that read: 'Notice to young offenders', 'Shower and cream to eradicate scabies', 'New opening times for the infirmary'? Did they really have to walk past it all again?

Yes. Because it's adolescence that dictates who you are, and this was the most important place in their lives.

They paused at the noticeboard hanging on the wall of the teachers' room: 'The Alphabet of Prison'. 'A for Attorney, B for Bars, C for Cell, D for Detention, E for Enforcement . . .' They smiled crookedly because they had participated in that project, which had been Pandolfi's idea. Even their basic vocabulary was different from that of others their age.

Finally, Frau called them back: it was time.

It was crucial, fateful, and a little bit illegal, seeing as ex-convicts aren't allowed to go back into prison – at least not without committing new crimes. A magistrate would never have given two people like Vargas and Innocenti authorisation for a tour of the institute. It wasn't Disneyland.

But Gilda had promised Marta 'a quick spin, just because it's you two', and they found themselves once again in front of the Door.

The Security Door.

The border between normal life and awful life.

Between the girls who were right and the girls who were wrong.

Gilda rang the bell. The guard inside opened the hatch window in the door, and the noises that immediately slipped out were familiar, grating, like sandpaper on flesh. A mixture of rap music, walkie-talkies, brass keys, rage. They noticed a couple of shabby-looking girls with greasy hair, their lost eyes concealed by fake eyelashes, sashaying down the corridor with cigarettes in their mouths. The eternal smell of smoke, ashes and the canteen; the sound of swearing and brawls over a bottle of nail varnish.

The guard, framed by the little hatch window, made to open it. It was all as clear and mechanical as the workings of a mortise lock. Instinctively, Emilia stepped backwards, and Marta said out loud, 'No.'

Gilda turned red. She raised her hands, almost in apology. 'Girls, you asked me for this. I would never have suggested it.'

'We know,' Marta reassured her. 'We were sure, weren't we, Emi? But now I realise I can't cross this threshold anymore.'

'Me neither,' Emilia said. 'I'm done.'

The guard, after a nod of the head from Gilda, closed up the hatch, sending the bolt back into the recess.

Emilia and Marta watched as the past was locked in again.

It was true that it wasn't possible to fix or repair it. But – and they only realised it now – the past was also something that was *finished*.

Now they just wanted to get out, and quickly. They said goodbye to everyone with big, hasty smiles: 'Yes, it was great, no, it was tremendous.' 'Ciao, bye, see you never.'

'Let's go get some lunch,' Marta proposed to Gilda.

'And let's not skip seeing Bologna; we've missed out on enough of it already,' Emilia said. Gilda took them to a typical restaurant, where they ordered lasagne, *cotoletta* alla Bolognese, panna cotta and a litre of wine, always chatting about the same topics – the latest crime news, the national teen gang crisis, the short-staffing of prisons and dwindling funds, changing magistrates, the penal code that hadn't changed – but with a levity, almost a joy, because it wasn't about them anymore.

Then they hugged Gilda with the promise of keeping in touch and went to Piazza Maggiore to take a couple of selfies. They took one with Palazzo D'Accursio in the background and another in front of Neptune's fountain with his balls in pride of place. Silly shots they wouldn't post anywhere, because why would you post as an ex-convict? The only thing that counts is life.

Now, on the train, the night swathed the landscape outside the windows in a heavy blanket. They were drained, exhausted, with sore feet and their makeup cracked like old plaster. But they felt at peace, like people who had done what they needed to do and knew it. They said nothing to one another because there was nothing left to say, nothing to lament.

They got back at gone eleven. Just as the train was slowing down into Central Station, Emilia felt her phone vibrating in her bag. She thought it was probably Mohamed, or her father. However:

This is an apology. I wasn't ready for the surge of joy that you are. I even bought a TV, which as you can imagine doesn't work. I hope you're well, wherever you are. Even if I miss you. Even if I'm ready now to live life with you, whatever it truly is.

Emilia closed the message immediately, as if it was burning her fingers.

She forced herself to bury it under other thoughts for the whole taxi ride home, during her shower, then in bed after Marta had turned the bedside lamp off. But she couldn't sleep.

At about three in the morning she slipped out from under the sheets and locked herself in the bathroom, in safety. She opened it again and reread.

Many times.

30

THE PARADOX WAS THIS: she couldn't think about the main event of her life. Couldn't recall it, couldn't recount it; nothing. She had to pretend it hadn't happened. Yet she felt it, unmoving and compacted around her heart, like a clot thickened in darkness, a piece of sharpened graphite. Dangerous, too. Lethal, like a quiescent tumour, an undetonated bomb. She had to hold on to it, be careful to not dislodge or aggravate it. Because if it was opened, if it exploded, the black would invade everywhere, and paralyse her.

The three times she had been forced to talk about it, she had mumbled the fewest possible words in the tiniest possible voice, dissociating from herself. During the trial, her trance state was such that all memories disappeared as soon as she left the courtroom. With Rita, years later, she ran through it with the same detachment with which she made broths during cooking lessons, or cleaned the communal areas. With Marta, finally, she had struggled through a stilted summary only because Marta had confided in her first and had threatened her that, 'if you don't, we're no longer friends'.

But now, at thirty-one years old, her heart couldn't take a fourth confession. Her darkness had to remain encapsulated inside her, isolated in her sarcophagus like the Chernobyl reactor.

That's why she hadn't responded to me, hadn't called. Despite how strong and irresistible the pull to do so was.

I knew now. The version told by the newspapers, by others, by upstanding citizens. But there was also her version. And love demanded that this version was expressed, that the unsayable was said, that the erased was remembered. But to remember, for Emilia, was worse than the fourteen years and four months in jail.

She had decided to stay in Milan, a city that – as stimulating as it was, and rich in things to do, and see, in people to meet – meant nothing to her, and to go on with her part-time job that she didn't give a rat's ass about, to fuck that nice boy she couldn't fall in love with, and to camp out in Marta's comfortable apartment that wasn't home, with no Alps outside the windows, and no scent of forest sneaking in through the cracks.

Despite all her armour, however, Milan was getting to her. The vast piazzas, neighbourhoods, streets – all that freedom to go wherever she wanted whenever she wanted – were giving the world back to her, but it was also poking at her dark knot; opening up the future and, at the same time, cracking open the trapdoor to the past. As if, at the end of the day, they were part of the same damned knot.

Then she was flooded with memories, which wriggled out from the deepest parts of herself at the least opportune moments. Quick clips, rough bits of footage. But clear, blinding. And they left her in ruins.

There was always Marina in those flashes, always the pine woods, the brooding sea, the petrochemical plant ensconced in haze no matter whether it was summer or winter. The beach bars mobbed but the beaches empty, the huts closed.

She was overcome, despite herself, by a gust of salty air, and suddenly it stopped being March 2016 and became January 2001: the end of the Christmas holidays. *She* had forced the lock and shut herself in a beach hut, all on her own. It came naturally to her – breaking the rules, violating private property, producing a condom from her pocket – because *she* was a capable, determined, brilliant girl.

Which was easy, thought Emilia, when you had everything. When your mother hadn't died, you were flaunting a generous C cup, you read out loud in class without stumbling over words and your average grade was a B even if you only studied for ten minutes a day and spent the rest of the time on the PlayStation. If she had gone no further than thinking these things, Emilia might have only spent nine or ten years in prison. But she had written them down, pen on paper. Even though she hated writing. Even though the secret diary she kept as a dorky little girl was scant and full of mistakes. Everyone had one, so she had to have one too.

Emilia could see the beach hut again from outside, the white and blue paint peeling from the wind and salt. She was the lookout, the servant. The extra in the sumptuous film all about the other girl. And the person inside with her wasn't some classmate but a fully grown, fully formed man. She didn't just do it with boys, spotty, awkward, clumsy. She demanded the maximum: a full life.

Emilia was her guard dog, the keeper of the secret. The fully grown, fully formed man was married. Unfortunately, it would later emerge that not only was he a paedophile, but that the day in the beach hut wouldn't be an isolated episode. That deserted early January in Marina di Ravenna, the turn events were going to take was as yet unknown. Love wasn't something they talked about; the twisted and murky friendship between her and *her* remained the most important relationship.

How would the *other girl* have lost her virginity without Emilia's cover? How would she have lived her intense and radiant life?

In the bookshop in Milan, Emilia was shelving paperbacks of Ariosto, Pellico, Manzoni. But in reality she was holding her old diary in her hands, the lock rusty, the key so thin you could bend it, the lined pages grubby with her terrible handwriting. It wasn't a memory; she was truly feeling the rough texture of the paper under her fingertips. The past was giant again, and it engulfed her, swallowed her.

She took the diary out of her rucksack, sitting on the wreckage of a pedalo that had sunk into the sand. The wind was strong and cold. As she waited for the two of them to finish, she sketched the view nervously: the red flag taut in the north-westerly, the white crests of the angry waves, the low black clouds. Then she unloaded:

I hate you.
You're a bitch.

Five scrawny words. Spat out in rage, jealousy, envy. That would then become an 'aggravating factor', proof of 'premeditation', and an additional five years.

And do you really believe that? she would reply today if she could. The diary of an adolescent? Don't you know that adolescence means both everything and the opposite of everything? That if I write I hate you, I love you too? That if I like kissing with tongues, I also think it's gross? That if I'm happy to be her friend, I'm also sad? That I'm me and, at the same time, I'm a stranger I'll never know?

'Emilia, what's up? You're shaking.'

Signora Emma's worried voice cut through time. Emilia landed heavily back in the present, the past slipping back swiftly under the trapdoor as the paperbacks fell from her hands.

She felt her heart blocking her throat like a big seashell washed up on the sand. She turned to face Signora Emma slowly, in a cold sweat.

'You're so pale.' She put a hand on Emilia's forehead. 'You're burning up. Go home.'

Emilia dragged herself to the back room and took her jacket and bag. Raising her hand slightly to say goodbye, she left hurriedly, unable to breathe. She could feel she had a fever, but she didn't want to go home to bed. The apartment was Marta's, not hers. She didn't have a place of her own anymore. She couldn't go back to Ravenna, she couldn't go back to Sassaia. She was held in such a ferocious vice that again she began to long for the young offenders' institution, the sentence that absorbed all thought, where there was no possibility of interrogating yourself, of finding yourself head-on with the black knot, because you were already paying, you were already full to the brim with anxiety meds and cuts: what else could you do?

She continued along the pavement, floundering like a castaway on the shore. They tell you: 'Off you go, you're free', but it's just a word. Like *bitch* and *I hate you* in a sixteen-year-old's diary. The truth is that you can't untie yourself from yourself. There's no way of turning back, rearranging things, of taking a deep sigh of relief and finally moving on.

If only she had been able to meet her one last time somewhere – a café, an underpass, this very pavement, anywhere was fine – and clear things up. She couldn't wait to touch down on a star, to become a soul, but what if then we just became worms and that was it? Emilia needed to resolve this. If you don't love anyone, you can say 'fuck it' and kill yourself. But love demands that you repair the irreparable.

Her head was pounding, and she was sweating so much that she had to unbutton her jacket. She set to sifting through the crowd that was bustling through Milan – the kids released from school, the models on their lunch break, the old people with their dogs – stubbornly searching for two blue eyes. And when she realised that she was actually searching for them, here, in the real world, she said out loud, 'Emilia, you're going crazy.' Then the earth beneath her feet suddenly slid and she lost her balance. She held on to a signpost in the metro, suffocating amidst the general indifference.

There was no way of coming out of the past, of looking again at those blue eyes, of stopping herself from falling. Yet she wanted a way, she needed a way.

She plunged into her bag. She scrambled for her phone, pushed at the screen with the last of her strength. She called the only person in the world who could grab her hand and pull her out of the dark.

One morning, when my lessons ended at ten thirty and I knew Martino was safe at school, albeit with that jerk Patrizia, I got in the Seat Ibiza, turned on the ignition and, without thinking, headed up the valley in a very specific direction.

By now the daylight lasted almost until teatime, which around here is at six, six thirty. The light, in its new intensity, illuminated the forest floor, melted the last stains of snow and warmed the buds on the branches. Was I disappointed that Emilia hadn't replied? Yes. But love was of no use when it came to obtaining, or solving. I'd understood that by this point.

It was of use when it came to accepting.

And so I drove slowly up the abandoned country road, slowing down at the hairpin bends between the mountains, over the tarmac corroded by all the snow that had fallen over the years and through the dented guardrails, the faded signs, which nobody ever came to maintain.

I turned right when I got to the crossroads, and felt a chill down my spine. That point marked the end of the tiny hamlets and isolated farmhouses and the beginning of the bare mountain. I was absorbed in it, remembering every pass, every sheer drop, not with my memory but with my muscles and nerves.

Yes, I accepted it. That Emilia would be of no use as someone to marry, start a family with, become like my parents with. But if it weren't for her, I wouldn't be making this journey.

I stopped the car in the middle of the deserted car park.

It had taken forty minutes to get there. I calculated that I had a quarter of an hour, no more, because then I had to go and collect Martino from school and give him lunch.

I opened the door, put both my feet on the ground. I looked at the void, face to face.

The hotels, the restaurants, the two-storey holiday homes in peeling white paint, their charming wooden balconies now covered in mould. They had been built in abundance in the Sixties, but their value had dropped after the massacre. Then, higher up, the ski lift, the impassable ridges, the pine woods. Finally, to top off the little forgotten village, was the Monte Stella cable car.

It was all there.

Dusty, blockaded, closed.

It looked smaller, I thought.

I left the car open, the keys in the ignition, my phone on the seat, and walked alone, in a T-shirt, towards the crocus-studded meadows. I raised my eyes and saw the surviving cabins still suspended in the sky, their windows cloudy or broken, covered in rust with birds' nests on the seats, and it didn't horrify or scare me. Just a prick of pain, of tenderness.

Monte Stella had become unreachable, except on foot for the few people who had the strength. The glacier lake nestled at the top had become a secret again, like it was at the beginning of time.

I stopped under the pylons of the disused cable car, halted forever by repossession signs. I filled my lungs with the light-imbued air, the scent of primroses, the life that was preparing to push through the earth, to start again where the bones of my parents were crushed. Because all the bad in the world couldn't stop a stubborn bud and its small but tenacious will.

I opened my lips and whispered: 'Screw you.'

Then a bit louder: '*Screw you. I'm still alive.*'

I was grateful for it, for the first time – grateful that my sister had turned back to recoup the little ring or whatever it was her boyfriend had given her; that her nothing love had saved us.

I let myself glide, running down the sweet hill of the mountain, my arms wide open like the eleven-year-old boy I had been. The grass was wet and tender, new. Perfumed by pastel yellow crocuses and pink and blue primroses. This was paradise, I was surprised to notice myself thinking. I laughed at the paradox of life. Tripping on a stone and rolling down, stalks and pollen in my mouth, nose, hair. Stopping against the roots of a beech tree.

I got up, completely wet, bewildered. Like I was just born.

I brushed myself off and walked back up the hill towards the car park: I had someone to look after now – something which wasn't my past.

'Papa.' Emilia collapsed on the floor, breaking into tears.

Desperate tears, like she'd never cried before. As if she needed to expel the whole Adriatic along with the beach bars, the petrochemical plant, the port, the sand, the pine needles. Not in a hallucination, not in a dream, with her strength at the end of its tether and fourteen years destroyed by jail behind her, no – she would never see those eyes again.

'Papa, I can't do it.'

'Where are you?' Riccardo immediately sensed the extent of her pain. 'I'm coming, I'll leave now.'

'No, stay where you are. But talk to me.'

'What's happened?'

Emilia looked up from the asphalt at the comings and goings of people: smiling, distracted, busy on the phone, rushing down into the metro. But she didn't see anyone. She didn't see anything.

'Do they still organise torchlit marches against me in Ravenna? Do they still protest the fact that I'm out? That I had the maximum sentence but it still wasn't enough?

Because it'll never be enough?' She shook her head, punching her fist against her forehead, hard, to hurt herself. 'How did you do it?' she shouted at him. The question she'd had in her throat for all that time, which now exploded. 'How did you do it, all these years? Because wherever I go, whatever I do, nothing fucking changes. And now I don't have anywhere else to hide.'

Riccardo was silent. Then, with a calm voice, he said: 'I've never hidden, Emilia.'

It was true. Emilia gripped the phone tighter, pushed it against her ear as if it was the hand or cheek of her father, and thought that he would always be there. In the same city, in the same house, the same office. Still as a nail. Resistant to any kind of bad weather, or stories in the newspapers. Obeying the same schedule, the same demands of life: bills, trips, projects that needed to be handed in on time. A tsunami had overcome him, had thrown everything at him: first widowed, then that day in June that had cracked his life in two. Because it wasn't just Emilia's life that was broken: it was also Riccardo's. And him? He had gone to work. He'd done the shopping. He'd looked after the house, the bills, his daughter in jail. He'd let people point at him, look, judge. Because surely many people would've said, poor man, what a terrible thing to have happened to him. But others would've said, what kind of father is he, to have brought up a daughter like that?

'I haven't hidden, Emilia, because you can't hide from yourself. You can deceive yourself, at best, but it doesn't resolve anything. You have to stop doing that.'

'What can I do?' Emilia shouted. But no one was listening. She was just embarrassing the people around her, who sped up as they walked by. But he'd never turned away. Even through the telephone, he managed to breathe next to her. 'Everyone's finding out. Even Bruno, even he knows now. He's disgusted by me, horrified. He told me to leave Sassaia.'

Riccardo emitted a long sigh. He was beginning to understand. 'Nobody has the right to tell you to leave anywhere, Emilia. And you might be shocked to hear me say it, but now I truly think you should return to Sassaia.'

'Impossible.'

'You think it hasn't been hard for me too? That I've never felt on the cusp of collapsing?'

Slumped on the floor by the sign, Emilia's heart cracked in the places it had cracked a thousand times. Because she had paid what she owed. But her father had paid for nothing.

'Did people say things? Yes. Were there people who crossed the street when they saw me? Yes. You know how cruel people can be, especially when they are scared by an ugly thing, a thing they don't understand, that's bigger than all of us. I haven't kept count of the acquaintances who have disappeared, even certain relatives. Especially at the beginning, when I would come out of the garage and have to wait for the journalists from all the TV channels that were always there to move out of the way. And I wanted to crush those busybodies under my boot, slap their stupid cameras out of their hands. But, Emilia,' Riccardo sighed again, 'we have to go on.'

Emilia closed her eyes and tried to digest those five words, to absorb them into her bloodstream, her tissue: *we have to go on.*

'Do you know what saved me? The thought that, even in that disaster, it was still you and me, together. And as long as we were together, all that suffering had a meaning. We could work with it. We could move through it, in time. Because, despite everything, you and I were – we are – a family.'

Milan no longer existed, Ravenna no longer existed. They were just father and daughter now, on the phone just like before the arrest, with no defences up, like when Emilia was born and he cut the cord.

'I always felt your mother at my side, when I was working all week, and then at the weekend when I went shopping for you, because I knew the week after was visiting week. They filled me with joy, those visits.' He started to cry too. 'I wouldn't wish it on my worst enemy, but it didn't matter because I was seeing you, Emilia: you were my daughter, you were you, even in the worst moments. And we would come through it because we loved one another. No crowd of journalists stopped me from getting on with my career, no inhabitant of Ravenna kept me from going on. My true friends, they stayed. And eventually I also found a partner. Emilia, please, don't keep running away.'

And then he said it, the phrase.

The phrase that wouldn't extract the unexploded bullet, the black knot – that was impossible – but would change its position.

'The best thing you can do, not only for yourself but also for *her*, is to not throw away this "after". Rebuild it.'

Emilia instinctively looked for her once more among the shop windows and restaurant terraces of Milan. Then she dried her tears and pulled herself up. She looked around, still in a daze, but also with a new certainty, a new strength.

'You're right.'

Since Emilia had learned to walk, and then to ride a bike, her father had let her fall and helped her up again. The road was quiet, now. People had returned to their offices. She wiped a hand across her forehead: it was sweaty but cool.

'I never thanked you.'

Riccardo started to laugh. 'You don't thank your parents.'

31

THE SCHOOL'S PEAK PERIOD of enrolments coincided with the arrival of Prof Mangiagalli, who taught front-of-house and culinary arts – neat goatee, blue eyes, marble butt tucked into snug jeans. So snug that he was quickly baptised with the name Lunchbox.

He was about thirty, with pecs that bulged through the fabric of his shirt and a wedding ring on his finger. Not that anyone was put off by that. A quickie with him behind the hobs was everyone's daydream.

But he was an upstanding man. Very strict, very serious, completely dedicated to his role as teacher of *lasagnette ai funghi*, carefully balanced trays of champagne flutes and good posture between tables. And suffice to say that they put great effort into shimmying, unbuttoning their shirts, giggling and winking – to no avail.

Every so often, when they perfectly garnished a carpaccio after hours of corrections, he'd let it all go: 'Well done,' he'd say in a tone midway between motivator and saviour, 'they'll be fighting to hire you in all the big hotels and Michelin-starred restaurants, *one day*.'

Yes, they sniggered: *why not*. As if they didn't know that the only jobs they could hope for on the outside were at state-subsidised neighbourhood cafés with eleven-euro fixed-price menus.

He never looked at them with anything but the look of a teacher as they rooted around him like a herd of starved teenagers, forced into a chastity they hadn't chosen. They had been left high and dry by the Neighbour, and now Marble Butt had arrived. Their gaze was entirely lewd shots, zooming in on his lips, close-ups of his zipper, a welcome distraction from the lessons which none of them gave a toss about. Marta wanted to be a scientist, Emilia an artist, and the others would've much preferred a health and beauty course instead of the boredom of front-of-house and culinary arts. Even if the *lasagnette ai funghi* was good, as were the ricotta crepes and, particularly, the risottos and escalopes which called for the extraordinary appearance of wine. A Tavernello of a mere ten per cent, but it was good nonetheless; after their allotted glug went into the pan, they passed the rest around, swigging it on the sly.

They cooked the Christmas and Easter lunches for the whole institute, and the incidences of self-harm decreased slightly. There was also talk about opening a restaurant connected to the prison: an ambitious project that made them feel they were ever so slightly more than nothing.

But Lunchbox, Marble Butt, whatever you wanted to call him, was much more enticing than any kind of training project. He was cool and blond like Brad Pitt. The evenings they'd spend conjecturing about how and in what positions he probably fucked his lucky wife took the same inflamed turn as the porno notes they wrote together to the Neighbour. They were all dying with the desire to reach out and touch it: his bulge. They were sixteen, seventeen, twenty-two – it was hard to keep sublimating. Their fantasies mounted, looming larger and larger: 'I'm gonna do it. I swear tomorrow I'm gonna do it', 'No, I'm gonna do it, I'll give him a nice blow job', 'Let's do it together'. Collective movies in their minds, fed constantly by new details passed every night from bed to bed in a whisper. Until, one morning, in the middle of the school day, Myriam broke the barrier between the possible and the impossible.

Stirring the soup, she stealthily wiggled her hips until they were rubbing against his. Then – fast, accurate – she ran a hand over the crotch of his trousers. She lingered in front of the others, who couldn't contain their shock and excitement. The gas sizzled, the oven toasted the croutons, and they were all overcome by a wonderfully raised heart rate. Until Lunchbox's face froze.

He untied his apron, staring at Myriam and the others with infinite disdain. He also took off his chef's hat and threw it violently to the ground. He walked at pace towards the door and called the guards in a loud voice, ordering them to take these brats down to the fetid basements of society where they deserved to rot. Finally, not yet satisfied, he knocked on Frau's office door with a hard fist.

The latest in a long list of crimes – 'sexual harassment' – was reported and sent for the magistrate's overview. In three days, Myriam would be sent to Rome, 500 kilometres away from her relatives, interrupting her academic career for the thousandth and final time. Because if you change city and institution, you don't just pick up school where you left off, and anyway, not all institutions have the same programmes. Nor is the right to education guaranteed if you've made a mistake and keep on making mistakes.

That interruption, in Myriam's case, was a death sentence for her already precarious future, as would become clear later from the dosage she injected into her vein – while Marble Butt was just assigned to another class, substituted with a paunchy guy in his fifties who was incapable of making anyone fantasise.

The fault was theirs: they couldn't complain. In fact, if they dared to, they'd meet the same end as Myriam, whose transfer had heightened tensions to the point of high alert. All lighters were confiscated and the guards no longer chatted, no longer joked: they just watched. The faces in the cells became long.

'School is a privilege that you have to earn,' Frau shouted in outrage, walking between the cells. 'School in here is a luxury, and you have to understand that.'

Vitriolic silence. Nails pushed into forearms until blood appeared.

Then Marta shouted, 'No. School is a right.'

The torch was lit, the fire inextinguishable.

And Frau turned it to ashes. 'My office. Now.'

'We're already being punished, and you're punishing us further for every little bit of trivial bullshit,' Vargas retorted when they were alone. 'And you think we'll become better like that?'

'Groping a teacher's willy is not trivial bullshit. If he touched your bottom, I'd have reported him on the spot.'

'We'll apologise to him, we'll write him a letter . . . But send us a boy from Beccaria every once in a while, so we can let off a bit of steam.'

'Be serious, because right now you can't imagine how tempted I am to send you all the way out to Pontremoli . . .'

Marta fixed her eyes on the framed face of the President of the Republic above Frau's head: a white-haired man wearing a tie, dignified, light years away from the miserable, rancid hardships of real life.

'I want to write to Carlo Azeglio Ciampi,' she announced solemnly. 'A letter to tell him that the right to education is not guaranteed in Italy's juvenile prisons.'

Frau's eyes widened.

'I want to ask the President – who is also my president, is he not? Not only the president of good girls. I want to ask him to make school the backbone of a sentence. Make it so that no academic course can be interrupted or denied, because otherwise being in here has absolutely no purpose.'

Marta, when she said certain things with her specific vehemence, was someone you'd vote for. It was a real shame that she would never, in her whole life, be able to run for office.

'You can't expect us to understand our mistakes – sorry, our crimes – if we don't even have erasers. You can't expect us to stop doing wrong if we only know wrong words, wrong examples, and bars at the windows. The sentence is of no use; culture is of use. And I know that you agree with that.'

Frau sighed. She closed her eyes. She cursed.

Then she passed Marta a piece of paper and a biro.

Now the defender of the right to education was sitting opposite Emilia in the kitchen, putting two steaming plates of fusilli with tomato sauce on the table. She had just finished recalling the story of Lunchbox and, drizzling olive oil over her pasta, concluded, 'Do you know what drives me crazy, Emi? That school isn't the backbone of anything, let alone juvenile prison. Masses of unaccompanied minors get thrown into cells because there's no other place to put them. They go from the same neighbourhoods to the same institutions. And in the end you and I, and Afifa and Yasmina and another couple of others who graduated were just exceptions in an ocean of lost causes.'

Emilia got caught on that word: *exceptions*.

Marta skewered three fusilli at a time and devoured them. She was always hungry and always thin: she seemed to never stop burning calories.

'You have no idea what I'd give to be able to go to Beccaria at the weekends and help those boys out. You can't imagine what I'd get up to if I was the Minister of Justice, or of Education . . .'

'Oh I can imagine!'

They laughed. The lamp that shone over the table created a special kind of intimacy. Emilia felt good in that house. *Apart from . . .*

'Marta.' Emilia tried to interrupt her friend's fervent flow, listing the initiatives she would put in place if she were a minister.

Apart from they were no longer cellmates, put there by life.

'Marta.' Emilia found the courage, her voice steady. 'I'm going back to Sassaia.'

Marta stopped talking, chewing, smiling.

'Bitch. Ungrateful bitch.'

'I am so grateful. You've caught me in my shittiest moments, you've helped me back up . . .'

Marta gripped her fork in her fist. She tried to plunge it back into the pasta, but her disappointment was too powerful. She shook her head. 'Always for a man.'

'It's not about him.' Emilia looked her in the eyes. 'I mean, he's not the reason.'

'He hasn't texted you, or called?'

He had, of course, more than three weeks earlier, but Emilia had been careful not to tell Marta.

'So why do you have to pull such a shitty move?'

It had never been easy for Emilia to confront Marta, contradict her, disappoint her. But the phone call with her father had, at least to some extent, renewed her.

Her pasta was going cold. 'You said it: we are the exceptions. How many people leave prison with a degree? We did it, we're some kind of miracle. But what was that degree for if I can't choose where I go in the world?'

'A shithole halfway up a mountain?'

'The only place where I've ever been happy – since my mother got ill. Since I became a failure. And I'm not going to give that up, as you say, *for a man*. Whatever he wants, I'm staying in Sassaia. I'll get my job back. My view of the Alps.'

'Do what the fuck you want, you're an adult.'

This time Marta started eating again, with the voracity of someone who was tired of letting others ruin her life.

'Just know that I'm not picking you up next time. Next time the goatherd reduces you to that pitiful state, don't phone me, don't turn up at my door. I won't open it.'

'Marta,' Emilia tried to smile at her, 'after six years of prison together, then another eight as pen pals, we're inseparable. Whether you like it or not.'

She didn't like it. She wanted to rage, because it was her deepest wound, now, that had been opened.

'He throws you out, insults you, humiliates you, and you go crawling back. It's a scene I've seen a thousand times. My father kicking my mum, locking her out in the middle of winter, because there wasn't enough salt in the pasta sauce, because the spaghetti was overdone. Hurling her out onto the doormat like a bag of rubbish, and what did she do? Cry and apologise.'

'Marta.' Emilia tried to take hold of her hand. She pulled it away.

'What do you think is gonna happen? You think he'll be able to look at you every day, every minute, without remembering what you did?'

At this Emilia jumped up from her chair and put both her hands flat on the table; she didn't intend to run away, ever again. 'I want to do what you do: look up when I walk down the street, tell the first person I pass where I come from, like you did with Habib at the station. Not hide, not make up lies. I want my own place. And if Bruno intends to be there with me, so be it. If not, Sassaia isn't his. I don't need anyone's permission to exist.'

She went into the bedroom and started packing her bag.

Marta knocked at the door half an hour later, opening it slowly. She looked exhausted. 'I'm sorry, I went too far.'

Emilia turned towards her. Open on the bed, half full, was the wheelie suitcase she'd bought from the discount store after the phone call with her dad.

'Do you remember when the President of the Republic replied to you?' she asked Marta. 'And you couldn't believe it, Frau couldn't believe it, nobody believed it? But it happened.'

Marta nodded.

'Do you remember when you graduated, what you said to me?'

Marta stayed at the door, leaning on the frame, precarious.

'You told me you had won, that you felt *free, happy.*'

Both of them felt a shiver run down their spine. The words 'freedom' and 'happiness' always sounded obscene on their lips.

'I want to try it too,' said Emilia.

She returned to filling her suitcase with the Milanese dresses her friend had given her, and the ones she'd bought for herself with the money from her brief stint in the bookshop.

'I'll be waiting for you up there, in the mountains.'

Marta closed her eyes. Emilia kissed her eyelids, pressing her lips to each one. She grabbed her bag, pulled on her jacket and left.

And Marta let her go, because that's what true friends do.

32

I WENT IN FIRST, to be sure. I checked that he wasn't lying in drunken ambush somewhere, ready to hit us with a bat – or worse. I opened the doors, inspected every room, taking in the state he had left things in. It was dirty and untidy, certainly, but it didn't seem like anything was missing. Only the cows had gone – there was a great silence from the barn next door; they'd probably already been sold. He wasn't there, which was the most important thing. I turned back to the open door and told Martino and Adelaide they could come home.

The arrest had taken Fiume Senior by surprise. He had gone down to the Samurai to drink and curse, but this time he'd found neither moral support nor credit for the génépis he'd brought with him. Piero was leaning over the bar and told him loud and clear that in this valley there was no place for men who beat their wives and children, and that he'd better leave if he didn't fancy being dragged into the woods to meet the same end as Brother Dolcino. The others, old and young, nodded from their tables and paused their games of Tressette to glare at him. If you don't report, people can know while not knowing. But if the truth is written in black and white, then there's no escaping from it. He retreated without protest, having understood, and went to sit under the bus shelter on the other side of the piazza, wondering what to do with himself.

This can happen in small isolated villages where the mindset hasn't changed for centuries: people badmouth and tease, but when the time comes they know how to truly help one another. Which is one of the reasons I came back and stayed.

Adelaide was still in a bad way, but as soon as she found herself back home, her face changed. She went straight to the kitchen and circled the table, regaining ownership of the pantry, the sink, the pots and pans. She filled one with water and asked if I'd stay for lunch.

'No, thank you,' I said. 'I have to be off.'

It wasn't true: I didn't have anywhere to be. But it wasn't easy to stay there and linger in the separation.

Martino was standing stock-still in the middle of the living room, rucksack on his back, jacket and hat still on, as if ready to leave again at any moment. I turned to him and tried to smile. He kept a sombre look on his face. But what could we do about it? If I wasn't his family and he wasn't mine?

'Let's name a day: Friday, Saturday? And every week, on that day, you come to my house for lunch.'

His mouth twisted: he couldn't be content with so little.

'You come to my house for lunch, and in the afternoon we'll go down to the city.' I raised the stakes. 'Gelateria and then billiards.'

Martino was difficult to buy, but his closed, pissed-off mouth was starting to soften. He touched the straps of his backpack, slowly took it off and let it fall to the ground with a thump.

'Billiards, fine. But no gelato: I'm not a kid anymore.'

He allowed himself to glance quickly around and recognise the sad, cheap pictures on the walls, the sofa covered in Misty's fur, the dusty carpet, the TV on the little table. Suddenly he ignored me, threw himself onto the sofa, grabbed the remote control and put cartoons on – the thing he had missed most at mine in Sassaia. I looked at him and thought: you healed me, little shepherd.

I went back into the kitchen to say goodbye to Adelaide. She had already laid the table. The sauce smelt delicious. Life had picked up where it left off.

'I'm off. If you need anything, I'll keep my phone on.'

'Mr Teacher,' she called as I was on my way out. There was nothing I could do to stop her from calling me that. 'Thank you,' she said, looking down at the floor, as if she was ashamed to have needed my help.

'It's you two who helped me,' I responded. And at that point I too looked at the floor, then turned to ruffle Martino's hair as he lay sprawled in front of *Power Rangers*, and closed the door behind me.

Walking back down towards Alma, I tried not to think about the empty house that was waiting for me. As I passed the Samurai, I realised that everyone had come outside to watch me with a strange excitement, strange little smiles. But I paid no attention: they were mad. We were all mad around here.

I returned to the alleyways of Sassaia, paying no attention to anything. Nothing seemed to have changed. I ate a sandwich, although I wasn't hungry, and then went up to my study to correct homework, keep my mind busy. I watered the cyclamens. Then, since it was only five in the afternoon, I decided to start the weekly laundry early. I put the basket on my back and went to the washhouse. Doing the laundry by hand in freezing water tires you out, and I needed that. I wanted to arrive at the evening exhausted and then fall asleep as soon as my head hit the pillow.

I got dinner ready at around seven, laying the table for one. It felt cold and dark in the room, so I lit the stove. I sat down at the table facing the street. That's when I saw . . .

The lights were on in all the windows of the house opposite.

That morning in the summer, Rita came to pick Emilia up very early – as the one responsible for her exceptional trip out, and the one who would be responding to any glitch in the plan.

'She can't turn up there in handcuffs, escorted by the prison police,' Frau agreed. 'And anyway, she deserves it, this opportunity,' Frau agreed again, adding the sign of the cross.

It was 2004. In recent months, Emilia's 'chain,' as they liked to say inside, 'had fallen off'. She had studied little and poorly. She'd botched her thesis. The only decent parts had basically been dictated by Pandolfi, and the rest could barely be called coherent Italian. She didn't believe in it anymore. She had believed in it before, in years gone by, when she had first started studying again. Even amidst the constant flow of poor souls around her, with the reduced and simplified programmes with fewer hours, in classes of just three or four inmates-cum-students, she had felt she could do it.

But now she was taking the final exam, which was the same one that other teenagers were taking – those who weren't inmates-cum-students. Kids who had covered the whole curriculum, and been able to do their homework in peace in their own bedrooms or at the library, without other people's music playing at full blast in the corridors, without crises, insurrections, fights, meetings with lawyers, without their mind always being on their sentence.

She would be treated the same, with the same external examiner, the same unknown teaching staff – just like the others. Only she wasn't *just like the others*, nowhere near. So the old Emilia returned, complete with cuts on her arms and a black outlook on life. What was the point in studying, in graduating high school? If once she got out she'd always be *the Ravenna girl*?

She got into Rita's bashed-up Punto and they drove out of the prison gates. Piazza San Francesco immediately opened up in front of them, flooded with light. Although her heart was heavy as lead, Emilia was still amazed: Bologna was so beautiful. It was never grey, anywhere. There were bicycles, posters for concerts, jugglers half-asleep at the traffic lights. Poplar blossom drifted down onto the avenues.

Rita didn't speak, she just turned the radio on. Emilia was too bewitched by the whole living world not sectioned up by bars to absorb the news. The prison staff always feared that inmates would escape during a trip out, and this would've been Emilia's opportunity: all she'd have needed to do was open the car door at the next red light, jump out and run for as long as she had air in her lungs and strength in her legs. Then she would've gone into a bar and ordered a giant spritz.

'Rita, I'm only not running away because it's you, you know.'

'We'd miss you.' She was driving calmly, but Emilia could see that she was on edge.

'If Venturi had brought me, I'd already be in Piazza Maggiore. They'd find me this evening, but I'd be shit-faced by then.'

'If that's all you want, I'll take you to the bar. *After.*'

Emilia laughed. 'Really?'

'Only if you're good. A little glass of Prosecco, then you immediately eat a mint. But you mustn't ever tell, even under torture.'

Emilia swallowed. She had to get something off her chest, and with Rita, she could. 'I'd rather do it in prison, the exam.'

Her social worker slammed on the brakes in the middle of the road, even though it was rush hour and she risked causing a huge pile-up. She turned towards her, purple in the face, shouting, 'Do you have any idea how much we begged the security magistrate? We were on our knees, swearing on our kids' lives!'

Emilia had one worry, one anxiety that was bigger than all the others. 'Do you think they know, the other kids?'

'No, Emilia, they don't.' Overwhelmed by the protesting car horns, middle fingers, curses and insults, Rita pulled up onto the kerb and put her hazard lights on. 'Listen. You are going in there as an external candidate. Like any other person who wants to take their final exam. Nobody knows who you are or where you come from. You sit down and you write your essay. That's it.'

'I'm shitting myself.'

'Vargas told me she hates you for having this opportunity that she didn't have last year.'

'I know.'

'So make the most of it! Do it for her, for the others. And most importantly, for yourself.'

Make the most of it was a piss-take.

The reality was that she had no choice. It had been taken away from her years before.

A quarter of an hour later, her legs jelly, Emilia walked into the Artusi Professional Hospitality Institute: not the prison branch, the real thing.

She recognised the typical form and colours of an Italian public school in the corridors, the classrooms, the windows.

The smell was so unlike prison – the smell of chalk, of young people, of teenage crises, of not having a care in the world – the same smell as her previous life. She merged into the flow of girls and boys a year younger than her, going in and out of classrooms in dribs and drabs. She found classroom 5B, where she'd been told to go, and holding her breath, crossed the threshold.

Her hands were trembling. Her heart was trembling. Many people were already sitting down, nervously fiddling with their pens and hiding notes to copy from in their pencil cases. Nobody looked up when Emilia entered. Nobody pointed at her or exposed her: *it's the monster, the monster of Ravenna!*

She sat down at a desk in the back row. She looked at the barless windows for a long time, the clear sky outside and the pollen suspended in the air, floating, letting itself be carried on the wind. Then a teacher arrived with the envelopes. She waited for the fateful time and then opened them, and gave Emilia her sheet of paper stamped by the ministry. She read and reread the marks on the page, unable to decode them. Her thoughts were like the pollen outside flying weightlessly, sticking to nothing. She chose a question on instinct: the short essay on art. Not because she knew anything about it, but because she liked the way it sounded: 'Light in Caravaggio'.

She took the lid off her biro and placed the tip on the line of the white paper. It remained there, in that position, at that possible start point, for an undetermined time. Then she looked up at the downward-facing heads of her unknown fellow exam-takers, who were wearing the same kind of jeans and T-shirt as she was. Their faces were focused, their pens moving fast; maybe they had one eye on the holiday they'd go on as a reward after results. And she was there, with them. No walkie-talkies, no keys, no heavy doors slamming. The light bathed the classroom like a calm lake. And her heart swelled, paused in a breathless wave of gratitude.

She would write a meagre page full of spelling mistakes, twisted lines of reasoning, and she'd still be the last to hand it in, so as not to lose even a millisecond of that silence.

She'd do pitifully, get the minimum mark. But, in that classroom, in that marvellous silence, the rustle of paper, of ink, of concentration, as she wrote her essay alongside everyone else, Emilia had felt like a normal person.

On Monday March 21st, 2016, at three in the afternoon, when she got off the bus and found herself again in the small square in Alma, in front of Rosa's grocery shop, the school, the church, the windows of the Samurai from which everyone was squinting out at her in surprise, she felt it again: that she was normal. Nobody else could know how beautiful, how rare, that word was.

So she raised a hand in greeting to the patrons of the bar, among whom was Basilio, who came outside to greet her with all the teeth he had, tears in his eyes. She lit a Winston and headed towards the steps, half-hidden by brambles which were no longer burnt by the cold but were now unfurling new leaves.

As she started to walk up Stra' dal Forche, pulling her wheelie suitcase behind her, her lungs steeped in smoke, her legs already aching from lack of practice, she couldn't help laughing.

There was no more snow. The branches of the beech trees, birches and chestnuts were sprouting buds. Some of the birds had returned to fill the air with tweeting and the flutter of wings. Ants were starting to emerge from the tree trunks.

When she got as far as the shrine of the little Madonna, she stopped and noticed some faded writing on the side that she'd never noticed before:

You'll find more in the woods than in books.
The trees and the rocks will show you what no teacher can.

The silence, she thought. That's what the teaching is. The silence and the light, and the winter that always comes to an end.

She started walking again, her nostrils full of the smell of leaves, stems and pollen; the wholeness that was beginning again, wilful and determined, because the important thing was to keep on living, at any cost – to find the courage to live.

By the time she reached the final stretch, Emilia was a breathless mess. The wheelie suitcase had been a bad idea. But, after the final bend, the black and white sign emerged from the trees and Sassaia materialised in front of her eyes, unscathed. Preserved in time, immersed in the light of Caravaggio.

I got up from the table and rushed outside.

With my long beard and dirty shirt, blood pumping at a ridiculous speed, I crossed the alleyway, looked at the door and thought: now I'll knock and someone else will answer. Riccardo, Aldo, an unknown new tenant.

I knocked anyway. Three decisive bangs that echoed across the mountains. The seconds rolled down like heavy rocks. I was stunned by adrenaline, by fear, by uncertainty. But my body knew.

The door opened, provoking a release of air from my lungs that was equal to or more than the air that had been ripped from me in 1990. Only this time it put me back in the centre.

Emilia was there, in ripped low-waisted jeans with the waistband of her knickers peeking out. There, in an oversized red and white checked shirt, half unbuttoned, no bra underneath. There, vibrating and raging even if she looked calm on the surface. There, with her real surname.

She wasn't wearing makeup and hadn't brushed her hair. She challenged me with her typically insolent expression, as if to say: *you saw? I'm back.*

Why? What are your intentions? I asked her silently with my eyes.

She replied with a smile. *You can't even imagine.*

In all this, she was inside and I was outside. She'd been right all along; words were of absolutely no use. Not for living, at least.

She grabbed my shirt and pulled me to her. She shut the cold out. We didn't make it to the first floor. There was no need to close the curtains or be quiet.

We fell onto the sofa, our bodies so incandescent I thought they might burst. For a moment the thought exploded in my head: I was about to do it with *a murd*—. The word died inside me, unravelling itself.

As I undressed her and her me, not just removing our clothes but all of the past and the future and the names and appearances and laws and conventions and rights and wrongs, I pulled my mouth from hers to say the only thing that I still hadn't said, the only thing that mattered to me that night: 'I love you.'

33

But the past was there.

It was definitely there.

And so was the future.

Both shadows crouched there beneath the furniture, in the alley outside the window, behind the doors.

Emilia lit a Winston. 'I don't want to give in this easily,' she said, tossing her hair back. She was naked, lying on her back on the sofa, her legs entwined with mine.

Also naked, I looked at her, bewitched, my head resting against the other arm of the sofa. I wanted her not to speak, not to get up; for us not to ever have to leave the warm and fragile cocoon of that moment.

But Emilia got up. With the cigarette hanging from her lips, she pulled on her knickers, her jeans and her shirt and walked over to the table where there was already a sketchpad and pencil laid out, ready to use.

She sat down and inhaled distractedly. Then she put her cigarette in the ashtray, opened the pad, picked up the pencil and, without looking at me, as if I no longer existed, started sketching with a methodical fury.

Although the fire in the stove was roaring, I suddenly felt cold. I got dressed, opened the cupboard and took out two glasses and a bottle of *nocino* because I sensed we might need it. And I went to sit across the table from her.

Her face was dark. She was hunched over, absorbed in the sheet of paper that I tried not to look at. Sweat was dripping down her temples and she was breathing fast, chaotically, her legs crossed and her hair falling over her face. She pushed it back behind her ears without stopping the movement of her pencil, too enraptured to look for a hairband.

I poured myself half a glass and rested my gaze on the useless television, the brass pots I had polished. I had no idea if she'd noticed the improvements I'd made to the garden and the attic, the tap in the bathroom that was no longer dripping. But this wasn't the time to ask. The clock said it was half past eight. Sassaia was like a star fallen down to earth, landed in a lost and inaccessible place. Emilia was smoking with one hand while the other didn't put the pencil down once. I listened to the scratching of the lead against the silence.

She looked up only when she had finished. First she evaluated the result with a severe face, then she stared at me with an urgent, shining intensity that I had never seen in her before. She turned the sheet around and placed it in front of me.

It was a portrait of a girl. She was very young, and some hair had escaped from her ponytail and fallen over her face, as if it were windy.

Her eyes were pale and shrewd. Her lips thin, tense in an allusive smile. I didn't recognise her. Emilia had also sketched her shoulders, her protruding collarbones, the straps of a triangle bikini.

'This is Angela,' she said. She pronounced the words carefully: 'Angela Massia.'

My blood turned cold.

She had said, *this is*, not *this was*.

I wanted to stop her and say: no, you don't need to do this. But my mouth was like sawdust, and I knew, deep down, that she did.

I knew that you can't love someone without knowing their whole story, especially the darkness.

'Almost fifteen years have passed. But I remember every mole on her back and every freckle on her shoulders. I remember the dimple she had on her chin and the two she had above her sacrum that the boys were wild for. Oh how I envied her them . . . they're still here –' she pushed a finger against her eyelid – 'bobbing above her bikini bottoms as she struts along the beach. Her eyes are here too, which were her best feature, along with her tits. It's all engraved here, branded, as if I've never seen anything else in my whole life.

'At the beginning I used to dream about her, so I asked them to up my dose. I would bash my forehead against the bars to try and get her out of my mind. The way she used to smile at me, take the piss out of me. I saw her, as if she was real, standing in front of me. Then they raised my dose so much that I stopped dreaming altogether. For a long time. And when I started again, I dreamed of

Sassaia. Which is the reason I'm here, getting in your hair.' She lit another cigarette and leaned back in the chair, looking out the window into the night. 'I was the last person to see her. I was the last person she saw.' She closed her eyes. 'You can't undo something like that.'

'Start from the beginning,' I implored her. 'Please.'

Emilia returned to sitting with her back straight and head high, composed. She took a sip of *nocino*.

'We lived next door to each other. She moved in soon after my mother died, and maybe I read this coincidence as a sign. We were also in the same class.

'We weren't very nice to each other; we were too different. But maybe that's why we were also drawn to one another. She had everything. I couldn't see beyond her good fortune: her still-whole family, her beauty, how secure she was in herself, or at least seemed to be. I envied her, but also admired her. Because if you're beautiful and smart, it must be because you deserve it, right?

'Anyway, she was also a bitch.' She smiled. 'I know, you're not allowed to say that about the dead, you have to say only nice things. But what can I say? She was. That's not all she was, of course. She was many, many other things. I knew her as well as I knew myself, or so I thought.

'She blanked me in front of the others at school, because she said I "ruined her reputation". When I went to the beach with her, I had to lay my towel down away from hers, even if we had just got ready together and peed together at her house.

'Sure, now I see it from here, from the age I am now, she was nasty like the rose in *The Little Prince* with her thorns. Among the few books that circulated in prison, *The Little Prince* was the most popular,' she added, in response to a look of surprise on my face I hadn't been aware of. 'Do you know it? *What is essential is invisible to the eye?* That bullshit? But when the only things in front of your eyes are complete shit, it sounds pretty good.'

What was visible to my eye right now was her, my love, making a devastating effort. And I too was making a devastating effort to remain there, where I was.

'Anyway, it was a complicated relationship. Imagine, my first kiss on the lips was with her, not a boy. "I'll teach you," she'd said, "you're so awkward." And then she made a massive fuss, as if she was making some huge sacrifice. But I knew that she liked it, and I liked it too. And inside I thought: for real, Angela, you're the devil. Without knowing that the devil was, in fact, me.

Maybe I was obsessed with her, like they wrote in one of the reports. In another they wrote that she, in my sick head, had taken the place of my mother. Of course, it's not like I had many other people in my life. No one I could actually call a friend. Guys? Go figure. Only you, of all the people I've ever met, has found me attractive. I didn't give a shit about school, or about dancing or piano or any of the things my mother made me do that I was bad at. She'd always say, 'The important thing isn't being good, but learning! It's not about excelling, but discovering!'

But you've seen the shithole of a world we live in. If you don't excel, you die. In that respect, I'd rather be in jail forever.'

She looked me in the eye then, perhaps to see the effect that kind of comment was having on me. But I was inert, pale, frightened; determined, however, to listen deeply.

'I know that you know nothing about prison. Nobody knows anything if they haven't been in there,' she added with a half-smile. Then, quickly becoming serious again: 'But right now it's Angela I have to talk about.

'Basically, she was this colossal cunt with a mother and perfect hair and an athletic brother who I fell in love with by . . . what do I mean . . . by osmosis? By law of transmission?

'Being with Angela meant always having someone in front of me who I was desperate to become, but never could, for which I both hated and loved her. I idolised her and envied her to death.

'The thing that most disturbed me to discover *after*, at the trial, was how insecure she really was. She had been seeing a psychologist, but she'd never told me that. In her diary she wrote that she felt inadequate, that she had too much pressure put on her by her mother, by school, by the world; she felt them breathing down her neck, pushing her to aspire, aspire, aspire. While in my eyes her mother was the best mother in the world. She'd dedicated her life to her children, to working today to make them into something tomorrow. And now, out of all the people who hate me, Angela's mother is the one who hates me the most. And I understand.

'There hasn't been a single anniversary of Angela's death on which she hasn't organised a torchlit procession. On which she doesn't buy an entire page of the *Resto del Carlino* newspaper to remember her daughter – for which I pay the price. I was given sixteen years, the maximum for a minor with an abbreviated trial. Which then became fourteen years, four months and nine days for good behaviour. And you can't imagine the fuss she made. She went on national TV, on the radio, wrote letters to the minister. And I wished I could explain to her that that year and eight months gave me not even a milligram of relief, didn't change and never will change anything. Neither for me or for her.

'But she had brought her into the world, she was her daughter; she had given birth to her, nursed her, rocked her, raised her, dreamed of a wonderful future for her. A surgeon, a businesswoman, Miss Italia, married to an equally successful man, with four or five children. And then this total imbecile – me – arrived, this wriggling worm who didn't even deserve to have been born, and destroyed everything.' Emilia shook her head hard. She reached her arms out. 'How can I find fault with that? How can I explain to her, one day, that I'm not a mother, I'll never be a mother, but that I think I know what she went through? Her devastation, her desperation? She'd never believe me.'

She lit a third cigarette, and I got up to let the smoke out. Really I got up to open the window and breathe.

'In December 2000, my last year of high school, Angela started seeing this guy. He was thirty-seven and had a wife and a little boy. He was a pig, really; depraved. But she lost her mind over him.

'It seemed too good to be true, you see? He worked in a used-car salesroom, killed himself at the gym, was always tanned and clean-shaven. You know those guys on dating shows? He was like that. Apparently he'd even auditioned to go on one, but didn't get picked.

'So he stayed in his hometown, had a family, and replaced his TV dreams with an affair with a good little girl. And I became nothing to Angela.

'She saw him every afternoon she could. Now she was fucking, no longer a virgin, she kind of moved up a level, while I . . . could only imagine,' she smiled with infinite sadness, 'I would have to wait for you.'

My eyes must have widened, incredulous. Emilia nodded, confirming that yes, I really had been her first.

'And that Emanuele guy?'

She stifled a laugh. 'The Neighbour? Oh, I'm a pretty good liar when I want to be.'

I looked at her, not fully comprehending. So Emilia had to reveal the true story of Emanuele and the little notes thrown through the bars – a parenthesis that made me laugh and broke my heart at the same time.

But we were sitting at a table with the portrait of Angela Massia in the middle for a reason. We couldn't laugh or go off on a tangent any longer.

'I was useful to her.' Emilia looked at the paper and straightened it because it had been nudged off its neat right angle. She caressed it with one hand. '"Mamma I'm going out with Emi", "Mamma I'm going to study at Emi's", and everything was suddenly possible. I was the excuse, the alibi, the key to hiding away with him in the car parks or pine woods of Ravenna. And when he was at work, or with his family, or with his friends, I became the replacement, the confessional booth, the armchair room in *Big Brother*. I was there to listen to her go on about how much she loved him, how cool he was, and how as soon as she turned eighteen he was going to leave his wife and marry her.

'She never asked me: and you? Do you exist?

'And I was jealous. I felt betrayed.

'And are these reasonable motives? Of course they aren't. Are there any serious, valid motives for what I did?'

She rubbed a hand over her face as if she wanted to erase it, her hair damp and stuck to her temples. She drank another sip of *nocino*, but then got up and went to get a packet of crisps because she didn't want to get drunk, wanted to remain lucid. I watched her and it seemed to me that, as she pulled the words out of her body, she was losing kilos and years.

I looked at the time: ten o'clock. Neither of us had eaten.

'You don't have to tell me everything tonight.'

'No, I do,' she responded, putting a fistful of crisps into her mouth. 'Otherwise we can't move forwards, I can't stay here. I'll never have a place of my own.'

'OK.' I nodded. I thought again of the story of the Neighbour, of her and the other girls she had named: Yasmina, Myriam and Afifa. 'Why don't you tell me about prison first? That's part of the story too, right? An important part. And I'd like to hear it.'

34

Between 10:30 p.m. and three in the morning, Emilia recounted her years in prison, which I've recounted in these pages. And I admit that I enjoyed those hours. Not that Emilia wasn't in pain – but her eyes were lively, her face morphing into a thousand expressions, her words washing over me like a warm stream.

'I don't know, or rather, I don't know anymore, what idea people outside prison have of young offenders' institutions. But I can tell you that where I was there were no mafia bosses, no scary Camorrists, and even the worst people were still just lost souls, deep down. We were all unlucky bitches.'

As she told her story, I saw her body flinch with emotion and her soul shine through in the way she gesticulated, the way she raised and lowered her voice, as if still inhabited by all those people: Vilma, Rita, Frau, even Venturi.

She also recounted an episode which perhaps had not happened long ago: the elections, when the volunteers arrived with forms and ballot boxes and those who had the right to vote went down to the visitor room. I want to mention it because those of us outside would never imagine it. Or rather we forget that those exiled, condemned, segregated people are still citizens.

Emilia told me that Marta was always so excited when the time to vote came, and how everyone felt so important on that day – everyone except the ones who were born in Italy without citizenship, who were justifiably enraged.

I felt like I could see and hear them, those girls. I felt like I cared deeply for them despite having only met them through Emilia's voice, because of the way she talked about them, the way she loved them. That was the most absurd thing about that long night – that it was overflowing with love.

'The breaking point was when our high school exam results came out. It was June 19th, 2001. We went to get them together, parked our scooters one next to the other in front of the school. All of our grades were there on display; the usual public humiliation for me.'

We were exhausted by this point, consumed by tiredness. Yet we both sat there, eyes wide open, fervent with attention.

'I'd done very poorly, failing three subjects – the usual kick in the butt – but I'd just about passed the rest. I was happy that I didn't have to retake the year, especially because it meant I wouldn't lose her. She, on the other hand, got all 9s.

'She had promised me we would celebrate together if we both did well. She had sworn to me that we'd go to Marina, meet the others and stay out late on the beach with a bonfire, guitars, joints and boxes of wine. I couldn't go without her invitation; I wouldn't be welcome at any party otherwise. She had even written it in my school journal. On the page of June 19ᵗʰ, she had circled the number and drawn an arrow with the words: "This will be our crazy day!"

'But when the day came, he arrived in his shitty yellow Opel Tigra – the chavviest car in Ravenna – with his swollen bicep resting on the window frame, his hair gelled, sunglasses on as if he was some secret agent who for some reason lived in our neighbourhood. She, obviously, spun around to me breathlessly and took both my hands. Like Judas. "Sorry, Emi, but I can't go anymore. You understand, don't you?"'

Emilia paused. Something very, very old re-emerged from the depths of her eyes. Something I recognised as anger. An anger that now was just a weak echo of the past, but that at the time must have been an untameable fire.

'I went home on my own and shut myself in my room. I spent the whole day in there with my earphones in, listening to Marilyn Manson.

'They were all happy. This obvious fact bounced around my head. They were all, all of them happy, apart from me. Everyone was celebrating the summer with someone else, they were all loved, appreciated, joyful, and I was the only one cut off; the only one not good enough, the only victim of this injustice. And I thought seriously about killing myself to make them pay. Only I was smart enough to know that no one would've cared.' She stared at me again, feverish. 'You've gone through worse, I know, and you're still good, you're still right. But not me, Bruno: I couldn't handle it.

'I've asked myself a million times: what is evil? I wanted to take philosophy at university purely for that reason. To find out.

'Is it a mistake that you make? A choice? Or is it a flaw in your system, a fault in every human? Is it madness? Is it an addition, a crazy cell that you're born with? Or is it a subtraction?

'I think it's a subtraction. Like a void that starts as a small crack inside, and then it digs away, and keeps digging, until it annihilates you.

'Pain doesn't improve anyone. Or rather, it can improve people who are already strong, who have support. I've always had an exceptional father, but I didn't accept his help; I believed I didn't deserve it, or that I was too weak to ask for it. I preferred to take pleasure in the hate, to rot in it. Which, really, is the easiest thing you can do – have it in for everyone else when really you're the problem.'

She stood up passionately without meaning to. Then suddenly she stopped and looked around, as if she had just landed and didn't know where she was. She laid two weary eyes on me.

'I didn't know how to forgive, Bruno. My mother, for her death. My schoolmates. Angela. Myself, for being what I was.

'I didn't know how to let things go.'

She sat down again, smoothing out the portrait of Angela, touching the edges of her face with her fingertips.

'When my father got home that night, me progressing to the next school year was something to be celebrated. I was there, sitting in the kitchen at the empty table, just like the night my mother died. I had believed that was the worst day of my life, but this one felt just as bad. And I didn't know that another would come that would be far worse. Because having something evil done to you – I know now – is much better than doing something evil to someone else.

'There's no escape from the evil you do to someone else.'

Her hands shook as she tried and failed to light another cigarette. I watched as she fought with herself and I felt excruciating pain for her. I took the lighter from her hand and helped her. Again I found myself wanting to say, 'That's enough now, let's go to bed.'

But after a couple of puffs, she found her concentration again.

It was four in the morning.

'On June 22nd, 2001, I wrote her a text arranging to meet. An SMS sent with my white Alcatel:

Meet me tomorrow at 2 on Stradello della Pesca? I need to talk to you, it's important.

She could have responded the way she had a thousand times before, with, 'No, I'm seeing Fabio.'

It was likely – extremely likely – that she'd blow me off.

But instead she wrote back:

OK, Fabio's working tomorrow anyway.

O

'On June 23rd, at half past one, I put a knife in my rucksack and left the house.

'A long knife, the longest one I could find in the kitchen.

'It took less than twenty minutes to get to Stradello della Pesca. I remember my bedroom was freezing. I'd had the air-con on full blast all morning because I was sweating like a horse. And when I got outside it was forty degrees. The tarmac was red hot, I could see it shimmering at the end of our road. The sun was at its highest point above my head. It felt like it was burning everything.

'Before getting on my scooter, I said to myself: what the hell are you doing? Go back inside and put the knife away.

'I'd always been capable of both understanding and wanting. Right from when I chose the place and the time of the meeting. It was just that – how can I put it? The understanding was disconnected from the wanting. No, it was the opposite. Because I understood no, but I wanted yes. I was lucid, conscious, I understood perfectly that it was a stupid thing. But this was also a film. That I'd been making for a long time in my head. And now I wanted to watch it.

'I put my helmet on and left. It was Saturday and there was traffic in town, but I overtook everyone on my scooter, riding past the market stalls rammed with swimming costumes and towels, the corner shops displaying their beach toys outside – buckets and sand moulds. I remembered stopping with my mother to buy them, new ones every year.

'This thought could have stopped me. But it didn't.

'There were so many colours, so much light, it was almost a party atmosphere. But I was like a slice of darkness circling under the bright light of the sun. Stuffed full of rage, I pushed my Phantom to its maximum speed. I played the film over and over again as I rode. The film of Emilia: an important person who nobody had ever noticed. Passing the cemetery, I wondered: where is he in all this?

'Papa, who comes to kiss you on the forehead every night before going to sleep? Who knocks on your bedroom door as soon as he gets home from work to ask how you are? Who always wants to talk to you, to listen to you?

'Papa, who doesn't deserve this.

'No, I wasn't going to think of him. I banished him from my mind.

'Too uncomfortable.

I was thinking only about myself.'

'I have to explain the Stradello della Pesca.

'Before Marina, before the beaches, the pier, the hotels, the *piadina* shops and the seafood restaurants, there's this stretch of dirty road that leads to the canal.

'It's a brutal place. You can see the petrochemical plant and the industrial port from there; dozens of cranes, warehouses, stacks of shipping containers, chimneys constantly smoking and tankers as big as craters on the moon. They take up the whole horizon. It's a cut-off place, just like how I felt. The road it leads to is full of holes and along one side runs a row of wooden shacks, with fishing nets submerged in the canal and little jetties for the boats. Families go there at the weekend to grill fish on their barbecues. And, on the other side of the road there's a pine wood. The most dense and untamed wood in Ravenna.

'I repeated to myself so many times on the Stradello with the forty-degree heat beating down on my helmet: as if I'd ever actually use this knife. I'm not unhinged.

'I had the impression I was playing a game. That I'd push myself to the line to see what happened, but I wouldn't cross it.

'But in my head I kept seeing Angela strutting over to the Tigra, leaving me behind like a piece of rubbish. And this image, I don't know why, got muddled with the image of my mother when she weighed thirty-seven kilos, already smelling of decomposition. It was just an excuse, that rage; I can see that now. The truth is that inside me there was a hole, a powerful abyss that was crouching, clawed and sharp-toothed, under my life.

'The wanting said: I'll show you that I'm stronger, stupid bitch. The understanding laughed: it couldn't take me seriously.

'I arrived at the end of the Stradello and parked up in the usual place Angela and I met when we had something shady to do, like smoking, necking wine, or talking about serious things. I saw straight away that her scooter wasn't there.

'The understanding said: *better this way – you dodged it.*

'The wanting replied: *see what this slut is like? Her little Fabio will have called her, he's free at the last minute, and she couldn't even find the time to send you a text.*

'Five minutes later I heard a scooter arrive and I turned around: it was her. Her Aprilia SR was kicking up dust.

'She pulled in next to me and turned the engine off. The thing I remembered most often, after, was the moment she took her helmet off. The naturalness of that gesture, which demonstrated how much she underestimated me, the trust she had in me. She didn't look at me, didn't even say hello. She checked her phone because her mind was elsewhere.

'Anyway, what was she supposed to expect from the stupidest girl in the class? That I had a knife in my backpack?

'My throat was dry, my mouth like sandpaper, my heart cold.

'I waited for her to finish sending her message, which was to Fabio, as would emerge in the investigations – but I didn't need an investigation to tell me that. Fabio, by the way, would lose everything: his job, his family. After the newspapers had published and embellished their story, I think he even left Ravenna.

'Anyway, I was staring at the enormous cranes in the port that blockaded the sea; the swampy water of the canal; the barges lined up in the distance. I wasn't breathing, not even when Angela got off her bike and finally deigned to look at me.

'"So? What did you have to tell me?" I didn't speak then either. Because I couldn't.

'The wanting told me I had to get us to an even more remote place. That I had to be cold and efficient like Jill Valentine in *Resident Evil*, as if this was a video game. Meanwhile, a few kilometres away, the cafés were playing endless music, the beach bars were full of families with children, and from the beaches spread a cheerful clamour that resounded throughout Marina.

'"Let's walk," I managed to say. "We'll go to the upturned boat." Outside was a pool of light. The shade of the pine wood was thick and cold as we ventured in, like it had been that first summer, when she had dragged me along with those two strangers.

'I still hadn't got that drawing out of my head; it would only leave me afterwards, in prison. Among all the things – so many, too many – that I couldn't forgive, the worst had been that afternoon in the pine woods when we posed topless for those two forty-year-olds. An obscene thing that she wanted and I didn't. Because she was an exhibitionist, she was beautiful, she was alive – and I wasn't.

'"You look strange," she said to me. My face must have been that colour.' Emilia pointed at a grubby white doily on the table. 'The understanding rose up and shouted: *leave now, find an excuse*. But the wanting could feel the weight of the knife at the bottom of my bag, under my beach towel.

'As we walked, brambles cutting our calves and a sea of pine needles punching holes in our flip-flops, Angela started telling me that her mother wanted to take her on holiday to Greece for Ferragosto, that she'd been going on and on about it, but that she didn't want to go because she didn't want to be away from her Fabio for two weeks. But I was hearing her as if through cotton wool. My ears were buzzing, making any external sound muddled in my head, weak, even the cicadas trilling like mad on branches so intertangled they darkened the whole sky.

'When we came out, the sun started to burn us again. I closed my eyes instinctively, half blinded, and I felt my legs giving way. My breath roared from inside, everywhere. My heart, however, was slow, really slow, as if it were about to stop.

'What we called "the upturned boat" was an abandoned wooden hull nestled into a bay at the point where the pine grove opened up onto the swampy water. A point where, if you screamed, nobody would hear you.

'I leaned against the boat, rubbing my eyes and trying to bring the place into focus despite the light. I raised my level of alertness so I could perceive any stealthy movement of an animal or person, any outline lying in wait in the darkness. A pine cone fell in the forest, making me jump. While Angela, peaceful, turned her face to the sun to tan it.

'Calm down, I told myself, there can't be anyone down here. Not in the daytime, at least. There were used condoms left over from the nights; cigarette butts, maybe syringes, like my mother always used to warn me about. The depths of the pine woods was a dangerous place, like the depths of darkness. The water was stagnant and smelt of spilled petrol, rot, endings.

'But from there, if I looked hard enough, I could see the sea.

'Half hidden, but glimmering with light. Beautiful, open, clean.

'But I didn't want to.'

'She was the only one who spoke.

But when she paused to ask me, "Anyway, what is it that you were so desperate to tell me?" I realised I had to find an excuse, and I started stammering, like in a horrible oral exam in front of the whole class.

'"Uh, it's about a boy . . ."

'"What? You've got a boyfriend?" She laughed. And that laugh irritated me immediately, made me deathly angry, and a lethal power rose up, like when you spend four hours in a row shooting in *Resident Evil*.

'"No way, I don't believe it!" Of course she didn't believe it; how could I possibly have a boyfriend? And it was indeed a lie, the whole meeting was a lie, our friendship was a lie.

'She started talking about Fabio again, and I was grateful for once because my stomach was filling up with nausea. I had so many things to say to her, but the words weren't coming out. They were out of my reach, like air, evanescent. I needed them and they weren't there.

'I realised, or maybe I only realise now, that if I'd managed to tell her the hate I felt, the anger, the love, however rotten, and that whole tangle of desperate feelings obstructing my throat, I would've saved her life, I would've saved my own life.

'But instead we sat on that hull covered in red paint that peeled like cracked skin. *Hope*, it was called – the boat – even if you could no longer read the H or the P.

'Angela was leaning back on her elbows to tan better, her eyes closed, hair tossed back. A pose that made her completely defenceless.

'It was forty degrees and my teeth were chattering.

'My entire vocabulary had left me, and yet she kept speaking. About what? Fabio? I don't know, because I could no longer hear her.

'I put my bag down next to the boat, on the opposite side to her so as to keep it hidden. I bent down, opened the zip and reached in to feel the handle of the knife under my towel, my suncream, the packet of sanitary towels because you never know. I had been a teenager for so little time. Or maybe I never really was one.

'I was sitting on the edge: it was a matter of centimetres, millimetres. Another pine cone could fall, a coypu could pop its head out of the water, someone on a fishing boat could come close enough to see us. But it was two in the afternoon and the world was empty. So I gripped the knife in my fist and, with all the strength I could muster, plunged it into her stomach.

'Then, since she started screaming, I plunged it into her neck.'

Emilia's eyes, now, were completely extinguished. Her tone of voice was flat. She sat unmoving on the chair, her hands resting on the table, white as a sheet.

'You do it. But you can't really believe that you're doing it.

'Half of you knows that you are, but the other half is convinced that in the end something will save the situation. That an angel will pop out, a fairy from a cartoon, that someone will start laughing and say: OK, joke's over.

'It's like a magic thought, like believing in Father Christmas again. You're sinking a knife into a person's body, your best friend's body, and she is thrashing around and scratching you and you're thinking, *OK, soon the ambulance will arrive, they'll take her to the hospital, and in three days she'll be fine.*'

Emilia clenched her fists and closed her eyes. I saw her body tense up in the effort to go on.

'She fought a lot. I climbed on top of her to keep her still with all my weight, the rotten wood giving us both splinters in our hips, backs and arms. She wanted to live so much, really wanted it.

'Of course she did. She was sixteen years old.

'I didn't want to strike her throat. But my heart had become so dark, so black, and there was so much rage that I no longer knew how to stop it. And my whole life flashed before my eyes.

'My mother taking me to Bagno Amore as a little girl with our netted bag of sand moulds, the chestnuts we collected here in Sassaia with Aunt Iole, the Sunday mornings I crawled under the duvet in my parents' double bed, in between them. Just like they say happens when you die. Because I was dying, with her.

'I watched as the light in her eyes went out and mine went out too. In that kind of dream or video game or film, which was actually reality. Her yellow sundress that had turned red, her two-piece swimsuit with Amalfi lemons on it, and her now struggling to breathe with her divided throat. Then I stuck it in further, this time out of compassion. And I saw those beautiful eyes give up the ghost, her soul slipping away. And I could no longer stop it.

'It's not possible, is it? To kill a person.

'Once she was dead, before I left, I hugged her.'

Emilia's eyes were now two black holes, her face terrifyingly drained of blood. She was absent, incapable of looking at me.

As the golden light of dawn filled the room, I burst into tears.

For Angela Massia who was no longer here, who died in that way at sixteen.

For Emilia who at the same age had killed a person.

For me, who didn't know what I was supposed to do. Get up? Stay? Bash my head against the wall?

I decided to get up. I lifted her by the armpits and helped her up the stairs, with great effort. I put her to bed. Then I curled up next to her.

Exhausted, I lay there, next to a murderer. And what difference was there between me and her? Nothing.

We were two human beings. What she had done, I could have done too. It was a possibility that we all had in our bodies, and whatever was inside them: a soul? An empty abyss?

Unable to sleep, I listened for a long time to the sounds of the forest, the birds, as the beautiful, moving world woke up again, started afresh after the winter. Suddenly I realised how fragile and wonderful the world was, all the good contained in us and in everything, and it was worth caring for at all costs.

So what was evil?

Not knowing how to forgive.

PART THREE

The Sea

35

THE GREEN SURROUNDING THE little Donato church was covered in dandelions, the wind blowing dustings of their seeds.

With my back leaning against the trunk of the only oak tree to offer shade, I remember watching them for a long time, those seeds suspended in the afternoon light, my heart full of fear but also, stronger than the fear – hope.

It was June 22nd, 2016. Later that evening, Emilia and I would head off on a trip with no return date, determined to take the time we needed.

Before talking about the trip, however, I want to recount the most significant events of the spring that had just gone. I don't want to leave anyone behind: we are a harsh, difficult community, but a community nonetheless.

First of all, the *Last Judgement* of Alma was finished.

What's more, Emilia and Basilio had managed to complete it in time for the Easter celebrations, which brought about an almost miraculous effect on my fellow citizens. The rounds of applause bestowed upon Emilia and Basilio when the priest called them up to the altar didn't bother either of them. They just nodded, smiling hazily, then returned to their seats.

The following day they started work in the nearby hamlet of Novella, a twenty-minute walk from Alma. Where they both really wanted to be, though, was Donato – thirty-four kilometres from Alma, the last valley in the province – where there was a small 500-year-old church that Basilio had fallen in love with as a boy. It would only take Emilia a minute to fall for it too: the wooden Pietà, in particular, had moved her to the extent that, purely so she could get to Donato in order to work on it, she'd learned to drive in just two months.

I accompanied her down to the city for her theory lessons and driving practice. We spent entire Saturdays and Sundays revising every possible road sign. With no car parks in Valle big enough to bash the Seat around in, we'd go down to the desolate open spaces between industrial warehouses in the city, to allow her to practise the clutch and me to practise patience.

But she did it, stubborn as she is. And so, from the end of May, she and Basilio could get to Donato to be near to the Pietà they both felt was astonishing, and a Danse Macabre that was rather rare around here.

I suffered a bit from the solitude during that period, but Martino came to mine for lunch every Friday, and then we went to the Samurai to play billiards under the gazebo Piero had put up for the summer season.

Then school finished and there was the usual big party on the riverbank. And I realise that *big* for a class of thirteen children might sound like an exaggeration, but for me it really was.

There were parents, siblings, cousins, old teachers, all with homemade cakes, biscuits from Rosa's, pizzas and fruit juice. And most importantly, Emilia was there.

She was dressed nicely, for once, in a flowery pink cotton dress that called attention to her femininity rather than her time spent in jail: we liked to joke about that. She met my pupils – she already knew Martino – and their parents, and Alma welcomed her warmly, of course not knowing her past but seeing her only for who she was now: clean hair, lighter eyes, the desire to contribute. I believe, after all, it's only right that the darkness be given to those who love us.

It was only Patrizia who blushed and lowered her gaze each time she passed her, even though Emilia offered, when the moment arose, to help her hand out the slices of cake. I laughed a lot at that scene, at Patrizia's sudden stuttering and Emilia's 'young Alma lass' willingness. I never told her who it was that gave me that article. What was the point? Some things are best left unsaid.

Finally, that last part of June came which is no longer work, but isn't yet the summer holidays. The days between exams and the results were so dull that I decided to join Emilia and Basilio, getting into the back seat of the Seat with a couple of books, a thermos and a sandwich.

They protested at first, taking it as an intrusion. They warned me, 'We don't want to be disturbed while we're working'. But I didn't even dream of going into the church.

I just wanted to stay outside and read in the shade of the big oak tree.

The hill that the Donato church sits upon is far from the main roads and the town; the only way to get to it is along a dirt track. The mountains surrounding it, unlike the ones in Sassaia, aren't close enough to touch; they expand and soften as they cross Valle d'Aosta. It's where both the province and the entire region ends, where mine and Emilia's little world ends and the beyond begins, blurred in a blue haze like the sea.

That day, June 22nd, 2016, I went along with them, even though I knew we probably wouldn't leave until gone midnight and so it would've been good to get ahead with the preparations: packing, sorting the flowers, doing the housework. But it was too beautiful a day, the sky clear and the wind sweet, and the little church had the power to calm anyone's mind, even mine in anticipation of that trip.

While they took care of the Pietà, the Danse Macabre and yet another Black Madonna, I pulled Martino Fiume's last piece of writing from my bag.

I had photocopied it to keep it with me, even if strictly speaking I shouldn't have. When I'd read it the first time, I'd gone straight to Patrizia in the staffroom and waved it in her face. 'He's going up a year,' I said. I hadn't spoken to her for five months. 'I don't give a damn how he's doing in maths, what his average grade is. Fiume is getting an A in Italian.'

'The Future' – that was the title. Imagine what you'd like to do, where you'd like to be, and who you'd like to become when you grow up.

Martino had worked hard on it: I'd watched him. Over where he'd always sat, at the desk at the back next to the window. But this time he tried his best, looking up from his sheet only to catch his breath. He'd only made a single mistake: *evrything.* And I pretended not to notice that missing 'e'.

That afternoon I reread it, lingering on the ending:

With Misty trotting at my side, I want to climb to the very top of Monte Cresto, on a day when you can see evrything, and from up there I want to say goodbye, or maybe see ya, to my valley.

I don't know who I am or who I want to be.

I'll decide one step at a time, listening to what life has to say.

At around eleven we closed our front doors and headed down Stra' dal Forche with our torches, rucksacks, hold-alls and flowers.

We knew there would be less traffic at night, and the most important thing was to arrive at dawn while everyone was still asleep. I had run through the journey countless times so I wouldn't go wrong, I'd learnt it from memory, but I had to keep telling myself anyway: it's OK, we're not late.

We stuffed the holdalls into the boot and carefully arranged the flowers on the back seat like sleeping children. At that time of night Alma was like a little nativity scene behind glass, trembling in the light of its four cross-shaped lampposts. I shut the garage, started the engine and we left the known world behind.

We drove along the country road that leads to Tartana, and Emilia half-smiled as we passed. Then we arrived at the toll booth and crossed the border. At that point she reclined her seat, stretched out and closed her eyes. I maintained cruising speed. The A4 was empty, with the exception of the odd lorry with a Polish, Hungarian or Slovenian number plate. The flat farmland sank into pitch black. I slipped through the night with the hum of the engine and Emilia's breath to keep me company.

Not until we got to the Milan orbital road did she suddenly open her eyes, as if she knew where we were. She pulled her seat back up and stared out at thc lights, the big buildings and billboards and whispered tenderly, 'Ciao, Marta.' Then she went back to sleep.

She needed to be well rested for the morning's plans. I just had to drive. I wasn't the protagonist, just the accomplice in this plan that we had been working on for weeks together, plotting down to the finest details. But my heart didn't stop racing the whole way.

When we got to Bologna I looked at her again: curled up on her side, her mouth half open and the relaxed forehead of someone who is calm for having made a decision. And I decided not to tell her, to drive past the memories and move onwards to the places in her life that I had never seen.

At 5:15 on the dot, just as planned, as a tide of still-pale light rose from the east, I parked the car a few metres from the side entrance under a row of maritime pines.

I woke her. 'Emilia, we're here.'

The monumental cemetery is an unscathed place, full of peace, and in this sense it is like Donato, like Sassaia, like all our valleys. Set apart from the city, it's an island of silence bordered by a canal, the petrochemical plant and open countryside.

Naturally it was closed at that hour. But that was all part of the plan.

Emilia pulled the hood of her fleece over her head and pushed the car door open.

'I'll help you climb over,' I said.

'No, you pass me the flowers and get back in the car, like we planned.'

The flowers had survived the journey. There were gladioli, daisies, begonias and dahlias, the most beautiful ones Basilio and I had planted, divided into two bunches.

We got out of the Seat and walked across the clay car park. The chapel and the flower kiosk were shut and there were no other cars around. As we reached the side gate that we'd identified on the map, I couldn't help raising my eyes: there were CCTV cameras, and they were probably working. But we had already thought about this.

'Even if they did recognise me,' Emilia had rebutted my objections, 'it's not like I'm going there to vandalise the tombs. I just want to lay some flowers without bumping into anyone.'

The cemetery opened at 6:30. We had also checked the daily calendar on the town hall's website: there would be a commemorative mass at 10:30 and the annual torchlit procession would begin as usual at 9 p.m. 'What are they going to do? Write another article about me? Fine.' She had smiled. 'It'll be the best one yet.'

I watched as she climbed over and jumped down on the other side. I passed her the flowers through the gate. The air was crisp, the light gently caressing the tombs in the silence. My heart was racing on her behalf.

'Be careful.'

Emilia grabbed the two bunches and nodded.

Before getting back in the car, back to my lookout post, I watched her walk off into the large cemetery, between the family tombs, the walls of white recesses and, further on, the porticos of the entrance to where the more illustrious people were buried.

She already knew her way. The gravel crunched under her trainers. Her footsteps were the only sound, the only sound in all of Ravenna.

She went to see her mother first.

She grabbed the handles of an iron stepladder and pulled it along to one column of recesses. She was resting in the highest one because she had expressly asked to be close to the sky. Emilia climbed up the steps with a watering can filled from one of the fountains, changed the water in the vase and swapped the old dried flowers for the fresh ones from Sassaia.

She looked at the oval with the coloured photo of Cecilia: a young woman, smiling, surrounded by old people in black and white, luckier people. But that will do for now, Emilia said to herself, you're here for something else.

So she caressed the stone and gave her mother a kiss, her lips warm on the cold surface of the glass. 'I'm going now. But I'll spend longer with you next time.'

Her mother wasn't the jealous type: she'd understand all too well the order of priorities that day. The light was still low and suffused, but it was rising in the sky with more and more intensity. She had forty minutes until the caretaker would get there.

Emilia climbed down, threw the old flowers in a bin and, with the second bunch in one hand and the watering can in the other, headed towards the middle of the cemetery.

She was looking for a pink marble angel. It was so bright it looked new, her father had told her, standing out against all the other statues: there was no mistaking it. He had already been there several times, obviously not on a June 23rd or a November 2nd, but over those fifteen years he had consistently brought her flowers.

For Emilia, on the other hand, it was her first time being there, and it couldn't have been any other way. As she walked along the main avenue that cut the cemetery in two, her heart beat loudly in her chest, as if she was about to be born again.

She recognised it straight away. It was the most beautiful one: a tomb covered in fresh flowers, cuddly toys and drawings. The angel that loomed over it had his eyes closed but was smiling.

Emilia put the watering can down. She held the flowers with both hands, instinctively bringing them to her heart.

'So, it's you and me again,' she said, her voice cracking.

She looked at the photo the family had chosen. Maybe it was from her confirmation: she was dressed all in white, with a crown of flowers around her head, her pure, promise-keeping face.

'I would've chosen a different one,' Emilia said, trying to smile. 'At the beach, in a bikini.'

It was almost impossible to be there, standing under all that sky. Emilia looked at the photo and let the tears fall silently down her cheeks.

'I'm thirty-one, Angela, almost thirty-two. And you're still sixteen.'

She looked for a vase to arrange the flowers. There was more than one – it must be her mother who made the effort to provide them for anyone coming to visit. Emilia filled one and put it in the middle, above the silver letters that read:

ANGELA MASSIA

†

01.10.1984 – 23.06.2001

Her eyes lingered on those two dates.

Then she sat down on the grass with her legs crossed.

It was 05:57. Her phone wasn't vibrating, which meant no one was coming.

She could take her time. Be alone with her on the surface of the earth and finally look for the right words.

'I've thought of all of them,' she said, shaking her head. 'I think I went crazy with it. But you're not coming back to life. I have to accept that.

'We'll never go out to dinner to clear the air, we won't smoke any more joints together, we won't swim at midnight. And we'll never go there again, to the Stradello.'

Her tears were drying out her mouth, misting up her view, but she wanted to look properly at the face inside the silver frame.

'I can't accept that you're no longer here. Because it's my fault. I decided, I wanted this. But also it wasn't me, but that poor girl, that stupid loser, that sad case I was back then. I hate her. Because she took you away not only from your mum, your dad and your brother, but also from me.'

She was determined to find all the words she had never been able to find, with the hope that, somehow, from somewhere, Angela would hear her. With the hope that, against all evidence, there was at least an iota of magic in the world.

'I got my high school certificate, and a degree in fine art. I wonder what you would've studied, in what city. Bologna, surely. We would've gone together. I wouldn't have seen the city only through windows covered by bars, and you would've become a doctor of medicine, or law. You'd have had a better boyfriend than Fabio, that I guarantee you. But I didn't let you become an adult. So now what do we do, Angela?'

Emilia covered her face with her hands. 'I robbed you of everything, even minuscule things, like going for a walk, the first sip of Coca-Cola, a kiss. It's an impossible thing to live with. It would be easier to die, to bring things to their conclusion. But I don't want to be a coward anymore. So I thought,' she uncovered her face and bit her tongue hard to stop herself crying again, 'that from now on, every beautiful thing I experience, I'll dedicate it to you. I don't want to run away from what I did to you, I want to remember it. And if I can't bring you back to life, then at least every day I live, I want to live it for you.'

She stood up. The sky was now full of light.

After she killed her, she'd come here. She'd run back to her scooter covered in blood, driven with no helmet, not looking where she was going, willing an accident. But her gut knew.

So she came here, she took the steps and sat at the top, in front of her mother's stone. She told her: 'Mamma, don't look at me, I'm disgusting.' She knew, without really knowing it, that she had to go to the police station, to *hand herself in, turn herself in*. That's what people said, wasn't it?

She knew it because otherwise no one would find Angela. Or maybe they would find her, but it would take too long, and some animal might have done more harm than she had already done.

But first she had to tell her mother she loved her. And take the Alcatel out of her backpack to call her father and tell him too, before ruining his life. She had left the knife there, though, next to the *Hope* that was missing its *H* and *P*.

Emilia put her hand into her fleece pocket. She pulled out the folded-up portrait that she had drawn that evening at the kitchen table in Sassaia. She opened it up and placed it next to the vase of flowers.

Then she kissed the glass of Angela's photo too and left just in time, five minutes before the caretaker opened the gates.

Dawn had protected them.

Epilogue

BEFORE HEADING SOUTH, we went to see Riccardo in the terraced house Emilia grew up in and which he had never wanted to leave. Angela's parents still lived next door and so Emilia lowered her hood-covered head as she got out of the Seat, and I instinctively shared her unease. The point of this trip was to repair things that could never be repaired, to tie up loose ends that could never be tied up.

It wasn't yet seven when we parked in front of the gate where Riccardo was waiting, impeccable even at that hour in a white linen shirt and blue trousers with a crease down the front. He made us breakfast and asked Emilia how it went, but she didn't want to talk about it. Her eyes were still red and swollen from crying.

'I've invited Camilla for lunch,' he told us. 'She's really looking forward to meeting you both, so you can't refuse. And,' he turned to me, 'I will not allow you to drive unless you get at least a couple of hours' kip.'

I was indeed so tired that my eyes were drifting shut and my head drooping towards my chest.

'I'm not taking him up.' Emilia looked at the stairs. She moved from the table to the sofa in the living room and

I couldn't help noticing how careful she was to stay away from the windows out of fear that the neighbours, *those* neighbours, might catch a glimpse of her. Even indoors, there was no refuge.

'I'll sort him out.' Riccardo led me up the stairs and along a corridor to Emilia's old bedroom.

When he opened the door I was assailed by a smell that I recognised. A mixture of my own room and Valeria's. The smell of a room left shut since high school.

Riccardo nodded towards the bed and I met his gaze. I looked deeply into his eyes: beaten down but still alive, luminous. *How did you do it?* I wanted to ask him. How did you always stand by her, unconditionally? How did you share the horror with her, how did you take on the burden even though you were, you are, innocent?

But I swallowed the questions immediately, because I realised that I already knew the answers. I was doing the same thing.

Riccardo smiled at me, as if he sensed my thoughts, and closed the door, bidding me to sleep well. I stayed there, alone with the dusty teddy bears and lowered blinds. The light quilt that covered the bed had a childish print of puppies and stars, and there were so many cuddly toys for a sixteen-year-old, squashed onto the shelves and the bed, bundled into a wicker basket. Her collection of books, on the other hand, was slim. Just a pile of school textbooks on the desk. On the walls, held up by drawing pins, were posters of the Spice Girls, Leonardo DiCaprio and characters from *Beverly Hills, 90210.*

I took my shoes off, sat down on the bed and it struck me how normal the room was. I tried to imagine the last time Emilia had looked at it, with what kind of eyes, with what kind of heart, before going down to the kitchen and taking the knife.

It was in that moment, with the daylight forcing its way through the blinds, that I decided that as soon as we were back in Sassaia, I would write it down. All of it.

Love is the answer. If you love someone, you can't ignore what they are, or what they've been. You can't divide them into parts and choose the parts you like. You have to accept them whole.

I needed to write because, ultimately, words help.

They help with living, remembering, understanding. Leaving tracks so as not to let ourselves die completely, so as not to let the people we love die. And because if one day we were to have children, it would be necessary for the truth to be embodied in testimony. We've ruled it out for now, both me and Emilia, but who are we – we who thought ourselves write-offs and then, finding one another, changed – to exclude something from our future before it's even begun?

When we set off after lunch, promising to host Riccardo and Camilla in Sassaia in August – there's certainly no shortage of rooms – Emilia told me about the cemetery, what she had said to Angela and how her words already felt too few, far too few.

'You'll go back,' I reassured her.

Meanwhile Italy flowed around us and changed. First it rippled and hardened over the Apennines, then turned a magnificent green through Umbria, and sprawled back out in Lazio as we drove between fields, medieval hilltop villages and flocks of sheep dozing in puddles of shade.

We drove around the edge of Rome and, even though we stuck to the roads alongside the mansions of the suburbs, the capital had an impact on us. A mixture of marvel at all its hugeness, its giant history looming over us, of childish euphoria and, almost, of gratitude.

We hardly spoke now, too absorbed in the new landscapes, the congested arterial roads heading out towards the sea, the sandwich kiosks along the roadside, the little markets that appeared at junctions, the Roman ruins between maritime pines: the work of the world. And we were part of it all.

I took one hand off the wheel, searched for Emilia's and squeezed it.

My sister was standing there on the pavement outside the door of the address she'd given me. Her face was covered in makeup, her hair dyed black with two purple strands, and she was wearing a leather miniskirt with cork-wedged high heels on her feet.

When I first got out of the car and walked towards her, she hardly recognised me. I, however, could've spotted her a mile away. Even if she had a few wrinkles now at forty-three, to me she would forever be the Witch of the Woods.

We hugged wordlessly, breathing together in unison for a while, and I pushed back the sobs in my throat because she always told me off for being 'soppy'.

Then we stepped away from one another, looking at the floor and coming up with comments on the heat, the traffic, the price of petrol, as we started to unload the bags from the car. We carried them up the three flights of stairs (there was no lift) to her two-bedroom apartment, pulled the sofa bed out and put our toothbrushes in the bathroom, our few items of clothing not worth unpacking.

We were in a rush, however, because we couldn't be late. Valeria was anxious: 'It's the best restaurant in Ostia, we absolutely *have* to be on time. A first course costs no less than twenty-five euros!'

I could see that this was her big moment. Who knows what kind of memorable evening she had spent in that restaurant, and now she was desperate to go back, to go back with us.

Emilia and I rushed to get changed, brush our hair, put on aftershave and perfume, and then followed Valeria along the Ostia seafront towards this 'super famous, super chic, super prestigious' place, where, indeed, we were greeted by elegant waiters who led us out onto a charming terrace to a table with candles lit on the linen tablecloth, and a little card that read PERALDO.

All three of us sat down and looked silently out at the sea.

I felt incredulous, overwhelmed by the reality of finding myself there, with the Tyrrhenian Sea in front of me, alongside Emilia and Valeria: my family.

It was still light. Before opening the menu, Emilia said, 'Will you excuse me for a minute? I need to make a phone call.'

Valeria and I nodded. 'Of course, we're on holiday.'

Emilia left her sandals under the table and ran away barefoot. We saw her wandering along the beach and then climbing up onto a row of rocks until she reached the highest one.

'Is that you, Rita?'

'Who's speaking?'

She didn't recognise Emilia's voice after all those years.

'Rita, it's me, Emilia Innocenti.'

Silence on the other end of the line, broken by a sudden exclamation: 'My God, I don't believe it.'

Emilia smiled. 'See how I keep my promises?'

The waves splashed her face as they broke, the salt fizzing in her nose and throat.

'Tell me how you are, where you are.'

'Right now? Do you want a laugh?' She looked at the sea. It was restless, shimmering, immense. 'On a big rock.'

'At the sea? The sea you hated so much and swore to me you'd never see again?'

'But it's not the Adriatic, it's the Tyrrhenian. You have to change, right? *Everything changes.*'

'When Pavulli told me you and Vargas went to see her in February, I wanted to throttle her. How could she not tell me you were coming? But I was happy anyway, because I knew it was good news.'

'I wanted to tell you something, Rita.'

'Tell me.'

Emilia filled her lungs with the wind and closed her eyes. 'I went to see her this morning, at the cemetery.'

Silence again, a silence that Emilia felt surrounding her like a hug.

'I took her some flowers, and a drawing.'

This time Rita cried; she allowed herself to.

'You were one of the most wonderful rehabilitation projects of my life.'

Emilia looked at the sea again, at the light that radiated off its surface. Living – it took extraordinary strength.

'Above all, Rita, I wanted to say thank you. Because if I'm here today and I'm phoning you up, it's because you lot didn't leave me alone. You never let me go, never stopped breaking my balls: Pandolfi, Vila, Pavulli, even Venturi. And you, Rita, especially you.'

The sea's moving, tireless surface shone as far as the eye could see. Two sailing boats crossed the horizon and the disc of sun that would be propped up on it, balancing there, for a few more minutes. Then it would sink. But it would come up again tomorrow.

'Thank you for reminding me that, even in me, there is good.'

Acknowledgments and a Note

I wouldn't have been able to write this fictional novel without a profoundly vivid meeting with reality. Or without the trust and generosity of the numerous people who allowed me to access Bologna Male Juvenile Detention Centre. The opportunity to get to know the boys in there, to listen to them and to offer them reading and writing workshops, was one of the most powerful experiences of my life.

For this gift I am grateful to Salvatore Busciolano, honorary judge of Bologna Young Offenders' Court and an irreplaceable travel companion.

I want to thank the juvenile judges, Luigi Martello and Francesca Salvatore. The director of Bologna Juvenile Detention Centre, Alfonso Paggiarino. The youth worker coordinator, Romina Frati. The teachers, Agnese Arena and Elena Manaresi. The social worker, Anita Lombardi. And all those who work in the institution who were of such great and touching help.

I am grateful to each and every one of the boys who took part in my workshops: I will never forget your names, your faces and your eyes. You taught me immeasurably more about life and humanity than I could ever teach you with my words and my books. I will always be rooting for your release.

And I thank Monica Malatesta, the first reader of *Cuore Nero* (*Dark Heart*).

I must add a note for my readers. Since this novel is a work of imagination and therefore permits it, I have taken various liberties: geographical, temporal and narrative. In particular, I must point out that the law that raised the maximum age for detention in an institution for minors from twenty-one to twenty-five didn't come in until 2014, but I backdated it so that Emilia and Marta could spend more time together.